THE COLLEGE CHRONICLES
Freshman Milestones

KELLY OWEN

*To John —
Because you are
the "original" rock
star! Hope you enjoy
these words!
Love,
Kelly*

Boxer Publishing
Charleston, SC

Boxer Publishing, LLC
3642 Savannah Hwy. Suite 116 #319
Charleston, SC 29455
www.boxerpublishing.com
www.thecollegechronicles.com

This is a work of fiction. Names, characters, businesses, places, events and
incidents are either the products of the author's imagination or used in a fic-
titious manner. Any resemblance to actual persons, living or dead, or events
is purely coincidental.

Front Cover Photography: Matt Owen
Back Cover Photography and Design: Kelly Owen

Owen, Kelly
The College Chronicles: Freshman Milestones / Kelly Owen
p. cm.
ISBN 978-0-9960617-1-1
Library of Congress Control Number: 2014941240
First Paperback Edition

To Matt:

—Always My Rock Star—

P. 68 mid - reigns
P. 134 Sumter "yard"
to the Union

176 comma
, Steve, and his...

COURSE SCHEDULE

FALL SEMESTER

COURSE SCHEDULE

SPRING SEMESTER

THE COLLEGE CHRONICLES
Freshman Milestones

FALL SEMESTER

Chapter 1

English 101
The Composition of Life

SKIP LINES . . .

Cadence stared in disbelief at the board's directions, the ones that accompanied her first academic command of college—compose an essay. Where were the inspiring introductions and philosophical lectures that made professors legendary? Alumni promised four remarkable years, but here she was facing a writing sample and the most pressing issue of the moment was remembering to *Skip Lines*? She had not imagined the first day at her dream school would begin like this.

She wasn't certain when she first had fallen for Charleston, but it was many years before the historic haven became a fantasy destination for the world; perhaps it was during field trips in elementary school when the port city's wonders lay open for exploration. The journeys here left her with memories of marshes, museums, gardens, galleries, even graveyards and ghosts; of burly carriage horses, rainbow buildings, beautiful beaches, the Battery, and the beaten hands of black women weaving sweetgrass into artistic marvels on the Market. She recalled two bridges that once jumped the Cooper River: one gliding smoothly into Mt. Pleasant where the stately Yorktown reposed safely in port; the other a rickety rollercoaster where riders clenched fists tightly in fear, sweating the climb to its double crest. Once over, wheels clacked louder and faster, rushing down Grace's aging joints while rusted railings raced by the windows. Only the courageous dared look down into the water's green-gray ripples. Cadence remembered this speedy thrill into the city and how the affair continued with her acceptance into Charlestowne College.

When the admissions letter arrived, she dismissed the possibility of attending any other school. With its cover picture of the Grand Lawn where a young woman sat cross-legged engrossed in a book, the college's brochure emitted a siren song. Cadence lived vicariously in that photograph and knew that one day she would be nestled beneath the protective oaks, surrounded by the sensualities of Charleston, immersed in the dream of college. Now she was in that photo, but the romantic image to which she clung was cruelly corrupted by a woman wanting written work on day one.

"Fail to skip lines and I will not read your work," the professor reiterated with the tone of a drill sergeant. Her penetrating stare, enhanced by the intense "V" her eyebrows formed, made the students feel they had entered the underworld.

She was scary, so Cadence wrote the instruction—SKIP LINES—on her left hand, underlined it three times, and peered again at the assigned topic: Choose the most important word in the English language and argue its significance. With little thought, the term came easily to her, so she focused on *loyalty* and wrote passionately of it gluing friendships, marriages, and businesses. Ideas flowed effortlessly, but her muscles burned furiously as her hand devoted lines to the word.

With confidence, Cadence exchanged her essay for a syllabus, which the professor reminded all students to read for the next class. Unimpressed with her introduction to higher education, Cadence quickly forgot this disappointment when she joined the masses flooding outside into the courtyard; under the magnificence of majestic trees and the campus's mesmerizing antebellum architecture, she drew in a deep breath and exhaled it with that particular brand of excitement that marks life in a brave new world. With her first class down and lines skipped, the chronicle of her college life began.

Biology was in the basement of the musty science building; on her way there, Cadence spotted her suitemate Penny with the signature freshman look of being lost. They had the same class, so they found the room together and watched as students filed into the lecture hall. Penny whispered about the number of good-looking guys she had already seen, and the two had fun observing some taking seats around them. At the front, a gray-haired, wiry man shuffled papers while graduate assistants distributed copies of his syllabus.

Precisely at the top of the hour, his dictation began: "This is Biology 110; I am Dr. Kinsdaw. Follow me through the syllabus, as it is imperative that you know the objectives, assignments, and expectations. My listed office hours indicate when I will be available. Otherwise, I am engaged in research, so follow my schedule if you need to speak with me."

He peered over the rim of his spectacles at them. "Next, you will see the required text. If you purchased the wrong one because of incompetence, you'll need to exchange it. Next are the objectives . . ."

The drone of his voice was like white noise that would lull them into sleep in classes to come. For the full fifty minutes, he drudged through the ten-page document, noting behavior policies, grading percentages, the work, the lab component, and just before releasing them, he called their attention to the sixty pages of reading on the formation of life for the next class.

With less than an hour for lunch, Cadence and Penny ventured to the cafeteria to begin the force-feeding of required meal plans. The meal hall offered soup, salad, sandwich, and dessert bars, but the oily aroma of Southern fare overpowered most sensory choices. Fried chicken, mashed potatoes and gravy, macaroni and cheese, and string beans submerged beneath glistening puddles of grease ensured sleepy comfort after consumption.

Grabbing a slice of pizza and fries, Cadence joined Penny and hallmates Madison and Malinda. As locals, they knew the area and each other well, and with their manicured fingers on the pulse of the city, they were quintessential Southern belles complete with accents, monogrammed accessories, and penchants for gossip. They shared a suite with Olivia, who hailed from Tennessee, and Ruthie, a flighty native of The Garden State.

"So have y'all met everyone on our hall?" Madison asked.

"Not everyone," Penny said.

"Nope. I met the resident advisor, Carrie. She seems pretty nice," Cadence replied.

"The RA?" Malinda grabbed a fry from Penny's plate. "Yeah, does seem nice. A bit nosy, maybe."

"Y'all know who's not going to be cool?" Madison held out her right hand to inspect her nails. "Those girls who live next to you, Cadence. They've already started playing that dreadful rap music. I can't stand it. And then there's all this singing and clapping and laughing coming from in there. It's so noisy already."

Malinda chimed in, "We're not going to put up with that. It's the whole suite isn't it?"

"Um, I don't know," Cadence said. "I haven't heard anything."

"Has your roommate?" Madison asked. "Now what's her name?"

"Corrine. Corrine Malloy. She hasn't mentioned any noise."

"Oh, yeah, that's right. I dropped by to introduce myself, but she was on the phone. Later, I came back by and she *was still* on phone. Imagine that, coming all the way here just to talk on the phone. I swear!" Madison laughed with a shrill not too dissimilar to nails sliding down a chalkboard.

"Well, it's only a matter of time before that thumping drives you crazy." Malinda took a long sip of her sweet tea. "Anyway, while we have the blacks representin' at one end, I think we have the dikes at the other."

"Really?" Penny leaned in. "How d'you know?"

"Because they're softball players, and their suitemates are into sports, too," Madison said.

"Who lives across from them?" Cadence asked.

"This girl named Darla from North Carolina. She wants to be a nurse. Her roommate's Natalie, from Florida," Malinda said. "From what we see, she's really into the gym and exercising, always wearing workout clothes. We haven't seen her in anything else."

As the selective social butterflies they were bred to be, Madison and Malinda had already met and assessed most of Albemarle Dorm's third floor. Following the orientation chat, Cadence left for music, her final class on Wednesdays.

A hundred or so students anxiously awaited the start of a course coveted simply because of the teacher. Their schedules promised Professor Glissan, an internationally recognized star whose specialty was creating music programs in developing countries. The entrance of a towering, dark-haired stranger hushed the buzz of anticipation, and like most instructors, he started with the syllabus, a document of unreasonable expectations, and a predeterminism that most before him would fail miserably.

"Everything you know about music is probably wrong. This is not a class in which you get to listen to what you want. You listen to what I assign. It's not about lyrics; it's about the notes. And that means *my notes*, not yours." His face oozed a smarmy smile.

"And please, over the course of these tiresome weeks, spare me your uninsightful contributions of what music you think we should study. I am *not* interested in the latest alternative rockers, studio-made imposters, or chart-topping talentless contestants. I'm not even interested in enlightening you about the subtleties of the discipline I have commanded for decades, but alas, we all must sometimes submit to the most ignoble of tasks. Such is my lot here. No matter. I will make the best of it." He easily made tyranny sound like martyrdom.

They waited for the music to make this circle of hell bearable, for tunes that would deliver them from fate's present cruelty, but despite the obvious subject, no music would be heard, just the humid, sticky breath that spewed from the despot on stage.

"Making the best of this class involves you fulfilling my demands as outlined on the syllabus. This class requires, among other tasks, your attendance at two musical events this term," he said.

Instantaneous visions of rock concerts filled their minds, but as if he could read their thoughts, he crushed these fantasies by clarifying that events attended must be from a list he had compiled, and yes, they would have to pay to attend these performances.

"Additionally, you will need to know what is expected of you at all times, so study the syllabus until you have committed my policies to your memory. And don't neglect to read the material assigned for Friday. That is all, unless any of you people have questions."

A lone, bold voice spoke up: "I thought Professor Glissan was supposed to teach this course."

"In the future, I would appreciate being addressed as 'sir,' 'doctor,' or 'Professor Brodsky.' This *is* the South, for those of you unaware of mannerly convention. As to your question, it is painfully obvious Professor Glissan will not bless you with an appearance this semester. For you groupies who wish to hone your skills under his tutelage, I suggest you hop a plane. He felt it more imperative to help indigent Africans with music than to fulfill his obligations as a supposed educator at this institution. You may, however, delay this course until his return in the spring, but alas, if he couldn't bother showing up this term, why should he in the next?" He paused for a reaction, and in seeing none, he said, "That will be all."

The misery that was Brodsky had only just begun, but dropping the course did not occur to most students. Changes were to be avoided at all costs since they were just getting routines established.

With three of five classes finished, Cadence could not wait to get started on what was already becoming a mountain of work. She had over a hundred pages of reading to complete by Friday and reports beginning in the second week. The threat of quizzes loomed for every class, and she needed to exchange her textbooks since she had bought the wrong ones. She intended to begin immediately, but a call from her mother arrested her progress.

Beginning with English class, Cadence recounted the day's events and would do so again at nearly the same time tomorrow. The call was a reminder of how much she already missed home, but she was too busy to dwell on the heartache of separation. After hanging up, she headed to the bookstore, a trip about as pleasant as being in the dentist's chair at any semester's start. Standing in an irritatingly long line with a weighty stack was quite uncomfortable, but the real discomfort was in feeling violated by price gouging. The business of book mongering was little more than economic rape as new books became used ones upon the moment of purchase.

While she waited for the exchange, Cadence watched the passing T-shirts and hats advertising every party, product, band, and sport imaginable. Although this unofficial uniform varied, there was a ubiquitous element—the palmetto tree and crescent moon—extracted from the state flag. With its spiky top and slender, jagged trunk, the tree was famed for bouncing cannonballs back at the British during the Revolutionary War, and since the palmetto remains undeterred by the Lowcountry's saltwater and sandy, dry soil, it epitomizes resilience. Citizens with a hubristic history of rebellion plaster the palmetto everywhere, in every color, on coozies, bumper stickers, and clothing.

Two guys standing in front of her bore the iconography on their fraternity hats and T-shirts. They completed the standard attire of Charlestowne College with khaki shorts, flip-flops, and sunglasses, which clung to their necks with rubber cords. Cadence studied them as she waited.

"Dude, what's up?"

"Hey, bo. What's up?" the other returned, using the affectionate moniker for all Southern males. A ritual pop from their colliding palms sealed the greeting.

"Nothin'. Just gettin' my books. What you takin' this semester?"

"Same shit I took in summer school."

The other laughed. "Oh man, that's rough."

"Yeah, I just couldn't see doing work during the summer. You feel me, bo? But I got a new prescription this semester, so I can focus on all the new subjects." He glanced at the lines of tanned legs surrounding him. "Know what I mean?" They laughed like hyenas in the bush.

"I hear you, bo. Anything up for tonight?"

"Yeah. We're getting together at Big John's. 'Round five. Start celebratin' being back here. Hell, some of us never left." He smirked at his own stupidity. "You gonna stop by?"

"I will. Catcha later, bo."

Observing the others standing around, especially girls who dared don heels in statements of outlandish fashion, Cadence was reminded of how many females she had seen stumbling through campus. Clambering over the undulating brick walkways, the fashionistas performed the city's most famous dance—the Charleston Shuffle, that haphazard movement caused by trips and stubs over broken masonry and cobblestone streets. At some point, everyone does the dance, whether in heels, flats, flops, or sans shoes, everybody lunges for the ground.

In addition to the accentuated calf muscles their heels forced, these girls were also marked by the glow of their tans which were enhanced by skimpy, strapless dresses. Cadence noticed how her fairer skin appeared a bright shade of white against theirs, and she couldn't wait to make it to the beach. Even though it was "fall" semester, summer's sun beckoned flesh from beneath clothes, and women all over the peninsula responded in worship. Cadence, too, would find her place beneath the scorching orb when she could make time for it.

That night, the buttery smell of popcorn lured Cadence down the hall to the open door of Enna and Myla's room. She joined a gathering of hallmates chatting about their days, tomorrows, and pasts. The advantage of going to school in a place away from home is exactly that—it's not home. No one knows who you are or, for that matter, really cares who you were. Lofty high school status becomes lowly anonymity and unsullied reputations replace soiled ones. Thousands of strangers remain oblivious to the personas of the past. It's a prime place for a renaissance, a reinvention, a remodeling, a *tabula rasa*— college offers them all, so tonight, their conversations steered safely toward mutual likes, dislikes, family details, schedule comparisons, and other feel good, fluffy topics that form the stuff of superficial bonding.

Sophomores Enna, Myla, and Althea were intrepid, intense women who shared deep appreciations for the humanities, especially art and music, and absolute loves for social causes. Signs, posters, advertisements, and propaganda for their political bandwagons plastered the walls of their suite. They chose their crusades carefully, but when they took up a fight, their fealty was unwavering and their passion, unmatched. Their trio was originally a quartet, but the fourth friend broke her promise of rooming at the last possible moment to move off campus. Unable to cement one of their own to complete the suite, their fortunes were left up to chance, and luckily, the spot remained unfilled.

After getting to know those who would live in closer proximity to her than most of her relatives back home, Cadence returned to her room. Strangely, Corrine was not on the phone but asleep by the time Cadence snuggled into bed. When she did, it was already her second day of college, and Cadence thought she was too excited to sleep—that is, until she heard the first of many fire alarms that would force the dorm's residents into the streets. Hundreds stood watching for any puff of smoke or flash of flame that could justify standing in their underwear while brawny firefighters secured the premises. The evacuation deprived everyone of an hour or more of sleep, and the pajama mob decided that the alarm-pulling offender should be burned at the stake. When Cadence's head finally met the pillow again, it was only for a few minutes until her alarm buzzed her into the routine of rising for classes.

She filed into Spanish and took a seat next to the window in the far corner. This class also began with the syllabus—that legal contract binding professors and students in an academic tango of sorts. Mid-way through the class, the guy in front of her passed a sheet back and whispered, "Sorry."

Cadence thought the apology odd until she saw only one slot left on the sign-up sheet for presentations on countries. She was the last person to receive the paper, so the only time remaining was the first presentation. Reluctantly, she wrote her name on the vacant line so that in one week she would present a report on Mexico, and during the next, the apologetic guy in front of her, Kirby, would enlighten the class about Chile. When she reached the syllabus's end, Professor Marquez gave a few last words.

"Today, I will speak English for you but thereafter, *no más*. You will learn by immersion. Instructions, directions, readings, and tests will be given in *Español*. Should you have difficulties I would encourage you to visit the language labs for assistance. *¿Comprende?*"

"*Bueno*," she replied to their nods. "Now, for the next class, remember to read the first three chapters, answer the questions that follow each, and prepare for the weekly vocabulary tests beginning next time. On that day, we will also start presentations on countries. And the first one will be given by . . ." her voice trailed off as she looked for the name. "Let me see . . . Cadence Cooper will present on Mexico. Okay? *Muy bien y adiós.*"

As they got up to leave, Kirby turned to her. "Sorry about leaving you with the last one. I was in Chile this summer, that's why I picked it, but I'll trade if you like."

"That's okay. I'll manage," she muttered. Before leaving, Cadence received an instruction sheet for the trial by speech she would face. Snippets of the requirements nauseated her: a ten-minute oral presentation in English; a two-page written report in Spanish, collectively weighted at twenty percent. Her stomach turned and kept churning all the way to her next course.

No one had the slightest idea what Freshman Seminar would entail, nor was anyone interested in sitting through fourteen weeks of this required course. Professor Elders's introduction and covering of the syllabus fit the pattern Cadence had seen from most of her instructors, except for the English one.

After Professor Elders told them of the assignment for next time, "Describe each class on your schedule, explain what you hope to learn from the courses and how you will achieve your academic goals," she was about to get down to teaching when a guy asked, "Is there a text in this class?"

The professor softly replied, "No."

That was all, so they sat with notebooks opened as the lights dimmed. Despite their readiness, no notes were taken, as what followed was so shocking that hands remained paralyzed above pages. Splayed before them was a series of photographs depicting anatomy marred by sexually transmitted diseases. Gone untreated, genital warts form masses that look much like fungi clinging to tree trunks, although Professor Elders described them as "cauliflower-shaped lumps." The photos of the ulcers hanging from white and black crotches, male and female, made her vegetable simile barely digestible. The fact that these lumps may be the result of HPV, the human papillomavirus, which can also cause cancer—even of the throat—was also difficult to swallow.

"Syphilis can wait years before it produces sores called 'chancres,' and a milky discharge begins creeping from the penis or vagina. Left untreated, the disease may progress into dementia." To illustrate the point, she a showed video of one deranged man writhing against restraints holding him to a hospital bed.

With eyes wide open to match their mouths, the students learned how silently developing gonorrhea and chlamydia often produce no symptoms. If they do, the diseases appear as nondescript conditions: urinary infection, abdominal pain, or discharge. The discharge from one patient's exposure made legs cross tighter and lips purse in disgust. Both blights can also hide in the warm, moist darkness of the throat and be transmitted orally. Gone undetected, they can lead to infertility in men and sterility in women, as a lonely woman devoid of children testified.

Just when they thought the lesson was over, another segment documenting life with HIV shattered the illusion that AIDS was no longer a threat. The disease's dangers had been largely forgotten thanks to the supposed cure created by drug cocktails, but people of all ages, especially young adults, with their medicines spread out before them spoke of the prescription schedules that make up their daily planners. When the drugs no longer work, the final stages of AIDS are horrific—the pathogen destroys tissues and organs, the body sucks itself in, replacing healthy forms with haunting, skeletal reminders of its awesome power. Heads turned away with each new image, but like the irresistible magnetism of a car crash, they couldn't help but look at the collision of disease and flesh.

Dr. Elders's presentation quelled horniness instantaneously. Clearly disturbed by the intrusion of documented risk on the possibility of fun, the freshmen were even more bothered by her follow-up statistics. She began with the national numbers. Young people aged 15-24 have five times the reported chlamydia rate and four times more for gonorrhea than the general population. One in five people living with HIV carries the virus unknowingly and numbers are rising. For a moment, the students were glad they had chosen a college in a smaller city until their instructor revealed the homegrown reality.

"You reside in the state that ranks among the highest in the nation for chlamydia and gonorrhea infections. Most people who have one have the other, so it's a double whammy after the 'wham bam.'"

She gave the rankings for HIV and AIDS, which again placed the Palmetto State in the national top ten. "Oh, and remember: diseases aren't only passed through sexual activity. Sharing needles or even rolled up bills when snorting drugs can lead to HIV or hepatitis C infections. Watch yourselves. We'll discuss what you've seen today in the next class."

She released them with a tart: "Welcome to the Holy City." As if emerging from war trenches, the shell-shocked freshmen were speechless. In their departing silence, one student broke the trauma: "Damn! That sure as hell wasn't in the brochure!"

Cadence thought of the photo that lured her here, of the girl sitting next to the tree—a tree without fungus, a student seemingly without worry.

The images of Freshman Seminar lingered with the coincidental presence of Petri dishes, microscopes, and test tubes that decorated the charcoal-colored tables of Cadence's next class. In a smaller room attached to a large, corpse-colored one were a few rows of desks to which the biology students were directed. Dressed in the signature white coat of all scientists, Alex, the lab director, detailed rules, procedures, and expectations. A student in her early twenties, she was pursuing her master's degree in microbiology while working as a teaching assistant. Cadence noticed the excitement in Alex's voice as she gave the introduction, which was a striking contrast to Dr. Kinsdaw's monotonous tone.

Before leaving, someone asked about the mix-up with the biology books, so Alex clarified the confusion, adding some of her own advice.

"If you're like me, you're probably a starving, poor student. If you're not, just wait; you'll figure out a hundred ways to cook Ramen noodles before you graduate. Be smart. Buy good, used books when you can, check the library for copies to borrow, and shop around for bargains. No sense in going bankrupt over the books since you're probably already in debt." A select few appreciated her lesson in economic Darwinism.

Already they needed a break, so when Cadence's suitemate Saida mentioned a stroll around town after dinner, the thought of work evaporated. Cadence reasoned it was only the first week, and her professors could not expect too much from them, so she quickly finished her reading and joined the jaunt.

Their tour took them onto King Street, that central path cutting a swath of luxury through the city. Perfectly displayed merchandise glittered, especially through the glass at Bob Ellis, where the group gazed longingly at shoes in colors that rivaled those in a box of crayons. Each pair reposed on its platform, like fairy-tale slippers awaiting feet to step into the expensive fantasy. The girls left the dream in their wake, along with the jewelry, clothes, handbags, lingerie, and other treasures each new window dangled. Interspersed between the stores were the bars and restaurants, of which they noticed upperclassmen reclaiming familiar territory and the buzzing business professionals who had never left.

Following the curve of King brought them to the Charleston Place Hotel where they licked their lip glosses at the ever-present lure of Godiva's chocolate-covered strawberries, glimpsed the shiny sophistication of Gucci goods, and peered into the dark elegance of the Grill. They sniffed the aromas that floated from its interiors and couldn't help but let their mouths drop at the colossal chandelier in the hotel's lobby. Soothing sounds of jazz from a café followed them as they glided across the white marble floor out of the hotel. In the famous City Market, vendors loaded their unsold wares into vans while more music floated from places where diners clinked wine glasses in the elegant establishments that made Charleston a culinary Mecca.

They took pictures on the stone steps of the towering Customs House, smiled at valets awaiting chances to park, and savored samples of fudge from the candy store. Eventually, they headed back toward campus, overshooting home to the supposed site of some parties. Turning the corner onto a narrow street, they saw the truth of the rumors. People were leaning over the rickety piazzas' bannisters, cramming into narrow yards, and drifting from house to house in what had become a block party.

Apprehensively, the group approached the first house, where a boisterous figure clutching an oversized red cup welcomed them to the party: "Helloooo ladies!" Flinging his arms widely, he indicated that the liveliest of houses, the one featuring the most kegs, was his kingdom.

"I'm Stu. Welcome to my humble party." He puffed out his chest like a peacock would its plumage. "Let's get you all some drinks." Slipping his arm around Corrine, he led them through a gauntlet of attendees, a motley group of no particular sorts that had one goal in common—celebrating the momentous accomplishment of a whole two days of classes completed.

When the opportunity to catch a buzz presented itself via a cup from the keg, Cadence indulged. Beer was a quickly acquired taste, and it felt right. On the porch, the girls toasted this rite of passage and the many occasions to come. With every half hour, the crowd grew larger, the music louder, and the binging more pressured.

Eventually, the drinks forced the need for a bathroom, so Cadence and Penny searched inside. Within the walls of that well-worn house, the thumping bass bumped bodies together on a makeshift dance floor. The alcohol-fueled ritual of hooking up intensified as hands explored haunches and tongues traded tastes. Strangers became vertical lovers in the blur of buzzes. As the night's steamy humidity forced skin from clothes, every grind of hips and pump of the keg ushered in the new era.

Directed upstairs by a partier who told them to go through the door at the end of the hall, Cadence was surprised to find no line for the bathroom, but when she turned the knob and walked inside, different kinds of lines met her sight.

"Come on in, and shut the door, will you?"

Cadence and Penny shuffled in as the guy who made the request dropped his face to a coffee table where a mirror reflected the ghostly powder disappearing into his nostrils. He threw his head back and inhaled every particle while the girl next to him tapped the glass with a razor and followed his lead. While she did, he grabbed a rolled up bill and held it out to the guests.

"Join us. Let's get this year started off right," the ringleader said to the approval of the group in the round.

"Yeah," the girl said in between snorts, "it'll make you so ready for classes."

"What is it?" Penny asked.

"Oxy, baby, oxy." The way the drug rolled off his tongue was seductive and a perfect accessory to his good looks.

Penny glanced at Cadence then to the users. "Um, what's that?"

Laughter sang from the circle. "Oh, I love the new ones. Oxycodone, sweetheart. Come on, try a line."

"That's okay. We thought this was the bathroom." Cadence reached for Penny's hand and pulled her out of the room.

group spoke of it. They occupied themselves with meaningless chatter about what tomorrow would bring, while silently wondering if his life would end here before it had even begun. Their "good nights" were more sincerely expressed than they would have been on an otherwise uneventful evening. As Cadence lay down to sleep, she thought of the guy with the ghostly face and vomit-laced hair and mouthed a silent prayer in hopes that he would live to celebrate again.

There was nothing to celebrate in her first class the following morning, and prayer was no help. The quiz was a painful, sobering reminder of the instructor's earnestness. Blank pages, save for the hastily scribbled names of their owners, reached the professor. Although Cadence had read the thirty assigned pages, she guessed only one answer and swore she must have gone over the wrong material.

After the quiz, the woman introduced herself. "I am Professor Mirabilis," she said, "Crys Mirabilis. In case you need the full name." She discussed the syllabus and completed the set of obligations that would map the semester. In hearkening back to the challenge given only forty-eight hours ago, she elaborated that *SKIP LINES* was merely a lesson within a lesson.

"It's a metaphor to live by. I am, after all, an English teacher, and metaphors are the modes by which we frame life's lessons. For you, 'SKIP LINES' may be no more than petty directions for a writing assignment, but for me, the words are a maxim. Skipping lines leaves room for thoughts between the lines. Those thoughts often have the most value, are the ones worthy of pursuit. Go for what's in between the lines—that's where the deeper thinking awaits." She paused to see if they were following her lines.

"Skipping lines makes space for what will come. It's often what we need in our overly crowded lives. Leave room between classes, events, and relationships. Leave time to reflect." She honed in on their haggard expressions. "Leave space even between drinks for those of you suffering the effects of gluttony this morning."

Cadence looked around to see the sly smiles of those who had ventured out last night. They appeared surprised that their professor would recognize the tell-tale signs of their hangovers. The memory of the alcohol poisoning episode flashed into Cadence's mind, and she wondered if the guy had made it.

"Otherwise, your life will be one crammed, chaotic, suffocating section on the daily page of life, and if you want many pages to come, well, learn to leave space. Part of that space comes from establishing one of your own, just as Virginia Woolf reminds us of the importance of a woman having 'a room of one's own.' Of course, it's vital for everyone to have this space. I know this concept may be escaping you since you're sharing your space with strangers." She let the words sink in before giving them the mental assignment.

"For the next few classes, I would like you to think about the concept of your 'space.' How would you define it? What are its dimensions? How have you come to occupy this place? Contemplate these questions as you begin our semester's first major reading: Jon Krakauer's *Into the Wild*, and keep in mind that space is not only physical. That's why you are here—to explore your intellectual space."

Although she still wasn't sure about Professor Mirabilis, Cadence thought this class was certainly much better than the first. While walking to biology, she pondered the place that stretched out from the Grand Lawn and its reflecting pool, that rippling water feature that seemed to feed the college's growth across the city. The campus boasted many monuments: not the stone statues that dot the landscapes of so many schools, but the aged houses, wrought-iron gates, and the haunting beauty of oaks offering shelter from the sultry southern sun. These were its best features. Its old beauty was magical, and in strolling beneath the historic canopy, Cadence realized that this was just one of many settings to consider, for back in the dorm, she shared a room with Corrine.

Cadence was not quite certain what to make of the person who now lived closer to her than anyone else in her eighteen years. At home, she had the liberty of roaming acres of space on her family's farm, and she had never shared a room with someone and certainly not a bathroom with three strangers.

What she could make of Corrine was limited to brief facts shared: she hailed from a small town in Georgia, liked country music, and spent most of her time talking to one person. Corrine came to college with a most cumbersome piece of baggage—a boyfriend named Jed, who would be coming to stay next weekend.

Even though Corrine had gone out with them last night, she spent most of the time on the fringes of conversation, her attention occupied by a continuous string of messages and calls. The boyfriend was none too happy that she was out and especially upset when the police and ambulance arrived.

When the group returned to the dorm, Corrine immediately slipped on Jed's old flannel shirt and dedicated hours to placating him with promises of not going out, not even on weekends. Cadence drifted in and out of sleep over the apologies and love declarations and awoke feeling foggy, a state that did nothing to help with Friday's challenges.

A case of *déjà vu* followed in Dr. Kinsdaw's class with most of the blanks remaining unfilled on another impossible quiz. Why did she really need to know the geologic time scale? After papers were collected, Cadence found solidarity in others' failing faces, except for one person whose countenance bespoke the pleasure of not only passing but of doing so with perfection. The girl's long, dark hair was pulled back in a neat ponytail. Her red T-shirt was the brightest in the class, and its left sleeve announced in white letters, *ALWAYS.* Blue jeans, a pair of running shoes, and a black backpack with a silver water bottle tucked into the pocket, completed her look.

Cadence's examination of her classmate's style was interrupted by the professor's inquiry: "Miss Cooper, do you know the answer to number three?"

Regrettably, her attention was refocused. "Sir?"

"Question three. What hypothesis posits that life was formed from chemical reactions to inorganic molecules?"

Her unopened book clearly spoke for her. "Um, I'm sorry. I, I don't know."

His expression dismissed her as if she were sediment, and he moved to the next target, the one who just held Cadence's attention.

"It's the primordial soup theory," the girl answered.

"Correct," he said, but before he could get to the next question, someone had a query of her own.

"Professor?" a voice in the front row began, "are we going to study creationism in this class?"

He stared at her as if she had spit in the soup recipe. "No, this is biology, not mythology. If you want stories about life's beginnings, I suggest classes in the religious studies department." His eyes brushed over a tattered black bible mockingly perched atop her textbooks before focusing his interrogation on a young man who had rolled from bed still sporting plaid pajama bottoms, slippers, and a T-shirt.

The professor tried summoning the bedhead from the sleep he had not left. "Mr. Rears, do you know the epoch in which we currently live?"

Mentally, the student was hitting the snooze button. "Uh, what's an epoch?"

Dr. Kinsdaw shot a look as stony as the rock layers the students were drilling through in study.

"Oh yeah, I got this. Biology!" pajama pants replied, rather pleased with himself.

Dr. Kinsdaw was unamused. Methodically, he found another student who answered, "the Holocene epoch," recognized it as the time since the last ice age, and clarified an epoch as longer than an age but shorter than a period. His students were quickly discovering that time in biology seemed more akin to an eon.

The doctor's lack of reaction to anything other than his research was aptly confirmed on the website "Evaluate My Educator," a fairly useful, albeit extreme tool for class selection. Cadence read about her professors after she signed up for them, and although some had scathing criticisms, she was more afraid of altering her schedule than of facing them. Come to think of it, some of the harshest comments had been about her English teacher, who had earned the title "Demon of Darkness." Cadence had laughed when she read it but now recalled the possible truth of one posted opinion: *Will make you work until you cry.* Cadence had not cried—yet.

When biology was dismissed, Cadence found herself to the right of the dark-haired oracle. She saw the word *RUNNING* on the other sleeve and rolled her eyes at the slogan. Cadence hated running but watched her classmate pull ahead in the pack moving down the hallway. The shirt's back boasted a 10K: Run against Racism in some place called Deland, Florida. Cadence was still reading the sponsors' logos when the shirt faded into the crowd.

The same group met again for lunch, but when they became lost in details of the night before, Cadence arrived late to music. A glare of disapproval escorted her to a seat. Dr. Brodsky seized the opportunity for humiliation.

"Note the beat, on-time, precise, unlike that of this one—

Miss . . . ?" He waited for Cadence's unwilling incorporation into his lecture.

"Cooper," she said, slouching low into the seat.

"Miss Cooper, you *will* be on time for my classes. If you are not, don't bother coming. This also applies to anyone who wishes to follow her preposterously poor example."

Cadence wished the chair would open up and suck her into oblivion. Just this day, she had managed to become the model student of incompetency: the daydreamer, the latecomer, the ill-prepared moron making Fs. The weight of the academic world was piling on faster than the freshman fifteen.

No quiz began the hour in music; Professor Brodsky had better torture for the hordes of hungover students before him. He blared the chants of Gregorian monks to decibels so barely tolerable that several excused themselves. In less than an hour, he surveyed centuries of sound from the Middle Ages, Renaissance, Baroque, and Classical periods. He stopped the montage with the latter, giving his subjects extra doses of Bach, Mozart, and Beethoven and with every change in music, he gave verbose descriptions of defining characteristics in a tempo faster than those listening could write, but the clock could not tick fast enough to release them from this fresh hell. Just as they thought the period was about to end, he topped the pain with a review quiz, beginning with their mastery of his policies. Cadence had skimmed the syllabus, so she failed to answer how many absences they could incur without penalty, what percentage of the final grade their exam comprised, and other nitpicky details of his doctrine.

He also questioned them on the past hour, but heads aching from deafness rendered it impossible to recall his points. With regurgitation not forthcoming, Cadence again turned in a nearly blank sheet of paper, as did a majority of her peers. She was going to offer an apology to her professor but didn't want to remind him of her lateness.

"Don't let him get to you. He's a jerk to everybody," a voice said on the way out.

Cadence turned to see a stranger with dark eyes smiling at her. "How d'you know?"

"I have friends who've had him. He's just trying to get rid of us—get the number of students down, so he'll have less to teach. Makes less work for him. Nice, huh?"

"Yeah." Cadence felt some dread lift.

"His intimidation makes students drop. Seems to work. Looks like half the class is gone already. Hang in there, unless there's another class you can get into."

"Don't know. I haven't looked. My advisor told me to take this, and my schedule is so fixed everywhere else. Guess I'll stick it out." She extended her hand. "I'm Cadence."

"Reena. Look for me next time. I'll save you a seat."

Cadence's depression from the day's failures evaporated with news from Saida of not-to-be-missed parties. Little did they know that there was always a party, always a buzz to be caught somewhere, but as moderation was not yet a lesson fully absorbed, they crammed their calendars with social activities. After all, freedom felt too good to pass up. They made the rounds Friday, but it was a bash thrown by the rugby team on Saturday night that went down in collegiate history.

The ladies arrived late to an already rocking party. It was a collection of cliques, but despite social affiliations, the greatest concentration of partiers was not in the house, but around the beer truck the team had skillfully driven into the backyard. Lines for the taps moved quickly, and with beer securely in hand, the freshmen began to enjoy the release incited by the foamy goodness. They surveyed the hook-up prospects, made seductive moves to the music, and Cadence amused herself when she realized she was listening for the songs' nuances. Briefly, she wondered if Brodsky would be impressed; she knew he wouldn't be.

After a while of making eye contact with various hookup potentials, Saida said, "Well ladies, I see what I want. I'll be back later." Like a lioness, she crept purposefully toward a pride of juniors to begin her game. Cadence and Penny watched her work for a while before returning to the truck for another round. As they walked through a gauntlet of guys to an open spot, they felt the sensation of elevator eyes. The attention lifted their spirits, and they talked flirtingly with a few who passed. They met more people than they could keep up with and answered the same questions of hometowns, classes, and hobbies. The time was great, and the euphoria of simply being in college—and at a party—was a high from which they did not think it possible to come down. It was an elevation to be outdone only by the party's hosts.

When the music stopped, all attention turned to the top of the beer truck where members of the rugby team, bearing only cups of beer, loin cloths, and bongos, took their positions. Eight guys carried the beat makers, except for one who stood in the center and commanded the attention.

"Who *is* that?" a voice purred.

"You mean Mr. Abs?" The guy oozed jealousy over what appeared to be a developing beer gut. "That's Adon, the team's captain. The rest of the Chippendales are players."

"I bet they are," another girl quipped.

"Oh my God. I'd love to wash my lingerie on his abs." She seemed to sway with derision while Cadence and Penny laughed.

It was as if some overzealous sculptor had chiseled beyond a mere six pack and endowed this special subject with eight. His muscles gleamed in the light and tightened as he spoke. Ladies swooned while boys glanced down in pitiful comparison.

Like a descendant of Dionysius, Adon began his ritual of waxing Whitman's poetry to the throngs below: "I celebrate MYSELF, and what I assume you shall assume; for every atom belonging to me as good belongs to you!"

The followers roared while his chorus repeated, "Celebrate! Celebrate! Celebrate!" and beat time on their bongos to the rhythm of this voice.

"I will go to the bank by the Cooper and become undisguised and naked, I am mad for the PLUFF MUD to be in contact with me . . ."

"Wooooo! I'll get naked in that stuff with you!" a drunk worshiper shouted to echoing laughter.

"Stop this day and night with me and you shall possess the origin of all the peninsula's treasures . . ."

"I'll stop with you anywhere!" said the one in need of laundering her lingerie.

He directed the next lines to her: "You shall not look through my eyes either, nor take things from me; you shall listen to all sides and filter them from yourself."

"I drink filtered beer!" some buffoon boasted.

The crowd groaned while Adon held his focus on the coed: "Do you guess I have some intricate purpose? This hour I tell things in confidence, I might not tell everybody, but I will tell you." He pointed his finger at her, and she froze as if she had been turned to stone.

"I am the poet of the body, and I am the poet of the soul. The pleasures of the Holy City are with me, and the pains of hell are with me . . ."

"Poet! Body! Poet! Soul! Pleasures! Holy! Pains! Hell!" the chorus atop the truck chanted and pounded their instruments.

"Press close bare-bosomed night! Press close magnetic nourishing night! Night of the SOUTH winds! Night of the large few stars in this SOUTHERN sky!" In exaggerated fashion, he shot his hands into the air, and red cups everywhere followed, their contents spilling over white rims to anoint the masses.

"Still nodding night! MAD NAKED SUMMER NIGHT!" The crowd went wild.

"Smile, for your lovers come!" The performers moved in a circle on the truck's roof, beating and repeating the words in a whirl of excitement. Pockets of people below clapped to the pounding and danced with frenzy.

The captain brought them to a hush. "I know I have the best of time and space—and that I was never measured, and never will be measured."

"It's *that big*?" someone yelled.

Adon grinned. "I tramp a perpetual journey . . . Not I, not anyone else can travel those milestones for you; you must travel them for yourself."

They hung in hushed silence on the words echoed from Papa Walt, but the quiet was not to be for long as Adon brought the revelers to a climax: "I too am not a bit tamed . . . I too am untranslatable, I sound my barbaric yawp over the roofs of CHARLESTONNNNNN!"

The roars shook eardrums, music fired from the stereo, and the beer truck dancers tore off their loin cloths, dancing in intrepid abandonment. Gyrations drew wild applause and with every rebel yell of approval, their pelvic thrusts grew more pronounced. With arms around each other, Cadence and Penny raised their drinks to the madness and to the first of many memories marking their freshman days of college.

"It's not a rugby party 'til somebody gets naked!" a supporter announced.

But a guy within earshot of Cadence and Penny proved that not everyone was impressed with the lyrical lesson. "Bunch of goddamn faggots if you ask me," someone said. "Spoutin' poetry and shit. How fuckin' gay can you get?" The words were meant to be heard only by his friends, but in his drunken state, this critic was unaware of how loudly he had spoken.

Turning to see the insulter, Cadence noticed the familiar emblems of the palmetto tree clones and heard his buddy say, "You got that right, bo."

"Come on, let's go get another beer," the bo instructed, but just as they moved forward, a wall of muscle blocked their path.

The biggest of the rugby players crossed his gargantuan arms. "So, you think my friends are fuckin' faggots?"

With humility long drowned in cheap beer, the bo laughed. "Yep, I sure do." His chest rose to meet his foe's. "What'n the fuck you gone do 'bout it?"

A wide grin and a few head shakes accompanied the rugby giant's reply: "Kick your ass."

Inches apart they stood, nostrils flaring, rib cages rubbing, testosterone poisoning the atmosphere. But no one moved— that is, until some violence-craving primate let a cup of foam fly. The anointment was followed by a deluge. Bystanders soaked in the keg-fueled crossfire quickly moved to safety. Beer mixed with blood splattered from shattered noses, and guys anxious to prove their loyalties surrendered to primordial urges, attacking enemies made in an instant. When a full beer bottle grazed Cadence's face, she grabbed Penny, and they ran against the pushes and shoves of males built like bulldozers.

In the exodus, they spotted Saida against a car with some guy in a full-on saliva swap.

"Come on, Saida, Let's get outta here!" Cadence pried her suitemate from the hookup and the girls quickly followed the horde moving in the direction opposite from the blue lights and sirens closing in on the mayhem.

It was well after midnight when the trio headed home. En-ergized by the cheap beer of charity and the expensive freedom of college, Cadence and her newly found friends practiced the week's lessons. Falling into a childhood game of motherly pro-tection, they skipped lines on the sidewalk, careful of cracks undoubtedly formed in the Holocene epoch, a time when STDs grew like fungi on trees in the nether regions of humanity. Like the unskilled performers they were thanks to many *cervezas,* they chanted ditties, ever unmindful of their pitches and tones, frolicking upon an old peninsula, in their very new space of living.

Chapter 2

Sociology 103
Introduction to Social Survival

"He died alone in a bus not far from the fringes of civilization but just far enough from it to make him yearn for human contact. In his final days, he penned a five-word philosophy for us to contemplate: 'HAPPINESS ONLY REAL WHEN SHARED.' With whom will you share your happiness?"

Professor Mirabilis's question was not meant to be answered immediately, but she tossed it out for consideration. The story of Christopher McCandless was one to ponder: a marginal man of sorts, he survived four years of college only to perish after nearly four months in the Alaskan wilderness. Where would the road take them after four years, and who would share the adventure with them? The answers, of course, remained unknown.

"Most of you will not be sharing happy feelings in the case of the papers I am about to return. Once I give these back, you must observe my twenty-four hour rule: You may not contact me about your paper for a full day. During this time, read my comments, review the chapters on writing you have been assigned, and begin thinking about your revisions. Writing is a process—your progression begins now."

"Does that mean they weren't good?" someone posed.

"They're what I've come to expect. In education, we now believe that learning is measured through standardization. We sacrifice your intellectual development in the name of test development. We value darkening bubbles over enlightening your minds . . . ." On she went but the students heard nothing. Visions of numbers—the grades and averages that defined their existence—scrambled in their minds as they stared at the white stack that would shatter their illusions of writing grandeur.

When the papers were returned, most met an unfamiliar letter, the sixth of the alphabet. Expressions of wide-eyed denial formed from the scarlet blot that damned their efforts. When the essay reached her hand, Cadence felt the immediate satisfaction of her first composition coming full circle—that is, until she turned to the last page. She had not prepared herself for any possibility that her writing would garnish anything less than an A. Her heart beat faster and a knot of nausea formed immediately. She flipped to the front of the paper, checking to make sure it was her paper. It was.

Your ideas show promise, but your writing should be much more specific. Use concrete examples, not hypothetical scenarios to develop points. Draw evidence from literature, science, politics, history, or popular culture in the revisions. Grade: F.

Squinting hard at the last letter in her professor's comments helped Cadence hold back the tears as she slid failure into her bag and sulked to biology.

None of Dr. Kinsdaw's attempts unearthed buried knowledge of middle school science. When the jargon of biology appeared on the board, Cadence assumed the role of a scribe—recording away while the professor explained the origins of life.

"Prokaryotes, the first cells . . . ." His voice had the immediate effect of inducing listeners with sleeping sickness, and the darkness of the cool lecture hall didn't help.

"Eukaryotes, possibly developed from symbiotic relations with the prokaryotes," he continued while Cadence fought to keep her lids up. "Endosymbiont theory. . . ." His explanation was long-winded, so she condensed the chaos: *fusion. Large pro. cell hugs smaller pro. cell. = community / symbiosis.* Hoping she would remember all that she wasn't writing, she felt a sense of relief when she glanced over at Penny, who was furiously scribbling every word. Relieved by her suitemate's efforts, Cadence felt that reviews would be much easier with the two of them working together.

"The next class will begin with the growth and reproduction of organisms. Darwin, Mendel, and the double helix of DNA will be part of the focus," Dr. Kinsdaw announced dismally.

In the shuffle from the lecture room, someone asked, "How can a professor suck the life out of this subject?" The question was met by collective sighs.

Although it was lunchtime and Cadence's meal plan forced her to eat, both classes had killed her appetite, so she decided to visit the library. The noise of tapping keyboards, purring printers, and table conversations made the library's bottom floors ones to avoid. With its mostly artificial light, the ground floor was cold and chaotic. The drone of copiers and whisperings of study groups drifted from the middle floors, but those seeking true solace climbed to the top, where a reprieve with long rows of tables lit by the warm glow of antique lamps and floor-to-ceiling windows awaited. This penthouse offered sweeping views of what was below: tin tops of houses glinting green, red, and silver in the sun, and steeples rising every few blocks, the arms of their crosses stretching majestically in the bluish haze. In the distance stood the towering authority of the medical school; its brown and dirty white blocks offered an uninspiring contrast to the healing potential within. Between these sights, the narrow streets jutted in gridded directions, with drivers, bikers, and walkers disappearing beneath the camouflaged canopies of oaks, palmettos, and magnolias. The trees stretched a green mile or two until they tapered off into the blue of the surrounding rivers.

Cadence climbed to this height to read more of her professor's criticism. She chose a seat near a guy engrossed in a massive textbook. Stacking the composition books neatly in front of her, she prepared to face the failure. The crowning glories of high school writing held little shine now as she stared, once again, at what she thought was a great paper. The knot from earlier returned, and tears welled in her eyes with each comment. For the two pages, barely a sentence was unscathed. *Us, var, v. var, ww, shift, and trans* littered the margins in ink so red that Cadence felt as if the paper had been splattered by her own blood. Next to every paragraph appeared *DEV*, so she reached for her grammar book to decode the hieroglyphics, mouthing "D-E-V" in her search for the translation.

"Development."

She looked to the guy with the big book. "Excuse me?"

He pointed to the paper. "Development."

Glancing again at the letters then to him, she said, "Oh, okay."

"You must have Mirabilis for English." He motioned to the stack in front of her. "Your books. She's the only one who teaches those." He slid the pencil he held above his ear and reached his hand over the table. "I'm Walker."

"Cadence," she replied, her voice shaky from the paper shock.

"First paper, huh?"

"How'd you know?"

"The looks of confusion, frustration—yeah, they're clear signs." He smiled. "What's the topic?"

"Um, we had to pretend the language is dying and choose a—"

"Word and argue why it's important?" He paused. "Oh, sorry, please, go on."

Not minding the interruption, she said, "Well, that's the assignment. You've had this one?"

"I did. "What's your word?"

"*Loyalty.* I thought it was a good paper, but Professor Mirabilis doesn't think so." Cadence twisted the red ink-stained sheets. "I don't agree with her. I made A's in high school English. She must not like my style."

Expecting a sympathetic reaction, she was genuinely shocked when he began to laugh. "What?" She stiffened in her seat.

"I said the same when I got back my first paper. It's none of my business, but you got an F, didn't you?"

When she nodded, he replied, "Me, too. I was so mad at that woman I confronted her right after class. Didn't bother to read her comments. Just saw the 'F,' freaked, and went after her."

"Really, what'd she say?"

"She reduced me to tears. I came in here thinking I was hot shit, having gotten all A's in high school, honor roll, AP classes, all that," he explained. "I let her know I worked hard on my paper and that I didn't deserve the grade. I even told her she could at least have written something positive."

"You did?"

"Yep. She gave me a moderate tongue lashing. Told me she didn't reward poor work and that she'd be lying if she told me my writing was good." He leaned back and grinned at the ceiling tiles. "No teacher had ever said anything that harsh to me. I was used to nothing but praise, but she taught me how to write. I ended up liking her class so much I took her again."

"Then she taught you to love punishment?"

"I guess so," he said. "Hey, if you're looking for an easy A, drop her class. If you want to learn, hang in there. Go see her, even if she seems intimidating. She'll help you."

"I might, but she's got that twenty-four hour rule. Told us that we can't talk to her about the papers for a whole day."

"Hmmm. That's a new one. Wasn't the policy when I had her. Maybe I was the reason for that."

"What word did you choose when you had her?"

Schoolboy mischievousness appeared in his smile. "*Sex.*"

Cadence's cheeks reddened. "Bet you had fun with that. How'd you write about sex without sounding like a pervert?"

"I wrote about how sex is used as power in politics and business, focused on tortured prisoners, destroyed politicians, child slaves, but you gotta look at both sides of your word."

"The negatives of *loyalty*, huh?"

"Hey, for as much as students bitch about Mirabilis, that's what she does—makes you think. Sometimes, I'd walk out of her class with a headache. A lot of students don't like her. But her kind of class is addictive, if that's what you like. My friends thought I was crazy for taking her."

Glancing down at her paper, Cadence thought that she, too, was crazy for taking the demon and that no class in which her first grade was an F would be addictive. Her fear of failure made her want to take a seat in another section.

"When are the revisions due?" he asked. "And I know you have them because she's all about revising, revising, revising. And she reads every word, so don't bullshit."

"She hasn't given us a deadline yet," she said.

"I know it doesn't seem like it now, but that F may be the best grade you'll ever get. It made me work so much harder to do better in her class."

"Did Professor Mirabilis lure you into becoming an English major?"

"No, not quite." He chuckled. "Historic Conservation. My minor's business." He answered her perplexed expression. "Hey, what better place to study preserving history than in a city founded in 1670?"

"What've you learned about this town?"

"Well, she was originally named Charles Towne. She has a lot of other secrets."

"That's a secret?"

"Well, I guess I felt like it was when I found that out. That's how I see studying history—as a bunch of secrets waiting for me to discover them. Doesn't matter if other people know them, they're still hidden to me." He removed his pencil from over his ear and tapped the book in front of him. "Who knows? Maybe one day I can show you around. Tell you about them."

"That'd be nice." She fingered the spiral wire of her notebook.

"So do you have any ideas on your major?"

When she indicated she had none, he said, "You'll figure it out. Are you done for the day, class-wise?"

"Oh no! What time is it?"

"Almost two."

"Crap! I'm going to be late for music." She shot up, grabbed her books, and rushed from her seat, but before she reached the end of the table, she turned to him. "Thanks for the advice, see you around."

Although she was out of earshot, the words, "hope so," chased after her.

Praying that she would avoid a chastising from Brodsky, Cadence raced through the humidity to the music hall. Sweat slid down her skin as she cautiously opened the door and listened. All was fairly quiet, so she crept in. She had made it, and true to her word, Reena motioned to Cadence over.

"I was worried he was going to crucify you again," Reena said.

"Me too. I got caught up in the library, talking to some guy."

"Really? Anyone interesting?"

Cadence was about to share the details but was silenced by the blast of music that popped them up in their seats. Brodsky materialized from the shadows to resume the week's torture.

"You'll note that in this first selection . . ." his voice boomed. Cadence tried, in vain, to detect the subtleties, to absorb the keywords of *pitch, dynamics, texture, form, and style.* Her notes were barely decipherable but proved better than Reena's, which were nonexistent. Instead, variations of the name *Blaze* surrounded by accentuating doodles were artfully inked on her page. Cadence pointed to the name and a grinning Reena wrote, *boyfriend,* and drew a small heart next to her answer.

Words here, scribbled definitions there, Cadence's page resembled a pile of Scrabble tiles. Brodsky must have been reading her mind when upon departure he announced, "If you possess too slow of an ear to hear the nuances of music and too feeble of a mind to process this information, then please, by all means, drop my course. You all are, gladly, dismissed."

With classes over for the day, Cadence thought she had time for a break but then remembered the assignments due, especially the presentation on Mexico in her Spanish class, so she returned to the library. When she rounded the corner to her previous spot, she was disappointed to see the table empty, so she began the task of translation. Even after two years of high school Spanish, Cadence couldn't recall the rudimentary skills necessary to string together a report. She stared in frustration at the task before her—a seemingly impossible one. Her professor had mentioned something about a language lab, so she searched through the labyrinth of the library's back rooms and found it.

Opening the door apprehensively, she was somewhat relieved to recognize the face of the dark-haired girl from her biology class. "Hello. Welcome to the language lab," she greeted, "I'm Isabella, but most people call me 'Isa.'"

"I'm Cadence. Aren't you in Dr. Kinsdaw's class?"

"Yes," Isabella said, "how do you like it?"

Cadence shook her head. "I don't. It puts me to sleep." She recounted the difficulties of that class and others, including the assignment that she knew would consume her schedule for the next twenty-four hours.

"I'm okay with the oral part, but I need help with the written report," Cadence said.

"Okay. I can assist you with that. No problem. Let's work over here." As they settled at a table for the task ahead, Isabella asked, "So, what's your report topic?"

"A presentation on Mexico for Dr. Marquez's class."

"Ah, Cadence, I'm from Me-hi-co," she proudly announced in her native pronunciation. Despite Spanish being her first tongue, Isabella spoke nearly flawless English.

Cadence couldn't believe her luck but tapered her enthusiasm with the embarrassing admission: "Listen, I don't know much about your country, only what I've read."

"That's okay. Let's see what you've researched. If you need more, maybe you could ask me questions, you know, like an interview or something."

For the next hour, the two engaged in an exchange of cultures. Isabella spoke lovingly of the wondrous beauty of her South. In her native Tequila, the calming blue tint of the mountains slides over the spiky splendor of agave plants that cling to the hillsides. Beneath the blazing sun, cows, horses, and goats seek the shade of oases that dot the countryside. In the town not far from her home, mariachi music and the smell of roasted meats wind through the bumpy streets. With every detail, Cadence watched the darkness of Isabella's eyes brighten and listened to the familiar longing for home. Cadence thought it strange that a Latina from a foreign land could describe a place that sounded so much like her own, a land where the ritual of farming was a daily practice and a drive through the town's center delivered comforting aromas of foods cooked with the love that only locals hold. The place Cadence called *home* could be a cousin to Isabella's: two romantic, adventurous, magical spots merely separated by thousands of miles.

So interesting were the stories that Cadence nearly forgot to write down the details. Eventually, Isabella asked, "If you're in Spanish 101, are there about twenty people in your class?"

"I think so."

"Well, you may want to make a handout, a flier, or something for each person. Like a fact sheet with some pictures. I have some that you could borrow. They may be a good idea."

"I hadn't thought of that."

"I also ask because my mother sent me a package and she always packs too much candy. Although I like it, I'm training for a race and it's too much. You could have some for your presentation. You know, a little something extra, authentic Mexican candy? Your classmates could get a taste of my country."

"Really? That would be so cool. You sure you have enough? I, I could buy some from you."

"I have more than enough. Your money is not necessary. I'd like you to have it. Okay? When I'm done here, I'll bring it to you. Where do you live?"

Hours later as promised, Isabella delivered the sweets from her room in Albemarle to one a few floors down. *Sinaloenses*, tasty-looking peanut candy bars, and *Arcoirises*, colorful pink and white marshmallow-topped cookies were the choicest items. The *Pulparindos*, hot and salted tamarind pulp candies, did not sound particularly appetizing, but the *rollitoes de guayaba*, sugar-coated rolls made from guava, looked positively loaded with energy. Overwhelmed by the gesture, Cadence thanked Isabella for the confections that would surely add some authenticity to the report. Before Isabella left to tackle the unrelenting load of science courses she took on as a pre-med major, she offered Cadence some survival advice.

"Listen, I was thinking about what you said about not being able to stay awake in Dr. Kinsdaw's class. There's a place with great coffee near campus."

When Cadence cringed at the mention, Isabella said, "I used to feel the same about the black stuff, but it helps me a lot. This coffeehouse has lots of good drinks. It's called c.a.t.'s. When I came here over the summer, I had to find somewhere to get my *café con leche*," she explained. "This place has the best, and the owner, Catissa, she's a special woman. *Muy simpática.*"

"Okay, I might try it," she said.

"You should. Well, good luck and *adiós*."

Although emboldened by Isabella's generosity, the feelings dissipated when the reality of an overwhelming workload set in. On top of her Spanish report, she had assignments for Dr. Elders's class, so she took up residence in the common room to avoid Corrine's incessant conversation. Wrapped in stress and fueled by the sugar of Isabella's homeland, Cadence began forcing her native tongue into a foreign one.

Around three in the morning, her head went down, and her body rushed deep into sleep. Riding Gunpowder, her rescue horse of five years, Cadence inhaled the freedom of a cool afternoon breeze as they powered over the pastures of the farm. Arriving at her favorite place of escape, an oasis of trees near the edge of the property, she slid off the horse's back. To her, the place was sacred for many reasons, one of which was the spot that held Snowy, her cat from childhood, who was buried in the hollow. When she found the beloved pet dead from old age in the barn, Cadence wrapped him in a blanket, laid him in her wagon and pulled it to this place. She spent most of the day choosing the right spot, mixing her tears with dirt, and mourning the loss of her furry friend. She would visit often, whispering young secrets to his ghost. This refuge held her best secrets, including the initials of her first love, carved into the tree that stood over Snowy's resting place.

As Cadence moved through the shade toward the natural diary of the marked tree, she lovingly traced the initials *B.S.* with her finger then looked to see the *CC + JR = BFF*, she and her friend, Jean, had cut into the trunk. With her eyes sweeping over other carvings in the tree's timeline, she noticed lines near the base, etchings she had never seen before. When she bent down to investigate, she found the marks to be a collection of chaotically moving scribbles. No matter how hard she tried, she could not make out their message. Just as she reached to touch them, Gunpowder released a spine-shivering whinny. Cadence jumped back from the tree and out of her dream. Wiping the cold drool from her face, she struggled to make sense of her surroundings. The stack of unfinished work clarified her location and the reality that she had many miles to go before she would sleep again.

When the sun had risen, she rushed to complete the presentation. Energized by the deprivation from her first all-nighter, Cadence stood before the class. Her nerves felt as if they were exposed wires emitting shocks and shakes during every second of her report. She knew it was a disaster, so she was genuinely surprised when Professor Marquez practically sung "*¡Excelente!*" and pronounced that the class had a high standard to meet. Cadence felt her classmates' eyes cutting her to pieces and hoped the candy Isabella provided would soothe their ire. Later, she especially wished she had saved some of the sweet stuff for Professor Elders . . .

"I hope your first week has been more pleasant than mine," the teacher began. Her stern expression was like a hand reaching out to slap each of them. "I have spent the past days defending myself for a complaint filed against me after our first class."

As if the seats suddenly developed needles, some students shifted uncomfortably while others glanced around for the one who had caused the pricks.

"Apparently, someone was *offended* by my presentation. Let me take a few moments to explain my pedagogy. I'm not a professor who lives in theory, who placates myself in some padded ivory tower and purports to teach about life. No. I choose to work and live in it."

She delivered her lecture on life, detailing her job as a medical counselor, where she saw people transformed because of poor choices, heat-of-the-moment decisions that left lifetimes of pain. She described the emotional, mental, and financial scars of living with incurable diseases like HIV. She explained the inhumane practices of insurance companies that refuse policies for those with preexisting conditions they received from loving and lusting unconditionally. She spoke of bankrupted lives and the legal culpability of disclosing positive status to a partner.

She reminded them: "This is the reality, the risk of being sexually active. These are the consequences. If this offends you, well, I guess life itself offends you. Then again, this may not be your life or life as you know it. I see before me people who have a lot of living to do." Without expression, they stared into the impassioned face of a black woman who knew about living.

"*Naked* education," she called it—raw material stripped of pretension, padding, and political correctness. She laid bare the dangers because she was not fooled by guises of their innocence: promise rings and abstinence assurances. Professor Elders spoke truth, and her delivery, however unpleasant, forced them to listen like the prospective victims research dictated some would become.

"One in four teens will contract an STD. Take our classroom as a microcosm of that. Hypothetically, five people here are carriers of a disease. But that number does not even speak to the silent numbers, and it's the unreported ones that concern me.

They wondered who among them was a statistic.

"If you think that college is about making you feel better about yourself, about being pacified, about reaffirming your beliefs, I suggest you rethink what higher education should mean." She watched to see if any of them were rethinking, but she could tell they did not know what to think.

"Three degrees ago, I knew I wanted to help people, and each day I step foot in my clinic, I do help those clients, but that work is *reactive*, not *proactive*. Those patients have already made the mistakes—unwanted pregnancies, sexual indiscretions, diseases. I don't want to see any of you on the other side of my desk in that office. This class, you all, you are the proactive part of my work. See, I can teach you to teach others about the dangers, but that's only if you want to be taught. If you don't want me as a teacher, then drop. If you are *not* here for a class that challenges you—drop. If you want to live in the comfort of ignorance, drop—*out of college*, because an education that does not transform you is no education at all."

Shock appeared on some faces, intrigue on others. "Education should be uncomfortable," she said, "because for many, survival is uncomfortable. If something or someone offends, ask yourself why. Fear or ignorance may be the answers. Or perhaps it's an unwillingness to admit that other people hold very different perspectives that run contrary to your experiences."

Although they were silently considering her points, they were also looking for the guilty party, searching for the offended, but whomever it was wore stoicism well. As quickly as the teaching tempest of Professor Elders had come upon them, it blew over. For the remainder of the class, they sat in a circle, listening to their responses about what they hoped to learn in college.

Because of her Spanish report, Cadence had spent little time on the questions, so she replied very generically, "as much as I can." When pressed for how she would achieve this, she could only come up with: "I don't know. I guess I'll figure a lot of it out as I go along." The majority of her colleagues had the same plan, and their professor adamantly warned against this haphazard approach, encouraging careful consideration of consequences.

For the week's remainder, work continued to pile up, less-than-stellar grades rolled in, and a case of full-fledged homesickness paralyzed Cadence. Her longing to return to all things familiar and to give up this collegiate dream burned deeply in that first month, but returning home was not really an option. Since she was the first to attend college on both sides of her family, nothing short of the apocalypse could remove her or the pressure to succeed. Still, she missed the simple pleasures she had taken for granted all these years—a stocked refrigerator, clean laundry, her own space, and of course, her family. In high school, teens often view parents as less-than-desirable accessories, but they become intensely longed for in those first days of college. In some ways, Cadence knew if given the choice, she would swap the freedom of her new life for the security of home without a thought.

Thought, and the deep kind at that, was a requirement for the discussions that came to dominate English. Professor Mirabilis would extract lines from the literature and hold them up for examination. While composition class relied heavily on books, Freshman Seminar had none since the issues of their daily lives became the text. Spanish consisted of call-and-response participation, an often embarrassing exchange when tongues raised on English got twisted in the quagmire of conjugation. Biology and music were miserable hours of lecture— one painful from sheer boredom, the other from the sadist who fed on their intellectual insufficiencies. Exercises in exactness were the tasks of biology lab, but Alex made the hours bearable, even fun. And so it went: those initial weeks that lay the foundation of four years.

With weekends already worshipped and welcomed, this one promised to be especially sweet since Friday was Penny's birthday. That night, Penny and her hometown friend, Jade, along with workout-crazed Natalie, her roommate Darla, Cadence, and Saida ventured out for a celebratory sushi dinner. Unlike the others, who wore flats for the jaunt, Saida braved the cracks and snags of Charleston's stones in heels. Her colorful sundress was flanked by the sassy skirts of the others. They reflected nicely against the fashions flaunted by storefront mannequins and mirrored by other would-be college models.

Although some were familiar with the slabs of uncooked fish laid over rice and the seafood-centered rolls dunked in soy, most were not. Sashimi and sushi presented new lessons in eating, and it took some persuasion for the inexperienced to try the raw delicacies. The ruby flesh of tuna with smearings of vibrant green wasabi piled on rice melted in their mouths thanks to the chemical cooking of soy. At first, Cadence was hesitant, but with Saida as a guide, the meal proved adventuresome. The farm girl marveled that she had gone eighteen years without this delectable staple, a cuisine that was an extreme departure from the charred meats and cooked-to-mush vegetables of her Southern heritage. Glad for this discovery, everyone was stuffed beyond comfort, except for Natalie, who claimed a bad stomach and opted for an undressed salad.

Unbeknownst to the group, Saida had arranged for her recent hookup to meet them. When Brian made his entrance with his roommate Paul, Saida feigned mild surprise. Joining the table, they downed shots of warm sake followed by swigs of Bud Light, while the ladies toasted with sodas. Afterwards, they headed out to a string of parties courtesy of the guys' connections. With the girls parading past the storefronts and restaurants of Market Street, Brian and Paul admired the views, with the former eventually taking Saida around the waist and whispering: "You're so sexy. I love a girl in heels."

Drawing back, she threw him a stern look. "A *woman* in heels," she said. Spurred by her feistiness, he cut a boyish grin and slowed so they dropped behind the group.

Ushered in by the clinging gazes of frat brothers, the first party had all required elements: guys in white long-sleeve shirts with conservatively patterned ties, fabric and leather belts, khaki shorts, and brown dock shoes. They all held the signature red cups, except for the older ones, who clenched customized tumblers that slowed the humid air's assault on their cocktails. Those who could not afford bourbon indulged in the keg. Despite their loyalty to light brew, many sported the emerging beer gut beneath the clean-shaven boyish faces that would carry them into brotherhoods of politics, law, and business.

Learning it was Penny's birthday, guys sent an abundance of drinks her way and the pressure to perform ritual shots began. They tried to persuade her into a keg stand. When she declined, an attention-starved coed promptly stepped forward. Some would remember her face, but many more would recall the fire-engine red thong she flashed when they hoisted her upside down. "Go! Go! Go!" erupted as they praised her example so others would follow. Nameless girls did and soon, the guys committed every style and color of panty to memory. To make the most of the fleshy exhibition, they fashioned a game of guessing underwear to girl. A guy who missed had to drink but all were rewarded when dresses lifted over thighs to confirm the guesses.

When the keg was exhausted, some brothers hit the bars, others paired off into rooms with their panty matches. Cadence and her group moved on, prancing from party to party until Darla and Natalie departed for the dorm and the rest carried on to the final stop, a cocktail party of sorts in a stately home. With three piazzas for each story, the house was the epitome of Charleston's residential grandeur. The crowd was a bit older, and though the freshmen felt out of place, Saida, hot on the arm of Brian, displayed no reservations about being there. His sister was housesitting, and although forbidden from throwing parties, she stretched rules regarding small gatherings, pretending the house was hers for entertaining. When her brother arrived with a juvenile crew in tow, Jennifer gave him an austere look, which he promptly dismissed, making himself at home and getting Saida and her friends drinks. From the porch, Cadence could see the garden below and ventured down to look.

The plants and flowers reminded her of those her mother tended to so carefully at home. Swaying down the path, she inhaled the honeyed perfume of gardenias, glimpsed the bursting pinks, purples, and whites of crepe myrtles, felt the bouffant puffs of blue hydrangeas and the towering red cocks of gladioli. In a far corner, she paused to admire an elaborate sculpture of a girl smiling at a flower. A closer look revealed a spider atop the flower, clutching what looked to be a butterfly. The sculpture's base held the lapidary: "What but design of darkness to appall?—If design govern in a thing so small." Pondering the poetry, she did not see someone approaching from behind, but his voice tugged at more than her ear.

"Don't mind me for saying, but their beauty doesn't even come close to yours." Cadence turned to meet the gaze of a well-dressed, slightly older guy whose handsome face was enhanced by his oozing charm. "I saw you strolling on the allée. Thought you'd enjoy a little refreshment in this suffocating heat. I hope you like it," With a smile, he handed her something the color of sunrise.

Struck by his thoughtfulness and not wanting to insult his hospitality, she took the cup. "What's this?"

"Our custom. We Chawwlestonians," he began, dragging out the pronunciation in his native speak, "we always like to welcome guests with a cocktail. This here's Dragoon Punch. Takes a few days to make and maybe more to recover from it."

Cadence peered into the cup. "Hmmm, sounds interesting. What's in it?"

"Oh, a little whiskey, rum, green tea, a few other special ingredients, lots of fruit floatin' 'round in there."

The dark shapes of sweetness certainly weren't floating, but they waited like sunken treasure for discovery. Convinced by his hospitable gesture, she took a sip.

He eyed her for a reaction, knowing what it would be. "I'm pleased you like it. I see you were admiring the sculpture?"

Cadence glanced at the little statue, whose smile now appeared a bit forced. "It's beautiful."

"The poem's by Frost," he said, with a professorial air. "But I think the piece is a bit ominous for such a lovely garden. Don't you?"

"I guess so." Uncomfortable with her lack of knowledge on the subject and feeling the effects of the night's drinking, she redirected the conversation: "This punch is really good."

With Cadence lured back into the comfort of a drink, they began the ritual of information exchange, which left him knowing much about her while she knew nearly nothing about him, except that he told her to call him "Will."

In the midst of their conversation, Jade rushed up. "Cadence, Penny's really sick." She pointed over to the garden's entrance, where a stone pillar held up the birthday girl. "Must've been the sushi. We're going home. You ready?"

"Yeah, okay. I'll be right there." Cadence looked longingly at Will, hoping Jade would catch the hint that she wasn't ready to leave.

"Beautiful, don't ruin my night by leaving," Will reached over to caress Cadence's arm and turned to Jade. "I'll be happy to walk Cadence home. Tell you what, why don't I call you and your friend a cab? My treat. That way, everyone gets home safely."

"You'd do that?" Jade asked.

"Absolutely." His phone materialized instantly.

Jade whispered to Cadence: "Wow, he's really nice."

Seconds later, Will assured them: "It's on the way," and true to his word, a cab arrived in minutes. He paid the driver, helped Penny and Jade into the car, and returned his full attention to Cadence as soon as it disappeared down the street. With her drink finished, she shook the cup to loosen the fruit.

Hearing his cue, he urged, "So, are you ready for the best part?"

"And what's that?" In his presence, she felt wanted—a sensation that hadn't come to her in a long time.

Reaching into the bottom of her cup, Will retrieved a piece of pink pineapple and held it up to her lips. Like a fish being baited, Cadence leaned in for a bite, but just as she reached the dangling fruit, he pulled it away. His lips widened. "Slowly, darlin'. Savor this little taste of my hospitality."

This time as he held up the piece, he slid it seductively across her lips, creating a sugary gloss he had every intention of removing. Her bite into the fruit released the pungency of concentrated alcohol. At her grimace, he offered his glass as a reprieve. He reached into her cup again and pulled out a cherry.

"Ah, the best fruit of all and my favorite." He swayed the fruit before her as if it were an offering. "This little bit of red symbolizes merrymaking. So, here's to making merriness, Cadence."

At the cue, she leaned in for it. Again, the alcohol had soaked to the core, transforming the usually sumptuous fruit into a treat she endured and one that left a trail of juice down her chin. She raised her hand to stop the trickle, but Will caught the wetness instead. Bringing his fingers to his lips, he licked the nectar freshly captured from her skin.

Captivated, she watched the work of his mouth, anxiously awaiting the kiss that would come as the distance between them quickly diminished. With their eyes fixed, Cadence was lost in his attention, so lost, that she did not see the shadow stomping toward them. Soon, she felt the dig of nails into her arm.

"Owwwwwww," she wailed, but pain instantly turned to into pleasant surprise. "Ennnnnaaaaaa," she slurred, "how're ya?"

Enna looked to Will then to their cups. "What the fuck is going on here?" She didn't wait for a reply but snatched Cadence's cup and slung its contents over the plants.

What normally would have been a buzz kill had little effect on Cadence. "Enna, chill! I'm just having a little fun. This is my friend, Will."

"Your friend?" Unamused, Enna pulled Cadence a few feet away.

"Look, Cadence, you're not going to hookup with that guy."

"Enna, I can handle my." Her burp arrested the sentence and a stumble punctuated her point. "Self."

Enna's grip tightened. "You're coming with me."

"No! I'mm nnnot!" Cadence jerked her arm from Enna's grasp.

"*Yes*, you are!"

Will slid between them. "Hey, what's your problem?"

"My problem, *Will?* Don't you mean, Wiley? My problem's you and your plan to take her back to that den of yours."

"We're just talking. It's really none of your business," he said.

"Just talking? Tell me, how long before she can't talk because she's unconscious? Consider her *my* business."

His eyes flashed a lethal anger, and Enna could hear the grinding of his teeth. "Fuck you! Go be a bitch somewhere else."

Enna met his wrath with laughter. "Is that the best you can do? Got news for you, Wiley, you might as well go home with your hand because she's coming home with me."

The look he gave her would have burned a heretic back in the day, but Enna simply deflected it. Standing firm, she said, "Yes, I know all about you—you fucking deviant. Fuck with me and I'll make certain everyone knows about you, if they don't already. When I'm done, you won't be able to pay a prostitute to give you a handjob."

He moved in close. "You fucking meddling bitch. You'd better watch your back."

As Enna watched Wiley slither into the darkness, her friend Rachel came down from the porch. With Cadence's condition deteriorating, Enna tried to get as much information as possible. "Cadence, who's with you?"

"Ummm, Saida, I think."

"Rachel, stay with her. I'm going to go find Saida." Her search would be to no avail. Saida had absconded with her male of the moment. Enna quickly returned, and with Rachel's help, they soon made it back to the room, but not to Cadence's. With Myla gone for the weekend, Enna placed Cadence where she could watch her. A few minutes after Rachel left, Cadence managed, "Ennnna, I thhhiinnkk I'm gonna be ssssick."

Like lightning, Enna had Cadence over the toilet. Wiley's concoction turned Cadence's muscles to jelly, and as her knees buckled, she bowed before the great porcelain god, offering up the night's food and drink. A river of red shot from her mouth and the pain of convulsing stomach muscles would have, under normal circumstances, been more than she could bear, but the same alcohol that had forced her on the floor also numbed the pain of puking.

Resting between wretches, Cadence busted into fits of laughter at what appeared on the toilet lid's underside—a sticker with a stick figure beneath a red strike-through and the warning: *NO DIVING*. For all their seriousness, Enna and Myla balanced it with healthy humor. While Cadence prayed to this altar, Enna brought her a cup of water, a wet facecloth, and graciously held back Cadence's hair. Few gestures prove to be as convincing a litmus test for friendship as holding a girlfriend's hair as she vomits. Undoubtedly, it is a measure of loyalty. In this intimate time, when the body pours itself out and philosophies of drunk love echo from the stall, true friendships are formed. After an hour, she was done, and with Enna holding watch, Cadence slept safely.

When the freshman awoke, her haze immediately turned to hurt, and a fear larger than any she had felt since coming to college began to steal her breath. Sheets she did not recognize and walls decorated with unfamiliar images launched Cadence upright, but dizziness struck her back down on the pallet. Her heart beat quickly as sweat broke from every pore.

A gentle voice brought some assurance: "Good morning, sunshine."

Cadence saw Enna smiling down. Lifting her hand to her head, Cadence moaned, "Owwww, I feel awful."

"I knew you would, but hey, you're better now than you would've been if you were waking up next to Wiley."

"Wiley?" Cadence struggled to recall.

"Your friend, last night?"

"My friend?" She couldn't put it all together immediately. Only snippets flashed in her memory. "Um, I remember a little bit of him, but vaguely."

"I don't expect you to remember much. That's the way it usually happens."

"What do you mean?"

"It's rumored that he drugs women and has his way with them. He gave a friend of mine a few diseases last year." Enna shook her head. "She had chlamydia, but the genital herpes will stay with her for life. When she confronted him, he turned the whole thing around, blamed her for giving him all that shit. Then he trashed her reputation."

Cadence dropped her face into her hands to hide her shame and soothe her throbbing head. She sat speechless while her mind mockingly flashed to the ruinous slides of Freshman Seminar.

Noticing her friend's lost look, Enna brought Cadence back from brink of possibility: "Hey, you're okay, except for the hangover. But be smarter than those assholes trying to seduce you. I'm just glad I showed up when I did."

"How'd you find me?" Cadence asked.

"I wasn't looking for you. Rachel and I were on our way home when we stopped by that house. I was talking with a friend when I saw him with you."

Enna filled in the night's details. When the recap was over, Cadence hoisted herself up and headed for the door, embarrassed at the night's blunders, but before she dragged herself to her own bed, Cadence thanked Enna who answered the gratitude with a smile and a nod.

Once in her room, Cadence stared at the stack of work on her desk, but the thought of reading made her brain ache even more. A few aspirins and water helped begin the recovery process, so Cadence settled into her bed like a caterpillar into a cocoon.

Hours later, she awoke to that irritating voice chatting aimlessly. Some crisis at work had prevented Corrine's boyfriend from visiting, but he promised, "Come hell or high water," that nothing would impede his arrival the following weekend. Their irksome love declarations intensified the hammering in Cadence's head, and with no hope of going back to sleep, she got up and staggered out for greasy food to soak up her body's toxins. After scarfing down a cheeseburger with fries, Cadence checked her mail. To her surprise, a care package from her mom awaited.

She opted to stay in the fresh air rather than return to the cave of Corrine's suffocating breath. Taking the box to the green space of Marion Square, she chose a cool spot in the shade and settled in. Frisbees flew as shirtless boys practiced their dives between bikini-clad sunbathers. The sunglasses of park goers reflected the bustle of activity that was the peninsula's beach—a scene providing a pleasant contrast to the already overwhelming assignments. She had so much to do, but the hangover from her social life dictated that she would get none of it done today.

Running her fingers along the package from home resurrected an immediate sense of sadness. In addition to the illness from her night's adventure, she was homesick. This was the longest she had ever been away, and the distance was wearing on her. The gifts sent by her mother and grandmother only increased that longing. Tucked inside were her favorites: her mom's sugar cookies made with icing so thick it was guaranteed to cling to teeth and tongue and her grandmother's orange balls, round rolls of gooey sweetness, made with orange juice and covered in coconut. With these were a few toiletry essentials, sets of sanity-saving earplugs, some candy, and a letter, the close of which read: *We are so proud of you. Made you some sweets to share with your new friends. Study hard, have fun, and be careful. Love always, Momma, Daddy, and Granny.*

The paper held the scent of home and the marks of her mother's distinctive cursive, an art she had encouraged Cadence to practice, especially in her time away.

She recalled her mother's words before leaving for school and now could feel their power radiating through the paper: "Cadence, write often about your experiences because some day, you'll appreciate remembrances of things past. Writing letters may be dead in this day, but do so and your memories will live. I promise."

Unable to withstand the weight of sadness, tears fell onto her mother's words, dragging their ink down the page and recording her moment of melancholy. Surrounded by hundreds of people in the city's park, Cadence couldn't remember a time when she felt so lonely. College was supposed to be among the happiest times of her life but sitting alone was immediate proof that she had no one to share it with. Everything was foreign, and all she wanted was the familiar: the flowery smell of her mom, a tender nuzzle from her horse, the protective gaze of her dad, the sweet sound of her granny's voice. The home that for years she had dreamed of leaving had suddenly become the only place she longed to return.

Chapter 3

Business Administration 101
The Principles of Practice

Every college has that haven for relaxation, reflection, recovery: a setting vividly engrained in the yearbook of memory. Fondly recalled by alumni, it stirs nostalgia, is revisited at reunions, and becomes the quintessential spot for fostering growth as much as any lecture hall on campus. For the family of Charlestowne College, c.a.t.'s was that place. Short for "coffee and talks," the shop silently boasted a devoted following and provided caffeinated support for the weary who slipped through its doors. Owned by a woman who became everyone's adopted mother, the coffeehouse occupied an old Charleston residence, transformed into a second home for students and the place for a day's first business.

In the space of a converted piazza, chic baristas served creations laced with Charlestonian lingo. Pluff Mud Mocha, Calhoun Cappuccino, East Bay Espresso, and Rainbow Row Refresher enticed guests, but the house special—The Lowcountry Latte featuring a shot of homemade pecan syrup—was the coveted concoction. Cup sizes reflected the city's architectural features. Smalls and mediums were listed as Charleston singles and doubles, after the house plan designs that made the city famous. The largest size cup, a "plantation," was aptly named after the grand tracts that were once the area's economic powerhouses. Catissa Crawford, the proprietress, served teas from the famed Charleston Tea Plantation, coffee by a local roaster, and hospitality from the depths of her Southern soul.

C.a.t.'s offered many escapes including those found throughout the house, especially upstairs in the consilium. Mostly bare, save for oversized pillows on the floor and an old cedar chest that held art supplies, the room's off-white walls featured writers' wise words, philosophers' perplexing ponderings, and customers' colorful comments. Doodles, drawings, and the occasional "good time" digits also canvassed the area. Every year, it became a scrapbook of sorts, with contributors returning to check for responses to their musings. Each August, Catissa made way for a new year of graffiti, restoring the room to a mostly blank slate, save for an initial line of inspiration that she chose.

For this year, a string of red cursive danced across the top of the walls, bearing a stanza from T.S. Eliot:

> *For I have known them all already, known them all:*
> *Have known the evenings, mornings, afternoons,*
> *I have measured out my life with coffee spoons.*

With J. Alfred Prufrock leading, Catissa encouraged visitors to answer the question: *How do you measure your life?* Some had begun to disturb this small universe with their deepest (and most shallow) thoughts: *I have measured out my life with bong hits*, wrote one. Another scribed, *In my life, I have known so much pain and pleasure that there is no measure.* As the semester progressed, words would climb like vines of kudzu from floor to ceiling and even onto French doors that opened to the piazza, a space where rocking chairs waited languidly, a joggling board offered courtship opportunities, and a hammock swayed carelessly at the far end.

While the consilium was for writing, the room adjacent to it was for reading. The sanitarium was quiet space. Large arm-chairs waited in all four corners, and the most comfortable couch imaginable faced the fireplace. Images of famous writers hung everywhere, with the Chandos portrait of Shakespeare staring out from above the mantle.

In following Isa's advice, Cadence paid the first of many visits to c.a.t.'s one afternoon. She had stopped by Isabella's room to share her granny's orange balls, a sweet exchange of appreciation, and invited her along, but Isabella had plans for attending an early evening mass and was off to a tutoring ap-pointment afterwards, so Cadence went alone.

As she sat with her house special, she took it all in. She loved this space. Of all she was growing to appreciate about college, she relished its freedom the most. The liberty of having no curfew, no one to tell her to clean her room or to do her chores, and the autonomy to make new discoveries. Like the house special before her—these were the joys of this new phase. She closed her eyes and inhaled the sugary steam, and the moment she sipped the perfect marriage of flavors, she knew the taste marked a necessity. Sitting with the cup of com-fort, she stared out of the window, lost in the fantasy of it all.

"Goodness gracious, what sweet imaginings."

The voice brought Cadence out of her dreamy state to the calming presence skirting her table. "Sorry?"

"Your thoughts, honey, you're really lost in 'em. You know, we have a room upstairs, the consilium, if you want to share them."

"I, I was just thinking about how great it is to be here."

"Why, thank you. I'm delighted you like my little 'ole cof-feehouse," the woman said.

"Oh, I meant it's great to be at college." The instant the words went out, she regretted them. "I'm sorry. I didn't mean that it's not great to be in your shop."

"Darlin' it's okay. I know what you meant. I hope you'll find what you need here—and freshmen do need a lot in these first weeks."

"It's that obvious I'm a freshman?"

"Oh, you don't stick out. I can just spot my new faces, and it's always nice to meet them. How do you like my house special?"

The steaming cup of perfection rose to her nostrils. "It's amazing."

"It's my grandmother's secret recipe for pecan syrup. I'm Catissa, dear, mother matron of this humble house." She extended her free hand while the other held a large, white mug with the shop's logo embossed in black and red.

"I'm Cadence."

"Cadence, ah, lovely name. As in running, biking, or musical Cadence?" Catissa grinned.

"Um, none of the above? I think my parents just liked the name." Cadence was unsure of her answer because she had never bothered to ask.

"Well, it's beautiful," Catissa said, spying the line forming at the counter. "Cadence, it's been my pleasure. I hope you'll come here often. If you need anything, dear, just let me know."

Although she wasn't sure if it was the coffee, Catissa's hospitality, or a combination, whatever it was wrapped her like a childhood blanket—a sensation shared by the devotees who established c.a.t's as a tradition.

When she returned to her room, Corrine was, as usual, on the phone. To block the incessant chatter about nothing, Cadence shoved her earplugs so far down her canals she may have been millimeters from brain matter. She opened her Spanish book, but the subject was quickly lost when she began analyzing the room that was not entirely her own.

The business of decorating had been largely uneventful, with Corrine contributing only to "her side." In a perfect roommate-matching world, amenities are split, accessories are shared, but colleges are not in the business of creating harmonies. More often than not, the pairings of strangers result in indescribable hells rather than the heavenly friendships promised in brochures and promoted in orientations. Sharing a room becomes a cruel social experiment that tests patience, designates possessions, and alters personalities. In so many instances, dorm life is nasty, brutish, but rarely short, as dramas lollygag over a term's long miles.

At first, Cadence had not made much of the fact that her roommate did not bring any amenities to school; she thought Corrine's family may have been financially strapped, so the luxury of a dorm fridge was a gift from Cadence's grandmother. The fridge sat in the margin of the middle, a reminder of her family's generosity and unwavering support. It was meant to be shared, but Cadence was the only one who kept refreshments in it. Lately, she noticed her food and drinks had begun to disappear, but in wanting to avoid tension, she said nothing.

Looking up at her wall, Cadence dwelt upon the photos she had taken in her high school photography class. It was a love she developed from her teacher, Mrs. Wright, who guided her through the camera's complicated settings and taught her to see subjects from unusual angles to harness light in making art from darkness.

One of her favorite black and white photos featured a close-up of Gunpowder's eye, and within this sphere, another circle appeared: the outline of her camera lens—the instrument so often poised between herself and the world. Although the camera was with her nearly every day of high school, she had not brought it to Charleston. By the end of her senior year, she was accustomed to shouts from subjects begging for their pictures to be snapped. She lugged around that camera so much that by graduation she wanted a break from the relentless *click, click, click* she was obliged to deliver as the yearbook's photo editor. When she packed for college, she left it buried in her closet.

Cadence's side bore a striking contrast to Corrine's whose walls were bare, save for the preponderance of photos that hung like portraits at a shrine. All were of Jed, and Corrine had arranged them in the shape of a heart; mementoes of their life together skirted the spectacle: a dried prom corsage, a cork from their first bottle of pink champagne, and his high school ID—a piece of plastic he had not needed in the five years since he had graduated. Beneath the collection sat a teddy bear, which Corrine clung to as if it were her child. She was holding it now as she, dressed in Jed's ragged flannel shirt and facing the altar to him, whispered into the phone, a technique that meant Jed was getting phone sex. Her commitment to servicing his long-distance needs was so severe that she couldn't be bothered honoring the promises in her roommate contract—especially the cleaning ones.

Cadence tried returning to her Spanish homework, but the vocabulary lulled her to sleep with a dream that featured the animal terms of her foreign language lesson. She found herself walking among the farm's residents. The oinks of the *cerdos*, moos of the *vacas*, and the clucking of the *pollos* delighted her, but it was her *caballo* that again became the dream's focus.

Another perfect afternoon played in fragments: the rush of the galloping power beneath her, the distinctive smell of his shiny coat, the squeaky grind of a leather saddle, all surrounded by the fragrance of freshly baled hay. Her long hair danced back as if some invisible force were holding it suspended. Gunpowder's mane bounced up and down with every stride. Eyes closed, she breathed in the sun's heat, the air's coolness. Lost in this freeing realm, she did not see the black hole looming ahead, the gaping mouth aiming to swallow her and Gunpowder. Seconds before the edge, she opened her eyes. Panic surged within and she pulled hard on the reigns, hoping to avoid the abyss, but it was too late—Gunpowder, frozen in the act of rearing, twisted off the edge with Cadence hanging haphazardly in the saddle. Her scream was arrested by a sudden *thud*.

"Cadence! Could you keep it down?" Corrine shouted with irritation.

Tangled in the comforter still clinging to the bed, Cadence pulled herself off the floor and staggered into the bathroom. A splash of cold water brought some relief, but she couldn't shake the fear that something was wrong, so she called her mother who reported that everything was fine. Coincidentally, Gunpowder had gotten out for a few hours, but they found him in the back pasture at the high fence that separates their property from the MacDonald family's. Their neighbors had a new addition, a California mare that was in heat, so Gunpowder had gone a-courtin'. Cadence laughed in picturing her stallion strutting his stuff before the new girl on the grass. She filled her mother in on all the week's upcoming work, especially a huge English assignment.

With the library project and paper for Professor Mirabilis looming, Cadence knew she needed help. After music, she decided to take her teacher's offer for assistance and found the office on the second floor of a dark, musty house. Since the professor was already in a conference with a student, Cadence waited, but despite the door being closed, the paper thin walls of this antique structure made Cadence privy to their conversation.

" . . . But I don't understand why you think this paper is so bad."

Professor Mirabilis patiently replied, "Please tell me what you would like clarified."

"Everything."

"Lana, you're telling me you do not understand any of my comments?"

"I'm not used to having so many bad things pointed out about my writing," she said. The remarks reminded Cadence of her conversation with Walker.

"In that case, I wonder if anyone has ever read your writing. Or have your teachers just placated you with inflated grades and illusionary praise all these years?"

Lana tossed her hair back. "I was an AP student if that's what you're asking."

"In English?"

"Yes."

"Then tell me, why are you in English 101?" Professor Mirabilis asked.

"I didn't pass the test because I'm a bad test taker."

"Well, I can't speak for your performance on standardized exams, but I can say that your writing needs work. For one, try to avoid beginning every sentence with the same word. Add sophistication by combining constructions to reduce choppiness, and use action verbs to engage your audience. Furthermore, you need a thesis." The teacher went on in a brief instruction on the business of better writing.

A few minutes later, the girl emerged. She did not acknowledge Cadence but already had her phone to her ear as she stomped down the stairs. "Mom? Yes, I just met with her—ridiculous. She was no help at all!"

While the disgruntled voice drifting up the stairs, Professor Mirabilis invited Cadence inside and wasted no time in offering suggestions and encouraging her student to think more critically about the complexities of *loyalty*.

"In some instances, Cadence, you may find that individuals become so blinded by their loyalty that they cease being able to distinguish 'right' from 'wrong,' 'morality' from 'immorality,' 'good' from 'evil,' or very simply, 'sanity' from 'insanity.' Finding examples to illustrate will help you see the complexities more clearly. Discerning the positives of loyalty is easy—I want you to consider the negatives. It is vital that you learn to look at all sides of any issue, especially in formulating an argument. Understand?"

"Um, I think so," she said. "If I don't want to write about this word anymore, can I change?"

"You're no longer 'loyal' to your chosen word?" The joke put Cadence at ease. "Absolutely. The paper is due after fall break, so you have time, but I'm curious: why do you want to change?"

"I'm not sure. I just think there might be a better one out there."

"Well, I'm sure you'll find another. It may not drop from above, but believe me, you'll know it when it comes. It's funny how great ideas just appear sometimes, especially when you least expect them." Professor Mirabilis's expression seemed to brighten in a way Cadence had not seen before. "Come see me when you need more guidance."

Cadence began packing her things, but Professor Mirabilis initiated some light banter about classes, activities, dorm life, home and hobbies. Surprised at her professor's interest, Cadence spoke as if she was chatting with a friend. The time proved well spent, and Cadence left feeling good about her paper and even better about her decision to remain under the demon's instruction.

What she was not so sure of was the decision she had made not to join a sorority. With September well underway, the campus buzzed with the activity of Greek life. Cadence often saw Madison and Malinda heading out to their engagements, as now their calendars were always booked. She remembered how earnestly Madison had taken the whole process when they met before school started. Since summer orientation, Cadence had considered the possibilities of rushing—endless parties, guy gatherings, weekend getaways, and bonds of sisterhood that would hold long after college. She had heard of the legendary social life, so she had registered for Rush Week and ventured with Penny, Malinda, Madison, and hoards of others in the days before classes began.

On the way to convocation, Madison prepped them on avoiding any discussion of the "Bs": boys, booze, bucks, and bling. Cadence found the advice funny since she didn't have any of those things to talk about, anyway. She did not find anything particularly funny about the rushing process. For her it was stressful, judgmental, and utterly unpleasant, even with the guidance of her recruitment counselor, also known as a "Phi Chi." At every house visit, she met the sizing-up eyes of sisters meticulously glancing over her every aspect. She felt like a sow at auction. Even though she was fairly unsure of joining, she went through the rounds: Open House, Philanthropy, Sisterhood, Preference and up until Bid Day. The week doubled as a progressive fashion parade, beginning in recruitment T-shirts and shorts and ending in an explosion of flowered sundresses, complete with heels and pearls that accentuated bronzed bodies.

Unlike many, Madison was made for this culture and prided herself in her identity as a legacy since her mother and grandmother has both been Zetas. In fact, so confident was she in her chances of joining this sorority that she embarked on "suicide bidding," entertaining no other preferences for her group of choice. It was risky but rewarding since ultimately, she received only one bid, which she wholeheartedly accepted, and thus, another legacy had been secured within the Panhellenic universe.

As Madison's shadow, Malinda managed to get accepted to the same sisterhood, so their bond became even more unbreakable. To her dismay, Penny did not get any bids, and Cadence secured one from a group she didn't feel any connection to. For all its promised rate of return, Cadence could not get past the time she would have to devote or the money; she could not ask her family for hundreds of dollars per semester considering how much they had already borrowed for her education. In the end, the business of rushing was better left to the belles and beaus willing to sacrifice themselves to appease the gods of Greek life.

Cadence found her decision aptly illustrated when one of the Greek minions burst into her Spanish class, ten minutes late and half-way through Kirby's report. Professor Marquez admonished his rudeness, but the frat faithful dared offered this excuse: "I don't understand how we are expected to make it to class and complete all this work while pledging a fraternity."

"*¡En Español!*" the professor demanded, but finding himself dumbstruck by loyalty that prevented him from studying the most basic terms, he simply muttered, "Sorry," and gave the floor back to Kirby.

As her classmate returned to his desk, Cadence grinned approvingly, and Professor Marquez congratulated him but in a less enthusiastic tone than when she praised Cadence. Each week, the reports comprised a countdown to the semester's close, and the first-years were quickly learning how college life was measured in presentations, papers, tests, and exams.

Although it was not even fall break yet, Professor Elders presented them with one more monumental measurement for the term when she announced the final project: "I hope most of you are beginning to discover this city's remarkable treasures, but in my experience, students too often focus on finding the next party. This challenge will get you out there chasing cobblestones."

The directions flashed from the projector: *Find the Seven Wonders of Charleston.* Their professor explained, "Going to college is more than sitting in classrooms, taking notes, and being tested. It's about the community around you—what it offers, what it needs, how it gives, and how you should give. You are residents here, and it's time to get to know your home.

Introduce yourself to her and once you find seven interesting, intriguing, funny, or just plain fun wonders, you'll share these and their significance the final week of class."

Ideas rushed through Cadence's mind—more specifically, images, which she would be at a loss to capture without her camera. She thought it too risky to ask her mom to mail it, so she decided to wait until after fall break to start the project. For now, she wrote *7 Wonders* on her hand, which remained for some days but faded with each hand washing and shower.

With the week wearing on, Cadence was looking forward to relaxing after Friday's classes, but way before her alarm clock assaulted her ears, the smell of bleach stung her nostrils. Opening her eyes, Cadence saw Corrine scurrying like a frightened mouse, picking up piles of dirty clothes and attending to long-neglected chores.

Cadence's eyes were barely open. "Corrine, what are you doing?"

"What does it look like I'm doing?"

"It smells like you're trying to fumigate the place. Why're you cleaning? Your turn was last week."

"Was it? I guess I got my dates mixed up." She kicked Cadence's shoes out of the way. "Jed's coming today, so I want the room to be clean for him. When you get up, tidy your side, okay?"

Cadence seethed. Corrine hadn't bothered to clean or pick up after herself since she arrived, opting instead to lie in bed and read teen magazines or be a phone sex service, but suddenly, there was sanitation urgency. Maybe Jed should come every week. With her roommate's chemical inconsideration dissolving any hope of returning to sleep, Cadence crawled out of bed. At least she would take advantage of a clean bathroom, but before she stepped in, Corrine said, "I just cleaned, so keep it in order, and let those others know, too." Cadence answered her with a door slam.

Friday's classes were a bit of the same. Cadence had begun to look forward to the interesting hours in English, except for one annoying aspect. Sometimes, when she'd look around, a guy named Corey would be staring at her, and on certain days, she could feel his eyes brushing up and down her back. She couldn't decide if he was zoning out or visually stalking her.

There was more mind-destroying monotony in Kinsdaw's class and harrowing harassment in Brodsky's. Dismissal from the latter only intensified enthusiasm for the weekend. Reena was looking forward to spending hers with Blaze: dinner and a movie tonight, followed by a trip to Columbia to see the state's celebrated Gamecocks play football. Listening to the excitement in her classmate's voice, Cadence couldn't help feeling jealous, as she had no plans for the next two days and no guy to share anything with on any day.

That afternoon, Corrine received the call—Jed had arrived. Like a damsel frolicking to meet her prince, she checked her hair, the room, straightened the pillows, and ran to the lobby. Minutes later, a stout, overbearing figure entered. Corrine, more interested in Jed's reaction to her domestic skills than in him meeting her roommate, offered a half-hearted introduction. It was as if Cadence had faded into the cinderblock walls.

"Corrine's told me all about you," he said.

Cadence thought the comment was strange. The two hardly spoke since Corrine's ear and the phone were one. In these few minutes of meeting, Cadence felt as if he sucked more air from the room than his girlfriend's pointless talking. When he extended his hand, Cadence was struck by his powerful grip, a crushing impression that lingered long after she pulled away.

Being in the room was beyond oppressive. When they weren't sucking each other's tonsils out, his fingers were clearly wandering her waist and below. Seeing they preferred a horizontal existence in hues of darkness, Cadence gave them privacy and spent as much time away as possible. Taking advantage of the vacancy still on the hall, she crashed in Althea's room on Friday but returned to the lust lair on Saturday with intentions of starting the project for Mirabilis due Monday. With no plans, she reasoned she had plenty of time to get it done, even though her professor had warned of procrastination with this laborious assignment. Luckily, Jed and Corrine had gone out, so Cadence decided to relax. With her earphones on and a magazine raised in front of her face, she was blind to the hand that snatched the reading, causing her body to jolt feet off the bed.

"Jesus, Saida! You scared the shit out of me!"

Saida laughed. "You busy? Obviously not. Hey, I'm going with Brian and his friends on a pontoon trip. We're gonna stay overnight and come back to Charleston tomorrow. Penny's coming. Wanna join us?"

Cadence could not get "yes" out of her mouth fast enough and immediately began packing the essentials. For good feeling, she brought along the materials for Mirabilis's project. An hour later, the three climbed into Brian's king cab truck where John, his friend, was waiting. When they arrived at the Isle of Palms marina, they met Barrett, whose dad owned the boat, Barrett's girlfriend Katie, and Luke.

The party platform rocked gently against the dock. It was a steely sight with a top deck that beckoned viewers and luxuriously cushioned seats everyone sank into. With all on board, they set off up the Atlantic Intracoastal Waterway—a snaky path running from Norfolk to Key West—and for much of the afternoon ride, the girls stretched out on the front seats, embracing the breeze, and exchanging waves and smiles with passing boaters. Greetings also hailed from dock sitters and their dogs. Everyone had cold drinks beading from the heat in hand, oil gleamed from browning skin, and mirrored shades reflected it all. Every particle of the scene painted one of life's perfect afternoons.

The saltmarsh's scent became more intoxicating with each channel marker, and the guys were especially proud to stand at the wheel and grin down on the bikini-clad beauties laid out near the bow. Of particular interest was Katie, the captain's girlfriend, whose overly large breasts became awkwardly fascinating. They became the conversation topic as the alcohol boldly ushered in the otherwise taboo topics of body parts and functions. Soon, all were exchanging opinions about breasts—sizes, shapes, bra brands. No one in the group was surprised to learn that Katie's breasts were implants, but everyone, except Barrett, was shocked when they learned of her means for getting them.

Arching her back with pride, Katie said, "They were a graduation gift—from my dad."

The guys snickered like schoolboys; the girls stared in unspoken awkwardness. Cadence looked to Penny then Saida, who leaned back with disgusted interest and asked, "Whose suggestion was it to get them?"

"It was kinda mutual," she explained. "See, he knew I wanted implants for a long time. When he asked me about a graduation present, I told him I didn't know what he could get me. He mentioned big gifts like a car, a trip to Europe, but wanted to make more of an investment in my future and hinted to something else I had wanted."

"What'd your mom say?" Saida wondered.

"She got a pair, too. We shared the experience."

"Did it hurt?" Penny asked.

"Oh God, it was awful, especially the recovery. Soooo much swelling and bruising and there were these drain tubes I had to clean; my nipples were crazy sore. I even had to learn to sleep on my back." She paused to dig out a bug stuck in the oil between the plastic mountains. "But hey, that's the price you pay for beauty, you know?" she said, flicking the insect from her French manicure.

Their judgmental looks revealed that they didn't know. Aware of their silent opinions, Katie said, "I feel much better about myself. I really like them."

"So do I, baby." Barrett beamed.

"I think it's awesome your dad got you boobies for graduation!" Brian said.

"Who the hell says that? 'Boobies?' What're you, in first grade?" Saida looked off into the distance where marsh mounds lay across a flattened horizon. Katie irritated her in the same way that her father's new wife did, the one he had left her and her mother for. When she looked back over to Brian, he grinned and gulped the remainder of his can.

The boat made slow but steady progress north, and the farther it traveled from Charleston, the more of the Lowcountry's pluff mud residents appeared. Gulls and swallows soared above the boat, hawks and eagles perched stealthily in trees, and herons and ibises stood on muddy banks. Sometimes, a pelican would swoop by on its way to the ocean, and the occasional herd of deer appeared in the fields lining the channel. Behind the pontoon, the sky exploded into fireworks of warmth: reds, oranges, yellows, but ahead, an eerie mouth of black shadows threatened to swallow them.

Each time Cadence would look back at the sunset, she felt John's eyes on her, and each time she peered deep into the wetlands, Cadence could swear eyes were watching all of them. Unlike the oaks on campus, these seemed sinister with their Spanish moss spiraling into the channel. Joining the companion of oaks were water-loving cypress trees, their veiny roots reaching like fingers into the murky depths.

When night had almost descended, so, too, did the mosquitoes. Bug spray replaced the sunscreen and everyone lathered up before they were sucked dry by the bantam blood suckers. Barrett turned off the main channel and steered the boat into a cove. He killed the engine and sounds of the dark encircled them. Bullfrogs and crickets created a cacophonous chorus. Amid the noise Barrett said, "Y'all want to see something cool?" It wasn't really a choice; he was going to show them anyway. "Everybody look past the bow," he instructed.

With their eyes fixed into nothingness, he turned the boat's spotlight into the nook. On the water's surface, the golden eyes of an alligator congregation shined like marbles. A swing of the light to the starboard and port sides revealed they were surrounded. The beady stares of the prehistoric beasts chilled them all and intensified their fears of falling overboard.

They continued on and some distance after the village of McClellanville, Barrett directed the boat off the waterway again, cruising to a quiet tributary he and his father had long visited on their weekend excursions. Off the beaten aquatic path, only locals knew of its serenity from the channel's traffic, so that's where he decided to drop anchor. While positioning the boat some distance from a cluster of trees, the guys were moving around when Brian let out a harrowing cry and everyone heard the splash.

"Brian!" John rushed to the spot where his friend had stood seconds ago. "Holy shit, man!"

They frantically scrambled to the port side. Luke lunged for the spotlight as they all screamed for the missing, but the wetlands only mocked them with their own echoes.

"Oh my God! What're we going to do? Brian!" Katie cried.

Saida stood in slightly shocked silence as the others shouted for him. The murky void of the marshlands swallowed their screams, silence heightened their fears. Hearts beat faster, sweat broke out on burned skin. Barrett snatched the light from Luke and held it to the water, but only its reflection was returned. After a few moments of particularly screeching calls, a dead quiet rested over the boat then out of the dark—"Boo!"

"You fucking asshole!" John said.

"What the fuck, man? That is *not* cool," Barrett exhaled everything before allowing himself to laugh.

"Aw, guys, I didn't know y'all cared so much. I was just havin' a little fun." Brian hoisted himself onto the deck with Luke's help.

Grabbing a towel, Brian moved toward Saida, who held a nonchalant reaction: "*Not* funny."

"You didn't come in after me?"

"Did you really expect me to?" she said.

"Well, I thought you might." He leaned in to kiss her, but she turned her face. "Guess not," he said.

"So now that we know dickwad here isn't gator bait, let's get some dinner going," Barrett said.

Steaks and veggies replaced the void that had made most of them sick to their stomachs. Roasted marshmallows slapped into the gooey goodness of s'mores reminded Cadence of summer camp, of stories over an open fire surrounded by what lies beyond the light. Giving into the nostalgia and taking advantage of the Gothic draping, she suggested a haunted tales session, so the eight began exchanging urban legends against the backdrop of the wild wetlands.

Toenails scraping on a car's roof thanks to the work of the hook man; the babysitter and the man upstairs; the killer in the backseat; the kidney thieves; and aptly, the alligator in the sewer: the campers exhausted the popular tales and moved on to ghost stories.

Having worked as a guide for one of Charleston's ghost tours, Luke seized the telling and filled his listeners with local lore. He described the city's many apparitions: the famous Nettie and Junious Brutus Booth of the Dock Street Theatre; the gentleman ghost and the headless torso, also called a *haint*, who make the Battery Carriage House their home; South End Brewery's Captain George who committed suicide in 1885 after watching his cotton shipment burn in the harbor. Luke managed to instill quite a few shivers in Cadence, Saida, and Penny when he mentioned a certain residence built on the site of the Charleston Orphan House.

"Have y'all heard strange singing or children's voices?" When they indicated they had not, he said, "In October of 1918, a few of the children played a practical joke and set a box on fire. The blaze spread quickly to the infirmary where 200 sick orphans were stricken with the Spanish flu. Four children died in the fire."

"So, what songs do they sing?" Penny asked.

"'Ring-A-Round the Rosie,'" he replied. "They'll also laugh. Oh and apparently, they have a thing for making the fire alarms go off. You gotta watch out for those mischievous orphan poltergeists."

"Here's a history lesson for you," Barrett began. "A few miles from here, just off the banks of the South Santee River sits the once great Hampton Plantation. Back in the day, it was occupied by the Rutledges, and one of their children, John Henry fell in love with the wrong girl—she wasn't a blueblood."

"Oh no!" Brian smacked his forehead. "They're ruined."

"Hey dick, don't spoil it," Barrett said. "Anyway, no matter how much he tried to convince his parents and hers that it'd work, they thought the marriage was doomed. To top it off, his girl wouldn't even elope. Didn't want to disobey her parents. For weeks, he was depressed, locked himself his bedroom or in the library where he'd sit in a rocking chair for hours. His parents didn't give into his sad routine. They sent him to Rhode Island to get over it. He had to return when his sister died of yellow fever, so he set off for Charleston and found out that his love had married someone else." Barrett gulped his beer.

"That's terrible!" Katie said.

"What's really terrible, baby, is when he got back to the plantation, he shot himself. But he didn't die until a few hours later." Barrett paused to let the eeriness set in. "Now, some visitors and park workers say they've heard a man crying, and house slaves used to report seeing the chair rock not long after his suicide."

"Creepy," Cadence said. "How old was he when he killed himself?"

"Twenty-one. Died in 1830," Barrett replied. "Imagine that—you love a woman so much you kill yourself over her. Now that's fucking loyalty."

"It sounds more like obsession," Saida countered.

"What's the difference?" Luke posed, but the question was one of those that just hung in the darkness. The day's exhaustion had finally caught up with them, so the couples paired off and staked their places on the boat. During the hours before, Cadence and John had exchanged beer-inspired kisses in moments when they sat together. When the evening's cool air settled on them, they snuggled toward the front. His touch stung her reddened skin, but she liked the attention. Drained from the trip, she arrested his hands when they set out to explore. He understood and reluctantly, controlled himself. "Can we spoon?" he whispered.

"Sure," she said, secretly thankful for the added warmth as the misty coolness began to settle on the blanket and the sun's burns added to her chill.

While those below were drifting into sleep, Barrett and Katie were delaying it. All day, every swallow of alcohol increased his desire and his need to get her on the top deck. Now she lay beneath him—relaxed and naked—as he slid his sloppy tongue over her, paying special attention to those strange, saline attractors. As he worked over her and touched her into wetness, she hungrily said, "Mmmmm . . . I want you inside of me."

His pride swelled even more at the fact that she desired him too, but that's not what he had in mind. "Not tonight. You know what I like."

"Again? But we always do it like that."

"Please, baby, you know what it does to me. I've been looking at your sexy self all day and just dreamin' about it. You've been driving me absolutely fuckin' crazy. I even told that ghost story for you. Pleaseeeeeee," he whined.

The words came easily, as did her consent from his flattering, so she prepared for what he wanted. Bringing her hands to the side of each breast, she pushed them in. As they rose up on her, he positioned himself above, and taking some wetness from between her legs, he spread it over his erection. When ready, he slid himself between the massive mounds, thrusting into the space she held steady for him.

When her hold would loosen, he commanded, "tighter, tighter," to which she responded by pushing them together more. He moved quickly in and out of her chest's makeshift vagina, clearly unconcerned with the real one beckoning from below. It took only a few minutes before the day's tension shot over her, and having finished, he collapsed by her side then passed out. She grabbed a towel to wipe her chest, and lying on her back, she looked up at the tiny stars, their powerful shine dominating the massive sky. Alone in the dark, she couldn't help but feel as if their natural beauty were mocking her from millions of miles away.

Hours later, Cadence opened her eyes to the morning light and to a sight that instantly paralyzed her. Feet from her, a long brownish-black snake—its tongue flicking in and out of its triangular head—rested in a patch of sun. She dared not move much, but gently reached behind her and felt for John. When he didn't respond, she whispered, "John! John?"

He wakened slowly and began to slip his arm around her. In panic, she squeezed it. "Don't move! There's a snake right in front of me!"

John lifted his head carefully over hers and spied the serpent. "Shit!" he said in a quiet shout, "it's a goddamn water moccasin. Be still. I'll be right back." He crawled away toward the boat's center and called up to Barrett: "Don't freak, man, and everybody else keep it down, too. There's a fucking cottonmouth curled up near Cadence. Where's the gun?"

Barrett hurriedly pulled on his shorts and slipped down the ladder. From beneath the console, he pulled out a 9mm and crept toward Cadence. The snake was quite unaware it was disturbing the boat's occupants, but as Barrett moved closer, it started to sense something was awry and in its characteristic nature, tightened into a coil. In reaching Cadence, he whispered, "Okay, I'm going to rest this on your arm. It's a tricky shot. Be absolutely still."

Cadence really did not want him to shoot the snake as she hated the killing of most creatures, but she was in no position to argue, especially considering the oozing machismo with a weapon crouched over her. As he indicated he was ready, Cadence shut her eyes tightly, stiffened her body and waited. Seconds later, the gun exploded into the coiled mass. The snake's body flailed about. Even though he had hit the head straight on, a skill perfected by years of target shooting with his father, Barrett shot it again for good measure. With danger dying on the deck, Cadence rolled away from the bow. Barrett and the guys took a few minutes to study the kill—its size, length, markings—then kicked the carcass overboard.

Turning to the others, their captain asked, "Who's hungry?" At first, the question didn't seem digestible, but soon, the grill sizzled with breakfast that readied them for the haul back to Charleston.

With every hour that slipped toward sunset, Cadence became anxious about the project due tomorrow. Sunning again on the bow but with more sunblock and John's hat, she pulled out the assignment hoping to make progress. A quick read of the directions revealed that she needed to be in the library to complete it. She assured herself she would have time since they were steadily making their way to the marina, or so she thought.

Unbeknownst to her and her friends, they were the surprise guests at a late afternoon oyster roast thrown by Barrett's dad, and sure enough, when the day was almost done, he stood waiting for them on the dock, a long extension of the massive mansion that reposed above the river.

When the boat slid up, he greeted, "Well, hello, pretty ladies." With a large, insulated tumbler of bourbon occupying his left hand, he helped each of them to the platform with his other. "Welcome. How was y'all's outing?"

"Really fun, Mr. Shaftesbury," Katie replied, "except for the snake part. Oh my God that was scary!"

"Snake part?"

"Tell you about it later, Dad," Barrett said. "This is Cadence, Penny, and Saida, and you know the others."

"Nice to meet y'all, and please, call me 'Earl.'"

The guests walked the manicured path up to the house, taking in the splendor of a landscape that dripped wealth with a heated infinity pool, ten-person spa, and sculptures of boats and fish decorating the lawn. Off to the side, under a massive oak tree, two black men roasted oysters over a large steel grate resting on four cinder blocks. Next to them, an enormous silver pot released the unmistakable smell of beer and spiced water. A Lowcountry boil with potatoes, corn, sausage, and shrimp was at hand. On the porch, a black woman was preparing to set out the staples expected for this culinary tradition. It was a small occasion, but catered as if it was much more. A bartender stood ready, while a lonely server waited for the work of collecting empty glasses and plates.

As they entered the house, a striking blond greeted them: "Well, hello everyone," she gushed. "I'm Frances, Earl's wife." Tall, slender, and several years younger, she was decked with diamonds that sparkled with her every movement. The most dazzling stone was a large ruby encased in more diamonds, and it prominently assumed a comfortable position between her overly large breasts, also apparent gifts from her husband.

Barrett addressed his stepmother with a warm smile and asked Katie to show the girls to one of the house's many bathrooms to freshen up.

"This place is amazing," Penny said.

"Yeah, it's nice," Katie said. "Barrett's dad owns a boat business. He's a distributor, but he comes from old money, too."

"What's this party for?" Saida asked.

"Oh, Barrett said his dad has some potential investors in town, so he decided to throw a little get together. You know, show them a bit of Southern hospitality."

Saida understood immediately and looked forward to meeting the group who had flown in from Miami, so she quickly primed herself to readiness and reappeared by the pool. When they stepped outside, Cadence again noticed the scene conjured by the oysters and the men standing over them. Something else about it kept beckoning her; eventually, she realized that she just may be looking at the kind of wonder Professor Elders expected for the final project.

"What're you staring at so intently?" John asked as he approached from behind. "Here, I thought you might like this." Slipping his arm around her shoulder, he dangled a cold beer in front of the scene and planted a kiss on her cheek.

Cadence grabbed the bottle weakly, her eyes remaining fixed ahead. "Um, I just think that would make a great photograph, maybe for a project I have for Freshman Seminar," she explained.

"Here, take this and get the shot." He handed his phone to her.

Cadence had never liked the idea of shooting with anything other than her camera, but she wanted the picture and knowing she probably wouldn't see this again—a setting that fixes itself in memory, that perfectly captures the local essence—she walked over to the roasters.

As she approached, the men looked up and smiled. She could see the sweat glistening against their dark skin and the salt stains that formed erratic lines across their denim overalls. They wore scuffed black shoes, big straw hats, and their enormous gloves held shovels with handles smoothed fine by years of turning shells. She greeted them and asked if she could take their picture for a school project.

"Why, most certainly, miss," one said. "You'd like us to pose?"

"Um, it'd probably be better if I could just get you in an action shot. Maybe turning the oysters."

"Oh, okay, ma'am. Let us git the burlap offa there," the other suggested and began removing the cover.

At this cue, she backed away and framed the two beneath the moss-laden tree on the marsh's banks. When she had caught the first of many wonders, she thanked them and returned to John, who now waited with the others near a long, ornate table made from the mollusks' shells and featuring two large holes with trashcans positioned underneath. Minutes later, steaming oysters lay piled on it, and all the tools necessary for this delicacy were ready for use. Mr. Shaftesbury invited his guests over and especially encouraged the girls to congregate around him.

"Do y'all like oysters, pretty ladies?" He didn't wait for them to answer before continuing, "Well sugars, let me show you how to shuck." The girls leaned in to get a better look at his hands working.

"Take a glove or a cloth like you see here," he said, "and choose an oyster. Now, I like larger ones 'cause they'll have more meat inside. The oyster's top is the lid, the bottom is the cup, and on that nice, grooved end is the hinge. With your knife, find the slot in the hinge and push it in there, give that blade a little twist and it'll pop open." He paused like a lab instructor watching his pupils experiment.

"Yep, yep, beautiful. Y'all ladies are naturals. Okay, work the knife around the shell and open it. Scrape the lid a bit so you can get all of that juicy goodness then cut the muscle and you're ready to slurp." He smiled, waiting again for them to complete their shucking.

"I'm a bit of a purist, so I don't care for trimmings, but some folks, well, they pile it on: cocktail sauce, Tabasco, and lemon. Dress yours up however you like, but I like them *au naturale*," and with that, he tilted back his head, opened his mouth, and the gray mass disappeared inside. "Mmmm, mmmm, that's good eatin'!"

Cadence tried it. Despite its salty, smoky, juicy aftertaste, she could not get past its slimy texture, which felt like a ball of snot in her mouth. Still, she tried a few more with the condiments but eventually decided these muscles were not for her.

After each novice had tasted the ocean's fruits, their host asked, "What do you ladies think?" Their sour expressions gave him the answer. "Well, they are an acquired taste, but for our family, that taste has been acquiring for a long time. You know, when it was first settled, Charleston was called 'Oyster-Point-Town.' That was way back in the 1600s. My family has been sucking down these aphrodisiacs ever since."

"I love them," Saida replied and grabbed another large shell from the stack, before giving her attention to one of the investors while Brian relaxed in the hot tub.

Although Cadence was having a good time, Mirabilis's project kept nagging her. She tried to brush it off, but the uneasy feeling created by its lingering deadline would not subside. After the late afternoon slipped into early evening, she was relieved when the group piled into an oversized SUV with the bartender turned chauffeur. She sat in the back next to John, and when they pulled up to her dorm, he also got out.

"I had a lot of fun," he said.

Anxious to get to work, Cadence halfheartedly replied, "Me, too."

"So, I'll call you and we'll get together this week?"

"Sure." Just as she turned to go, he touched her arm and came in for a kiss, which Cadence rushed to end.

"I have to go. Bye!" she said with too much enthusiasm and scampered over to Saida and Penny.

"Hmmm . . . Cadence," Saida teased, "looks like someone's smitten with you."

"Um, maybe. I guess we'll see. Penny, what about you and Luke?"

"Nothing," Penny responded with disappointment.

As they made their way up to their hall, Saida pulled a card from the bust of her swimsuit.

"What's that?" Cadence asked.

She smiled. "Oh, just a business contact."

"You got one of those men's numbers?" Penny asked. "What about Brian?"

"What about him? There's nothing wrong with expanding my network." With that, Saida and Penny unlocked their door while Cadence made a brief stop in her room then hurried to the library.

Relieved when she recognized a few faces from class struggling with the work, Cadence got down to her own networking. The students hastily moved through the weeks-old assignment of answering twenty research questions. Even though they had not invested the necessary time in the project, she and her colleagues felt satisfied with the rushed result and were confident that when returned, their efforts would garner impressive numbers because of their teamwork strategy. Before they were completely finished, another procrastinator arrived bearing libations from c.a.t.'s. Learning that this student was meeting others from Mirabilis's course, Catissa sent over a tray of coffees to help the freshmen through the night. Cadence was the lucky recipient of one. When she pulled off the lid, the familiar smell that began the previous week helped usher in the next. In sipping the warmth, in holding that cup of Southern comfort, and in picturing the weekend's wonders, she felt, for the first time since coming to college, that she just might have found home.

Chapter 4

Music 105
The Appreciation of Sound

Souls should soar, ears energize, and minds move to inspirations conjured by a great song's cadence, but this was not to be for those in Professor Brodsky's course. He taught them the unfortunate truth that it takes only a single teacher to destroy a love for a subject, and for a crowd passionate and eager to learn the mysteries of music, this was a difficult lesson.

In spite of his efforts, he would not be entirely successful in killing their desire to make music; their love of it would transcend the course's trauma incurred. The playlists of their lives would continue to walk them to class, to woo them in love, to usher them through pleasures and pain, delights and despair. They knew this latter condition well when his arrival announced afternoons of agony. By the semester's end, he would extinguish any interest many had in knowing more about one of their most defining pastimes.

His cruelty was an obstacle they had to pass before the weekend's relief. For college students, this usually begins on Thursday, with Friday merely becoming a rest between social engagements. Beyond freshman year, most students knew to schedule classes later in the day to assure plenty of recovery time; savvy veterans managed to achieve the coveted Tuesday/Thursday schedule. Unfortunately for Cadence and her friends, this type of insight can be gained only through trial and error, the latter being abundant during those first months, especially in Brodsky's section.

Reena and Cadence spent each class trying to ignore the machinations of the musical monster. They pretended to take down his every word but wrote notes to each other. During their exchanges, Cadence came to notice faint, white scars on the inside of Reena's right wrist. Her watch covered the lines, but their ghostly ends peeped from beneath the band.

Today, Reena felt Cadence's stare and answered her friend's unspoken query by writing—*cutter*, which Cadence responded to with a question mark.

I cut myself, Reena wrote. *I used to.*

Before Cadence could ask why, the music came to a deafening silence. They had unleashed the beast. Brodsky's voice slapped them out of the shadowy prison, and as it did, the envious eyes of those secretly wishing expulsion followed them. Once outside, Reena and Cadence looked at each other with dread before howling in laughter. To make the most of their untimely departure, they headed to c.a.t.'s.

In finding the sanitarium empty, the two plopped on the couch across from the portrait of tragedy's grandmaster, and Cadence asked about the history on Reena's wrist.

"Around seven years ago," Reena began, "my mom started dating this guy. She got really close to him really fast. Before, we did everything together, but when he came along, suddenly, it was just me and the babysitter. It hurt a lot, so I began cutting."

"Um, so, one day you just picked up a knife and started to cut yourself?"

"A letter opener. I usually cut myself with my mom's letter opener."

"Oh, how . . ." in struggling for the right words, Cadence glanced up to see the Bard's eyes meeting hers: "very dramatic."

"But my first time was with a piece of metal in the bathroom at my middle school. I was in there crying. In walks this older girl, you know, the kind everyone looks up to." Reena took a cautious sip of her coffee. "She asked what I was crying about, and when I told her about my mom and some other stuff going on, she told me to grow up, that there was a better way to deal with shit. She walked over to the window where the blinds were hanging, placed her wrist against the end of one and pulled. I'll never forget her look."

"Painful?" Cadence guessed.

"No, well, at first it was but only for a second, then it was relief, like ecstasy. So, I tried it." She held up her arm. "And numerous cuts, scars, and three therapists later, here I am."

Reena's lines etched themselves in Cadence's mind. "Are you still friends with her, the girl who showed you how to cut?"

"Funny, we never spoke again, but when we'd see each other, she'd always smile at me, you know, like we had a secret between us. Actually, she had a lot of secrets. She moved on to embedding—putting stuff under her skin like paper clips, pencil leads. I heard she got an infection and had to have her arm amputated and that she spent time in a psych ward. Crazy, you know?"

Cadence nodded. "And your mom and the guy, are they still together?"

"No. He split when he saw how apparently psychotic I'd become. Said he couldn't deal with such a drama queen desperate for attention. Told my mom to get me some help—that it was only going to get worse when I got to high school. He was right. It didn't get better until I had some shock therapy."

Taking in her coffee and the trauma, Cadence again glanced up to Shakespeare, who appeared to be listening intently, as if he were collecting material for his next great work. Cadence thought of Ophelia, Hamlet's love who was driven to madness and ultimately, a watery suicide. Looking to her new friend, Cadence could not imagine being shocked into normalcy or enjoying self-mutilation.

"Are you and your mom okay now?"

"I guess so. She was mad but also very upset about what I was doing. We have a love-hate relationship. Right now, it's at the love stage. That is, until the next guy. She's extreme. Latches onto the next dick that swings her way, but she wasn't always like that. I think my dad fucked her up."

"What does he think of all this?"

"Wouldn't know. I've never met him. Honestly, I haven't bothered to ask much and she hasn't offered much."

Listening to the mysteries of her new friend's past made Cadence appreciate her own relationship with her father. Cadence knew how hard he worked to give her a good life. He had been through tough times when the unpredictability of weather forced the farm into financial troubles. At nature's whim, the family business could be at the mercy of drought, flooding, disease, and insects, yet despite these challenges, her dad kept it going. During difficulties, silence kept an eerie hold around the barns and workshops; even the animals didn't talk as much, but she always knew better times had arrived or were ahead when the unmistakable twang of Willy Nelson drifted from the barn's wooden walls. She suspected her dad used the legend's voice to resurrect the farm's life, and the thought of him now made her long for those sounds that signaled home.

Reena and Cadence talked into the afternoon, and when Wednesday ended and Thursday began, everyone could taste relief except for Cadence. Her grades told the story of too many nights out, so she needed to study, but when John called wanting to see her—as he did too often since the pontoon trip—she told him of her plans. Although his pursuit was becoming slightly annoying, she invited him to the library. On the top floor, she chose a well-lit table near the window. He put her books down and pushed his seat as close to hers as possible.

"I'll be back in a minute," she said and disappeared into the stacks. Although the book she needed was not where the computer promised it would be, she found a sea of titles encircling her. She wondered how thousands of people could be so intensely interested in subjects that they would take the time to write books about them. Title after title drifted down from the shelves and with each, her mind considered a different direction the paper could venture. Occupied in thought, she let out a cry when John's arm coiled around her waist. Her frightened response broke the quiet, but John's lips silenced her.

She pushed him back: "What're you doing?"

"Hopefully, you. You said you'd be a minute."

"I got lost looking at all the books. Some really cool ones are here."

"Books are so boring. I hate reading. I'd rather be spending my time on a boat or doing something else."

"Don't you have studying to do?" She didn't try to mask her irritation.

"I am studying—you."

Pressing her against the shelves, his hands moved like octopus arms over her body while his scratchy lips, made raw and dry from too many water days, dragged across her neck. While he kissed his way about her, she was scanning the spines of titles when her eyes locked in on one—*The Book of Knowledge*. The title's final word was precisely why she came to Charlestowne College. A satisfying grin accompanied her discovery as she reached for the volume and stopped John's advances.

His hands slapped his jeans. "What? What's wrong?"

"Nothing. *This* is what I have been looking for." She held up the book longer than necessary while he read the title.

"I have some knowledge for you." His lips came again for her neck.

"Very funny," she said, moving out of his way. "Let's go. I have what I need."

He followed her back to the table, and since he had no intentions of studying, his presence became increasingly irksome. Hoping for a way to get rid of him, Cadence was relieved when he offered one.

"Hey, these guys I know are having a party. You wanna go?"

"I'd really like to, but I have to get this work done. I've got to pull up my grades before mid-term. But you should go."

"So I guess you don't want to?"

"It's not that I don't want to," she lied. "It's that I can't, but really, you should go."

"Okay, but call me when you finish. I'll come get you."

The kiss he left her with was one of arid desperation. When he was out of sight, she wiped her lips and breathed relief that she would not see him for the rest of the night and hopefully, for the week's remainder. She needed to tell him she wasn't interested but hated the awkward "let's be friends" conversation. In the semi-quiet of the library, she settled in to redeem her grades and force in the knowledge of texts laid before her. She ignored her phone which began filling with messages from him. Hours later, the feeling that she couldn't cram any more information in her skull's limited space signaled it was time to go.

Back at the dorm, she was about to step into her room when Saida and Diana, a new friend from religion class, were leaving for a night out and persuaded Cadence to join them. Outings with Saida were too tempting to resist, so Cadence swapped her jeans and T-shirt for a miniskirt and blouse. Corrine was on the phone with Jed, and in a moment of wanting connection, Cadence thought of asking her to come, but with the roommate occupied in the same never-ending conversation, Cadence decided to save the invite. Saida and Diana were waiting in the suite for her, and when Cadence walked into the room, a pink colored drink seemed to jump into her hand.

"What's this?" Cadence asked.

"Colorful and tasty," Saida said.

"Why don't you tell her why you're drinking a 'colorful and tasty'?" Diana teased.

"To help with my UTI."

"Your what?" Cadence asked.

"My urinary tract infection. I'm taking antibiotics for it, and I'm supposed to drink a lot of cranberry juice."

"Yeah, but I doubt the doctor prescribed the vodka to go with it," Diana joked.

"No, but alcohol kills germs. That's logical, right?"

"How'd you get a UTI?" Cadence asked.

"From sex." Saida grinned. "Musta been rockin' that boat too much. But I'm done with him. He's so immature and boring. Cums too quickly. In fact, I've given him the name, 'Brian the boring boner,' and worse, he likes to fuck with nothing but his cowboy boots on. Oh, sometimes he puts on his cowboy hat. I'm glad we're not making a video."

A giggling fit seized all of them. The imagery was almost too much, and Cadence knew that if she ever saw Brian again, she would find maintaining a straight face difficult. The girls swapped stories of past boyfriends' strange habits, and each sip of their pink prescriptions brought a sense of revitalization. Finally ready, they ventured out to see what the night would bring.

College Pit was the kind of dive that forever ingrains its sticky, soured beer aroma into memory; paradoxically, it was also the kind of place where the amount of alcohol consumed prevented many from remembering the events. More often, nights ended here before they even began, thanks to a game of hide and shoot. The minors flocked to the restroom in groups, and ducked behind each other to take shots, chug beer, and hasten the feel of liquid empowerment. Some had already secured fake IDs, and they reveled in the illusion of maturity those pieces of plastic granted.

For the friends, College Pit would become the place to revive esteem, where they could flirt and play the field without really investing in the game. They sought attention and were showered with gazes that made them feel attractive, even if the interests were dead by morning. They simply wanted to be wanted, needed to be needed, and this dump was fertile ground for hooking up. It was here that many began climbing to the first rung of the ladder of lechery, and no one enjoyed the ascension into vice quite like Saida, who was always about the conquest and took no shame in her exploits. Her mother had become so aware of her daughter's sexual exploits that birth control was dispensed like vitamins to Saida, so that she would not, in her mother's words, "make those same mistakes."

Now that she was done with Brian, Saida was on the prowl, and she began scoping the bar the moment she pranced past the bouncer. Soon, Saida zeroed in on her target for the night; by morning, he would most likely become another entry in her diary, the female equivalent of a boy carving counts in his headboard. As Saida waltzed off, Cadence and Diana stood looking available in hopes of attracting some older guys who'd help keep the buzzes going. It wasn't long before Saida had the connection they all needed. She managed to secure them a few shots, which they duly downed by ducking behind the clusters.

While they came here for the forbidden fruit of alcohol, what they really indulged in was the music. Like celebrants to Bacchus, they danced to the rhythms that flowed from the stage where a band new to the area, Stone Miles, was being initiated into the scene, even though they boasted a following thanks to a summer of touring. Emboldened by the liquid courage coursing through their veins, Diana and Cadence took to the floor while Saida returned to her man of the minute.

In the bouncing and flailing that sometimes comprises drunken dance, Cadence bumped into a guy doing the same. He raised his arms above his head, and despite the massive sweat stains in his armpits, she stepped closer for a flirtatious exchange of moves. Diana, seeing the action, wanted in, so both assumed a side, warmly sandwiching the sweaty fellow between them. They exchanged smirks and sloppily formed seductive expressions between playful grinds until a sulking figure latched onto Cadence's arm and dragged her from the floor's fun into the sobering silence of the rear patio.

"I thought you were studying. You don't look like you're studying now. Why didn't you call me?"

Cadence looked around at eyes training in on them. "I just didn't."

"So, you just decided to come here instead? And, and dance with some, some random asshole?" John struggled to mark his territory.

"Not exactly. Saida asked if I wanted to come out. I did, so here I am."

"But you didn't bother to call or message me?" He stepped closer to her. "What the hell, Cadence?"

"John, calm down. Don't make a big deal out of noth—"

"Don't fucking tell me to calm down! I thought we had something going. Do you still want to be with me?" He threw his arms about as if he were a child denied candy.

The smell of the bourbon on his breath was lethal, but the alcohol had forced a question for which there was only one real answer. Cadence looked around to see even more spectators entertained by the fight. She breathed in. "Not really. I just don't want a boyfriend right now."

Her words delivered a swift kick to his groin, but he remained standing. This time, he looked around to see a multitude of stares fixed on them. A point needed to be made.

"Fine! I was tired of you anyway!" His voice echoed with a bit more disgust than he probably meant, and he stomped off through the crowd.

Standing alone, Cadence sensed pity being showered on her when Diana came to her rescue with two shots of purple liquid and handed one to Cadence.

"Hey, you singin' the blues yet over that one?" she asked, motioning with the drink in John's direction.

"Not at all."

"You are now!" She clinked the stunted glass of "The Blues" with Cadence's. They swallowed the blueberry juice and Southern Comfort mix and headed back to the dance floor.

With the buzz singing in her head and the tensions with John and the term upon her, Cadence shed her inhibitions. As she twirled, the light caught her hair and drew the eyes of the lead singer. He watched as his words incited her movements, and before him, she let go—dancing with alcohol-inspired abandon mixed with a splash of dramatic stress. Under the spell of his voice and with the band's pounding persistence, she swayed like a seductress to sensations issuing from his lips and instruments.

She not only liked what she heard; she loved what she saw: when the lyrics reached a point of intensity, his eyes closed tightly and his body pulsated with a virility that made him instantaneously desirable. His moves, while seemingly calculated, worked with a spontaneous fluidity perfectly in tune to harmony.

For hours, the band rocked the revelers until every body before the stage formed a pool of dripping exhaustion. The evening had spun by so quickly that all were surprised when the bouncers turned on the lights and turned off the party. Many made their ways to beds—some strange, some familiar, and most, lonely, as were the ones that Cadence, Diana, and astonishingly, Saida, went home to. Clambering down King Street, they reviewed the night. Cadence was especially giddy when the subject of the lead singer arose. They all expressed approval and teased at the raunchy possibilities of being his groupie as they lifted fantasies about rock legends up to the stars before laying their dreams down on their pillows.

The morning began with fog—not on Charleston's streets, but in the heads of those who had walked its paths just hours before. Cadence managed to swing by c.a.t.'s before English, and with her caffeinated attempt to clear the fuzziness, she settled into her seat. As she waited, she looked down to see the prominent black "X" on her hand, so artfully drawn by the bouncer, and noticed that others wore similar markings. The ubiquitous letter was a badge of honor, a symbol of underage defiance, of surviving shots in bathrooms and under tables, funnels of foam, and nights spent making memories they could not clearly recall.

Class was well underway when the door creaked open. Cadence looked up from the reading and thought her eyes were deceiving her. Standing with the same dreaminess that had mesmerized her only a few hours before was the singer of Stone Miles.

"Good morning, Rock Star."

"Hey, professor. Sorry I'm late. Couldn't find the room." His lame excuse produced eye rolling for the instructor.

"Have a seat," she said, pointing to a spot beside Cadence. As he slid into the desk, he nodded recognition at Cadence who tried to focus on her teacher's attempt to lead them through the final frontiers of *Into the Wild*, but the more the professor dragged them through the book, the more lost they became. Brains were simply not functioning, and she knew it.

"Rock Star, are you so dazed from last night's performance that you forgot your text?"

He grinned. "I did. Sorry." His charm was disarming, even to the demon.

"Well, you're not suffering in the haze alone. From the looks, smells, and cheap hand tattoos, I'd say the weekend began last night." She shook her head with amused disapproval. "Be careful, people. You may find yourself thrown into the wilds of jail. Keep in mind that one of McCandless' flaws seems to be that he lacks balance. His vision of extreme living costs him his life, so don't let your extreme indulgences cost you yours. Balance your academic demands with your social ones."

The class was impressed by her talent in connecting some random book theme to the immediate circumstances of their lives but seemed oblivious to the fact that to stand before them as an instructor, Mirabilis had to attend college first.

"Rock Star, don't forget your text next time. Perhaps if she is willing, Cadence may share hers with you."

Cadence didn't even think of denying the request. She was glad to share anything with the guy who had rocked her night. With his desk next to hers, she pushed the book over to him. He touched her arm and whispered, "Thanks."

It was good she was sitting because she felt weak even as an energy of attraction shot through her. In trying to make up for his incompetence, he studied the pages, while Cadence studied him. She watched as he scanned the notes she had written in the margins, but his reading suddenly made her uneasy since her innermost thoughts lay open for ridicule. Just as she began to regret her agreement to share, he picked up her pen and wrote, *DEEP*, beneath one of her thoughts.

Holding on to every brush of his arm against hers, she followed the contours of muscles that held one of her possessions (she would definitely not sell back this book) and performed a close reading of his hands. She even savored the smell of fabric softener, drifting from his clothes as it worked to mask the odor of beer still seeping from his pores. It was an overwhelming olfactory mixture she wanted to sniff even more, but when class ended, he disappeared.

Stepping into the hall, Cadence's disappointment turned to delight when she saw him staring in her direction.

"Hi, I'm Schilar. That was real cool of you to share your book."

"Anytime," she said. "So, you have Professor Mirabilis? I thought you were a junior or something."

"Nope. I'm a freshman. I have her at eight. I overslept this morning, so she told me to come to this class. I'm glad she did."

The flutter feeling erupted once again when she saw his eyes searching hers. "Why's that?"

"'Cause I got to meet the girl I noticed from last night." He continued dropping other flirty lines as they walked to their next classes. After minutes that Cadence wanted to last for months, Schilar asked, "Do you have any plans for the weekend?"

"Not really. I mean, some studying, but nothing major," Cadence said with restrained delight.

"You wanna get together?"

"Sure." Now her ears seemed to be deceiving her. She gave him her number and headed to biology while he left for astronomy. As he appeared smaller gliding down the hall, her smile grew larger watching him. In the high from the excitement of a rock star's interest, nothing could bring her low, especially her two least favorite classes that blocked the weekend's second beginning.

Cadence was looking forward to Schilar's call and hoped to hear from him soon, but he worked on guy time, so her phone did not ring. The possibility of the call held her in good spirits until she remembered that Jed was visiting Corrine again. Cadence felt sure the school should charge him a boarding rate. In addition to his irksome presence, he walked around in his boxer briefs, was incapable of putting the toilet seat down, and insisted on calling Corrine "puddin," which completely ruined a dessert Cadence had loved since childhood. To avoid them, she sought refuge with Enna, Myla, and Althea, who were enjoying a musical movie marathon. With the night's theme of "Heels Gone Wild," they began with *The Wizard of Oz* moved on to *The Rocky Horror Picture Show* and ended with *Grease*. Cadence found the event quirkily amusing, especially as her friends knew every word and gesture to every song and would earnestly try, on especially stagy numbers, to outsing one another and the performers.

The next morning, Cadence joined Isa in a trip to the Farmer's Market. Their tour began just past the fountain at the corner of King and Calhoun, where enticing smells emanated from the crepe and omelet stands, the latter operated by an affable Irishman. As they approached, he was slinging a spatula across a hot grill. "What's the story, beautiful ladies?" His accent was simply irresistible. "Can I interest one of ya in a fine omelet?"

Unsure of the offerings, they began reading the board, but the delectable combinations created indecisiveness. Sensing their difficulty, the egg maker addressed Isa first: "For you miss, how about I make you my favorite—a Mexican fiesta?

Eggs, cheddar cheese, black beans, salsa, toppin' of guaca-mole."

"*Perfecto*. Do you have any jalapeños?"

"Ah, a spicy Latina, aye? I do, and I'll add some extras for you, love. And for ya?" He turned to Cadence: "I'll make a farmer's special for you."

Finn piled the ingredients on the grill, and as he worked, they learned he hailed from Dublin and had been working jobs around the city in hopes of opening an Irish pub. The market gig and waiting tables were the means for achieving his dream. Beneath the tent, he moved to the tingling energy of Celtic music that conjured images of his Emerald Isle. When the cooking was done, Finn plated the creations, and although he moved to his next orders, he kept his eyes on them to ensure he garnered another "Mmmm" reaction from satisfied customers.

After breakfast, the two strolled through the tents, savoring local treasures: blueberries, raspberries, and blackberries. Heirloom tomatoes, cucumbers, squash, peppers, eggplants, and corn—nearly every shade of the vegetable rainbow lay on tables beneath tent after tent of enticement. Cadence picked up a package of sun-kissed strawberries. Inhaling the sweetness through vented plastic, Cadence found the smell transported her home, to afternoons when she'd pluck the delectable treats from her mother's garden and eat them while standing barefoot in the black dirt. Unable to resist, she bought the pint and anticipated enjoying them throughout the week.

When the two had circled the market's art booths, Isa departed for a tutoring appointment and Cadence to her dorm. In the stairwell, she passed Natalie looking painfully thin in gym clothes.

"You headed to work out?" Cadence asked.

"Yeah, I have spin class this morning," Natalie said. "Then yoga this afternoon."

"Jesus, Natalie. How many exercise classes do you have?"

"Only four. Wait, no, five. I also have two dance classes and aerobics during the week."

"Natalie, don't you think you're overdoing it? Is it possible for someone to exercise too much?"

"Oh, I don't think so. Exercise is good for you. Besides, that freshman fifteen was really starting to show. I was looking terrible."

Even though she had known her for only a short time, Cadence thought Natalie had looked great, up until now. The healthy curves had given way to a sickly skinniness. The drama of weight loss had begun to show on her pale face. Not wanting to make her hallmate more self-conscious at her haggard looks, Cadence said nothing as Natalie left to burn the guilt of illusionary fat.

Cadence was almost to her room when another hallmate, Ruthie, stepped out with a beach bag. Although the two did not know each other well, they had shared a few short conversations and would sometimes chat if Ruthie was hanging out in Enna's room. Ruthie was catching a ride with her friends Christy and Stephanie and when invited to go along, Cadence finally had the chance to make it to the sand. Ignoring Jed and Corrine who were lying naked beneath the sheets, Cadence put her strawberries in the fridge, changed into her swimsuit, and grabbed all the necessities for a day at the beach.

Shortly, they were in Stephanie's car headed to "The Edge of America," as Folly Beach is also known. The ride out was over a thin strip of land flanked on both sides by miles of green and brown marsh surrounded by bluish gray water. Halfway across the isthmus, an abandoned boat appeared on the right shoulder of the road, a grounding courtesy of Hurricane Hugo, the catastrophic storm that struck in 1989. Unlike the other debris that had been removed, this one stayed and served as the island's unofficial message board. Deaths, births, birthdays, anniversaries, holiday greetings, community events, charities, love letters, welcomes . . . no occasion had not been announced on the boat's side. New messages magically covered old ones, and on this day appeared the question: "I love you, Jodi. Will you marry me?" The message made Cadence wish someone were writing her sweet words.

It wasn't long before Christy and Stephanie were rolling out chairs on the shoreline while Ruthie and Cadence spread down towels. Once set up, Cadence went straight for the water. It had been ages since she experienced the gritty sensation and thrill of the ocean rushing over her. She dove into the salty freshness of an incoming wave and surfaced on its other side. Playing like a child, she rode a few in, ever careful of the invisible hand within a wave that manages to steal swimsuit tops. Still, she took the risk of flashing those on the shore to frolic in the simple fun made just between her and the water.

Plopping on her towel, Cadence dozed while Christy and Stephanie watched the motley parade of bums, surfers, bikers and bikini-bearing babes. Ruthie was caught somewhere between her hallmate's quiet relaxation and the others' chatter. She was restless and finally whispered to Cadence: "Hey, I know some guys who live a few houses down, wanna go crash their place?"

Telling the others they were going for a long walk, Ruthie grabbed her bag, and the two ventured over a mile to a shack a few rows from the beach. The yard was fairly unkempt, and the house's peeling blue paint reminded Cadence of some shabby island abode like the kind seen in paintings of tropical, faraway places. Surfboards lined the porch, and the hums of reggae drifted from inside. Ruthie knocked briefly before stepping in where a wall of marijuana smoke met their nostrils.

"Hey, Randall," she said, in a tone that was more of a question than a statement.

"Ruthie? Good to see you, and you brought a friend—nice."

"Yeah, this is Cadence."

"What's up, Cadence?" he and the others greeted while she managed a smile hooked with uncertainty. "So where you from? I know Ruthie's from the big city."

"A small town, upstate. I grew up on a farm." As soon as she revealed this tidbit, she regretted it.

"Hey man, I'd love to have a farm," one began. "I know what my cash crop would be." He laughed and took a hit from an excessively large joint. "But seriously, a farm, huh?" He smirked. "Well, I guess being from a small town, all this is new to you."

"Um, excuse me? What is?" Cadence looked around for the newness she was missing.

"This ganja, the blow, our party supplies." Randall pointed to the pile of drugs in a large cigar box on a table made of a stop sign atop cinderblocks.

Cadence loathed the stereotype of the naïve country girl who comes to discover the evils of the city. She never quite understood the ignorance of those apparently oblivious to the obvious fact that drugs are grown and honed in rustic realms.

"You're kidding, right? I'm surprised you don't have more hard-core stuff. Where I come from, these are appetizers. Heroine and meth are the big ones."

"Whooaaaa . . . ," the half-baked ones chimed in.

"Well, if that's what you like, then let me make a call." Randall dug the phone from his pocket.

She didn't want him to call her bluff, but she certainly didn't want her mug shot plastered on the local news for a drug bust with these clowns, so she relented, "Don't call anyone. I don't want any."

"Oh, but I think you do, and it's a great suggestion, right Ruthie?"

Ruthie grabbed the joint passed to her. "I'm up for anything. Sounds like a good time."

She closed her eyes and hit the fatty as if she were trying to suck its contents into every cell of her body. In resisting the urge to exhale, Ruthie made that awkward noise, between a sneeze and cough, and her puffed cheeks made her look like a gorged chipmunk. She let go into a hacking fit, recovered, and walked over to Randall who handed her a can of beer. Cadence grew uneasy when the group stared at her to smoke since she had no desire to rekindle her affair with the infamous Mary Jane.

Although her hometown qualified as small, the high school was infested with drugs, as were the parties she attended. She could count on both hands how many times she had gotten high as compared to the activity of some, whose uses resulted in expulsion, homeless drifting, crime, even death. She had already buried a few friends from drunk driving accidents, overdoses and suicides—the latter a last resort for those whose lives had been sucked out every time they sucked in the promise of a good time. Cadence had known enough of these scenes to recognize a place she did not need to be.

"Hey, Ruthie, let's check out the backyard," Cadence suggested. "Maybe we can catch some sun in a lounge chair or something. Grab a beer and join me."

Moving toward the outside, Cadence stepped cautiously through the kitchen—a true male hell hole with weeks of dishes piled high in the sink, a trashcan completely hidden by overflowing waste, crumbs and crud dried into the table. The entire area hosted a colony of flies, ants, and more tellingly, the riotous palmetto bug—a prehistoric pest of legendary status down South, capable of flight and transforming normally calm people into crazed individuals. Cadence watched these roaches and their insect acquaintances dance in and around the pyramid of garbage as if it were some sacred temple. The stench was beyond horrendous, and the floor was covered with a sticky film that looked like gray paint, an adhesive so effective it threatened to make shoes permanent fixtures. She held her breath and continued to the backyard where she gagged the moment fresh air hit her nostrils. Thankfully, Ruthie was not long behind her.

Cadence got straight to the point. "Let's get out of here. It's not a good scene."

"That's not fair. You don't even know them. We just got here. Give it a chance."

"Ruthie, how do you know them?"

"Um, a friend from back home hooked me up with them."

"So, you *don't* know them?" Cadence looked back into the house with irritation. "This is shady. We don't need to be here—let's go."

Ruthie started to protest, but a glare from Cadence stopped her. When they walked back through the hall, Cadence noticed a fluorescent glow from one of the bedrooms. Through the cracked door, she saw the unmistakable jagged edges of spiky, deep green leaves. On the wall above the plants, Bob Marley's image doted lovingly on the marijuana, his dreads reaching down as if to stroke the plants to maturity. On their way out, Ruthie muttered a disappointed goodbye, but a short distance from the house realized she had left her beach bag and went back for it. She took a little more time than seemed necessary, and when she returned, her daze was more pronounced and her chatter definitely more influenced.

When they reached the beach spot where the four had set up, they found only their sand-dusted towels. Cadence and Ruthie looked to see if Christy and Stephanie had moved, but they were nowhere to be seen. Cadence checked the street for the car, but it was gone.

"Are you kidding? They left us here?" Ruthie suddenly seemed more sober.

"Yep," Cadence peered out over the water. "Nice friends, Ruthie. How d'you know them?"

"Well, they're not really my friends. They're in my study group for econ, and yesterday they mentioned they were going to Folly, so I asked if I could bum a ride."

Cadence watched helplessly as an ominous black cloud barreled toward the sun. "Great, it looks like we're going to get caught in that." Just as she pointed to the rolling mass of darkness behind them, a bolt of lightning struck the mainland and thunder ricocheted.

"We could go back to Rand—"

"No! Let's head toward the pier to the hotel. Since you're so good at bumming rides, maybe we can get one back downtown."

The pier's shadow grew lighter as the sky got darker, creating a gloomily beautiful picture. A few surfers relished the waves whipped up by the advancing tempest but Cadence and Ruthie suffered through the slings and stings of sand as it danced to the storm's energetic command. In heading for safety, the girls passed a surfer emerging from the water who was quick to warn: "Hey ladies, storm's almost here; you may want to take cover."

"We're trying, but our ride left us," Cadence said. "We need to get downtown."

He rubbed his salt-smeared face. "I'm headed that way. Be happy to give you a ride."

The rescuer led them to his brown jalopy—a typical surfer coach complete with brand stickers, duct-taped seats, Sex Wax stuffed in the cupholders, and enough sand on the floor mats to make a mini beach inside. It smelled of coconut and vanilla, the trademark cologne of waveriders. A crank of the car flooded it with the reverbing of a guitar that made the music seem as if it were being played underwater. The driver reached to turn it down when Cadence asked about it.

"Classic surf music. I'm kinda old school like that. This is Dick Dale and the Del-Tones. Most people have heard of the Beach Boys, but I like the ones who came before, you know, the influences. My favorites are Johnny and the Hurricanes and The Storms."

"Those seem appropriate considering the weather." Cadence joked as the wrath of a late summer's storm bore down on them.

When they had driven through the chaos into the calm, their driver talked more about his aquatic addiction. He preferred surfing at The Washout but chose the pier today for a change. He was headed downtown to his job delivering pizzas for Norm's, a famous joint that had provided thousands with pies and pitchers of cheap beer since 1979. As he described the place, Cadence pictured the distinct red awning on the corner that she had passed a few times.

Not long after their conversation began, it ended when he dropped them in front of Albemarle. Reaching into her bag, Cadence pulled out all the money she had on her, five dollars, and handed it to him: "For gas. It's not much, but it's all I have."

Waving the cash away, he suggested she order a pizza with it. As he drove off, she heard the distinctively wet sounds of surf music drifting from his car. Unlike the lively tunes that marked their arrival, there was tension-filled silence between Cadence and Ruthie on the way to their hall. They barely said goodbye before Cadence went in for a shower and a nap. Later in the cafeteria, she ran into Ruthie's roommate, Olivia, who asked about the trip.

"Um, I've had better."

"Ruthie told me you got left there by some girls from her econ class. Did you all get in a fight or something?

"No, Ruthie wanted to hang out with some guys she supposedly knew, so we went to see them for a while and those girls hauled ass."

"Oh, so you went to a party?" Olivia asked, fingering a new and very expensive handbag.

"Well, I wouldn't call it a party, but they might have. It was shady to me."

"I've heard Folly can be a bit shady," Olivia continued.

"Anywhere can be," Cadence said. "Where's Ruthie?"

"She went out again as soon as she got back. Mumbling something about going to find some people who were into fun. Think she went back there? To . . . what's his name's?"

"Randall's? I don't know."

"That's right. Randall." Olivia glanced at her watch. "Well, I gotta be going."

Before she left, Olivia told Cadence of a few hall parties in the dorm that evening, so she just floated from one to another. The night was largely uneventful, and she retired fairly early with earplugs, an eyemask, and her pillow pulled over her head. She had hoped the night would bring a date with a rock star, but it didn't happen, and the next day didn't look very promising, either.

She was enjoying Sunday's serenity having the room to herself since Jed and Corrine were out for Sunday dinner and their afternoon farewells. In reviewing Spanish vocabulary about food, Cadence came across the word for strawberries, *fresas*, which reminded her of the pint in the fridge. Her mouth began watering before she opened the door, but once she peered inside, all she found was the empty container and a puddle of chocolate syrup from a bottle lying on its side.

Slamming the door, she threw the plastic across the room then kicked Corrine's bed, which only brought her to near tears from the throbbing in her foot. *They're just strawberries. . .* she kept thinking, trying to keep her rage in check, but the more she tried to persuade herself to calm down, the angrier she got. After all, it wasn't just the fruit—it was much more than that—it was everything about her inconsiderate roommate and her boyfriend who gave her the creeps.

Her eyes targeted the photos of Jed, who, poised on the wall, just smirked at her. Raging, she ripped one of the treasured pictures from the wall, tore it to shreds then threw the scraps in the toilet. She had never appreciated the *whoosh* of a flush quite like she did at that moment. Just as she began thinking of other small revenges, a whisper in her head reminded her: *They're just strawberries . . .*

She calmed down and laid on her bed, trying to return to the Spanish, but this time, the afternoon's quiet was disturbed by consistent thumping from next door. Cadence slammed her textbook into the wall three times, which was returned with three bangs seconds later. She tried again: *Wham! Wham! Wham!* It was met with *Bang! Bang! Bang!* It sounded as if they were using a metal bar against the divide. The thumping continued until Cadence couldn't take it anymore.

The towering individual who opened the door was Jacinda. Cadence had met her earlier in the semester, but the extent of their communication had been a few lukewarm "hellos" in passing. Now, she glared at Cadence who asked in a less-than-pleasant tone: "Could you *please* turn that music down?"

"No, I sssuuuuurrrrre won't!" As her friends snickered from behind, the impending figure grew bolder: "It's okay for y'all to blast that country music all weekend but you can't handle my rap? I don't think so." As she said it, her head moved with that charismatic sway that marks the dramatic delivery of a black woman standing her ground.

"I don't know what you're talking about. That must be my roommate and her dumbass boyfriend."

"You think I care? Now get away from my door. It's not even quiet time, so why don't you take your ass over to the library if you want some peace and quiet." The door slammed in Cadence's face with a force that rattled the hall.

Back in her room, Cadence felt the fury intensifying when she realized that Corrine was capable of ruining an afternoon without even being in the building. She was shaking so substantially that she could barely answer the phone when it rang.

"Cadence?" an unsure voice posed. "It's Schilar. You okay?" He paused into the silence. "Sorry I didn't call earlier. A last minute gig came up and we went out of town."

"Oh hi," she replied, crossing her arms in an effort to stop her trembling.

"Is this a bad time?"

"Yes." She rubbed her forehead and took a deep breath. "I mean, no. I'm having some roommate issues. It's not a bad time to talk to you. I'm just really pissed." She really had no idea what she was saying, but when Schilar asked her to meet him at the fountain in ten minutes, she knew exactly what to answer.

Quickly, Cadence brushed her hair and threw on her favorite red lip gloss that tasted like the fruit that was no longer in her fridge. For the second time this weekend, she was at the fountain. While she waited, she listened to the palm fronds swishing with melodious friction above the hum of traffic. Some distance away, a street musician sat beneath a palmetto, making a saxophone moan a seductive melody. She let the sounds work their calming magic and before long, Schilar rounded the corner, and her heart jolted when his smile made her feel like she was in the spotlight.

He approached her with a simple "hello" and a touch to her arm before suggesting they go for wings. "Not afraid to eat them on a date are you?"

"Is this a date?"

"If I say 'yes,' does that mean you won't eat wings in front of me?"

"I'll eat them no matter what you say."

Over a tray of spectacular flavors, the two meandered easily through conversation about their hometowns, likes, dislikes, and of course, about the common denominator of classes, especially the one that brought them to this moment. Mirabilis's class was a favorite, one that stimulated them beyond its walls and that fulfilled the dreams they had imagined of what a college course and professor would be like. In connecting with the material, particularly the book about McCandless, they discussed what fascinated them and their teacher about the enigmatic individual who perished in Alaska.

"You know, he had this unsettled part of his soul, this agitation, and that's the kind of feeling that keeps people searching. It takes balls to follow a desire so profound that it leads to death," Schilar said.

"Or to fully living? In that last photo, he didn't look like he had any regrets, you know, the one where he's holding his farewell note?" Cadence posed. "I wonder what kind of picture I'd take or even what I'd write."

"I'd pen a song," Schilar answered definitely. "What I'd like to know is the answer to the question you wrote in your book: *What would I take to the wilderness?*"

A pleasurable shock stirred inside because he remembered her words, had read her thoughts, and wanted to know more about them. "Is there a limit to the items?" Cadence asked.

"I don't know, it's your question. Let's say . . . top three items."

"Well, the first would be my camera," she began, "and I'd take my horse, Gunpowder, and a journal."

"Your horse, Gunpowder? What's up with that name?"

His question diverted her down a memory lane. "Well, he's black, fine, and quite powerful, like gunpowder, but truthfully, in sixth grade, our teacher Mrs. Young read us 'The Legend of

Sleepy Hollow.' That story with Ichabod Crane and the Headless Horseman?" She watched him nod recognition. "Well, that's the name of Ichabod's horse. That creepy tale has always stuck. Gunpowder had 'fire' in him and some of the devil, too. My horse isn't devilish at all, but he certainly has fire, and he's been through hell."

"What d'you mean?" Schilar leaned in.

"He was abused by his former owner. Beaten, starved, and left to die in a back field full of broken down trucks and tractors. Some asshole thought he should put the horse out with the rusting shit. Anyway, an animal group rescued him, and my parents got him for my birthday."

"You must be heaven to him after all that hell."

A flutter shot through her heart. "Okay, so what would you take into the wilderness?"

"I'd take my guitar, named 'X,' a compilation of all my favorite songs, and a radio with a long antenna and a year's supply of batteries."

"That seems like more than three items," she protested. "And hang on, your guitar is named 'X'? What's that mean?"

"It means I haven't found a name for it yet, so the letter marks the unknown."

With every word he spoke, her brows seemed permanently arched in interest. "I know guys name their cars, but their guitars? Who's done that?"

"Lots of musicians. One of my favs, B.B. King, named his Lucille. See, there was this bar fight that caused a fire that killed two people. King ran back into the burning building to rescue his instrument. The next day, he found out the fight was over this woman named Lucille, so he named that guitar and all the others he's owned since after her."

"That's cool. Do you have any names in mind for yours?"

"Yeah, maybe Wilma," he said. Her giggle made him smile. "From *The Flintstones*. After a jam one day, my buddies and I were watching TV when that cartoon came on. We had smoked and were laughing at Fred's big feet and how he had to cover so many miles in a car with stone wheels. There we were, stoned, laughing at Fred's big-ass feet and all the miles. Someone said, 'Stone Miles' would make a great name for a band, and well, here we are."

They talked on about college, and he asked about her other courses. She reeled off the list along with her opinions of each. Most were favorable until she reached biology and then Brodsky's course when she revealed her hatred for her music class. Disappointment swept over Schilar, and she regretted not liking it more. She described Brodsky's machinations, about being thrown out, and how much she dreaded those three afternoons every week. The only person who made the time bearable was Reena. In talking to someone who was so deeply entrenched in the subject, she wished Schilar taught the class.

As if he had been inside her head, he said, "Maybe I should give you some private lessons, to offset the damage that jerk's doing." She felt the flutter again. "In fact, if you don't have to go home, why don't we start your tutoring tonight?"

"What do you have in mind?" she asked calmly against a storm of pleasant possibilities brewing inside.

Half an hour later, the two were sitting at a small table inside the Music Farm, a cavernous venue where talent is nurtured, honed, and harvested by dedicated hands. Here artists nourish audiences with their raw, unadulterated, unapologetic love of music. Nothing else produces the sounds that resonate from this intimate hangar, and those who have been rocked behind its brick know what it means to have music dropped right into their souls. This was the classroom where Schilar took Cadence and where, by the night's end, he'd be a guest lecturer.

Schilar was surprised when his friend James called him to the stage, but such were the rock star's skills that he was ready to deliver without preparation. The shiny red Fender he grabbed was his own, borrowed by his buddy for the evening, and the guitar with the unknown name aptly projected its player's desire and fueled every note he crooned. During his performance, just like the one Cadence had seen some nights ago, he closed his eyes, surrendering vision to the power of certain lyrics and drawing inspiration from a darkness only he could see. Several times, he sang toward her and sealed the refrains with a wide smile to all, but his eyes, well, they narrowed on her.

In those instrumental minutes when the six strings were the only voice, she could tell he longed to write the perfect song, to deliver notes that dripped like nectar into ears and nourished the body's every fiber. Watching people sway to his mesmerizing voice, she knew that one day he would. To her he was a professor of passion, a true practitioner of the discipline, even if he still was a student.

When the set was complete, she clapped so deliberately that her palms turned as red as the guitar, which he handled as if it were the Holy Grail. With the show over, the crowd exited quickly, and Schilar came over to their table where Cadence was preparing to leave.

"Wait," he said, touching her arm gently, "the night's not over." He led her to the stage where they were soon joined by James and a few other musicians. Soon, everyone had an instrument, including Cadence who held a tambourine.

"Okay, you've got an ancient piece of magic there," Schilar said. "These jingles are called 'zils.' Let me show you how to make them sing." He was an expert in demonstrating the different rolls: the shake, spinning jingles, two handed, and the fingers. "We'll tell you when to come in, but really, just listen. Open yourself to the rhythm, appreciate the sounds, and you'll feel when it's right to play."

She nodded and tried to settle in for her musical debut. Sensing her uneasiness, he leaned over. "Oh, and remember one more thing—you look wonderful tonight."

The tambourine almost betrayed the shaking inside her, but the jam session began, and for hours, they were lost in the undulating momentum of the music. It was like a lab with the experimental ensemble blending, mixing, and fusing their knowledge. Accents, doubles, beats, forms, modulations, keys, ranges, and styles bent and twisted to their fingers, and Cadence witnessed the spontaneous overflow of powerful riffs shown in each player's expression of ecstasy. She could not stop smiling, and even though she had trouble keeping time, Schilar and the others congratulated her on joining the ranks of Jim Morrison, Stevie Nicks, and Robert Plant—legends who charmed the ring of rattles.

On the way back to her dorm, Cadence and Schilar talked more about music and the friends he had made through it. He told her it was the universal chord, one of true connectivity, because rarely do people part as strangers when they've shared in the friendship of a song. She liked the idea but hoped the two of them would part as more than friends, and her hopes were realized when he bid her good night in the best way possible—silently.

There was even a rhythm in the way he kissed as the subtle movements of his tongue issued their own song; it was one she did not want to end or at least one that she wanted to replay over and over and over because she knew she'd never grow tired of the way it made her feel. Even his hands were placed perfectly in the curves of her neck, and his fingers delicately cupped the edge of her face just as if he were tenderly stroking his beloved guitar. When his lips—soft, supple, and smoothly honed from his craft—finally pulled away, she felt invigoratingly numb. She wasn't even sure she would be able to make it up the stairs.

Surprisingly, when Cadence entered the room, Corrine wasn't on the phone but seemed dead to the world. The intoxication of an incredible night tucked Cadence into bed, and the evening's songs worked like lullabies luring her into slumber. All was quiet on the hall. She was just beginning to slip into sleep when she heard whispering at first then singing. It sounded like children, and as the eerie seconds moved hauntingly by, she recognized a familiar song from her own days in the schoolyard:

> *Ring-a-round the rosie,*
> *A pocket full of posies,*
> *Ashes! Ashes!*
> *We all fall down.*

Fearfully frozen in the rising warmth of her bed, she shut her eyes tightly and clenched her sheets lest the spectral melody makers show themselves. Silence soon returned, but too scared to sleep, Cadence's mind began playing over the musical mysteries of late—a cantankerous professor torturing his students with classical tunes; restless spirits frightening freshmen with childhood rhymes; and a romantic rock star with a melodic personality and a wandering soul, who was strumming his way into the rhythm of her heart.

Chapter 5

History 100
Unforgotten Events

In the muted light, their eyes fought to take in and decipher the black and white image. Some elements appeared clearly: a race track, people in formal attire, but a large, blurred mass appeared in the foreground. The professor called it a "visual argument" and revealed how they were surrounded by this rhetoric every day, perhaps not to the extreme she was presenting, unless they were willing to open their minds to view the more difficult ones. The implicit argument they saw was taken at the precise moment Emily Davison threw herself in front of King George V's horse, Anmer, at the Epsom Derby in 1913.

Professor Mirabilis let the photograph speak for seconds before breaking the silent history and filling in the details: "Her head struck the horse's chest, knocking her unconscious. She died four days later from substantial internal injuries. Her gravestone bears the creed of the Women's Social and Political Union, the suffragette organization she joined in 1906. 'Deeds not words' echoes from her resting place. So, how do you consider her deeds?"

"Heroic," someone said.

"Insane," another offered, and a line of descriptors were heaped upon the adjectives of Davison's deed.

"So, most of you see this as an argument that implies courage, equality, passion, sacrifice, mixed with a bit of lunacy?" she asked. "Anything else?"

"Yeah," a deep voice responded, "terrorism."

Discomfort hung in the air.

"Interesting, Dillon. Please explain."

"This woman, did she think about what would happen to the rider? Did she even care? What about the horse?" He scrutinized the photo. "And what about all those other people watching? Did anyone else get hurt?"

"Very keen observations. In truth, she *was* quite militant in her efforts to bring about equality for women," the professor said before elaborating on Davison's actions.

In her fight for women's equality, the suffragette attacked a vicar she mistook for Chancellor of the Exchequer, David Lloyd George, at whose house she planted a bomb in 1913. She was arrested and imprisoned for stone throwing, window smashing, and arson. The group of which she was a member saw violence as a means to equality.

On race day in 1913, Davison brought down the horse, but he was unharmed in the collision and finished the race riderless. Jockey Herbert Jones, already an accomplished thoroughbred rider, suffered injuries from the incident including a mild concussion. He claimed to have been haunted by Davison's face for some time but laid a wreath in her honor at the funeral of another suffragette, Emmeline Pankhurst. He retired in 1923 and committed suicide in 1951, although it remains unknown if his death hearkens back to Davison.

The gravity of Davison's deeds swept through the room.

"What you all see here remains somewhat of a mystery, as history often is. Some spectators reported that Davison accidentally stepped in front of the horses, thinking they had passed, as it was tradition to cross the course and walk to the finish line when the steeds ran by. Others claimed she shouted, 'Votes for Women' and carried a placard bearing these words, or that she was attempting to attach a suffragette flag to the horse. Some said she was bent on suicide, although she had purchased a return train ticket. Many consider her a martyr."

"What do you consider her?" Dillon asked.

Deep lines appeared on the teacher's forehead as she contemplated the question. "A leader. A woman responsible for the rights I enjoy. Someone who worked to ensure that the women in this class and in all classes have opportunities." Her eyes moved from face to face. "But I'm torn over the means. Her example makes me ponder those who commit violent acts for political or social reasons. How are the actions perceived and by whom? Are the circumstances of repression so great that violence is the only effective means?"

"Was it effective for her?" Dillon wondered.

"Good question. In the immediate time context, the answer seems to be 'no.' Some historians argue that her actions made men even more cautious in granting women the right to vote. They saw a well-educated woman resorting to sensational and dangerous methods, and they were concerned what women who were not as educated might do. Universal suffrage for British women was not gained until 1928. Arguably, it's a result of women achieving some independence when they secured jobs while men were fighting in World War I." She gave Davison a final appreciative glance before moving on.

All photographs are memento mori. Few understood the next slide's phrase until she translated the Latin embedded in Susan Sontag's words: "*Memento mori* is Latin for 'remember that you must die.'"

Each face strained at the mental difficulty of digesting a mortal reality—that all photographs measure life's time limits, for every figure appearing so alive in those images will, in fact, someday be dead.

For the remainder of the hour, Professor Mirabilis presented visual arguments excluded from sanitized history books. The scenes were so haunting, so disturbing, that they would remain burned into her students' consciences just like the images on exposed film.

Cadence left class feeling awkwardly struck and surprisingly empowered. From behind her camera, she had been creating visual arguments for years yet never knew. Now, separated from the mechanism that helped make her own history, she regretted leaving it at home and could not wait to bring it to Charleston after fall break. While she imagined the possibilities of framing scenes in the city, the shots of Davison, lynchings, and war-weary survivors kept flashing through her mind, especially during her other classes. Even into the afternoon, she was considering the implied arguments of her own photos when she absentmindedly answered a call from a number she had deleted long ago.

"Hey, remember me?" The simple words threw her heart into an irregular rhythm.

Wishing she didn't, she replied anyway. "Yeah. What's going on?"

"Nothin' much. Just thinking about you. It's been a long time," he said.

"Yes, it has. What do you want, Damien?" She tried to sound disinterested, despite the slight smile creeping across her face.

"You've been on my mind a lot lately. I want to see you. I'm in town to see friends. Let's get together."

Although a voice inside screamed to decline his invitation, another said, "Sure," before reason had a chance to trump emotion.

"I'll pick you up at eight."

"Um, don't you need to know where I live?" she asked.

"I already do. See you in front of Albemarle. Bye!" He ended the call with the same confidence she had found to be a charm and a curse in their years together.

The second she hung up, a wave of regret swept in. Schilar had mentioned his band was playing tonight and she should stop by. She had just broken this immediate future for a reunion with the past, but she reasoned this was not a date, just two old friends meeting up again. It was a chance for her to get some perspective on a history that felt unfinished.

As the hours approached when she'd see him again, her thoughts turned to her freshman year with Damien, who had been her first true love—the one whose class ring she had put on with pride and removed with humility. The one she had given her virginity to under "forever" conditions. The one a supposed friend of hers had done the same for only weeks later. The news was devastating, but his apologies, his groveling, his acts of redemption forced her to forgive, so she did. Undoubtedly, she loved him and had even envisioned a future with him.

At the time, it had not occurred to her that life could go on without him, as it inevitably does. After his betrayal, she was stricken with the sickness of love lost. Darkness clouded her days, she refused food, eating only when the waves of nausea subsided. Tears streaked the melancholy lines of her journal and followed her to bed where they soaked into her already stained pillow. Few distractions could console her, but aimless drives, cigarettes, and the occasional buzz helped the hurt. Eventually, he flowed out of her life, pushed by the entries she wrote and survival anthems she adopted as her own mantras. What would begin as singing would digress into screaming then to pitiful sobbing. He was gone for the most part, but the sediment of him rested at the bottom of her heart, waiting to be stirred in the flood of his return. She was beginning to feel that surge now, but instead of fully giving into him, Cadence vowed to put up a resistance, to tread cautiously over what had been a dangerous but alluring abyss.

Seeing him again was a dress-up game of revenge, so she focused her attention on looking unforgettable, especially since she had never forgotten the afternoon when he walked away after she had discovered the other girls also occupying his time, some of them from the new city he and his family were moving to. Cadence had waited for the time when she would see him again, when she'd flaunt confidence in his face and make him miss what he so easily gave up. With the perfect look and the better-off-without-him aura she assumed, she watched the clock count down.

Five minutes before eight, she left the room where Corrine scurried about like a servant preparing the arrival of her king. Passing the open door of Enna's room, Cadence was pulled back by her hallmate's voice.

"Nice miniskirt, Cadence. Where're you headed looking so sweet?"

"I'm meeting a friend from high school."

"Bullshit. You don't dress like that for 'a friend.' Which ex is it?"

Cadence resist grinning. "His name's Damien."

"Ah, and you're out to make him realize what he doesn't have anymore?" Enna asked to Cadence's nod. "If he doesn't realize it now, he obviously thinks with the miniature head most guys make decisions with. Maybe you shouldn't be wasting your energy on an idiot."

"Maybe not. We'll see," Cadence said. "What're you doing?"

"Notes for a history project. I'm swamped. I may meet up with some friends later."

"What's the project?" Cadence asked.

"It's on sixteenth-century martyrs. I'm burnin' it up, actually." Enna cackled like a witch over a cauldron.

Glancing at her watch, Cadence saw that it was already past eight. "He's probably waiting for me. Have fun with your martyrs."

Downstairs, she found that Damien wasn't waiting, and she felt stupid for wanting to see what had become of her former heartbreaker. After hanging around for ten minutes, she turned to go back inside when the red sports car sped around the corner like a flaming chariot. As she walked toward it, the breeze caught her hair and flung the strands around in a whirl. He was watching her as she was watching other girls stare at the car and the handsome driver behind the wheel. Getting in was like stepping into a portal to the past. His cologne transported her to the time when her clothes carried his scent, but as she inhaled the memory, she found it strange he hadn't changed.

"Hi," He leaned over and kissed her cheek. Cadence accepted it with indifference. "You look amazing. Haven't changed a bit."

Secretly, she relished the comment but didn't acknowledge it. "I see you still have 'Big Red.'"

"Sure do. It's a great car. We've been a lot of miles together in it, haven't we?" He winked.

Reclined seats, fogged windows, lost clothing—Cadence felt the warmth of flashbacks. The car was a yearbook, one that locked up memories like a diary beneath its red cover. She slipped back into its seat with ease.

At the base of the Ravenel Bridge, he turned on and up the songs from their soundtrack. The music added more nostalgia to her sensory tour of years past. With the sun laying its last bit of light over Charleston, Cadence looked out over the water to Fort Sumter. Although it appeared tiny in the distance, the monument still stood mightily between the river and ocean: an island of bricks, stone, and mortar that had refused to yield to the Union, to hurricanes and heat, salt and the sea, and to time's torture.

On the drive out to the Isle of Palms, they did the usual catching up, filling each other in on persons of interest, their families, other connections. She learned that he wasn't up to much these days, just working sales in the town he moved to after their breakup. Tellingly, he had a girlfriend within a week of moving there and continued with a succession of them, up until now.

When they pulled up to the party, Cadence reached to open the door. "Wait," he whispered as his hand caressed her cheek. Slipping it around her neck, Damien pulled her mouth to his. Before, she had loved his kisses, even craved them, but now, having experienced one of the most incredible lip locks of her life a few weeks ago, she thought Damien's method sloppy, formless, and clumsy. She kept her tongue largely to herself.

"You taste so good. I've missed you." His voice held a tenderness she wanted to believe.

The party scene was typical of then and now: every hand held a can of beer or cup of concoction and throughout, bongs and pipes packed with pot passed around intimate circles. Some floated into back rooms and returned with flared nostrils bearing snowy traces. As the hours passed, partiers came and went like the ebb and flow of the tide. Cadence secured a spot on the couch where Damien joined her, and they talked more about the good ole days until he excused himself. Even with a buzz, she maintained a sharp awareness and thought it odd that in this huge house he ventured upstairs to a bathroom. The voice inside her head kept mocking her with that irritating adage of history repeating itself and whispering a certain singer's name. In dismissing this nagging noise, she spied a head of long, red hair moving in the direction Damien had just gone. Cadence got to her feet.

The upstairs hall was dark, save for a sliver of light peeking from behind a partially closed door. No one was in the bedroom but Cadence followed the light coming from a bathroom. Creeping to it, she peered in to see Damien in a tongue-twisting embrace with the redhead. Pulling her head back by her hair, he placed his mouth against her neck and began to suck. She seized the bulge against his pants as his hand slithered up between her legs. The redhead moaned to his working fingers, which he eventually brought to her lips. She licked them with obedience, watching as he took them one by one into his own mouth before sealing their fluidic history with another kiss.

A deluge of deception came flooding back. Cadence moved to fling the door open but didn't. In her silent restraint, she heard the redhead whisper: "Don't go far. I'm staying here tonight, and I've got a place reserved for you."

Cadence rushed back to the couch. Moments later, Damien appeared above. Before rejoining her, he grabbed a drink then strutted toward her with a grin bigger than the bulge she had just seen. She rose to greet him, and just as he stretched out his arms to wrap her in them, a prodigious slap stopped his advance. His grin lay crumpled in a corner, and the noise of the party came to a hush.

His eyes darted about. "What the fuck is your problem?"

"*My* problem? I don't have a problem. *Your* problem is that you're still an asshole! Take me home now! I wouldn't want you to miss your reservation." She could hardly believe the voice coming to her. Damien reached for her, but Cadence slung his hand away.

"Get your filthy hands off me!" Turning to leave, she noticed the redhead at the top of the stairs, smirking down at the scene.

The screaming started before they had made it off the island and ended when they reached the peninsula. For miles, she released years of hurt he never got to hear, and it seemed to reach a pitch as they crested the bridge into downtown. Her fury forced him into silence.

A little after midnight, she effectively slammed his door on their past and any future. "Don't ever call me again." She didn't wait for him drive off but heard the car behind her and imagined what she couldn't see—Damien watching her walk out of his life.

Riding the rejection high and feeling so strong in her skin, Cadence knew all along whom she wanted to be with. If she hurried, she could probably catch the end of Schilar's show. Breathless but invigorated, she approached the dive in time to see him step out. Still some distance away, she was about to call out to him when a girl emerged from the bar and took her place beneath his arm. He hugged her tightly to him. Falling back into the shadows, Cadence spied the rock star stumbling away with a groupie. With the evening's elation dead, Cadence went to bed but could not sleep thanks to a heavy heart and the voice of reason mocking her missed opportunity.

By morning, the freeing feeling of deserting Damien was quickly hampered by thoughts of Schilar. When Cadence rolled over, Jed was staring at her from Corrine's bed. She shuddered and turned back to the wall but could still feel his eyes crawling up her back like a spider beneath her sheets. Although he had stayed only two weeks ago, she already hated these visits. Feeling like an inconvenience, a stranger in the space of two lovers, she wished she had another bed to sleep in.

Unable to withstand the creepiness, she got up and set out to get some work done. Studying under her favorite tree on the Grand Lawn was difficult since she stopped too frequently to watch passersby and listen to the *clop, clop, clop* of horses pulling carriages packed with tourists. Squirrels scampered about, while aspiring artists sat nearly motionless before their canvases, capturing life amidst the gray buildings and black ironwork. Ultimately, the only subjects she ended up studying were the beautiful distractions of Charleston's everyday life.

Returning to her room, she momentarily forgot the "other" roommate was in town, but in opening the door without warning, she was given a searing reminder. Country music slapped her ears and the sweaty scent of sex smacked her nose. A naked Jed was pulling Corrine into him from behind—but on the wrong side of the room. The dog-imitating lovers had piled Cadence's pillows beneath Corrine, whose face was also buried in one atop Cadence's bed. Jed slightly shifted toward Cadence, grinned deviously, and continued his grunting and thrusting. Quickly, Cadence shut the door and stood alone in the hall — shaken, shocked, and sickened.

The thought of their sweat and secretions defiling the one place that provided her security made her beat the door with derision: "Get off my bed! Do you hear me? Get your naked asses off of my bed!"

Minutes later, Corrine cracked the door and shot her roommate an annoyed look. "We're done. You can come in now." Cadence watched as her roommate—wrapped in a quilt Cadence's grandmother had made—dropped the covering on the floor before climbing into bed with Jed, who wore a sickly satiated smile as he reclined beneath the shrine.

A knot formed in Cadence's throat, and tears welled in her eyes, proof that the only thing she had control over was her escape. Unable to speak, she quickly snatched her comforter, bed linens, and blanket, throwing them into her basket. She held her bottom lip in a bite the entire time, but as soon as she slammed the door, she released it and a flood rushed down her face.

Her refuge was by means of the Laundromat several blocks away. At first, the whirring sound of machines and thumping of dryer drums were externalizations of her distress. Even a sign spoke for her: *Careful! DO NOT OVERLOAD!* Too late. She was done. As the machines washed away the stains on her possessions, Cadence's feelings spun from anger to depression. Awash in tears for most of those hours, she found them drying by the time she dumped her renewed laundry on the table. The place was empty save for an attendant glued to an ancient comedy on a dusty TV. Taking extra care to avoid wrinkles, Cadence folded her clothes and linens as her mother had taught her, and in those fresh, neat stacks, she discovered some restoration of order and control in her disturbed universe.

As she walked away from the wash house, she thought of calling Schilar but cringed when the nauseating image of his

arm around that girl surfaced in her mind. She felt she had nowhere to go and seriously considered calling her parents and
asking to come home. Wrapped in her own blanket of self-pity,
she was startled to hear her name as she passed by a row of
houses.

"Cadence! What're you doing? Laundry on a Saturday?
Girl, you've got to get a life!" Reena was leaning over the railing of a piazza.

Cadence's eyes grew wet above the basket filled with evidence of an unplanned task. Even from a distance, Reena knew
she'd said something wrong. "Hey, I was only kidding. Come
up and join us. You look like you could use some company."

Before her classmate could resist, Reena was already down
the steps leading Cadence to the second floor. The house was
one of a horde that had, like so many other historic singles, been
divided into various residences. They stepped into a room of
people watching the Gamecocks play football, and when Reena
introduced her friend, the room echoed a greeting in unison.

As they entered the kitchen, Cadence thought it strange that
the refrigerator door was wide open, but as Reena moved closer
to it, a head surfaced from behind it.

"I was wondering where you'd gone. I should have known,"
she said. "You going to share that with me or do I have to beg?"
Reena pointed to the bottle in his hand.

"Beg, huh? I'll make you do that later, but for now, I'll
share." Electricity bristled between them, intensified with their
kiss, and lingered long after their lips parted.

Reena turned to her friend. "Blaze, this is Cadence. We're
in Brodsky's class together. You know, the music class I told
you about?"

"Oh yeah, *that* class. Hi. As she said, I'm Blaze."

"What can we get you to drink, Cadence?" Reena looked to Blaze, who was already moving back toward the game, with his bottle of beer. Her eyes followed him with slight disappointment. "Anyway," she continued, "what would you like?"

Cadence was indecisive, so Reena, being a self-proclaimed "beer girl," chose for them. Reena popped the caps on two brown bottles, each adorned with a red label featuring a black palmetto tree, and handed one to Cadence, who studied the picture.

"It's local. Have you had Palmetto before?" Cadence indicated she hadn't, but she welcomed the cold comfort as Reena described the brewery's portfolio of beer. "This is a pale ale. I think it's really good. They make an amber, lager, and some others."

"I just thought beer was beer," Cadence said, feeling a little embarrassed at her ignorance of a subject that seemed so simple.

"I used to think that too until Blaze taught me about the different types," Reena said. "The guys are big fans of this brewery. It's not too far from here and is pretty old. Goes back to the 1800s."

Cadence looked down at the glass artifact she held. "That's cool."

"Yeah, there's some history majors in this bunch, so they were telling me something about the original business going bankrupt in the early 1900s with Prohibition and all that. Some guys decided to start the new one in 1993." Reena could have been a guide on a brew tour.

"You're just full of interesting knowledge."

"I pay attention, sometimes," she said. "If the subject's worthy and the teacher's interesting, right?"

Breaking the lesson at hand with a wordless toast, they clinked their bottles with Reena suggesting a sojourn on the porch. "I'm really not into football. Not a fan. I mean, I don't find a lot of excitement in watching men run around after their balls."

The girls climbed into a ratty hammock on the porch, and as the roped retreat swung slowly, Reena leaned back, closed her eyes and breathed in the rare moment of relaxation. Considering the chaos Cadence knew Reena had been through, she seemed so comfortable, calm, carefree. They chatted for a few minutes before Cadence asked how Reena and Blaze met.

Happiness spread across Reena's face like a rainbow; its iridescence did not fade as she told of their short, romantic history. Like an actress slipping into a memoir of her most defining moments, Reena relayed how, during the week before school started, she set out on a mini-exploration that took her to the top of the Ravenel Bridge. Standing on the observation deck, she was taking in the view when a group of guys on bikes rounded the corner. As they passed, the handlebar of the last one snagged her purse strap, sending the rider and the contents of her purse to the concrete. Blood dripped from his elbow and knee, but he pulled himself up and helped gather her things. She assured him she was okay and after apologizing, he rode off toward Charleston. Later that afternoon, she stopped in the park and was immersed in *Wuthering Heights* when a rogue Frisbee kicked dirt onto her book. Soon, the figure with scabbed wounds cast a shadow over her pages.

"Hello again." From behind his sunglasses he gave her a sweeping gaze and looked to what she was reading. "How's Heathcliff?"

"You know it?" she asked.

"I only remember him. Forced reading in high school. Funny though, the cover of my version was yellow with black stripes and written by someone named Cliffs." He threw the disc back to his friends. "I'm Blaze."

When she told him her name, he lingered, unable to resist the attraction, but before he returned to the game, he asked for her number, which she willingly surrendered. Reena was too surprised when he called a few hours later and invited her to a party that night. She didn't hesitate in hanging out with a handsome, older guy who didn't seem to care that she was new to the area and college. Because he lived only a few blocks from campus, he walked to get her that evening, and when they set off for the party, tension rose between them—desire so intense that neither revealed it for fear that it wasn't reciprocal. Hours later, they learned it was, but only after their eyes continually locked from every point across any room, and until finally, their lips met in a fiery kiss that marked their genesis.

Except for his job as a pharmaceutical salesman that took him on the road when he wasn't in class, they were mostly inseparable. Sometimes, he ventured home to Charlotte on the weekends to visit his parents, but the remainder of his time he split between class, work, and Reena.

After the story, Reena focused on her happenstance meeting with Cadence: "So, what's up with laundry on Saturday?"

"It simply needed to get done."

Sipping her beer, Reena eyed Cadence with skepticism. "Since when does a simple load of laundry include a comforter?"

Struck by the keen observation, Cadence related her strained history with Corrine and the day's events, a process that proved cathartic. She was just finishing when Blaze stepped onto the porch. "What've you two been discussing?"

"Oh, just stuff that makes life difficult—boyfriends, laundry, roommates from hell." As Reena answered, the others came outside, including Blaze's roommates Peter and Ian and their girlfriends Jenny and Annie. A few other friends also joined.

"What's that about roommates from hell?" Annie, a junior hailing from Atlanta, asked. Cadence gave a brief recount of the incident.

"That sucks that she's banging her boyfriend on your bed. But at least she's not banging your boyfriend. That's what my roommate did last year," Annie said. "Worst of all, I found out about it during finals. Was so upset I blew all my exams. I'm still paying for that. Thankfully, my parents understood."

"What happened to your roommate?" Jenny asked.

"Got pregnant." Annie smiled. "Came from a real religious family, so she had it. Of course, being the selfish prick that he was, her sperm donor wanted her to get an abortion, but she didn't. Moved back home to go to a tech school. He pays child support now. Sucks for them."

The possibility of being parents cast a pall over the conversation which continued when Mark, a neighbor from down the street, chimed in. "Wait until you live with a meth addict. Happened to me last year. Fuckin' crazy! He dabbled in marijuana and coke before, but it only took one meth hit and he was full-blown addicted. He lied, stole from us, and eventually, dealers were banging on our door day and night wantin' money. It got so bad, we had to turn him in. He got busted."

"Wow, ratted out your roommate?" Lily asked, a freshman who lived on campus with a friend from high school.

Mark looked at her coldly. "We had no choice. There was no reasoning with him. We did what we had to do to protect ourselves. Shit, when you start sleeping with a gun, the situation is already too far gone."

"How's this for crazy?" Jenny began. "My roommate freshman year was obsessed with me, so much so that I thought I was going crazy when I couldn't find certain pieces of clothing. More specifically, my underwear, my *dirty* underwear."

A collective "eeewwww" echoed.

"Yeah. She'd been taking my underwear from my laundry basket. Honestly, I thought I was losing my mind because they kept disappearing. When she was out of the room one day, I searched through her stuff. In the back of her closet was a shoebox and inside were my underwear. What's even more disturbing is that I even found some tucked inside her pillowcase."

"How gross," Reena said. "Did you say something?"

"Damn right, I did. She denied the whole thing. Told me she didn't know how they got into her closet or pillow, that maybe someone was playing a joke. I just let it go. I wasn't going to argue with a psycho. For all I knew, I could have ended up in pieces in that closet."

"Ugh. That's a horrible thought," Annie said.

"Yeah. Eventually, I realized I would see her around campus near my classes when I knew she didn't have any, and she'd show up at places I'd be off campus. Always wanted to know who I had been with and where. I'd tell her stories about being out, thinking I was bonding with her, but in reality, she was checking up on me. When I told my mom, she called the school and they moved me into another dorm."

"And where's this crazy bitch now?" Lily asked.

"Fixated on someone else? Hopefully on meds? I see her from a distance every now and then, but she steers clear of me. I found out she had spent time in a psych ward in high school. What a freak."

Cadence noticed Reena pulling at a piece of the hammock's rope that had come unraveled before taking a long sip of her beer.

"I know about obsessions," Ian said. "My roommate had one—with his hand. He jacked off all the time under the covers thinking that I couldn't hear him. I made it a point never to touch anything of his or even shake his hands. My suitemates and I gave him the biggest tube of lube we could find for his birthday. Damn if the gift didn't make him do it more!"

The laughter lasted and the outlandish stories continued, until Peter broke the mood by saying, "If our roommate was here, he'd tell the whopper."

"No, he wouldn't," Blaze said, looking at Peter in a way that suggested silence, but he had already stoked their curiosity.

"What? What happened," Reena asked.

"His roommate committed suicide freshman year. Hung himself in the closet. Spring semester." Peter swigged his beer. "I lived on that hall. He had been acting kinda strange, but everyone chalked it up to grades, maybe a girl. One minute he'd be happy. Down in the dumps the next. Just manic. One Saturday afternoon, when everyone went out to throw some discs, he did it. Didn't leave a note or anything." Peter looked off into the distance while the others stared at the cracks in the porch floor.

"That's sad." Mark peeled the label from his bottle. "This is a strange question, but I gotta know. Is it true that if your college roommate kills himself that you get a 4.0?" Everyone held interested disgust at a question that was the stuff of legends.

"No, it's not true," Blaze said.

One by one, they shared heinous experiences of living with strangers, and for each tale told, Cadence was thankful for the comparative therapy. Although she had washed away the spoils Corrine and Jed left on her linens, it would take more than a trip to the laundromat to cleanse the dirt of these roommate memories. Like veterans trading stories of war, nearly all recounted the gluttonous roommate who ate every morsel of food and drank every drop of stashed liquid. A few relayed memories of the licentious ones whose semesters consisted of non-stop copulation, while others told of extremes: roommates too clean, too dirty, too obsessive, too compulsive, too reclusive, too inclusive. The cornucopia of disturbing disorders made for lively conversation as each relived the experiences in sleeping feet from strangers.

After they had exhausted their store of stories, Peter suggested dinner. "Our roommate's getting off from his shift at the grocery store. I'll get him to bring home some stuff." While the arrangements were being made and drinks refreshed, Cadence began gathering her things.

"Hey, where d'you think you're going?" Reena's tone was almost scolding when she saw Cadence with the basket. "The fun's just beginning, and you're skipping out? I don't think so." She grabbed the laundry from Cadence. "Surely, you don't need any more quality time with your roommate and her boyfriend, do you? You don't strike me as the threesome type."

Cadence couldn't help but giggle in disgust. The offer to stay was just what she needed, as were the fresh bottles of beer Blaze slipped into their hands.

"Cadence was thinking of leaving," Reena said.

"But you're not, right?" he said before joining the guys around the TV. Not too long after Cadence settled in to stay, the roommate arrived. When everyone went down to unload the bounty of beer and food, Cadence saw a familiar face smiling at her. Just as Reena was about to introduce them, he took the lead: "Hi, Cadence. What a nice surprise."

Reena's attention volleyed from one to the other. "You two know each other?"

"We've met before. Did you get that paper worked out?" Walker asked.

His memory brightened her expression. "I did, thanks."

"Good, then we have something to celebrate. Can I get either of you anything?"

They held up their nearly full beers. "Okay, then," he said and motioned for them to go up the stairs. Walker called up to Blaze: "Okay, Chef Boyardee, let's have a pasta plate special! I'm starving."

Reena looked at Cadence. "What? We met in the library the first week."

"You were studying, were you? Hmmm . . . what was the subject, chemistry?"

"You're one to talk. You and Blaze are on fire." Reena busted out laughing as did Cadence. "Cheesy, I know. But I couldn't resist."

Cadence's otherwise dark day was lightening. They took a seat in the living room with Lily and chatted about subjects Cadence and Reena already covered. When Walker passed them on his way to the kitchen, he briefly became the topic of conversation with Lily commenting on his relative hotness and prodding Cadence as to her opinion.

The topic soon shifted, and the group rambled on about life until the chefs dished out the dinner. Blaze was a great cook, and the impromptu Italian feast was completed with cheap red wine and garlic bread. For dessert, they pulled a chocolate cake from a box, sliced it up, and topped the pieces with coffee liqueur and canned whipped cream. Ian and Mark took advantage of the can and killed a few brain cells doing whippets, which prepared them for some outrageous dares in the after-dinner entertainment.

"Reena, truth or dare?" Peter asked.

"Truth," she answered.

"If you could have sex with anyone in history, who would it be?"

"You mean other than the obvious?" She puckered her lips at Blaze. "Hmmm . . . that's a good question. Let me think. Um, dead or alive?"

"Well, if you're into necrophilia," Peter joked. "Either, but we hope they'd be alive."

"Okay, um, I would have sex with . . . Beethoven."

Everyone laughed while her living lover looked on in shock.

"I could inspire great symphonies," Reena explained, "and be his 'immortal beloved.' Like he wrote in those letters: 'My angel, my everything, my very self.'"

"And did you learn that in your terrible music class?" Blaze asked.

Reena's eyes connected with Cadence's. "You know, we did. But not from the teacher. Some senior asked Brodsky about the story and how important inspiration is to musicians. He didn't acknowledge the question, but the guy got the details in before the asshole shut him up. It was fantastic. So, my definitive answer is Beethoven."

"Just because you fuck him doesn't mean he's going to be inspired by you or love you," Annie said, with all the bitterness her past would allow.

"Oh, I'd make sure he was inspired. He'd love me and be moved to write amazing songs about our incredible days and nights—music that would endure the ages," Reena said with a confidence that intrigued most, especially Blaze. With her truth accomplished, she looked to Cadence, who chose "Truth."

"Where's the wildest place you've ever had sex?"

Flashes of the past fired through her mind. There weren't too many outlandish settings where she and Damien had shared intimate time: in his car, atop a pyramid of hay, but there was one that was slightly unusual. "On a tractor," she said.

"Yee-haw!" Ian joked, to the laughter of all, except for Walker, who grinned at the farm girl's admission. Cadence directed the game to Annie who continued with truth and was asked, "Have you ever kissed a girl?"

"Well," Annie began, "yes, and she was amazing—red hair, funny, smart, tasted like watermelon lip gloss . . . ." Her confession left the guys wanting more. "And Ruby could play kickball like it was nobody's business. We kissed in third grade. We were best friends and wanted to know what it would be like. So we did."

"Ahhh, that doesn't count." The flirtation with lesbian fantasy clearly left Mark unsatisfied. "Okay, have you ever French kissed a girl?"

"That wasn't the question, Mark, but I'm a good sport. No, I have not," she replied, "but I have French kissed a woman, and it was fabulous!" Annie's semantic game was more than they could stand. They longed for the dirt, but she wasn't willing to dig up any. When Annie propositioned Mark, he wanted a dare, so she said, "I dare you to stand on your head and drink that beer."

Mark glanced down at the brown glass. "Done. But I need someone to hold my feet."

"I got you, bro," Ian jumped up to steady Mark's feet, which were already making their way into the air. A deep breath later and the beer was going up his throat, in his nose, and down his forehead into his hair, but he managed to drink most of it. When his feet met the floor again, he steadied himself from the stars stirring in his head before asking, "Li-ly, tru-th or da-re?"

"Dare!" she said with too much enthusiasm.

"I dare you to throat this bottle." He handed her the one that had just been on his mouth. There was still a little beer left in it.

She took the brown object with confidence and demonstrated a technique practiced on bottles and perfected on a number of male receivers. After gently gliding her tongue around and down the bottle's head, she took to the task of throating it. She worked diligently and with such precision that the jaw of every guy, save one, dropped. Slightly past the neck's curve, Lily unthroated it slowly, only to go back down for her grand finale of throating it to mid-point, before slinging it back without hands and swallowing what remained. A round of applause followed her performance, with the guys showing slightly more enthusiasm than the girls.

"Walker, truth or dare?" Lily posed and when he accepted the latter, she said, "I dare you to spend five minutes locked in a closet with Cadence."

Instantly, the game's risk rose, as everyone but Cadence was quite aware of his girlfriend's jealousy. They all looked at Walker who was willing to resist the potential backlash for some time with Cadence.

Lily led them to a tiny closet in the hallway, and the players had barely crossed the threshold when her hasty shove forced them into the cramped darkness. Junk on the floor made standing difficult so each gained footing by maneuvering limbs across the other's space. With his lips inches from her ear, Walker whispered, "So Cadence, we meet again."

She laughed. "Yeah, but I think the library was a bit more comfortable."

"Oh, I don't know. I think most places could be comfortable with you, maybe even a tractor."

The blackness kept him from seeing her blush, but he clearly sensed her uneasiness. "Just kidding," he said, "so, how are you?"

Cadence told him about taking his advice in going to see Professor Mirabilis and how helpful it was. They chatted easily about classes and their lives' happenings since the first time they met. So wrapped were they in conversation, they didn't hear Lily stealthily approach and fling the door open. She glared at their compromising position since Walker was forced to stand with his arms against the wall behind Cadence, a configuration that made him appear to be making a move. He stepped out then helped Cadence, while Lily cut her eyes at him reproachfully. Brushing by her, he returned with Cadence to the game.

"Ian, truth or dare?" Walker demanded.

"Dare, man!"

"I dare you to strip to your underwear, tie that red blanket around your neck like a cape and 'fly' to the corner and back."

Dropping his jeans, Ian revealed Superman boxers. As he grabbed the red blanket from the back of the couch, Mark slipped a dollar into his friend's underwear. When the super-hero was ready, everyone filed onto the porch and hooted wildly at the sight of Ian running with arms outstretched in front of him down the street. For good measure, he imitated the Man of Steel's various flying poses, complete with balled fist, the one arm tucked position, and the popular sway. A few passing cars honked, and Ian ran as if he were off to save the world. He returned out of breath and in need of another beer. The game went for a few more rounds until boredom indicated a change was needed.

Their wooden coffee table already bore the scars of previous Quarters sessions. That night, they added to its dented history. Well into the morning they went, until the couples began venturing off for more games. Soon, only Mark, Lily, Walker, and Cadence remained. Cadence moved into the bean bag, and as soon as she nestled in, the conversation lulled and her eyes shut.

She awoke mid-morning beneath the superhero's cape, a blanket she had not placed on herself. No one else was up and she left Lily asleep on the couch.

When Cadence returned to the scene of lewdness, Corrine and Jed were gone. It was the same routine as last time: church, Sunday dinner at a local buffet, and then a prolonged goodbye before he got into his truck for the hours-long drive home. Cadence savored her roommate's absence, but when Corrine returned, the tension did, too. Corrine said nothing about the incident; then again, how could she? Her ear was plastered to the phone as she verbally escorted Jed all those miles during his drive back to Georgia. Cadence sought sanctuary in the library but being alone did little to console her. She sat in misery until a voice lifted her out of the trance induced by her biology book.

"Here you are. I've been trying to find you." She looked up to see Schilar smiling down at her. "I missed you Friday night. Been trying to call. What's up with your phone?"

There was nothing wrong with her phone, other than it had been on silent. When she saw that he had called, she didn't want to talk. As much as she wanted to respond now, she really had nothing to say, so she let the uncomfortable silence speak for her.

"Hey, you're not going to talk to me? Did I do something?"

She had hoped the sulky looks she shot him would make him see his wrongs, but they didn't. The pain and mistakes of the past days surfaced. "Maybe it's more of who you did."

His face filled with confusion. "What *are* you talking about?"

"I met up with an old friend Friday night. Afterwards, I came to catch the end of your show, but it was really late. I was almost there when I saw you come out with some blond and walk off with her." Her eyes narrowed. "I guess rock stars do have their groupies."

He shook his head. "So you think that since I had my arm around her that I must have gone home with her? That I give into every supposed groupie who shakes her hips in front of the stage?"

She didn't answer, not even when he took the seat across from her.

"What if I told you that she was an old friend who dropped by to see me and that I was walking her a few blocks to meet her friends?"

"I don't know that I would believe that story."

"Well, you should. Her name's Sherry. She's from back home and was in town to see her sister. When you didn't show by the end of our gig, I figured you weren't coming, so I walked her to where her sister was working."

Cadence wanted to believe him and really had no reason not to, especially when he reached for her hand and squeezed it. "Look, I'm not here for you to accuse me of things I didn't do. I don't want that."

She bit her lip as a tear slipped down her face. "Well, what do you want?"

He let go of her hand and stood up. The sound of the wooden chair sliding across the floor was like her heart grinding to a stop. She knew, as clearly as if it was projected in black and white, what it implied—they had ended before they had begun. But he came over and forced her up from the chair. Softly, his arm slipped around her waist. She felt the breath leave her when the warm security of someone she wanted to know more of took hold. He wiped her wet cheeks, brushed away the stray strands of hair that clung to them, and planted a soft kiss on the right one.

As her head met his chest, she shook inside. All of his tender deeds were followed by the power of a few words: "You, Cadence. I want *you*." The whisper stole what remained of the oxygen within her space, replacing it with a visual reminder that marked the end of a weekend that began in relative misery. In giving her heart to him, she fiercely hoped that the tragedies of her dating past would not be repeated. She needed a new history—one which would be an obvious reminder of the sheer and undeniable fact that she was, at this moment, very much in the pleasures of the present.

Chapter 6

Freshman Seminar 101
Learning Strategies

Biologists Do It in The Field. Cadence watched the T-shirt's slogan move through the crowd in front of her. *I hope they do something exciting in "the field," because they sure don't do anything interesting in class,* she thought. She dreaded the trek to a lecture so uninspiring, so dull, so utterly painful to endure that surely, it had to be a prologue to one of Dante's hell circles. If it were possible to die of boredom, she expected the coroner to be called into Dr. Kinsdaw's course any day now, and the consensus was unanimous each time the students filed out of it.

"God, I fuckin' hate that class!" the same guy declared after every session.

"I'd rather shovel horse shit than listen to him for an hour," another added with a long, slow, southern drawl.

"How much longer do we have?" someone asked, and "Too long," was always the reply. Each time they exited the class was a testament to survival, but all were uncertain of surviving their first midterms, which lurked like predators ready to pounce.

Cadence was starting to enjoy the pains that came from learning, even if most of them were incurred through the arduous activity of studying, skills she had to hone since high school had left her largely ill-prepared. To lessen the suffering, a group met to prepare for their first serious episode of academic bulimia—that educational disorder in which students are force fed professors' words then induced to regurgitate them. No digestion, only binging and purging urged by teachers who care only to see their lectures reappear in written form.

With coffee and energy drinks spread before them, six members of the biology brigade began preparing for Dr. Kinsdaw's exam, a test so famed for failure that even upperclassmen groaned at its mention, but five minutes into the study hour, they became sidetracked when the question of favorite class was posed.

Cadence immediately answered, "English," with more enthusiasm than she intended.

"English? Ugh. I *loathe* my English class! Who d'you have?" Olivia asked.

When Cadence told them of Professor Mirabilis, Jade said, "Oooooo, my suitemate Lana has her and hates that teacher."

"Oh wait, I've heard of her," Diana piped in. "She has some bad rap, like being Satan or devil whore, and it's impossible to get an A?"

"I think you mean 'Demon of Darkness,'" Cadence said. "Well, she is hard. I don't know about getting an A. So far, I haven't gotten one, but the readings and discussions are so interesting."

"My teacher's nothing like that. Tries to do discussion, but if we open our mouths, this scowl forms on her already screwed-up face," Olivia said. "She looks right through you at the wall and corrects everyone. Apparently, her ideas are the only right ones. She's such a bitch! I can't wait to finish taking these stupid English classes. I'm getting Cs on everything, and I don't know why. She just gives you a grade, no comments."

"Have you tried talking to her, like going to her office?" Diana asked.

"Yeah, same dismissiveness. It's like she doesn't know what she wants. Acts like it's a chore to teach and we're all so stupid that we're not even worthy of breathing the same air. She's just horrible." Olivia buried her forehead in her biology book, which rested next to another new, designer bag.

In the roundtable discussion, they each related their opinions of their professors and the nicknames bestowed upon each. In the same vein as Olivia, Penny was subjected to the "Hater from Hell," a woman who epitomized unhappiness. It seemed she hated everyone and everything and that her sole purpose in life was to fill the world with gloom and doom. Past and present students were convinced that she'd die alone, a brooding, crazed woman surrounded by cats, and more than a few hoped it would happen soon.

"Super Sucky Summarizer" was the title given to Darla's teacher. Darla, the usually quiet nursing student who lived with Natalie on Cadence's hall, described how this talented educator would assign reading then summarize the material or worse, reread the homework in a slow, maundering manner—three days, every week. But the reward for the drudgery was that everyone received A's on every assignment, as long as their papers had words on them. Their observations on inefficient instructors were not confined solely to the English ones— incompetence abounds in higher education, so they continued swapping opinions of the good, the bad, the beautiful, and those not so pleasing on the eyes.

"Oh, here's one. My psych professor writes on the board with one hand and erases what he's just written with the other. We've been taking pictures of the notes before they're gone. How ridiculous is that?" Jade asked.

"I should take a picture of my religion professor, so I can stare at it when I'm not in class. He's the sexiest teacher you could ever imagine. The course is soooo good," Diana said. "It's a philosophy of religion course with Dr. Sessions, but Saida and I call him 'Dr. Sexy.' He's tall, wears these brown, tweed suits and round glasses. He's so fine, but the best part— when he's teaching, he gets so excited, so wound up, that he stutters. It is so cute." She ran her fingers through her hair in a dreamy fashion.

"I don't have any sexy professors," Penny said.

"Neither do I," Olivia remarked, "but my English teacher sure could use a makeover. I mean, I'd start by giving her a heart, but after that, she needs some hair color for her ashy, split-ended locks, eyebrow work, some make-up, and oh God, those long, brown, flowery skirts and socks with sandals!" She tapped her book against her head, the jingling of her shiny new jewelry accentuating the complaint. "I find myself mentally tryin' to fix her up."

"Maybe you should start by sharing some of your accessories. God, Olivia, how do you afford that stuff?" Jade pointed to Olivia's designer purse and jewelry.

The face of Olivia's new watch shined like her expression. "I picked up some tutoring jobs and treated myself."

"Maybe we should start the fashion patrol on campus and Olivia can be head cop," Diana doodled in her notebook. "We could cite them, give 'em thirty days to transform, then make them appear in fashion court. If they're not up to trend, we put them on probation."

With the conversation digressing, Darla brought the subject back to seriousness: "How is it that we're here complaining about how many of them can't teach, especially when we're paying so much money? Aren't they *supposed* to be professional teachers?"

Her questions and their lack of answers revealed their ignorance of a system they were paying exorbitant amounts to be a part of. Since they were in a study session, they embarked on a research project of distraction: looking up the basics of higher education.

They discovered that a large portion of classes at most colleges and universities were taught by adjuncts, part-time instructors who are hired on an as-needed basis. To teach at a college or university, their professors needed a master's degree at minimum, but in order to gain a teaching position for life known as *tenure*, most needed a Ph.D. They did not know these three letters stood for "doctor of philosophy," which seemed strange since who'd study philosophy these days? These degrees meant study in anything but law, medicine, or divinity. They also learned of the ladder professors climb to achieve tenure: assistant, associate, professor, then distinguished—a difficult career journey because of the infamous "publish or perish" pressure that forces educators to pump out research books and articles or face losing their jobs.

"So that's why they've always got their office doors shut or they're in the library buried under a stack of books?" Olivia asked.

"Wait, let me get this straight. My parents and I pay for my education, which goes toward their paychecks, and I get shitty classes with professors who don't care about teaching because they're too busy poring over their own papers in fear of getting fired?" Darla said.

Jade tossed her pen on the table. "That's bullshit! If we're the reason they're here, they should be focused on us, right? Shouldn't they know how to teach?" Jade remarked.

"You'd think so. After all, what would they be doing if they weren't teaching? Researching?" Diana asked.

Darla answered, "I doubt it. What's that saying? 'Those who can, do, and those who can't, teach.' That's obviously not true. Think of the professors we have who can't teach. What they're *doing* is proving they can't. My parents are teachers. It's hard."

"Yeah, you've got to have it together to teach. Most people can't organize themselves enough to take care of one or two people, much less a hundred or more. My economics professor never knows what chapter we're on then scares the crap out of us when he asks for things that aren't due yet!" Jade said.

"Uh-huh. The worst is spending all night studying for a test, and when you get to class, the professor's like, 'Oh, I'm sorry, I thought your test was next class.' What the hell? That happened the other week in art class. I crammed paintings and periods in my head all night. I was jacked and ready to let fly; then the bimbo bitch told us she forgot the test was that day. What? You made the stupid syllabus!" Olivia said.

Pondering what makes a teacher great, they continued to let the discussion distract them from focusing on multicellular organisms or cell structure and division. Sexual reproduction could also be a very stimulating topic, but they had little interest when it came to the asexual pollination of plants. Talking about their professors was much more fun and encouraged procrastination.

Their symposium resulted in the consensus that a great teacher must have passion or at the very least—a pulse. Fire stokes interest and intrigue, with students suddenly finding themselves not necessarily wanting to know more about the material but curious as to the mysterious attraction that drives teachers to lifetimes of studying a subject. And while all agreed that passion was an essential trait, they thought professors also needed to know what they were professing. Students know the difference between knowledge and nonsense, expertise and embellishment; however, distinguishing is impossible when the words from the teacher's mouth don't qualify as English. Native fluency was an absolute must; after all, they were attending college in America, and a few of them were more than a bit lost with professors who could not convey the information in plain, simple English.

The girls continued their build-a-professor seminar by insisting that compassion, concern, common sense, communication skills of the modern sort, and some ounce of comedic sense were all necessary components to the type of leader they'd love to learn from. And just when they thought they had exhausted the topic, Diana asked, "So, what do you all think Ph.D. really stands for?"

They thought for a moment before Penny answered, "Pathetically Horrendous Dictation." Nods and chuckles went around.

"How about 'Promised Helping of Displeasure?'" Olivia added.

"For Dr. Kinsdaw's class, it means 'Pretty Horrific Day,' every day!" Jade said to unanimous approval.

"Same goes for Dr. Brodsky's class, but I'd make it 'Partial Head Death,' because I feel like a part of me dies in that hour," Cadence added.

"Not for Dr. Sessions's class. I'd love for him to teach me with his Ph.D."

"Oh God, here it comes," Jade said.

"Powerfully huge dick," Diana said with a toss of her hair and a sly look of pursuit.

"You and Saida are too horny, too much of the time," Cadence said.

"Is there such a condition?" she asked.

"Yeah, it's called being a 'nympho,'" Jade said.

"We'll, I'll add that to my résumé." Diana laughed.

"I can't wait for fall break when I get to see my two Ph.D.'s," Darla said.

"Your parents?" Cadence asked.

"No, my pretty happy dogs. I miss them soooooo much!"

Expressions of longing for the joys of home filled the small space. With hundreds of pages paving the road before sleep, they returned to the major task ahead—developing their own strategies of study.

By mid-semester, Professor Mirabilis's students had such good rapport with her they felt comfortable asking questions outside the scope of English. Because she always arrived early, she spent the extra time chatting about classes, extracurricular activities, and any topic they wanted to broach.

Sensing it was a good time to ask a question he normally would not, Dewit posed, "Hey, Professor Mirabilis, I was looking on that Evaluate My Educator site. Um, there's some pretty bad stuff written about you."

She smiled like the devil in disguise she was rumored to be. "Is there? Some freshly negative comments? I wouldn't know. I don't read it anymore," she replied. "I grew tired of rants, complainers pointing out problems but no solutions, and often doing so using incorrect grammar."

"So they got to you?"

"Well, contrary to my reputation, I'm not fully inhuman. As much as I don't like reading about how awful I am, I do on the official evaluations."

"Why do they call you the 'Demon of Darkness'?" Dewit asked.

"I earned that title in the most hellacious of ways—busting a number of students for cheating. Don't you think the name fits?"

"Um, not really. I mean, I can see why people say you're hard, and they get mad when they don't do well, but that's pretty harsh."

"Thanks, but I rather like the title. In fact, I've come to embrace the identity." Bringing her index fingers to the sides of her head, she cut her eyes beneath makeshift horns. The class laughed.

"So you like being called 'Demon of Darkness'?" Dillon asked.

"Sure. It's powerful. As a 'demon,' I share ranks with remarkably infamous company—Satan, Hitler, Pol Pot, Stalin, and other notorious tyrants. When I die, I'll go down in the record books for the pain I have caused countless students because of my insistence on honesty, hard work, and developing strong writing skills. Quite the crime to merit this hellish identity, yes?"

No one answered, preferring to keep their opinions quiet until after evaluations, but more than a handful were ready to admit, albeit reluctantly, that English was their favorite class.

As the history of her reputation came to an end and class began, Professor Mirabilis seized the opportunity to capitalize on the discussion: "While we are on the subject of words and their potency, does anyone want to guess why I now call myself the 'demon of darkness,' when it was originally used as a disparaging comment against me?"

"Because you wanted to be badass?" Dewit asked.

"Nice try, but not quite."

"Because when you use it, you take away some of its sting. It's like that reading about the 'n' word you had us do for today," another student offered.

"Precisely, and a very nice segue into today's topic. If you want your writing to be extraordinary, you must understand how even single words wield tremendous power," the professor explained.

Centering on an essay explaining how African Americans took the term *nigger* and used it to describe members of their own communities, the professor led the students through another engaging hour. She described how blacks made a derogatory word their own, transforming its power to become a noun signifying affection, possession, and chastisement. In her own very minimal way, Professor Mirabilis took a title of hate and made it her own, rendering it illegitimate for future users. Anyone calling her "Demon of Darkness" did not faze her, especially when she knew it not to be true.

In expanding their knowledge, she told them of the epithet's soiled etymology, of its neutral beginnings as the Latin term *niger*, meaning "black," a descriptor for the skin color of people dragged in chains from their African homelands to this very city. The trade in black ivory was a lucrative business, and as the country's slave trade capital, Charleston was the port of entry for some forty percent of those brought to work and die in America—estimated between 10-20 million—for cash crops like rice, cotton, and indigo. The word, along with other less desirable speech, was shouted across the fields, paddies, and plantations of this otherwise genteel setting. Professor Mirabilis reminded them that the roots of the nation's racism burrow deeply in the dirt and psyches of Lowcountry life.

Unfortunately, this word was not new to Cadence. Growing up in the rural South, she had heard it—on the farm, in stores, among her family and friends, at school, even spouted from the mouths of the most earnest Christians. She even thought about the distinction between a *nigger* and a *colored* that some insisted on making. In contemplating what her teacher shared, Cadence began to face an uncomfortable reality. From the mouths of those she knew, the only difference between their word choices was that circumstances of time, place, and polite decorum, albeit hypocritical, dictated one over the other.

She remembered when, as a child, she was helping her father and the workers repair a shed. Her job was to pick up nails and other debris and to keep cold water in the cooler and the water cups filled. It was a typical searing summer day, and when they were all summoned for midday dinner, a needed reprieve from the punishing heat, everyone washed up and began going inside the house, except for Clovis, a hired hand from down the road, who took a seat on an old stump beneath a tree in the backyard. When Cadence asked why Clovis was not eating with everyone else, one of the workers told her: "Because niggers don't eat at the table with us."

She still could hear the matter-of-factness in his voice, a tone so stark it defined moment in which she was made aware of the obvious reality of Clovis's dark skin. Somehow, this made him unworthy of sitting at the family's table, a normally welcoming piece of wood at which nearly every visitor to the home was asked to join. She was the first to finish her meal, so when excused, she took her plate to the sink where out of the window she saw Clovis sitting alone in the shade. When no one was looking, she snatched an extra piece of pie and snuck out of the house.

His weary eyes seemed to brighten before his face did. "Thank you, Miss Cadence," he said, taking the dessert from her small hands. Cadence stood before him, not knowing what to say but sensing something was amiss in the gentle smile he offered her.

From the past to the present, her thoughts turned to Dr. Elders then to Isabella. Cadence knew that more than a few people in her hometown would have something to say about a black woman teaching college freshmen in a seminar about life. She wondered how many times her teacher had heard *nigger* hurled at her, how many times she had felt the jabs and jolts of hate-filled language and what it must have done.

She thought of her friend from Mexico and contemplated if wounding words had ever made Isa think less of herself. Had she developed a resilience to terms used by those in Cadence's hometown to describe the migrant workers who made whites' livelihoods possible? *Wet-backs, border niggers, spics, tomato pickers*—the list was long and ever-growing. The more she thought about it, the more ashamed she became. In her ignorance and immaturity, she recalled words loosely used around friends, a means for acceptance among one race at the expense of another. The damage that must come from being attacked based on the natural tattoo of skin color was a perspective those with ivory complexions did not know.

Even though she was lost in her own reflections, Cadence's attention surfaced to hear Professor Mirabilis reiterate the importance of pages, paragraphs, sentences, phrases, and more tellingly, of a single word.

"One word—however simple it may appear—can penetrate the complexities of the psyche in ways that can instantaneously render a person powerless." She paused as they absorbed her words. "While it takes a single word to destroy, it often takes many more to restore."

As was her circular method of teaching, the instructor began bringing the class back to the beginning—but on this day, she did so in a way that none of them had anticipated.

"It's fitting we should begin the hour discussing my 'Demon of Darkness' designation since I'm about to illustrate how I obtained it. I have your library projects ready, but they will not be returned today. Here's why . . ."

The harangue lasted five hellish minutes, but the time seemed like eternity, and the psychological trauma would burn for almost as long. Although Professor Mirabilis stipulated the assignment was to be completed individually, some students ignored those basic instructions. After reminding the offenders of the Honor Code and restating the clear fact that most college work was not to be done cooperatively, she reserved her most scathing words for the seconds before their dismissal.

"When you cheat, you prove that first, you are either too lazy or too stupid to complete your own work. I will let you decide which you would rather be perceived as, but if it is the latter, then clearly, admissions misjudged your abilities. Second, you have insulted me by thinking I am too stupid or careless to catch your dishonesty. Let me assure you—I am neither. So, for those of you who cheated, you have until Friday at 5 p.m. to confess your deceit in person in my office. After this deadline, I will do everything in my power to ensure that you will no longer be a student at this school." Sparks seemed to fly from her eyes before she snapped, "Class dismissed."

Apprehension and embarrassment stalked them for the week. Their teacher's tongue-lashing had left even those who had not cheated doubting their innocence. Nausea coupled with cold sweat swept over Cadence. She had procrastinated, and upon returning from that weekend on the boat, she realized it would take her all night to answer those twenty questions, so she worked with others. They compared blanks. Answers were swapped, shared, copied. In no time, the assignment was complete and sweet sleep, enjoyed. Guiltlessly submitted, the assignment had not been given any more thought, and she certainly did not anticipate that an instance of collaboration could end her freshman experience. Faced with the prospect of expulsion, admission was her only option. She was scared, the clock was ticking, and her short life in college was about to get even shorter, so after music, she gave into the pressure and trudged to the office to declare herself a *cheater*.

The demon had scared the daylights out of so many that the line to see her stacked down the stairs. With half a class ahead of her, Cadence settled on a step and awaited her turn at judgment. Along the stairs, students exchanged nervous looks and whispers of denial. Ignorance was the first defense, but deep down, they all knew that this was no excuse. None had taken the directions seriously or banked on being held accountable for cheating. Why would they? Cheating had become a cultural commonality. Presidents, politicians, preachers, parents, even professors did it—why was it any different for these pupils? Most of them did not see what the big deal was until they came face to face with the judge who would make them see, even if the cost was their college futures.

Red-marked faces and wet eyes heightened the anxiety. The instructor had broken these people, and when it was her turn,

Cadence entered the office and instantly sought the chair, her knees so weakened by guilt and fear they refused to support her body. Professor Mirabilis looked sternly at Cadence who floundered immediately. With streaming tears and shaking voice, she admitted all, telling only that she worked with students in other sections. She could not recall their names but offered an immediate apology and prayed for absolution. Through blurry eyes, she saw her teacher reach into a drawer; Cadence expected expulsion papers, but to her surprise, the demon produced a box of tissues.

"Your deceitful actions are unacceptable, Cadence. After fall break, I will inform you of your punishment, which may include an appearance before the Honor Jury and dismissal from this institution."

Cadence felt as if the life were being drained from her, a sensation that continued to weaken her after she left the office. She could not imagine the shame and embarrassment her parents would feel over their only daughter getting kicked out of school for cheating. If the worry from being busted for cheating was not enough, the immense pressure of midterms pressed fully on everyone. Tension abounded, and some professors, seizing on the opportunity to enhance the stress, added more work. Brodsky was in the lead, demanding a report on the major influences of one musical artist, a subject he never really seemed interested in until that senior piped up about Beethoven's love. The sadistic one seemed to be punishing them all for answers because of one question. They would have to comply, of course, or Brodsky's favorite chord, the F flat, would create cacophonies on their transcripts.

Professor Elders also laid on more work but of the different sort. She wanted to arm them with one of the most important documents of their professional existence—a résumé. As Cadence began compiling the list of her accomplishments, she suddenly felt inadequate. What had she achieved in eighteen years? According to the mostly blank page, the answer was virtually nothing. Other than the occasional babysitting job, being a member of a few clubs, and her past photography position, she could not fill a sheet of paper to get a job. As of late, the only experience she kept thinking of was being a cheater. The résumé writing proved to be an exercise in existential depression.

Having anticipated the trouble most of her students would have with writing a résumé, Professor Elders gave them another assignment. "There's no time like the immediate present to begin your future, so I want you to join a club or organization or sign up for a volunteer opportunity within the next week. Get out there, people. Offer yourself to this college and this city in service, and in return, you'll get experience for those résumés."

When Cadence researched the possibilities for joining some group, she discovered the student newspaper, *The Gator,* was seeking photographers, so she went to the office bearing nothing but determination and need. The editor, TJ, was an intense young man who aspired to cover adrenaline-overloading places where war, strife, and turmoil dominate daily life, but for now was covering the relaxing beats of Charleston and the campus. He gave Cadence a trial assignment of photographing the gospel choir's performance that evening. With a camera borrowed from the paper and equipped with a press pass for stage-front shooting, Cadence set out for what she thought would be some people singing.

What she found was a brand of music that defied the pain and suffering from which it was born. Swaying in unity, clapping in common, rocking in synchronicity, the choir projected the soaring triumph of the spirit across the auditorium. With a soulful style fired from the smoldering kiln of human bondage, gospel evolved from slaves who used hymns and spirituals to pass the long hours, to worship God, to send messages, and to strengthen their resilience against the baking heat, insect swarms, overseers' whips, and the vitriol hurled at them. They shielded their ears against the language of hate with tongues devoted to glory and greatness. Hearts filled with love, not loathing, kept them strong and always with faces that looked skyward toward home. Cadence moved her viewfinder from singer to singer, snapping shots of the choir as a whole then waiting for a more dynamic photograph, something that would secure her a place on the newspaper's staff.

As she scrolled through the pictures, the next song began— a solo *a cappella* by a voice that chillingly warmed the room the instant the first note slipped into sound. The mouth belting out the lowest and highest notes of "Swing Low, Sweet Chariot" with electrifying energy belonged to Jacinda. *Magnificent* came to Cadence's mind as she captured her neighbor in mid-song, hands outstretched in glory, with the humming choir swinging supportively behind her. Cadence wished her work could convey more than the image, but every art form has its limitations, so the photo's viewers would have to imagine the missing senses. With her own senses heightened by the music, Cadence left feeling uplifted, liberated, restored—such is gospel's strategy in teaching weary souls how to remain strong.

The following afternoon, Cadence presented the photos to TJ. Without hesitation, he welcomed her to the newspaper and ran the shot of Jacinda in the next issue. Happy that she could fill a line of her résumé with "staff photographer" and that she could check off a musical attendance requirement for Brodsky, Cadence was thinking of the future shots on the way back to her dorm, so she didn't see two furies stomping toward her. When she finally looked up, she recognized Lily from the girl's certain relationship with a beer bottle, but the other was a stranger now blocking her path.

"So I understand you like being locked in closets with other people's boyfriends?"

"I'm sorry, what?"

"I'm Melissa, Walker's girlfriend, and I know you two were in the closet together." The accuser crossed her arms and tapped one foot against the bricks.

Cadence looked to Lily, who lurked like a troll behind the stranger. "We were playing a game. It wasn't my idea in the first place."

"I don't give a shit whose idea it was. You were in there with him." Melissa was so close Cadence could feel the girl's hot breath. "Look bitch, I know you were all over him. If you know what's good for you, you'll stay the fuck away from him. If I see you near him again, I'll kick your ass!"

Melissa executed a pivot that she must have practiced daily and began strutting away when she suddenly spun back around.

"Oh, and you should really see someone about that herpes case of yours. Those breakouts can get nasty and you wouldn't want to spread them to anyone's boyfriend."

Before Cadence could recover from the shock and muster a defense, the two were snickering from a distance. Fear of the rumor began to make her ill, and on top of that, she couldn't believe she had just been threatened by someone's obviously psychotic girlfriend. For as much as college is supposed to be about adulthood, Cadence had managed to piss off one of its children.

Dread only increased when Cadence heard her name being called. She shuddered to think about what was next, but luckily, it was Enna whom Cadence filled in on the drama.

"You've got to be kidding." Enna shook her head. "I wouldn't worry about it. If she touches you, she can be taken care of. And don't sweat the rumor. It'll die as quickly as it was born," Enna said, turning her head slightly to avoid the plume of smoke issuing from a guy walking in front of them.

"I guess so. I thought college would be different than high school."

"You'd like to think so, but it never ceases to amaze me how many never graduate from there—mentally, that is," Enna said. "It sounds like this Walker guy has got himself a girl-*fiend*." She swatted away another cloud of nicotine. "You know what else *never* ceases to amaze me?" Her voice was rising noticeably.

"What's that?"

"People who don't know how to smoke a cigarette!"

The offending subject in front of them, a guy in flip flops, shorts, and a T-shirt advertising his survival of some party weekend, removed the stick from his mouth. "You talking to me?"

"Yeah, I was. If you're going to pollute this clean, crisp fall air the rest of us are trying to enjoy, at the very least, you should learn how to smoke."

"What the fuck are you talking about?"

"Dude, simply sucking in air to your mouth and blowing it out isn't smoking. You need to suck the shit out of it. Inhale deeply, get that cancer way down in your lungs. Drag it down to your toes. Otherwise, you're just another wannabe smoker trying to look cool when you really look like a dumbass."

He stepped inches from her. "You mean like this?" He inhaled long and hard and deeply and blew the smoke right into her face.

Looking deliberately into his oversized sunglasses, Enna inhaled his attempt and blew it back at him. "Yes, like that."

He took one final inhale before stomping the butt into the stones. "You're a cunt."

"So I've been told, but at least this cunt taught you how to smoke. That's probably more than you can say about the others."

As the schooled one sulked off, Cadence remained bewildered; it seemed there was no one that Enna was afraid of confronting. In fact, she was going with Myla and Althea to protest the slaughter of seals, sharks, and other aquatic wonders in Florida over break. The three would pound the pavement of tourist destinations hoping to educate the material masses on the corporate rape of the natural world. Their causes were intense, and Enna would readily defend any worthy one, sometimes without reason and always without reservations or regrets.

By this time of the semester, students certainly felt like protesting the oppressive atmosphere caused by mid-term exams. The campus was rife with academic anguish, conditions generated from exam anticipation, which actually proves worse than the tests themselves. Although the agony of test-taking lasts only a few days, the nightmares last well into old age. Like her pupils, Professor Elders admitted to test dreams: running late for an exam or missing it altogether; not knowing any of the answers; not having a pen or pencil; being the only one left in the room or not even finding the room.

She also explained that now, as a teacher, she dreamed of forgetting to make or bring the exam; of giving the wrong one to the wrong class; of not getting her grades in on time; of not finding the room. Perhaps the nightmares would subside for all of them since she was not giving a midterm but encouraging them to prepare for the end-of-term project.

Most of Cadence's exams involved multiple choice mania: cruel minutes of indecision when answers dwindle from two outrageously ridiculous choices, to two outrageously identical ones. The choice becomes a coin toss between A and C and no matter which feels most right, it's usually the one that is most wrong. Such was the case in music, biology, and a portion of her Spanish test, which mostly covered vocabulary and conjugation.

Professor Mirabilis's exam involved Cadence's first experience with a blue book, a cheap construction of large-lined, white paper stapled between a pale blue cover. Not too unlike the rudimentary booklets made in kindergarten, blue books were a requirement for some professors who would not consider reading responses if they weren't written in these. Working through the multiple choice, short answer, and essay questions, Cadence filled three blue books in her purge, leaving her weak and uneasy but hopeful that her answers proved how much she wanted to stay at the college.

In between studying and test taking, she spent time with Schilar, who was a most interesting subject. Hanging out in his dorm, Cadence met his roommate, Steve and his girlfriend, Nikki. Unlike Cadence's roommate experience, Schilar and Steve got along well, though they were not originally paired.

"My first roommate, Willie, lasted only a few weeks before he had to move out," Schilar said. "He had issues, potty issues. Seriously. Poor guy. He couldn't use our toilet or any public one, specifically to do number two."

"Awe," Nikki replied. "That's terrible."

"I know. Guy was totally miserable. Full of anxiety, actually *blocked* with it. He had some disorder. What was the name of it? Um, it was called parcooooo . . . um, parcopresis! That's it. How's that for vocabulary?"

"So what happened to him?" Cadence asked.

"He had to get a place by himself. Needed his own toilet. Actually, from what I've seen in our bathroom, it doesn't sound like a bad idea. Our suitemates are gross."

About a month into the semester, Schilar and Steve had problems with their party-scene-infatuated suitemates. Several nights a week, Parker and Dale, loaded on liquor and looking to cause trouble, would bust in, turn on the lights and music, and wail on a sleeping Schilar and Steve, who both had to make eight o'clock classes. The rest-destroying ritual went on until, complaining one morning to his psychology professor, Steve received some of the best advice of freshman year.

"Return the favor. Wake them up, make some noise, mirror their methods. They'll get the message," the instructor said. So Steve and Schilar did and with impressive results since now Parker and Dale leave their suitemates unmolested during ridiculous hours.

"That sounds great, but I don't think it would work for my roommate," Nikki said.

"Oh, yeah," Steve said, "maybe I should help you with that problem."

Nikki punched him in the arm. "I bet you'd like to. My roommate walks around naked. And it's not when she's just getting out of the shower. It's *all the time.*"

They laughed, but Nikki wasn't amused. "I know it sounds funny, but it's really awkward."

"Does she get dressed for class?" Cadence asked.

"I wouldn't call it that," Nikki said. "If there's an opportunity for her tits and ass to hang out, she takes it."

"Have you said anything?"

"Oh, yeah. Know what she told me? 'Not everyone can walk around nude, but luckily I'm one of the few who can,'" Nikki said. "That's right, she's not even *naked*, she's *nude*. And then she had the nerve to tell me that if I didn't lay off the eating, I'd be one of those people who couldn't walk around nude."

"Do you?" Schilar laughed.

"No, I don't, but according to her, I can, until the freshman fifteen goes to my ass. Yeah, that's my roomie experience. I never realized how many weird people you meet in college, and I never thought one would be sleeping across the room from me."

Cadence was again relieved that she wasn't alone in having issues with the stranger she lived with, but the remedy Schilar used for his suitemates wouldn't work for her since staying up talking on the phone or making noise would mean her own sleep loss. Perhaps a solution would present itself to create some desperately needed silence.

Schilar's room was certainly not silent. An incessant thumping issued from every corner of the building, so background noise seemed to whisper from the giant posters of greatness—Hendrix, Pink Floyd, the Dead, Marley—that were surrounded by fliers in rainbow shades announcing Stone Miles's shows.

Cadence realized just how much Schilar must have seen traveling for gigs. He would add more pieces to the wall after fall break since the band was hitting the road for some concerts.

In addition to the imposing figures that towered around his bed, a large quotation in blue ink appeared scrawled across a white strip of paper: *Rock is the foundation that rolls the musical soul.* Schilar was providing some sort of rock upon which she could rely, considering they both shared the dread in waiting for Professor Mirabilis's answer. They discussed the ways their fates could roll with others who had cheated. Most were convinced the demon would damn all of them, but Cadence and Schilar thought the punishment would be reasonable, and they maintained some faith that all would not be lost. Each received a post-break summons to her office, so until then, they would occupy places in purgatory during what was supposed to be a restful time at home.

It had been nearly two months since she had seen her parents, the longest separation from them Cadence had ever experienced, and although anxious to return, she also wanted to see more of Schilar; he apparently wanted the same.

"I wish I could spend all of break with you," he whispered during their last night together before departing. When Cadence asked what they would do, he replied, "Oh, the kind of stuff that inspires great songs."

Waiting in front of her dorm, they exchanged kisses, clinging to each other in a touching goodbye. She could hardly believe that half of first semester was gone, but right now, she beckoned time to move at molasses pace, so she could spend it wrapped in his exciting calmness. But time—yielding its power for no one—sprinted on, and Julie, an acquaintance from Cadence's hometown, soon pulled up to give her a ride. While looking over Schilar's shoulder in one final embrace, Cadence saw Jacinda coming out of the dorm, her face lit by a tremendous smile. In her hand were copies of *The Gator*, which she passed to the driver, a young man with shaded eyes, leaning coolly in the seat as if it were a recliner. Cadence listened as the thumping reached a peak then softened as the car cruised away. After a departing kiss and promises of calls from Schilar, she was on her way.

Cadence and Julie filled the drive with favorite songs as well as chatter of the memories, mistakes, and mishaps of their strange new lives. As the miles lessened between them and home, they anticipated what was to come: pampering by parents with home-cooked meals and line-freshened laundry; endless licks and love by pets; familiar sights and scenes, and best of all—that night's parties. In those remote fields of the community's farms, they would discover how so much and so little had changed. Stepping into that time warp of returning home, Cadence would revisit the monotonous methods of farming and see how life had carried on in her absence and because of it. In truth, she savored the break from the grinding class routine, a brief respite only she would enjoy. For rest was foreign to those who toiled relentlessly to give her the extraordinary experience of being not only a freshman, but more aspiringly, of one day being a college graduate.

Chapter 7

Spanish 101
Elementary Conversation

Hideous shades of blue and black marred his face, evidence of pains penetrating deeply; his hat added to the shadows, and with downcast eyes, he dodged the stares that accompanied him to the seat in front of Cadence. In the days following their return from break, Kirby had discovered another side of the Holy City and bore the remnants of a night hard spent. What hurt more than the attack was the assumption that he had been in some fraternity skirmish or drunken brawl. When Professor Marquez tried to make a light joke about the dangers of extracurricular activities, the humor didn't translate, especially when Kirby corrected her interpretation of his wounds: "With all due respect, professor, I was mugged."

Blankness came over her face, and she muttered an embarrassed apology then quickly directed attention to conjugating the future tense while Kirby stared a hole into his book. As soon as they were dismissed, Cadence leaned forward. "Hey, you okay?"

Giving her a full look at the extent of the attacker's wrath, he answered, "Yeah, but I've been better. Thanks for asking. Did I miss anything the other day?"

Because the Spanish class had covered a lot of material, Cadence agreed to grab coffee and meet after her classes to help him catch up.

Although an unwanted requirement, Dr. Elders's course became a strange attractor—that rare college class when an instructor makes a course real. She conveyed the material genuinely in terms they understood, always making pragmatic connections to the professional world. As is often the eccentric case of college, life's happenings can suddenly appear in the texts of class, but as this course had no book, experience was still reflected despite the absence of pages. Coincidentally, on that day, the topic was crime, so the class listened as a captain with the police force, Officer Sully, delivered the local statistics on drugs, robbery, assault, rape, and murder. He offered strategies to avoid being a victim, and having just seen Kirby's face, Cadence paid more attention than she normally might have.

"People, you gotta be smart. Don't walk alone, especially at night. Young men, this goes for you too. I know some of you think that because you're guys it won't happen to you, but I've seen the pulverized faces of too many who thought they'd be okay walking by themselves." He watched as some of his audience leaned back with confidence.

"Believe me, the cold muzzle of a gun or knife blade will shrink your masculinity in a bullet's second. And intoxication increases your chances of being a target. That liquid courage gets flushed right out when a criminal has you in the crosshairs."

When his serious crime talk ended, Officer Sully took questions from students eager to tap his knowledge regarding ticketing practices, possession laws, and other justice trivia to use in their defenses. The officer entertained their inquiries, answering each with light chidings that warned of a college degree's virtual worthlessness when accompanied with a criminal record.

While Freshman Seminar was generally easy to comprehend, biology required frustrating precision. Although

Cadence's lab results did not always turn out as they were supposed to, Alex showed her how to learn from the mishaps and not only made lab bearable, she managed to make it fun. Students wished she taught the class, and some asked why she couldn't. As a lowly graduate student, Alex wasn't allowed to have a class of her own, but someday she hoped to stand in the front of a lecture hall and deliver a more exciting approach to biology than what she had experienced.

So far, she successfully led them through conversions of the metric system and measurements, tutorials in using compound light and binocular dissecting microscopes, making wet mount slides, and identifying the characteristics of a specimen. Today, Cadence was the specimen, so after scraping the inside of her cheek with a toothpick, she rubbed the sample on a dry slide and stained it with a drop of methylene blue. After positioning a cover slip over the drop, she placed the slide on the stage. The smallest parts of her being appeared—a haphazard network of circular shapes, colored in every shade of azure. She glanced at her textbook and peered into the viewfinder. No evidence of herpes. She smiled. Observing the tiny blue chaos reminded Cadence of Kirby's face, so she completed the lab by locating the nuclei, cytoplasms, plasma membranes and the granules of her cells and recording all the appropriate measurements for her report.

Kirby was sitting on a bench off on the lawn's perimeter when Cadence arrived. Like so many migrants from the North, he was lured by Charleston's siren song. Picturing themselves lounging on its beaches and lolling through its historic lanes, most do not realize how quickly the honeymoon can end and how just beneath her seductive surface lurk the dangers of any urban environment.

"Here's your tall black." Cadence cringed as she handed him the cup. "That's intense."

For the first time in a few days, he laughed. "What can I say? That's me. It'll match my face."

As Kirby began to copy his classmate's notes, Cadence asked about the attack. He recounted how, on the way back to his room after being in the library, a guy jumped from behind a wall, held a gun to Kirby's back, and demanded money. When he told the thief he had none, Kirby soon felt the ground when the criminal punched him down and delivered swift kicks to his face and stomach. The thief snatched his wallet before disappearing into the night. With disappointment, Kirby stared across the lawn to the top of a church spire jutting above buildings in the distance: "Nice, huh? So much for Southern hospitality."

"Hey now, I'm Southern."

"You don't have much of an accent. It's not as pronounced as the others I've heard."

Unlike so many people she was raised around who carried the deep, distinguishing drawls, she didn't. "Not everybody from the South talks like a hick. I guess I left mine back on the farm."

"A farm, huh? That's cool. Was it fun growing up there?"

"It was, but I always wanted to live in a city. Felt I was missing out on something," she admitted.

"Like what? Overcrowding, no parking, pollution, noise, muggings . . . the stuff of my hometown, Boston?"

"Never been there. I haven't been anywhere up North. Then again, I've never even been on a plane."

"Really? Never? I can't imagine not ever flying. My parents have made me travel with them since I was a child."

"What's it like? Being on an airplane?"

Kirby thought for a moment then his face brightened. "It's like riding in the belly of a fire-breathing dragon. I'm always surprised by the power of a jetliner—a piece of aluminum rocketing through the clouds on flammable liquid. It's transcendent."

"Honestly, Kirby, who talks like you?"

"What do you mean?"

"That sounds like poetry what you just said."

"Words, Cadence, it's all about the words. But back to your question about flying. Nothing will change your perspective about how fearfully wonderful the world is like staring out of an airplane's window."

"Where have you been?"

"A lot of places, but I can't remember some since I was so young when I went to them, but in the last few years, I've been to Russia, Italy, Hong Kong, Australia, Brazil. This summer I was in Chile."

"Why were you there?"

"My dad. He's in the petroleum business, so he's constantly on the road. Or maybe I should say 'in the air.' Sometimes, I tag along. I'm fortunate; I get to see a lot of amazing places," he said. "If you could travel, where would you go?"

Cadence looked to the clouds, which she could see better since the trees had begun to shed their leaves. "Don't know. I've never really thought about it," she said. "Maybe Mexico. This girl I met, Isabella, the way she describes her home makes me want to go there. It sounds so beautiful."

"It is. I've been there, too," Kirby said.

"Is there anywhere you haven't been, Mr. World Traveler?"

"Sure—Antarctica." He laughed.

"When you get there, send me a postcard," Cadence said. "So, you've been all these places, but what do you think of Charleston?"

"I really like the city. I love that I can be walking down the street and strangers say 'hello' or ask how I am. If I'm at a store, the clerk or someone in line will start conversations with me. People are so nice," he said. "But the way I feel about the school is another story. I don't feel right here. I know I haven't been here that long, but I can't seem to find my place. I'm trying this fraternity thing, but I don't think it's gonna work."

"Why not?"

"Because I don't want to drink every night or play kiss-ass to some brother so they'll let me in. It's a bit extreme the lengths that some people go to be part of something. I mean, the life sounds alluring, but I don't know if I want to give up so much to have it."

"Have you tried hanging out with anyone else—like your roommate?"

Kirby shook his head. "He barely leaves the room."

"Mine too," Cadence said. "She's afraid of making her boyfriend mad, so all she does is talk on the phone. Does everything he tells her to and on the weekends he's bunked up with us."

"That sucks. Mine's not quite like that. He's addicted to videogames, plays them all day and night against people from all over the globe. He only stops to eat and go to the bathroom. It's so pathetic. Me and my suitemates call him 'Sadstick.'"

"Sadstick?"

"Opposite of 'joystick.' This guy came to college to sit in front of a screen twenty-four seven to play a game? I don't get it."

"Me neither. So, what else don't you like about this place?"

"Actually, and I hate to say this to you, it's pretty lonely here. I had these visions of what college would be like, but really, it's not what I thought, even in my courses. Some of the classes are boring, and the students are no better. A lot are too hungover or stoned to offer any intelligent comments. Maybe I just got in the wrong sections. I, I don't know. Maybe it's me." Kirby gulped the remainder of his coffee and closed his notebook. "Hey, I need to get going; I have to meet some classmates for a group project."

"Yeah, I've got some stuff to do, too."

"Thanks for the notes, Cadence, or perhaps I should say 'gracias,' and next time, I'm buying coffee."

"De nada and muy bien," Cadence said and set off as well.

When TJ told Cadence to get a feature photo for November to recognize National Running Safety Month, she wasn't sure who would be the subject. It had briefly escaped her mind that Isa was an avid pavement pounder, but in learning of her friend's need for a model, Isa obliged.

In the imposing company of its Greek-revival mansions, The Battery had become Isa's favorite running route of late. She enjoyed the waves lapping on the storied wall and the winds weaving over the harbor's waters. She especially liked keeping pace with the dolphins as the mammalian wonders would often feed feet from the wall as she ran. Isa couldn't help but stop and watch their graceful dives and the way their shiny backs glistened like jewels on the river's surface.

Cadence agreed it would make an ideal feature, and it did. Framed between two palmetto trees, Isa's striding silhouette appeared in the golden glow of a fall sunset atop that seawall, but its radiance would be muted in *The Gator's* black and white pages.

In retracing their route back to campus, Cadence asked, "So, what *is* it about running that you love so much?"

"Perhaps you should ask me what I don't like."

"Okay. What *don't* you like?"

"Nothing. I love every aspect of it," Isa said. "It helps me stay in shape, but I do it because I can, because I want to, because I love to. When I put my running shoes on, I'm free for as long as I want to be. It clears my mind, helps work out problems. Sweat is cleansing. *¿Comprende?*" Isa asked, in her dual-language habit.

"Maybe. But how do you work problems out?"

"I focus on what's outside so I can work out what's troubling me inside. I don't even listen to music when I run. I want to be aware of all that's around and within me," Isa said. "I get into these habits. Right now, I pretend that people or things I see on my run are my problems. I use colors, especially, like someone's shirt. A blue one could be a situation that's depressing me, or a red sign will be causing my anger, so I'll sprint by it harder and imagine whatever is concerning me is gone when I pass it."

Isa had poetry about her; perhaps it was her seductive Spanish accent that could make even running sound ruggedly romantic. When she spoke about her pastime, she infused descriptions with passionate involvement. She measured her life in strides, coming to know the intimate feel of every city by the way her feet delicately struck its passages. In treating her runs as adventures, Isa especially loved the slow tours of places she ran, where each block presented sensory memories, and every step unlocked treasures. Charleston had given her the lemony smell of blooming magnolias mixed against the brine of the marshes and traffic puttering below palms' clattering canopies. She spied gardens tucked beyond shadowy, slim passages and graveyards brightened by patches of wildflowers. Dogs sometimes ran the abbreviated lengths of their black iron fences with her, while others barked from piazzas and windows. On occasion, men in suits with bowties watched her pass while talking away behind office windows. Most people fly by the scenery never bothering to look at and learn the details, to absorb the special accents—but not Isa.

One feature she found a special fascination with was the clumps of silvery-gray tendrils hanging from trees like tattered sails. She sometimes dodged them on her running routes, and while stopped at a corner one morning, she grabbed the mossy mess and was pleasantly surprised. Its dry, velvety texture was not unpleasing to the touch, and she marveled at how hundreds of strands entwined to form a tangling that was not to be undone.

"I see you have an interest in Spanish moss?"

Isa turned to see a man in an oversized sunhat rising from the tall, green depths of his garden. "Yes, I guess," she said. "What did you say this is?"

"Spanish moss. Grows on most trees around here. Is this the first time you've ever seen it?"

Isa studied the wiry plant. "I think I have seen it before, but this may be the first time I have noticed it. It's a funny name."

He laughed. "Well, that's history for you. The Native Americans used to call it 'tree hair,' but it reminded the French of the Spanish explorers' long, black beards, so they took to calling it 'Spanish beard,' as an insult."

"That's an insult?"

"Oh, a man's relationship with his facial hair is sacred. And back in the day, a beard symbolized masculinity. It meant the difference between a man and a boy." He grinned as he rubbed his smoothly shaven face.

She smiled. "How do you know all this?"

"Too much time on my hands?" He held up his dirt-laced gloves and laughed. "I'm a trivia addict and an avid gardener. I just like to learn about what I take care of."

Isa reached up to touch the moss once more. "I like that very much. Thanks for telling me about it," she said, letting the mass go and stepping back into her stride.

Not only did she share this running discovery with Cadence, but Isa also talked of her native Mexico, of how it is not known for fostering a running culture, except for the legendary Rarámuri. These people of the Northwest were famed for covering ultra-distances, even up to 200 miles, through the rugged terrain of Copper Canyon. In relaying a joke that crosses many borders, Isa said if most Mexicans see someone running they think the person's trying to get away from *la policía*. But changes were happening, and a few years ago, someone started a running club in her town.

"I'll never forget my first run—it was up the hill, going out of town toward the volcano that overlooks Tequila. It was hot, and I had to walk, run, walk, run. I made it, but I wanted to run without walking, so I began to run every day, and well, here I am," Isa said. "Someday, I'll go back as a doctor and start more running clubs. My people need health, help, and hope, and running gives me that." The way she spoke of the dreams she was running after made Cadence long for the type of clarified direction her friend possessed.

When the two departed, Cadence remembered that she had quite a few miles of her own to log at the library, so she stopped by her room to gather books for her study session. Everyone was out, and all was quiet for once, but just as she settled into the silence, a harrowing scream splintered it. The shriek came with such force that it instantly lodged chill in Cadence's spine. She dropped her textbook and ran into the hall. Just as she did, Jacinda emerged from her room, wild-eyed and seeming as if she had no bearing of where she was. In her hand, she held a phone, its face live with a connection, one that was contrasted by the deadness across her own.

Frozen in agony, she stared at Cadence, and without warning, Jacinda let go: "Whyyyyyyyyyyyyy?"

Between uncontrollable sobs, she repeatedly wailed the question and answered it with screams of denial. When Jacinda dropped to the floor, her phone tumbled across it. Cadence rushed over, laying one hand on the wounded girl and picking up the phone with the other.

A loud voice chattered from the device. Pulling it to her ear, Cadence heard, "Jacinda, baby, I don't wanna be the one tellin' you dat yo brutha's gone. You feel me? But we're gonna get the muthafuckers who done 'dis. Jacinda, baby, you der?"

"Jacinda, she . . ." Cadence began, her hand tightening on the girl's shoulder. "She can't talk right now. Who is this?"

"Who's dis?" the voice countered.

"I'm, um, her neighbor. At school," Cadence said. "I'm the only one here."

"'Well, I'm her brutha's blood. Yo, tell her, tell her 187s gonna reign down on those Latino fuckers. Got me? Just tell her!" The line went silent but the noise from Jacinda continued.

Before Cadence could think of what to do next, their RA stepped from the stairwell.

"Nooooooo, noooooo, my God, noooo," Jacinda continued as Carrie rushed over for an explanation. Cadence answered her with a blank stare.

"I, I don't really know," Cadence said. "Um, I think her brother's dead."

Carrie was already on the phone with campus counselors, and when Jacinda's phone rang, the RA took the call from one of the girl's relatives. The sad story had become all too typical: a young black man with his life wide open closed off all prospects for a future when he joined the TNT gang, short for Thug Nasty Tribe. In their testosterone-filled world where status is measured in guns and drugs and women and where the crisis of manhood is fueled by any insults to reputation, Jacinda's brother got caught up in their territorial war with a Latino gang, the *Almas Diablo* or Devil Souls. As bullets flew, body counts went up, and today, Dizion became another senseless statistic. What his gangsta life left was a gospel-singing sister reduced to a crumpled, crying heap and a family bearing the scars of a lost soul they couldn't save; in the troubling days to come, they would all need music of the spirit more than ever to lift them back to life.

When the counselors took Jacinda to wait for her aunt to arrive, the hall was somewhat quiet again, save for the whisperings. Cadence resumed her journey to the library. Although the mound of work she encountered the first week had been replaced by new mountains that were no less towering, everything now seemed reduced in light of Jacinda's loss. Choosing an isolated spot, she tried to distract herself with work and was well into her assignments until someone else showed up and began gabbing on the cubicle's other side. With concentration gone, Cadence began packing.

"I so know what you mean. I've met so many total losers," the voice said. "Pathetic clothes, horrible music tastes, and don't even get me started on the freaks and faggots. Oh, and the fat asses—cottage cheese thighs and muffin tops. Seriously, there are some ugly people here."

Cadence stood up to go, but as she did, her book smacked the floor. Reaching for it, she spied a pink and green polka bag—the supposed stylish one's tote. Cadence didn't see anything forward about a bag that resembled so many others.

"Girl, I know. My roommate, I can't stand her. *Greasy.* Can you believe they'd let her kind in this school? Ha, ha. I know. She should totally be picking tomatoes, but hey, at least she helps me with my Spanish." Hearing enough, Cadence left for bed.

The patter of rain on the window was a soothing contrast to the sounds Cadence had heard the previous night. Fittingly, the morning began in the dreariness of a storm since today she'd meet with Professor Mirabilis to learn the punishment for cheating. It was a perfect day for sleeping, but courses called, and professors would be unsympathetic to tardiness because of rain; however, when the heavens opened on the Holy City, it seemed as if God rescinded on the promise not to destroy the earth with water again. Noah's ark would have been apt means of transportation to class or work. After all, this was the Lowcountry, and a steady shower sweeping over the peninsula combined with high tide produced soggy sights at every block. Sewers vomited their vile contents, and manhole covers became mid-street fountains. The city was rife with drivers drunk with stupidity. Steering their cars into murky waters, they'd end their commutes by taking refuge on the island tops of their vehicles until Samaritans helped push them to safety.

Having an umbrella offered little protection against sheets of rain coming down sideways. Cadence might as well have gone barefooted since her shoes were like sinking boats taking on water. She envied the prevalence of rubber protection wading around campus. Available in every pattern and color, rain boots offered more than a stylish fashion statement; these essentials to surviving the rising tides should have been an orientation gift from the school.

Despite the deluge, classes went on, and when she ventured out from the darkness of music the skies were still gray. With every step closer to her English teacher's office, Cadence's heart beat faster and her stomach hung on knotted edge. The initial sickness had subsided since her confession, but an uneasy sense had riddled her for much of break, and now the time had come to hear her academic fate.

"Here is what will happen . . ." Professor Mirabilis explained that Cadence would receive a zero on the assignment and a report would be filed. If the accused felt that her teacher was in the wrong, she could request a jury trial, which, flying in the face of a full confession, might be academic suicide. Once all paperwork was signed, the violation would sit in Cadence's record, a closet skeleton of sorts, the bones of which would remain undisturbed unless another honor infringement opened that door. When she finished going over the procedure, the teacher looked to her student for questions.

One remained for Cadence: "Will my parents find out?"

"Not unless you tell them. College professors are prohibited from discussing any aspect of your academic performance with anyone, including your parents. Privacy laws known as FERPA protect you."

Relief replaced Cadence's tension as soon as she heard she wasn't going to be expelled. She thanked her teacher and vowed to restore her trust. Leaving the building, Cadence was met by the sun's regenerating rays. Everything glistened with post-rain freshness and because she also felt renewed at having been spared from banishment.

Come to my room when you get this! Those were the only words in the note hanging on Cadence's door. Intrigued by the command, Cadence walked into Isa's room and nearly tripped over a stack of bags. Sitting cross-legged on the floor, Isa chattered away in Spanish and motioned for Cadence to wait.

As she did, Cadence studied the wall behind Isa's bed where photographs of rolling hills, forest trails, beaches, and mountains espoused mottos and mantras for each dreamy landscape. *Don't run like the wind—run to create it,* said one while another posed, *Running is not about chasing sunsets; it's about meeting the next sunrise.* Race ribbons, medals, and trophies decorated the shelves above Isa's desk, and pictures smiled from the bulletin board, including a larger one of a good-looking guy whose cheek was graced by the shiny obsidian beads of her rosary. A calendar sported a series of colorful numbers, the recorded distances of Isa's efforts. This week, she had logged twenty-three miles. Cadence winced, realizing that while she was sleeping, Isa was cruising the sidewalks for an easy three before the sun peaked over the harbor. Tomorrow, Isa's calendar noted, "Cock 5K." It sounded like some kinky athletic experiment.

Isa's natural décor clashed with her roommate's side, which featured colors that connoted a preppy high school heritage.

Pinks, greens, and other pastels in polka dots infected the comforter like a pox. Everything matched in a manner that bordered on obsession, with much of it bearing the irksome marks of identity—monogrammed initials. The curvy, exaggerated letters of the alphabet splattered across possessions reminded Cadence of a dog marking its territory. In the uniform code of bright colors and fancy-scripted letters, "F-A-E" clung to pillows, a blanket, a purse, jewelry, a sweatshirt—even a drink coozie was not left dispossessed. Cadence felt suddenly uncomfortable as she remembered the purse and the racist remarks of the girl in the opposite cubicle.

"She likes those monogrammed things," Isa said, hanging up the phone.

"I couldn't tell," Cadence replied.

"She says her mama gave them for her graduation. What do you think of her initials?" Isa asked.

"F-A-E?" Cadence asked. "Not much. Why?"

"Her name is Frances Eleanor Ashley," Isa revealed. "So her initials are really F-E-A."

"What're you getting at?" Then remembering the Spanish word for *ugly*, Cadence laughed along with Isa. Perhaps she didn't need to tell her friend what she heard after all.

"Enough of the language lesson; are you ready for a road trip?"

"Road trip?"

"*Sí, señorita. Un viaje por carretera*! To Co-lum-bía," she said. "*Mi hermano* lives there. There's a race tomorrow. You want to go tonight, hang out, and I'll run in the morning?"

Cadence hesitated. "Wait, does this mean I have to run the race, too?"

Isa laughed. "Only if you want to, but you'd like to go to the football game, *no*? My brother has tickets. So?"

Cadence punched the air with her fists. "Yes!"

"¡*Excelente*! My friend Maria is going home, so we can ride with her. There's room for one more. Do you know anyone who'd like to come?

She knew several, but Reena and Saida had plans already, so Penny gladly accepted the invitation. The timing couldn't be more perfect for Cadence since Schilar's band was on the road and Corrine was preparing for Jed's arrival. Cadence hurried to pack and when she had finished, she stripped her bed of its every linen, gathered her valuables, and stuffed everything into the closet, which she secured with a chain lock she had bought. She didn't say goodbye, but slipped out of her room and across the suite.

While Penny prepared for a journey with Cadence, Saida was off to Miami on a first-class ticket courtesy of her business contact from Barrett's party. As she was packing alongside her roommate, Saida threw a pack of condoms in her purse, and she left her contact's business card on her desk. Not long after Saida departed for the airport, Isa, Cadence, and Penny piled in Maria's car, excited to leave behind the coast for a weekend inland.

Along the way, Cadence learned that Penny was from a large family in Ohio. The youngest of five girls, she wanted to get away since all her sisters had gone to in-state schools. It took much begging to convince her parents to spend more on her education, especially since she had never been to the school prior to arriving as a freshman. A friend who visited Charleston described the place as extraordinary, and the more Penny read about the school, the more enamored she became. Although she remained undecided in her major, she was interested in psychology and thought about being a high school guidance counselor or even a sports psychologist. This latter interest had especially developed as of late since she had been hanging out with a few guys from the half-rubber ball squad, a jovial group who liked to practice partying even more than they did their game. In fact, she had ditched their bash for this weekend trip, but took the time to tell the girls everything she had learned about the sport.

Before becoming students of Charlestowne, most had never heard of the sport said to have its roots in the early 1900's in a slum area called *Little Mexico*. Originally, the game was played with mop or broomstick handles and a rubber ball cut in half. Teams consist of three to four players who rotate positions as catcher, batter, and pitcher. With no strikes or base running, teams score singles or home runs by hitting the ball to designated point zones. Games are usually three innings long, have very low scores, and like any event involving balls, a devoted following of enthusiasts sacrificed their paychecks and passions for their beloved boys.

"Are you telling us that the half-rubber team only has three or four people on it?" Cadence asked.

"Oh, no. The overall squad has twenty players, I think. They have sub-groups that alternate around the fields," Penny said.

"Um, I may be missing something, but what makes it worth watching?" Maria glanced at Penny in the rearview mirror.

"It's so cool and so hard. Because the ball is only a half one, it will curve, dip, drop, soar, and flutter. The guys like to say that a half-rubber ball will do anything except move in a straight line."

"Gosh, Penny, you sound like their ambassador," Cadence teased. "And you said this was created in Charleston?"

"Ren, he's kinda the star pitcher, said it started in that Little Mexico place. But he also said there was some dispute with Savannah. They claim it was born there. That squad's our guys' biggest rivalry."

"Isa, have you ever heard of 'Little Mexico?' In Charleston?" Cadence asked.

Isa turned toward the backseat. "I only know of BIG Mexico." She laughed along with the others.

In a little under two hours, they crested a hill and glimpsed the motley collection of rectangular and squared shadows of the capital's skyline. From a distance, there is nothing especially remarkable about its vision print. Its tallest structure is a light and dark blue striped product of modernity that dwarfs the State House's copper dome and Corinthian columns. Even though it does not occupy the distinction of being the state's oldest city, which Charleston holds, in 1786, it beat out the holy one and was designated the capital for its central location, a midlands meeting ground that still brings residents of the Upcountry to meet those of the Lowcountry.

The other important meeting ground in the capital is the campus of the University of South Carolina (the only "USC" most Southerners acknowledge), which sprawls across the city and out to Williams Brice Stadium, home of the Gamecocks. Fans publicly dub themselves "Cocks" and proudly wear the garnet and black colors, a cult following that includes those who have never stepped foot on the school's soil or walked its halls in search of a degree. They find special liberation in chanting "Go cocks!" without fear of reprisal. Cadence had considered becoming a part of this cock nation, but as many in her high school were going to the state's largest university, she wanted to move farther away, to break from repeating the past.

Columbia runs on the pulses of politics, football, and those folks who make this concrete slab between the rivers their home. Among those was Isa's brother Roano, a graduate student in his final year of the business program. Isa was not only looking forward to seeing him, but to meeting his new girlfriend. When Maria dropped the three off at a small house, the epitome of tall, dark, and handsome greeted them in the driveway. Roano reminded Cadence of a Latin looker she had seen only weeks ago . . .

In search of wonders for her seminar project, Cadence had ventured out, and since Blaze was gone for business, Reena accompanied her. Nighttime shooting was tricky, but Cadence had gotten some great pictures of lighted displays, all holding an array of items out of wallet range. Eventually, they came upon South End Brewery, and while they did not see Captain George's ghost peeking through the windows, they did spy the seemingly supernatural moves of Salsa dancers who appeared to float across the floor.

Cadence and Reena watched dreamingly as two of the sexiest specimens ever to heat up the bar's Salsa Night demonstrated how the Latin dance of lust should always be done. With hair shining like black pearl, lips so red they seemed smeared with blood, and sparkling heels so high she looked poised on swords, the woman beamed like a goddess. Each time the man flung his partner, her flame-colored dress stretched through the air then suddenly retreated to wrap her curves. His tight black pants and silky, half-buttoned shirt invited a body built for vertical and horizontal dancing. Every time he touched her, his muscles sparked with definition, but the best was when, in the lightning-complex moves of the dance, she brought her leg up to meet his hips—pseudo sex that was definitively on fire.

In them Reena saw desire beyond what she knew. "Someday, Blaze and I will dance like that," she whispered.

"Don't you already?" Cadence asked.

"Not out in public," Reena said slyly. "He's pretty private. But I'm working on that. Maybe we can take lessons and he'll get over the shyness."

Considering what Cadence had seen between them, she didn't think of Blaze as being especially shy, but she had not been around the couple very much. What she did know was there was a searing attraction between Reena and Blaze, the same kind kindled on the dance floor before them.

Now, in seeing Isa's handsome brother, Cadence wondered if Roano danced; he did not, but proved an excellent cook when Isa requested a Mexican fiesta as her pre-race meal. Over dinner, including the salty sweetness of margaritas, Cadence and Penny heard how Roano and his sister came to the States. When he was a high school junior, he met a graduate exchange student studying the tequila industry in their town. The more Roano found out about the business program, the more he wanted to venture out in search of a life beyond what their town offered. He earned an undergraduate degree from USC then went immediately into the business school. From visiting her brother, Isa also became enchanted with what America promised and chose Charlestowne because of its proximity to the medical school. The conversation of where they all came from and where they all wanted to go took them well near midnight.

Crawling out of bed for the race was a test of Cadence's discipline, but she, Penny, and Roano got Isa to the 8 a.m. start and positioned themselves at the finish line. Cadence had no idea how long it would take Isa to run three miles, so she was pleasantly surprised when after fifteen minutes, the first of the male racers began crossing the line, and in the eighteenth, two females sprinted toward them. By a few yards, Isa trailed a blond woman, who was well on her way to winning, when suddenly, the wind caught a spectator's plastic streamer. The scene seemed scripted in slow motion: the debris floated in front of the leader, wrapping her feet as if they were tangled in barbed wire. A gasp arose from the crowd, when she tumbled to the pavement, but before anyone could get to her, Isa was there. The woman lay on the ground, waving away spectators who tried to assist.

Blood ran from her knees, and the woman with the bib number of 362 attempted to stand but could not until Isa positioned herself under her competitor's arm. Other male and female runners darted by them, anxious to take the top places. The injured woman's sunglasses hid the tears, but the finish line was in sight. Just as they were about to limp over the threshold together, Isa let go and fell back. The woman crossed and was immediately led to the medical tent.

The crowd cheered, and Cadence looked over to see Roano filled with an almost fatherly adoration. When Isa walked over, she brushed off the drama and directed her attention to going home, showering, and the afternoon's tailgating, where Roano's girlfriend, Verena, would meet them.

Cadence's family had no traditions with football, which was clearly a departure from the garnet and black scene sweeping the stadium. A spellbinding spectacle, tailgating transformed parked vehicles into food and drink trucks. The entire area was a never-ending bar and a virtual buffet with weekend chefs slinging spatulas in cook-off contests to determine whose ribs fell most effortlessly from the bone, whose burgers dripped the most juice, and the most important distinction of all—whose barbecue was truly king.

Roano and his roommate, José, a criminal justice grad student, made the arrangements and supplied provisions. They encouraged the girls to stay close to the car if they wanted to indulge because undercover cops would be everywhere. Otherwise, they were free to car hop and turn heads as they sashayed up and down the rows, so they walked and talked as men and gatherings of guys invited them to stop. Sometimes they obliged, but mostly they just smiled and moved on, relishing the attention. They were largely ignored as they passed the fraternity tents; most brothers were fixated on the pearled ones. The trio giggled and searched for other interests.

As they paraded the grounds, Saida was doing her own parading in Miami with Miguel, recently divorced and looking for some fantasy and fun. He got that and more with Saida on the streets and between the sheets. He savored being on the arm of a younger woman who made him feel virile again, especially when the eyes of other men grazed her wherever they went. In exchange for the pleasures she afforded him in his new bachelor life, he treated her to designer bags, jewelry, and a pair of thigh-high stiletto boots.

"You must wear them for me and nothing else," he told her in front of a blushing salesclerk.

"I'll wear them whenever I want," Saida said, turning on the spikes before the mirror. "But I'll take your suggestion into consideration."

Later that evening, Miguel turned down the lights, turned up some Latin tunes, and with champagne and strawberries beside the chair he settled into, Saida took his suggestion. Pressing the right spike against his chest, she watched him watch her wearing nothing but those black leg gloves. He inhaled her scent and handed her a glass. She had been taught the taste of expensive champagne, but through instinct, she knew how to seduce with it. Dipping her finger into the glass, she brought the wet treat to his mouth, rubbing the liquid gloss on his lips then forcing her fingers to tangle with his tongue. When she felt he had just enough to keep him on the edge, she'd take another sip, intentionally allowing the sticky sweetness to spill from the glass, down her throat, over her chest and eventually, between her legs. Knowing the price of fine champagne, Miguel did not waste any, and as if examining every finite detail of a business contract, he worked meticulously over her, gathering every drop of Saida's proposition until she grew tired of standing and led him to the linens.

The sight and sense of her would remain imprinted in his memory, distracting him in board meetings, during office dealings, while driving, and in conversation with anyone, especially his ex-wife. Thoughts of her would be first on his mind in the morning, last on it at night, and even comprised the stuff of his dreams. He'd awake aroused, in a pool of sweat, fooled into feeling she was there next to him. He would reimagine how, at first, the leather around her legs was cool, but within seconds, it had warmed to the heat of them; how he felt the sting of stilettos when she firmly planted them in his chest as he entered her and when, thrusting his middle-aged self into the fleshy folds of this coed, the boots' texture began recording their time together in sweat. Soon, her ankles hugged his ears, and he pictured the way she stroked her breasts as he was above her, the way her silver eyeshadow sparkled on her closed lids, and how her tongue circled her lips while he worked in and out. Even though she was only a college freshman, she fucked like a woman with seniority, leaving him completely spent on those sheets and wanting more. He had tried to keep going, to extend himself as long as possible, but she was too irresistible, so he found himself coming up short on time, but thought she'd be satisfied with luxury trinkets of their tryst.

Only a few of the steamy details would be divulged to her friends when Saida reunited with them at the weekend's close. Until then, Cadence and Penny were enjoying the tailgating show and observing the sizzling chemistry between Roano and his girlfriend.

When the girls returned to the car, Isa's brother was in a liplock with Verena, a woman so stunning she was almost too gorgeous for words. Not only did she look as if she stepped from a fashion magazine, she was nice, really nice, and asked all about the girls' studies in Charleston and their interests.

Verena held a degree in fashion merchandising, had done some modeling for a local agency, and now worked retail. She met Roano at a gallery opening a few weeks ago. The more she talked, the more the girls approved, and they all thought it sweet how she'd peck him on the cheek and whisper words in his ear that made him smile.

When it was time to make the pilgrimage to the game, Roano and José packed up the car, and everyone filed toward the stadium, where they continued to stare, giggle, and guffaw at the array of characters around them. The game was exhilarating, loud, rowdy, and just plain fun; it was made even better when at half-time, Roano slipped his arm around Cadence's shoulders.

"It's really nice to see my sister with such a good friend. It makes me very happy." He squeezed Cadence to him. "I worry about her."

"Don't worry. From what I can tell, your sister can really take care of herself."

"I'm her brother. That's my job. I worry about the future, about anything that could happen." As he looked over to Isa and Verena talking, the weight of his arm seemed to get heavier.

"Your sister's great, and I'm sure she'll be okay. I'm glad I met her."

"Cadence, I'm glad, too. Come visit me anytime," he said, "perhaps even in Mexico someday."

"I think that'd be fun," she replied. "But maybe not as fun as a Gamecock football game." She joked as Roano laughed and hugged her tightly.

The Cocks's victory ensured the party would continue, not that a loss would have stopped it; the fiesta went on when the group returned to Roano's place that afternoon. Verena went home to freshen up and would meet them all later, so after power naps, showers, and food, Roano shared the fine distinction between tequila and mescal. He taught them that tequila was made only from blue agave while mescal could be made from many plant varieties and sometimes is distinguished by the worm in the bottle's bottom.

"If there's a worm, it's an especially bad bottle," he warned. "And it's not even a worm, but insect larvae or, as we say, a *gusano*."

"Is the bug some kind of tradition?" Penny asked.

Roano laughed. "Sadly, no. Back in the 1950s, some guy stuck the worms in as part of a marketing strategy. Tourists loved it. So mescal has been tarnished with the worm ever since. But if you're like me, tequila is your *tóxico*." He poured them shots. "Okay, let's lick, shoot, suck!" With salt and lime, he showed them the ritual of a tequila shot.

The girls suspected that the shots weren't such a great idea; in fact, they knew it, but the spirit of the moment and the fun of shouting, "Olé!" persuaded against worry. On they toasted, and on they celebrated straight to a house party only a few blocks away.

Partying is a universal language spoken by people from everywhere and that's what they found at the bash thrown by international students complete with a Latino band, kegs, and a bottle of tequila. Cadence couldn't believe all the languages she heard floating about: Spanish, Russian, Italian, French and German, even British accents abounded. Occasionally, passionate talk masked tongues she did not recognize and teased her ears. It made her want to push her own tongue beyond its American limitations.

Not too long after they arrived, Verena showed up looking more incredible than she did at the game. Isa and the others had liked her earlier, but they were beginning to dislike her simply because she was one who could be tarred and feathered and still come out looking fabulous. Clearly, there was no ugly day on her calendar—ever. No females really wanted to be in comparative distance near her and especially not in photos, but guys did, especially Roano.

The girls roamed around the groups and eventually stood by watching dancers of different styles take the yard's floor. When the band announced an upcoming limbo competition that was

bound to get dirty, Isa and Penny went to the keg for refills.
Cadence was waiting for the action when she struck up a conversation with a native of Argentina.

"Who're you here with?" he asked.

"Um, my friend and her brother. He's over there." She
pointed to Roano, who was standing with Verena leaning and
laughing on his shoulder.

"Ah, Roano and his *barba*?" The guy laughed.

Cadence laughed, too. "His Barbie? That's funny."

He looked at her as if she had a plastic doll head. "No, his
barba, you know, his *beard*?"

So much was being lost in translation, especially with the
tequila. "I'm sorry. I'm not following. His what?"

"Oh, señorita. *¿No comprende?* A beard's a person used to
cover for someone who's gay." He gestured with his cup toward Verena. "She's Roano's." When he saw Cadence's
stunned expression, he knew he shouldn't have revealed it.
"Hey, but it's no big deal." He walked off just as her friends
returned.

"Who was that?" Isa asked, handing Cadence a beer.

"Oh, just some guy." Cadence gulped her drink to avoid
conversation.

"Anyone interesting?"

"No," was all Cadence wanted to say.

When the band resumed, competitors lined up for the limbo
pole. Everyone cheered and clapped at the participants who
lowered themselves to ridiculous levels with each pass. The alcohol helped most meet the ground flatly, but there was one
who persevered, even after tequila shots: Roano won the limbo
challenge, proving that he was a good dancer after all.

With Verena on his arm and the tequila bottle in hand, he strutted over to Isa and her friends to salute his victory. "Who wants to do a shot?" Turning to his girlfriend, he asked, "Would you like a body one, my honey?"

"Mmmm, sounds good," she replied. "Too bad you don't have any limes and salt."

"Ah," he said, "*un momento*." Roano stepped into the house and was only gone a short time before returning with lime wedges and a salt shaker.

Giving him a playful look, Verena tilted her head back. He licked her neck, sprinkled the spot with salt, and offered a lime wedge to her lips. "Ready?"

Her teeth held the fruit while his tongue found the spot on her neck again. Stealing back the salt, he took a shot from the bottle and connected with Verena's lips to suck the lime's pulp. Everyone—except for Cadence—cheered them on.

Penny looked over and nudged her suitemate. "Hey, you okay?"

"Um, yeah," Cadence looked down into her drink. "Must be the tequila."

"Olé" Penny said, clunking her plastic cup against Cadence's.

The next morning, there was truth in Roano's humor about tequila. It was the poison hitting Cadence in the head like a hammer. The pain was excruciating, and opening her eyes only made the hurt worsen. She was sandwiched between Isa and Penny, a formation directed by Roano who made certain his younger sister and her friends safely crashed in his bed. He took the couch while Verena slept at home. Isa, being especially un-accustomed to liquid overindulgence, felt as if something worse than death had settled in her. Cadence and Penny were quite certain that if Mexicans drank tequila regularly, they must be the steeliest people in the world to survive those horrid hangovers.

Anticipating their conditions, Roano stirred up a pitcher of Horchata. A rumored cure for a hangover, the drink is a reviving blend of rice, milk, and cinnamon. Roano hoped it would combat the cycles of sickness: hot, dizzy, settled—repeat. Cadence was uncertain if she could keep the concoction down, but swallow by swallow, she did. Luckily, being young and spry, the three easily bounced back from their temporary debilitations. It took most of the morning for some sense of normalcy to return, and when they felt up to it, Roano treated them to meals of Southern comfort at a local tavern called Yesterday's. While there, he called their attention to the bar, where a group of men stood talking and eating popcorn over large beer mugs.

"Those are some of the journalism school professors," Roano observed. "They usually come in after class several times a week. I'm surprised to see a few of them here for brunch. Sometimes, their students join them."

"Really?" Isa said. "I think it'd be weird drinking with your professor."

"It's actually interesting," Roano said. "You'd be surprised what you learn about your teachers when they're not in a classroom."

"What have you learned?" Penny asked.

"Well, my accounting professor dumpster dives. He rummages through garbage bins for stuff," Roano said. "We were at happy hour one day, and he explained why he had to leave. Businesses dump trash at the day's end, so he was going to forage."

Penny scrunched her nose. "That's gross and weird."

"Not as weird as my management principles professor. She has a side business selling bondage equipment, S&M stuff. So many guys in class want to go in the store but they're too scared." Roano laughed. "Yeah, I've found out a lot from sharing drinks with them. Sometimes, people will surprise the hell out of you." He looked at his sister who beamed at her brother.

The journey home was longer than the one that took them there as weekend traffic stalled their progress. They swapped opinions of the parties and compared the capital city to that of Charleston, ultimately glad they were heading back to the coast. As their eyes searched for markers counting down to their destination, their ears learned of an incident that would haunt them always. While they were partying just a few blocks from Five Points, a young woman named Leda stepped out of a bar and a darkness that would hold the mysteries of her disappearance. No trace, no clues would ever surface regarding her perpetual absence. Posters of her image would cling to poles and boards for years, begging for someone to break silence and reveal the secrets of her fate. When the girls heard the story, an eerie quiet settled in the car, and especially on Cadence, who thought deeply about secrets and silence long after she caught sight of the bridge welcoming them safely back to the peninsula.

Chapter 8

Women's Studies 261
Gender and Conflict

An elderly man with a scraggly beard carried a baby splattered with red paint. He had nailed the doll to a cross beneath the words: *Jesus Was Innocent Too!* By his side, a wizened woman brandished her unshakable belief on a sign: *God is Pro-Life—Are You?!!* They marched on the outskirts of a small parking lot, tucked behind overgrown azaleas and beneath palmettos. Other protestors accompanied them including a middle-aged couple with their brood in tow. The children held stuffed lambs smeared with ketchup, while the parents wielded a series of grisly photographs chronicling aborted embryos at different stages. *CHOICE* appeared above each of the four images. One of their teenage daughters held a poster: *Abortion Makes You the Mother of a Dead Baby!*

Cadence had not foreseen herself standing outside an abortion clinic, but on this Saturday morning she was. Alone, she faced the hostile crowd as they tried to change the minds of those entering the building. A lone security officer stood guard in the shadows. Cadence raised her camera and began to shoot, an action the protestors welcomed as it would raise their activist status among fellow demonstrators and their heavenly status in God's eyes. This was, after all, a fight for the glory of life.

Cadence suspected TJ wouldn't run the photos of the poster carnage, but with the scene's limitations, she shot them anyway. She waited for something to happen, and it wasn't long before a girl, who appeared to be about her age, rounded the hedge into the lot. As soon as she came into view, the crowd howled like a wolf pack upon prey; one screamed, "Baby Killer!" and the old man shouted, "You'll be judged for this day!" The girl was making steady progress toward the door, but when she saw the camera, she stopped. Through the zoom, Cadence saw the girl's torn expression with merciless clarity. Determined not to be a part of the gauntlet of condemnation, she swung the view toward the racket, and in framing their fury, she pressed the shutter on the picture that would make the newspaper's next front page.

The image that hung in her mind for the weekend was that of the girl with struggle in her face and consequences on her mind, who, on an otherwise quiet morning, had to pass the judgments of people who knew nothing of her situation or cared to know beyond what they felt was their duty. All they saw was a girl getting an abortion—a sinner who needed to be brought to God's terms, and as self-appointed bailiffs, they were just the ones to escort her to the Almighty's court. Cadence sensed the girl did not want to be there, and not by any creative inventing could she imagine anyone wanting to be. Her out-of-class field trip was uncanny preparation for the week's unscripted topics.

In class, Professor Elders hurled the "F" word at all of them, but the one she used is so despised, so tainted with the trappings of rebellion and liberty, so connoted with hate that even those who stand as examples of its definition disown it as an identity. At its mere mention, eyes roll, grimaces form, and heads shake in dissension. Such was the reaction the instructor received when she wrote the damned term on the board: *FEMINIST.*

The tension was exactly what she expected. When she inquired if anyone in the class was a feminist, surprisingly, the one hand that lifted belonged to a quiet guy who sat in the back.

"So other than me and Preston, no one else claims to be a feminist?" she asked. The majority stared at the word, singled out on the board, embattled against their resistance. Seconds passed before the teacher broke the silence: "Talk to me. Let's start with the connotations. What comes to mind when you hear or see this word?"

Her question hung like dirty laundry no one wanted to air. Eyes darted for a spokesperson before someone offered, "I think of someone who hates a man."

MAN-HATER materialized below the offending word.

"Okay, good start. What else? Anyone?"

"How about 'bitch?' I always think of feminists as being total bitches, always screaming about their rights," one girl said.

Picking up from her cue, another remarked, "Don't they burn their bras and stuff? Oh, and they don't shave their legs and pits, right?" A few colleagues laughed.

"Aren't feminists lesbians?" someone added.

"Yeah, dikes," another said.

BITCH, UNSHAVEN, BRA-BURNING, DIKES: their responses filled the board's normally empty space. It was difficult to believe the words were written in a classroom, poised for discussion. They wondered where this teaching moment was headed and how Professor Elders was going to get them there. It was bound to get ugly.

"Obviously, there are more connotations to the term than this, but I'd like to ask the only other admitted feminist here, why he claims to be one. Preston, would you mind telling us why you're a feminist?"

The usually quiet but always-attentive student straightened his posture. "Because my mom would kick my ass if I wasn't."

"And why would she do that?"

"'Cause women deserve equal rights." His approval rating immediately went up in the eyes of his female peers.

"How many of you agree with Preston's view?"

Every hand in the class went up.

"Well, then by definition, you're a feminist, which is a person who believes women should have rights equal to those of men and believes in gaining these rights through social, political, and economic changes." As she explained, she saw some faces accept the identity, at least in definition, while others still resisted. "Oh, and in case you're wondering, you can shave your pits and your legs and still be a feminist. Guys, that goes for you, too."

From there, Elders led them through an abbreviated history of feminism: from the first wave of the nineteenth century in which Margaret Fuller and Susan B. Anthony fought for suffrage, Sojourner Truth worked for slavery's abolition, and Margaret Sanger struggled to secure reproductive rights.

Radical rebels of the second wave in the 1960s and '70s protested the Miss America pageant, or the "cattle parade," as they viewed it. This 1968 event began the myth of bra burning, but activists tossed only "oppressive" feminine items into a trashcan. Friedan, Steinem, Millett, Davis, hooks . . . these women demanded sexual and reproductive rights, equal pay, workplace opportunities, and an end to discrimination.

In the late 1990s, the third segment erupted thanks to the power of cyberspace and girl-only punk bands. Known as Grrl feminists, these agents of global social change flaunt femininity and have reclaimed derogatory terms like *bitch* and *slut* for the universal empowerment of women.

Before dismissing them, Professor Elders closed her lecture by saying, "Keep in mind that the history of women's rights is not confined to the last hundred years or so; this is a centuries-old fight and an ongoing one, but we don't have enough time for the rest today. I leave you with this to ponder: if the philosophy of equal rights has held true in these three waves, why are so many people, especially women, reluctant to call themselves 'feminists?'" Their minds circled back to the connotations.

Later after lab, Cadence stopped by Reena's room to review notes for Brodsky's test. While they worked, Reena's roommate, Miranda, got an update on her hometown from her younger sister, Maris, who had flown in for a visit.

"So what about parties? Been to any good ones lately?" Miranda asked.

"Well, there was this one last Saturday. A rainbow party," Maris said hesitantly as Reena looked up from her book.

"Hmmm, sounds interesting. What's that?" Miranda asked.

Maris's eyes darted about. "Maybe I shouldn't tell you."

"Why not?" Miranda inquired.

"Because you might tell mom, and I'll get in trouble."

Reena waited to see if the girl would talk. "You want me to tell her?" All eyes turned to Reena. "At a rainbow party girls put on different shades of lipstick and give boys blow jobs. Each guy tries to get as many rings of color on his dick as he can. When it's done, they compare their rainbows," she said, to the jaw-dropped faces of Miranda and Cadence. Maris lowered her head.

Miranda grabbed her sister's shoulders. "Oh, God, Maris, you didn't! Please tell me you have respect for yourself!"

"I, I didn't. Honest. Some of my friends did. They were all bragging about it. And the boys really like them."

"No, they don't like them," Reena explained, "they like what they do for them. Do you understand the difference?"

Maris fidgeted with the edge of her skirt.

"And they probably have no idea that they can get an STD of the throat, right?" Reena asked.

"Oh gross!" Maris said.

"Yeah, which reminds me Cadence, I haven't told you. And Maris, this will be good for you to hear, too. Cadence, you know Lily Tuggenlow. Maris, she's this girl who makes a point of showing off her blow job technique on bottles and probably practices on a lot of guys. May have even gotten her start at rainbow parties. Come to think of it, she probably invented them. Anyway, she has a very nasty case of gonorrhea of the throat."

"Ewwwww," they all chimed.

"How d'you know?" Cadence asked.

"She had to contact some individuals with whom she's had relations. They have to get tested, and well, you know how guys talk. My boyfriend told me, and he heard it from one of those affected. Or should I say 'infected.'"

"Speaking of Blaze, are you going out this weekend?" Cadence asked.

"He's on an extended business trip; then he's going home to see his parents. He'll be back in time for Halloween. We're going dressed as Romeo and Juliet."

Shakespeare was not the topic of English on Monday morning, especially when Professor Mirabilis caught ear of whisperings and wanted in on the conversation. There had been rumors of an incident: a party, heavy drinking, hooking up, and now some guy was being accused of rape. She reminded them of a story's dual sides and that the details were sketchy, but she decided to pursue the teachable moment.

"One of my friends teaches at an institution observing October as Rape Awareness Month, so why don't we make everyone aware of dangers now? Personally, I think we should be cognizant of this no matter the month, since according to statistics, someone in America becomes a victim of sexual assault every two minutes."

She gave them some types: date, acquaintance, drug-facilitated, statutory and mentioned that rape on college campuses most likely occurs with an acquaintance and that alcohol is the number one factor in facilitating sexual assault.

"Now, let's make this information a bit more real. Raise your hand if you or someone you know has been a victim of sexual assault."

Hands went up until three quarters of the class made the cold statistics tangible. Uneasiness crept over Cadence—her hand was up. It had been only a week since her suitemate became another statistic.

Cadence had arisen early on that Saturday to work on her seminar photographs. The bathroom was dark and quiet, so she walked in, but immediately, the rush of muggy air hit her. She flipped on the light. A sniffle came from behind the curtain.

"Hello? Saida? Penny?"

More sniffles followed a failed attempt to muffle a cry.

"What's wrong?" More sobbing met the question. Cadence slowly slid back the curtain. Wet and shaking, Penny sat in a bath, her face buried in her knees and her clothes floating at her feet. Cadence grabbed a towel and wrapped it around her friend.

"Shhhh. I'm here." The tears of her suitemate began soaking Cadence's shoulder. "Penny, talk to me. Tell me why you're upset."

"What's going on?" a sleepy-eyed Saida asked as she opened the door. With some urging, Penny arose, retreated into her robe, and sunk to the floor beside her bed. Eventually, she got out the details, the few she could remember . . .

It was an ordinary evening of hanging out, winding down from the week, passing the time as students do. Penny and some other girls were listening to music, dancing, and playing cards with guys from the half-rubber squad and some of their friends visiting town. She had been flirting with Ren and he seemed interested in her, too. They started with beer a moved on to moonshine—someone's concoction smuggled in from Savannah. Penny didn't know when the other girls and guys left, but they did. Soon, she was alone with Ren on his bed. They started kissing. Countless shots later and she remembered more kissing, touching, then—blackness.

When Penny awoke it was still dark outside. She was naked, curled in a sheet on the floor. Ren was asleep in his bed. Somehow, she found her clothes, but her bra and underwear were missing, so she pulled on what she could, steadying herself against the splitting in her head and ache in her stomach. Hearing her stir, Ren slightly turned toward her and whispered, "good time last night—lotta fun," before rolling back over to sleep.

It was her first and last walk of shame. The only problem was that she couldn't remember what she should be ashamed of, but her body bore the feel of violation, even if her mind wasn't providing the details. She knew she and Ren must have had sex because the soreness between her legs was more than she could stand and made any movement difficult. But there was something else, another raw, burning discomfort indicating they had done much more.

And that was really all she could tell her friends. She cried because she didn't know. Saida tried putting it together. "Penny, if you don't remember anything, if you blacked out and were unconscious, then he raped you."

"I don't know. I just don't know." She threw her face into her pillow and let out a long, pitiful wail. Saida and Cadence closed around her.

"We need to get you to the doctor," Saida said.

"Noooo, I don't want to go. We'll get in trouble because we were drinking, and if I go to the hospital, my parents will find out. I just want to go to bed."

"Penny, what if you're pregnant? Or he gave you something? You're going to the doctor." Jumping up, Saida began gathering clothes for her roommate.

Before long, the three were headed to the emergency room. Saida signed in Penny and in hushed whispers told the attendant she thought her friend had been raped. She asked about insurance and the charges, and the attendant assured her that the rape examination would be free, surprisingly, a program the state had in place for victims. Soon, Penny was called to an examination room, and the nurse took down the history of the girl's medical life and checked her vitals. She asked one of her friends to remain for the exam, so Saida stayed and held Penny's hand through the hours-long ordeal.

The doctor entered and began collecting evidence for the medical exam and rape kit. The procedure was standard but some steps were already compromised. He could not gather Penny's clothes for evidence because they were contaminated.

Taking hair specimens was also difficult because she had bathed, so they did the best they could. Oral, vaginal, and anal swabbing preceded the drawing of blood, which would be tested for HIV. Next, they scraped her nails for possible skin samples in case she scratched her attacker. With Penny's feet in the stirrups, the doctor noted the area's pronounced swelling and the vaginal tears—definitive evidence of rough intercourse, and he recorded that she had been sodomized.

To prevent pregnancy, he prescribed the morning-after pill and as a further precaution, gave her antibiotics against gonorrhea, chlamydia, and syphilis. Since she had not been vaccinated before, he administered a hepatitis B injection. He told her if she had been exposed to herpes that he could give her nothing. Time would tell. Drugs could manage outbreaks but not cure them. Additionally, she would have to be retested for HIV for up to a year. The hospital would send the blood work in for testing, and the results would be ready in a few weeks. He also suggested counseling as soon as possible and a follow-up appointment with her gynecologist. Lastly, it would be up to her to decide if she was going to report this to the school and to the authorities for possible prosecution. It was all too much to think about. She just wanted to curl up in her bed, which is exactly what she did—for weeks.

At Penny's request, Saida and Cadence told Jade, and the three checked on Penny daily, encouraged her to go to counseling, file a report—do something other than languish in the despair. They considered calling her parents but felt that would be overstepping their bounds, so they held her as she cried, and cried with her when she revealed she had been saving her virginity for the right guy. The way she imagined her first time was going to be perfect, but the flawlessness of her vision was ruined by the reality that she was waking up in a perfect nightmare. Because she would do nothing, they could do nothing, but be there.

With her thoughts drifting off about Penny, Cadence had missed much of the class discussion. In tuning back in, she heard Professor Mirabilis mention the illusion of safety that accompanies too many students in college. Perhaps it's the sense of invincibility programmed in the genetic code of the young.

She asked, "How many of you are willing to put your life, your health—psychological and physical—in the hands of 'friends' you have not known for very long?"

Most of them had done it already: parties with strangers, drinks poured, drugs traded, the hasty hookups. Many had already experienced too many murky mornings when their minds struggled to place together pieces of the previous night's puzzle. How many of them had stumbled the streets, crawled through the corridors, or simply crashed when and where their bodies gave up consciousness? The unfamiliar ceiling, the putridity of a post-drinking mouth, and the skull-smashing headaches. The freedom was literally intoxicating and on occasion—enslaving, especially when the liberty left scars resistant to healing.

"So, what's the best defense against campus rapes of the kind rumored? On what and whom can you depend to protect yourself?"

The answer was uncomfortably obvious.

"What defense does anyone—female or male—have who cannot recall what happened because of alcohol or drugs? What argument can be made if the events of the night are shrouded in mystery? Sadly, the types of rape cases I cited at the class's beginning, when alcohol or drugs are involved, become classic 'he said, she said,' scenarios," Professor Mirabilis warned.

She pointed out the difficulties prosecutors have in getting convictions for these crimes. Many won't take cases they know they can't win. Even evidence can be skewed, with bruises, cuts, and tears distorted to mean someone likes it rough. In the hands of defense attorneys, they spin semen to indicate ejaculation not rape. Sometimes in the process of trying to build a case, victims experience being violated all over again, especially if it goes to trial. As is too often the situation with female rape victims, lawyers tear those women apart in the halls of justice. Even if a woman is a virgin before the assault, she'll be made into a slut in a court of law.

"And a university's administration is not necessarily the authority that will deliver justice," she said. "An academic court is not the ideal place to try and rectify a criminal matter. An institution may pursue cases, but the results are rarely satisfying for the victims."

The unfortunate reality of what her teacher was saying and the relevance it held to Penny disheartened Cadence. It was one of those classes that had strayed from the syllabus because of need, but the instructor reiterated points about arguments, evidence, and the multiple interpretations that can prevent one clear perception of any event. At the end of the hour, Professor Mirabilis returned to the point that ushered in the discussion.

"Fifty minutes of this hour have passed, so according to the numbers, 25 people have had their lives forever altered because of a sexual assault."

The uneasy feeling had not left Cadence, and it was only exacerbated by thoughts of her suitemate. She wondered what had happened and if Penny would be able to bring charges. The muscles inside of Cadence continued to twist and she suspected it was because of more than the subject matter. In fact, she was sure the discomfort was cramps, slowly wringing deep inside. As is often the case with women, her suspicions were confirmed when she went to the bathroom before biology and saw nature's unmistakable mark.

"Damn," she said, feeling helplessly unprepared. Toilet paper would have to be a make-shift solution.

"Baby, you okay in there?"

"Um, not really," Cadence answered.

"You get an unexpected visitor?"

"Uh, yes ma'am," she answered. Seconds later, a tampon materialized from beneath the door. "Thanks," Cadence said. When she emerged from the stall, the custodian was wiping the sink.

"Honey, sometimes it creeps up on you." The woman smiled. "I keep those handy 'case of accidents."

"Thanks. I, I haven't had a chance to buy any," Cadence said.

"Grrrllll, don't I know it. I always say if men had they periods, tampons be free!" She chuckled. "And birth control, too! They'd be handin' the things out on street corners like candy!"

Cadence smiled at the joke, but the truth in this wise woman's humor wasn't funny at all. The convivial woman named Blondella had a point. What else would be free and without controversy if the burdens of biology fell on men? Cadence thanked her for the assistance then went to the class she was already late for. She would try to pay extra attention since Penny was skipping out, but would also be distracted by sitting next to Isa, especially considering what Cadence knew about her brother.

The issue of whether or not to tell Isa what she heard about Roano and his supposed "girlfriend" had been weighing heavily on Cadence since their return from Columbia. Considering Isa's devotion to her Catholic faith, Cadence wasn't sure how her friend was going to react when, or if, she found out. She wondered how long Roano had been masking his homosexuality and if anyone else in his family knew. For the time, she decided to remain quiet about what she had heard.

As they were walking out of biology, Isa remarked, "Cadence, I want to ask you something." Cadence's insides twisted again.

"I haven't seen Penny in a few classes. Is she okay?"

"Yeah, um, she's just been really sick," Cadence said, thinking of a way to change the subject. "I think she's getting better and will be out for Halloween. By the way, what are you going as?"

As the unofficial holiday of whoredom was approaching, girls and women throughout the city began shopping for costumes. Somehow, Halloween marks an occasion when even the most demure ladies dress like drabs, parade like prostitutes and assume personas of ever-tempting succubi. Enna referred to it as "Whore-o-ween" but was not beyond participating, especially when it meant countering the scores of strumpets prancing the streets. She decided to recruit five individuals for a group costume.

Cadence became convinced her friend must have been hiding out in Professor Elders's class since Enna wanted six people to go as the three waves of feminism: two figures for each period. Enna's whole suite was in as well as Althea's friend, Chloé, so they needed two more. Cadence thought of spending the evening with Penny, but Jade's parents were vacationing in the mountains, so she took Penny to get away. Having no plans for most of the evening until Schilar finished playing a Horror-ween show, Cadence agreed to be a part of the group and to find the sixth member, but everyone she asked declined this costume, except for Miranda who finally agreed to go as a third wave figure. Since neither was exactly sure what the most recent adherents looked like, Cadence and Miranda researched to discover that some Grrl feminists boasted lipstick, high heels, and push-ups bras. So as not to look as if they weren't in costume, they made T-shirts with Cadence's reading, *This is what a feminist looks like!* and Miranda's asserting, *Believe it or not, my short skirt has nothing to do with you!*

Althea and Chloé donned the constrictions of Victorian dresses and went as Sanger and Davison, the latter complete with a stick horse. They provided a striking contrast to Enna and Myla who sported bell bottoms and went sans bras and make-up to represent the '60s. On a poster, Enna had stapled copies of the covers of famous feminist publications: *The Second Sex, The Feminine Mystique, The Bitch Manifesto, Feminism Is for Everybody, Sexual Politics, The Beauty Myth,* and *The Female Eunuch.* Myla's featured the backside of a naked woman who wore only a cowboy hat; dashed lines divided her parts into those of a butchered cow: rib, loin, rump, round, and the sign said, *BREAK THE DULL STEAK HABIT.*

Stopping into c.a.t.'s to get the night started, the six were greeted by Catissa, the Good Witch, who raved about their costume choices and gave them complimentary cups of the night's special brew: candy corn lattes. Her baristas dressed as characters from Oz, with one even bringing her pet schnauzer to play Toto. Catissa encouraged everyone in Cadence's crew to spend a moment with the Tarot card reader.

Entering an area draped in black organza, Cadence sat across from the gypsy woman and immediately felt a foreboding sense. The candlelight flashed the gold shine of the diviner's dangling earrings, and her bejeweled hands affectionately fingered the black cards, each one featuring a silver pentagram, eight of which she laid, face up, in a circular seasonal pattern on the table. Poring over the configuration, she stared deeply into the animated figures purportedly whispering of this student's life.

"Hmm, the Ace of Cups over autumn reveals a new way of feeling. The beginning of emotion and inspiration is upon you." Bringing her fingers to her lips, she paused in contemplation. "Now, the Sun influences your winter card meaning that your search for knowledge continues and it's strong. In divination, this card is a Major Arcana—those things outside of our control, so this may be knowledge you do not pursue or do not want; it just comes to you. The Empress ruling over your spring means a cycle will come to an end." When she was finished, the reader peered at Cadence as if all predictions were obvious.

Cadence stepped away with that unnerving feeling that usually accompanies encounters with the occult. She tried filling in the ambiguity with details of her life but got as far as school and Schilar as the new feelings before determining it was too taxing to continue divining her future from a few cards.

When the six hit the streets as the three waves, they were not exactly received well, but they marched on, and after moving from some small gatherings, the ladies of liberation came upon an epic block party. They circled the premises a few times and settled beside a group dressed as fairy princesses. In contrast to the classic images of childhood play, these costumes left

little to the imagination, and these six could be more aptly identified as Little Red Riding Hooker, Slut White, Raunchy
Rapunzel, Sinful Cinderella, Sleeping Bawdy, and the Licentious Mermaid.

Enna could feel the disapproving eyes of Rapunzel, so when
she returned the look, the blond one asked with an upturned lip:
"Um, what exactly are you?"

When Enna told her, the obviously drunk tower prostitute
remarked, "How very radical of you. I had heard that feminists
were a bunch of dikes." She laughed and her girl clan joined.

Enna laughed, too. "How very bimbo of you. At one time,
the only work you'd be able to get was the way you're dressed.
That or being a nun, which clearly you wouldn't qualify for at
all."

The laughing ceased, but Enna continued, "You can thank
feminists for your college existence. Oh, and if you ever find
those heeled feet in the padded stirrups of a sterilized clinic,
thank a feminist for making sure the doctor's not mutilating
your uterus and for allowing you to be something more than
barefoot and pregnant."

Rapunzel's red nails flashed on her hip. "Do these feet look
barefoot, bitch?"

Enna's black nails flashed back. "Not at the moment blon-
die, but if your strumpet wear works, those stilettos will be on
the floor before midnight."

All the factual and fictional bitches stood their ground, but
in not wanting to waste their costumes on a bunch of feminists,
especially since they had not been put to the full use of fantasy
yet, the fairy tale floozies relented and sauntered off in search
of their proverbial princes on white horses. Enna and the others

made a toast to girl power and continued critiquing until the party was winding down.

Technically, it wasn't Halloween anymore when Jack the Ripper snuck up behind Cadence and delivered a killer kiss.

"Hey! You scared me!"

"That's the idea." He pulled her to him again. "Ooooo, I love a feminist in costume."

"It's not just a costume," she replied.

"Even better."

"Aren't you supposed to prey on prostitutes?" she asked. "We've seen a few tonight."

"Yeah, but I'm trying to raise my standards." For hours after midnight, Schilar swept her among the crowd until growing tired of it all, the feminist went home with the ripper.

The next afternoon, Cadence was enjoying the semi-solitude of not having Jed around, until an elated Corrine entered with a smile and a new ring. As her roommate pranced around, Cadence found herself asking, "Really, it's none of my business, but don't you think you're a little young to be getting married?"

"You're right. It is none of your business but no, I don't think I'm too young. My parents got married when they were eighteen."

"How long have they been married?"

"Eighteen years," she proudly replied.

A short knock preceded the entrance of Saida. "Sorry to interrupt, but do you have a few tampons I can borrow? I don't feel like going to the store to get any."

"That's gross, Saida. I don't have any you can borrow, but you can have some," Cadence said.

"Funny, smart ass. You know what I meant." As Cadence got the necessities, Saida asked, "So what's up with you two?"

"Oh, we were just discussing Corrine's engagement."

"He popped the question this weekend?"

Corrine held up her hand to reveal a diamond that looked more like cubic zirconium than the half carat he claimed it to be. "It was so romantic. We were at dinner at the buffet, and when he brought over desserts, the ring was stuck in the top of my lemon meringue pie."

"Well, congratulations! Guess you've got a lot of planning to do. Have fun with that!" Saida shut the door with a smirk.

Left alone again, the roommates returned to the awkward silence but not before Corrine asked, "So what do you think of Jed?"

Rather than add to the tension already apparent, Cadence said, "He seems nice," and left it at that, but she knew him and his kind, and knew them well. A good 'ole boy, raised on a strict diet of God, guns, and backwoods culture, Jed believed a woman's place was in the home, so he worked hard to restore Corrine to the proper path dictated by the limitations of her gender. This country boy would rescue her from the city and the evils of elitist professors and fanatical feminists by convincing her she was miserable. Somehow, he made the happenings in a small town more significant, more exciting than those of the city. He convinced her she was missing out on life so that she would abandon the new one dangling in front of her. Back in Georgia, he was building a home repair business and needed help. A place for her had been made—all she had to do was accept.

Together they would pursue their American Dream, raise their children in the steadfast tradition of family values and grow old teaching their grandchildren the importance of faith without question. With each other, their pursuit of this fantasy would be far ahead of clueless college students whose debts from these years of freedom and frivolous classes would make achieving the picket-fenced house, cars, and vacations an immediate impossibility. With her choice made, Corrine returned to her work of wedding preparation. Bridal magazines and event planning brochures replaced course materials and textbooks. With the promise of marriage well underway, she had little interest in her education and no interest in anyone who tried to tempt her from the path of happily ever after.

Chapter 9

Biology 110
Organism Basics

A white chocolate skeleton is not the kind of gift one expects from a friend, but Cadence received this sweet homage to death from Isa in celebration of *Dia de los Muertos,* a day in which family and friends gather in remembrance of lost loved ones. In addition to the chocolate, Isa gave Cadence a fascinating skeletal figure called *La Catrina.* Wearing a long dress the color of blood and striking a vogue pose as if she had something sassy to say about the beyond, this ghastly lady symbolizes Mexicans' willingness to laugh at death.

"We're all equal in the end," Isa explained. "No one escapes it. She reminds us of that." So intriguing was the present that Cadence found herself staring at it often, pondering the secrets of life, death, and beyond.

Following biology one morning, Cadence met Jacinda in the hall. She had returned to school after burying her brother and trying to rest, but her family had gotten little reprieve since Dizion's funeral had been disrupted by gang members. Although supposedly in attendance to pay respects, the crew carried guns and threatened to shoot up the place. When they were asked to leave, a fight broke out and the police were called. Several members were arrested for probation violations, and now the family feared a backlash. The events had so wracked Jacinda that she looked as if her spirit had been trampled upon, but she managed to maintain strength for her family, especially her younger siblings. When the two saw one another, Cadence hesitated in speaking but decided to anyway.

"Hi," Cadence said delicately. Her neighbor said nothing. "Um, I just wanted to say that I'm sorry about your brother."

Jacinda's eyes fell to the floor then up again to Cadence. "Thank you."

"I, I know we haven't gotten along before, but if I can do anything . . ."

"There's not much anyone can do. It's all in the Lord's hands. He'll make it right." Her expression held a quiet confidence. "At least I don't have to worry about him anymore. He's gone home, he's safe." Her voice began to quiver, so she bowed her head and walked away.

Although Jacinda said she had one less worry, Cadence's had been multiplying, especially in thinking of Penny whose condition was worsening. She shunned classes, counseling, and her closest friends, and when she did attempt some sort of normal activity like going to eat, she moved like a zombie. When she was not comatose, she swung all over the emotional spectrum: from anxiety to anger, depression to detachment, crying to calmness.

Finally, the nurse called with the test results. HIV exam: negative, at least for now, but she would have to be tested again in the coming months. When she asked about the rape kit results, the nurse said those had not been tested and would not be unless she decided to file a police report. If DNA was present, the authorities might be able to match it with her attacker. Penny didn't need a DNA test to identify this person—she knew exactly who he was.

To escape temporarily from the hall's anxiety, Cadence settled in a library study room, determined to write her English paper. In twelve hours, the words were due, but they would not come. The computer screen just glared at her, so Cadence tried to get her thoughts out another way, but the lines stared back at her like bars on the page of her yellow paper, and they shrieked with derision at her failure to fill them. When a sentence did appear, it was all wrong, so she'd rip the page from the notebook and tear it to shreds. The task was enough to drive anyone mad, and the library quickly began to feel like a prison, but the real prison was her mind. It wanted to break free from this academic insanity, to engage in some task more productive than writing an argumentative paper she had waited until the last possible moments to revise.

After a while, she had gotten as far as writing *Knowledge is* on one line, and a few more down, *Schilar* appeared. She did not know where to begin and regretted not remaining loyal to her original word. The unsavory feeling of another F began to creep slowly around her. Just as the fear threatened to engulf her, Saida opened the door.

"I'm glad I found you. We need to talk. It's about Penny." Her voice held a seriousness Cadence had never heard before. "Diana was hanging out with some people tonight, and they started talking about this girl who got a train pulled on her by some guys. A few of them have been bragging about how they all had turns with her and how one hit it to fifth base."

"Fifth base?" Cadence asked.

"Anal," Saida said, "but there's more. They used one of their bats on her; it's like a mop handle or something."

"Oh God. How many were there?"

"I don't know; Diana said it sounded like there were a lot. They didn't use names, but the girl has to be Penny. Cadence, we've got to tell her. She has to do something. I'm going to call Jade. I think the three of us should break it to her."

Later that night, the news that she'd been ganged shattered Penny again. They were certain the scream was going to attract attention, and it did. Seconds later, there was a knock at the door, and when Saida answered it, Carrie was there. Knowing they all needed help, Saida let her in. In sobbing fragments, Penny relayed it all again, but this time, she told them of her nightmares and how she kept seeing the blurred faces of different guys above her. She thought they were dreams, but they were really flashbacks of the assault—her mind's way of uncovering the buried secrets. Carrie assured everyone she would help and that starting tomorrow, she would go with Penny to file a police report and get her set up with counseling.

When Cadence left her suitemates' room, it was early morning, and with the library closed, she again made the common room a home and pulled another all-nighter in revising Mirabilis's paper. The surrounding drama directed some energy into her work, but it also caused distraction, and she found her ideas wandering into a writing wasteland.

In those wee hours, she didn't care about what her professor wanted, and instead of writing about knowledge, she wanted to talk about assholes and rape and pain and justice. Down the hall, one of her friends had been irreversibly wounded, and here Cadence sat, composing some absurd paper that had nothing to do with real life. The more she thought about it, the more pissed she became, and the tapping on her computer's keyboard increased exponentially as the morning marched on.

By sunrise she was exhausted, and apathy toward the paper and class replaced her usual interest. She could not discern exactly what she had written, and it didn't matter now. All she wanted to do was turn it in and be done. She felt relief when Professor Mirabilis took the essay, but a burdensome feeling returned when the teacher devoted the class to a peer editing workshop.

"No one becomes a better writer without revising—no one. In essence, it is the most important part of the writing process, and one that we certainly don't focus attention on enough. This is when you seize the time to shape and polish your words so they deliver the rewarding experience your readers deserve," Professor Mirabilis told them.

After revisions, the final copy would be due in a week. Those who came to class without the assignment were promptly banished—with stern warnings to get it done. At least Cadence had turned in something, so when she received a colleague's paper, she did her best to read it with the critical eyes of an English professor.

She couldn't understand how Professor Mirabilis did it. Grammar, mechanics, and punctuation rules, style, structure, evidence, documentation: Cadence could barely stay focused on one, much less all of these elements. Her mind drifted as she tried to follow her peer's argument that *milk* was the language's most important word. While Cadence was certain a lactose-intolerant reader would give the paper an F, she was thinking a D, maybe for the vitamin? Nothing made sense, so she was relieved when the class ended and her paper was returned with surprisingly helpful encouragement from her colleague:

Good choice of a word. I think you're right about some knowledge being "bad" like when someone's a victim of rape. I can't imagine anyone wanting that kind. Maybe give a real example like a legal case or someone's personal experience for support.

In the furious fog of last night's composing, Cadence had not realized she had written thoughts of Penny into her paper and made a seemingly useless assignment matter. Luckily, she would have some time to work out the argument and strengthen the research.

It took all the strength that Penny could muster to walk into the office of campus police to tell her story. The interview was a trauma in itself as she tried to provide a coherent account of what happened. Her blackout rendered a complete picture impossible, so she did the best she could as Carrie held her hand. Penny gave the officer Ren's name and relayed the rumors she had heard, but did not know anything else. The officer would have the kit tested and launch an investigation.

With so much going on, Cadence did not want to shoot a night scene, nor did she have the time, but that's what TJ wanted. Armed with pepper spray, she ventured out on the campus's main walkways. It wasn't late, but it was dark enough to see the fog slowly dropping to the earth like a stage curtain falling at the end of a play. She wanted to get an unusual shot, an angle from above, so she entered a building that held offices for the religious studies department. Perpendicular to the street, the old house had porches on all levels, mostly sheltered from view. It was fairly private and quiet since office hours were over and no one was working late. Cadence positioned herself at the end of the third floor's piazza with a view of the corner and the street intersections beyond. Like a field photographer camped to capture an exotic animal, Cadence waited. She'd know the photo when she saw it. Half an hour later, a group of girls passed beneath light, and although she clicked the camera, she wasn't happy with the shot and decided to linger.

The moment never appeared. As she was preparing to leave, a light came on in the office closest to her. Not wanting to startle the professor, Cadence crept quietly from the spot, but just before she passed in front of the window, the scene behind the partially drawn blinds made her pause. Two figures had already begun shedding their clothes. An opened purple blouse revealed a black lace bra, the same color as the woman's panties, garter belt and stockings, which were visible when the older man pulled up her skirt and slid her on the desk. Wrapping her long legs around him like an anaconda, she squeezed the life of him into her.

Cadence stepped back, fearful of crossing the window's threshold lest they catch her on the porch. She knew she may be accused of trespassing and wondered if she could be charged as a peeping Tom. Considering the cheating incident, she didn't need any trouble, so she crouched down in her spot and waited for the muffled moaning to stop. She was pretty sure it was over when she heard, "Oh God! Yes!"

Not too long after, the light turned off and a door shut, but she waited until the lovers appeared on the street before she moved. She watched the woman's white lab coat billow as she scampered into the night while her companion headed in the other direction.

Cadence slipped from the porch into the hall, noticing the office belonged to Dr. Heath, and that hours were *by appointment only*. She grinned at the late meeting she had just come upon and at the "night life" shot she missed, so off she went in search of a picture the public could view.

By the weekend, the plague had fully descended upon the campus. As biology proves, there is no better test for the immune system than the college realm, and the bodies of most coeds fail when it comes to fending off a virus. Stress, over-drinking, poor eating, little exercise—all ensure that once one student is infected, it's a guarantee the contagion will spread in this public Petri dish.

The only person not sick was Isa, who attributed her immunity to running. With her entire suite suffering, Cadence was partially grateful for the illness, as it meant that Jed would not be making his pilgrimage to Charleston. The girls all took turns vomiting in between chugging energy drinks and sleeping. Saida and Cadence were hoping Penny's nausea was because of the virus and not the rape since the trauma had already inflicted enough damage. At the week's start, Cadence was beginning to recover sufficiently when she received a call that weakened her even worse than the tiny assailants running rampant in her body.

Her mother did not want to alert her daughter but had to because of the girl's intense love for the animal. Rather than have Cadence learn of Gunpowder's disappearance from others, she decided to tell her. After all, her hometown was small, and news, especially of human or animal tragedies, travels faster than blood through veins. Ms. Cooper did not like keeping things from Cadence and hoped the girl could give them ideas on where the horse may have gone.

Her father and his farm hands had already searched the pastures, and Baxley, the most trusted aide, had scouted the miles of barbed-wire fence looking for a breach through which Gunpowder could have escaped. He found none. Neighboring farmers were alerted to look out for the missing steed since the possibility was entertained that he could have jumped the fence in search of the mare again, but there was simply no evidence of that, and Gunpowder had never displayed any escape tendencies.

When Cadence heard the news, she felt her heart immediately leave her body for home and was determined to follow it. She became convinced that her horse would come if he heard her voice, so she immediately prepared to go there and began thinking of ways to tell her professors why she would not be present to take tests, turn in assignments, and attend their lectures. Did a missing horse constitute an excuse? Would her professors understand? She believed her presence would bring Gunpowder home and that her absence had driven him away, especially since she had left him again after fall break. She had to leave, so she sent messages to her instructors explaining she would not be in class for the week's remainder because a family emergency had called her away.

But by that evening, the mystery of Gunpowder's whereabouts was solved. Baxley had been scouting the property's far reaches when he noticed vultures circling above an oasis. Cushioned between the long, fingerlike roots of the trees lay Gunpowder. Unable to fight whatever ailed him, he had gone to the pasture and surrendered in the sleepy hollow. When Baxley saw the animal's stiffened body, his thoughts flew immediately to Cadence. She would be crushed, and although he wanted to make the drive to deliver the news so he could be there for her, Cadence's mom thought it best to let her know immediately—to end the worry and to save a journey to the coast. As soon as Cadence heard her mother's voice, she knew.

The cry was not too different from Jacinda's, which had echoed in the hall only a few weeks ago. Saida came rushing in when she heard it and managed to get from Cadence that the horse was dead. Aching memories began immediately: of his powerful gallop across the rolling hills, his sassy trot in prancing up to the barn, his high-pitched whinny, and his lips loose and drooling over his favorite snack of an apple. She longed to look into his eyes again, just like the last time she did over break. In those glassy orbs, her reflection always appeared small, but she glimpsed a largess of love instead of the hate he should have held for humans. She marveled at his capacity to forgive, to trust, and to live with a greatness of spirit again.

Saida checked on her often, as did Penny who cried with Cadence over their losses, and although different in cause, they shared pains and voids that could not be filled. When they learned of their friend's hurt, Enna and Reena stopped in to visit, but Cadence could barely talk. Snippets of conversation were punctuated with breakdowns during which her friends just sat with her. Isa came bearing soothing teas and nourishing breads from Catissa. As instructed, Isa made them two cups and gave the bags to Cadence to place over her eyes for the swelling. Seeing Schilar only upset her more, so he gave her space but kept close contact. In a rare moment of selflessness, even Corrine asked if she could get her anything and managed to lower her voice slightly while on the phone.

Cadence did not get out of bed on Thursday nor did she eat. Weakened from the sheer sadness of a beloved pet lost, she could not bother with classes, so instead of a notebook taking down her thoughts, her pillow recorded her anguish. By nightfall, the lids of her eyes, balloon-like and swollen, felt as if they could burst from the pain driven from her heart into her eyes. Amid the sadness, Cadence received another call from her mother, one of several she had made to her stricken daughter.

Even her father, ever a man of brief words and well-practiced in animal deaths, offered an attempt at sympathy: "Baby, if you don't have 'em, you can't lose 'em." The words only made her cry more.

Cadence's mother also shared the vet's diagnosis. Gunpowder's death was caused by Equine Herpesvirus or EHV-1. Although the steed had been vaccinated, there was no protection against this neurologic strain. The vet was confident in the findings from the necropsy, but if there was any doubt, the fact that the horse on the neighboring MacDonald farm was also dead from the same virus reinforced it as the culprit.

Cadence mustered the strength to attend Friday classes, but she felt especially inadequate because she did not have her English paper ready. Dread pushed heavily on her when she saw her classmates' copies poised on the corners of their desks. Professor Mirabilis moved through the aisles collecting them, but when she came to Cadence, the student only shook her head when asked if she had the assignment. "See me after class," the teacher commanded.

Hours drag in times of sorrow even though the instructor made some fun with Margaret Atwood's metafictional short story "Happy Endings." Mentally removed from all the work's scenarios, Cadence looked helplessly at the blurry words, not daring to lift her head. She tried with all her will to stem the emotional flood building behind her eyes. The reading was coincidentally appropriate, especially for the line indicating the only authentic ending to any story: *John and Mary die.* Cadence listened to the simple certainty being repeated three times in rapid succession and had little choice but to reflect on its unrelenting truth in the wake of Gunpowder's fate.

When class was dismissed, she remained to hear the punishment for her late paper. After all, college professors were notorious sticklers for deadlines, and not even the apocalypse was an excuse for lateness. Professor Mirabilis waited for everyone to leave before addressing her student.

It took only the sound of her name being formed into a question for the dam of tears to break again. As much as she did not want to cry again, especially in front of this teacher, she could not help it, as even the slightest flashes of her horse forced an expression of her sorrow. She managed to communicate that he had died before her hands hid her face. Her crying shook her so powerfully that Cadence barely sensed the arms wrapping warmth and understanding around her. Professor Mirabilis said nothing. Sometimes, even English teachers know of death's extradictionary nature, of language's limitations in times like this, so she offered an empathetic embrace as her student yielded again to the ache. Nearly breathless, Cadence said, "I'm sorry."

"You have nothing to be sorry for." The teacher reached for a tissue but this time, the paper was for a different kind of tears.

Cadence wiped her face. "I, I don't mean to cry in front of you."

"Why? Because you need to grieve? Cadence, never apologize for that."

She nodded and between breaths stammered, "I . . . don't have my paper, but—"

"The paper's not important right now. What's important is for you to deal with your loss. We'll work out a due date later. Now, before you go, is there anything I can do to help you?" she asked.

Cadence indicated there was not. Of the three teachers she faced that day, only Professor Mirabilis was surprisingly concerned to see Cadence walk into class. In observing the water-drenched eyes, hunched shoulders and downtrodden countenance, the professor read the body language of loss very clearly.

Still in an emotional stupor, Cadence didn't want to do anything over the weekend. She did let Schilar take her out for pizza, which she barely touched before returning to her room to wrap herself in despair. Collapsing into the hollow of her bed, she breathed in its dark security. She pushed her earplugs in far and slept as if she had died from heartbreak.

The next morning was one more day removed from the initial news, so feeling a little stronger, Cadence intended to tackle some assignments. Just a few days of not working had set her back substantially, so she had to use as much of the Saturday as she could. Stopping by for her mail on the way to the library, Cadence was surprised to find a single envelop instead of the usual credit card enticements that clogged the box. In it was a handmade postcard, twice the size of a standard one, bearing a quotation from Percy Bysshe Shelley's "To a Skylark":

> *We look before and after,*
> *And pine for what is not:*
> *Our sincerest laughter*
> *With some pain is fraught;*
> *Our sweetest songs are those that tell of saddest thought.*

> *Yet if we could scorn*
> *Hate, and pride, and fear;*
> *If we were things born*
> *Not to shed a tear,*
> *I know not how thy joy we ever should come near.*

On the opposite side of the card, in delicately written script appeared the message:

Cadence,

Despite the English language's impressive lexicon, words are insufficient during this difficult time. I am saddened to learn of the loss of your horse, as your pain reminds me of all the dear pets I, too, have lost. Their unconditional love, loyalty, and liveliness exemplify what we should all aspire to provide. In celebrating our best of times and worst of times, they teach us of how life is to be enjoyed, to be cherished; they reveal, as Shelley does, that experiences of sadness make our appreciation of happiness possible. I hope you will recall the majesty of your magnificent animal and be comforted by the fond memories you undoubtedly have of him. Although time will be the only remedy for your heartache, I am here should you need me. I often find that putting pen to paper in moments of melancholy does much in the way of healing. Share your pain on the page— once trapped between the lines, it eases with every sentence.

With my sincerest condolences,

Crys Mirabilis

Cadence inhaled deeply, drawing strength and solace from the very source that penned the card. Tucking the treasure into her English book, she headed to the library for what would be hours of focused work, punctuated by minutes of memory, seconds of sobbing, and moments of rereadings from Shelley and Mirabilis.

The following week was one of perpetual catching up, so Cadence first focused on her paper revisions and managed a critical argument on the dualities of knowledge. She took her peer's advice and researched rape, and what she found concerning punishment for attackers and the residual effects of a sexual assault was highly disturbing. In writing the piece, she hoped that the case involving her suitemate would defy the statistics and stories she read.

As her eyes moved across article after article, her mind filed away fragments of information: Rape often occurs during those first few months for freshmen—"the honeymoon" phase; many victims are virgins; alcohol works as the weapon of choice for assailants; most campus rapes committed by a small percentage of serial rapists—repeat offenders; those found guilty almost never expelled; Jeanne Cleary Act requires colleges to report campus crimes; Jeanne Cleary: raped, tortured, strangled in her dorm room at Lehigh University in 1986; a culture of victim shaming, blaming, scapegoating thrives; drunkenness + sex = rape = dangerous rule. *Awareness, prevention, responsibility, adulthood, risk*—words Cadence saw over and over in her reading. By the time she finished, her head was spinning from learning about so many cases with so few resolutions, mired in so much confusion.

English was not the only class she had fallen behind in; biology lab was another casualty, so she made arrangements for a Friday afternoon make-up. No one was in the lab except for Alex and another teaching assistant, a long-legged, black bra-wearing woman in a lab coat whom Cadence recognized.

Before Cadence's awkward expression was noticed, Alex welcomed her back and began explaining the task: "For the lab you missed, we examined bacterial cultures grown on the Petri dishes, the ones you all swabbed from areas around campus. As you'll see, there are some dirty people around this place. So, let's look at a few of those."

Even though Cadence was not a germaphobe by any means, the cultures were enough to give even a semi-sanitary person reason to slather on hand sanitizer. Keyboards, treadmills, classroom desks, backpacks, ATMs and door handles were rife with E. coli, salmonella, staph, Hepatitis A, and pneumonia. In most cases, these spots were 400 times more contaminated than a public toilet seat, so it was little wonder that the campus had been stricken with plague. But the most surprising find of all was a swab from a washer in one of the laundry rooms.

"There are roughly 100 million E. coli in every load," Alex explained, "because every piece of underwear has about 0.1 gram of fecal matter. There's poop in your laundry."

Cadence winced. She would have to convince herself of the illusion that her clothes were clean and uncontaminated. "Alex, does being a research assistant change the way you live?"

She laughed. "Not really. I've been aware of much of this for a long time. In seventh grade, my science teacher Ms. Gresham had such an interesting and exciting way of looking at microbes. It was infectious, as nerdy as that sounds." Alex began tightening the lids on a stack of Petri dishes. "But to an-swer your question, we have changed our Beer Pong game. Those balls have some of the nasties we've talked about as well as listeria. So, we wash our balls and the cup—but not in the laundry, of course."

When Cadence finished her report, she prepared to leave but in noticing the other lab assistant was gone, she asked Alex if the woman studied microbes, too.

"Nina? No. She studies DNA sequences. Bit of a brainiac, actually. So's her husband," Alex said. "They're on track to be an academic power couple."

"What does he do?" Cadence asked.

"He's a psych professor, but she hasn't seen much of him lately. He's up for tenure and in prep mode. I think he's buried in paperwork, articles, and schmoozing with colleagues. Why'd you ask?"

"No reason. Just curious about what y'all do." As Cadence began gathering her books, Alex suggested one more task.

"Isa told me about your horse. Cadence, I'm sorry to hear about his death. The virus that killed him is myeloencephalopathy. A colleague of mine is working on a vaccination for that strain, so I asked her to send me some slides. If you want, I'll show you what was inside of him. It may help you understand what he was battling and why even the strongest equines usually don't survive this."

Under the light of the microscope, the germ that had taken down Gunpowder appeared hatefully beautiful. Despite its minuscule size, its impact was tremendous. As much as she resisted the feeling, she couldn't help but admire its power to kill a beast a million times its size. The usually invisible superbug glowed vibrantly in neon green. Despite the artificial color, the virus seemed to pulse in frozen brilliance, sucking in the color of life while sucking it out of the animal it killed. Multiplying like the voracious agent it was, it had grown until it consumed the entire cell, just as it had consumed miles of Gunpowder's tissues. In the end, Gunpowder did have the devil inside him after all—a lethal demon that worked insidiously to strip him of his spirit and his life. Cadence now understood what drew Alex to this field, and these hours alone in the lab foretold that one day the graduate assistant would have a classroom of her own.

The weekend before Thanksgiving, Cadence was overcome with the stress of how far behind she had fallen from missing a few classes. She had to finish her English paper and get photos taken for her seminar project. In knowing what she needed,

Schilar borrowed his roommate's truck, and together, they set out in search of Charleston's wonders, which were not difficult to find. In a city with so much history, every crevice caused by time's ravages creates beauty worth capturing. They saw it at each corner, and street by street, bridge by bridge, they embarked on a dizzying tour of places and faces that would be the features of her presentation.

After a day of constant clicking, they completed the photographic scavenger hunt with coffee from c.a.t.'s. Upon seeing Cadence, Catissa hugged her long and hard, and smiled approvingly when Cadence introduced Schilar. After a short chat, the couple retired to the campus's Grand Lawn, where in reviewing her work, Cadence was satisfied until Schilar took the camera for his own appraisal. He noted there was something missing and turned the lens on Cadence, who resisted being on the other side.

In his cheesiest voice, he begged, "Come on, baby, talk to the camera. That's right, give it some love."

A smile was finally documented on the face that for far too long had held a frown. Beneath the umbrage of oaks, the two stretched out on the grass, a freshly sprouted variety that was already defying the deadening attempts of the approaching winter. Not a word passed between them, but the quiet spoke loudly about a carefree day of connecting with the city whose soil they now rested upon. Gazing up at the rosy tint of a cool November sky, Cadence pondered the art above, the powers that painted it, and the cosmic circumstances that brought her and Schilar to share this view.

Later in his room, Cadence would also wonder about less serious topics, namely the origins of the most colorful wall decoration in the suite: a yellowed sheet of paper hanging next to the toilet roll dispenser. Poised above the *Playboys* and man magazines was the ultimate identifier of the most basic of human functions—*The Shit List.*

The guys studied it more than they did their textbooks and enjoyed expanding their vocabulary for practical purposes. It was not unusual for one of them to announce: "Just had a 'Ghost Shit,'" which is aptly described by the guide as: *The kind where you feel shit come out, see shit on the toilet paper, but there's no shit in the bowl.*

Other types that visited the bowl were *The Corn Shit*: a self-explanatory sort; *The Lincoln Log: the kind of shit that's so enormous you're afraid to flush it down without first breaking it up into little pieces with the toilet brush; The Ritual Shit: occurs at the same time each day with the help of reading material.* Above all of these and the other types like *Wet Cheeks, The Second Wave, The Brain Hemorrhage, The Floater,* the kind most cited in this suite and in bathrooms across campus was *The Notorious Drinker's Shit: the kind of shit you have the morning after a long night of drinking. Its most noticeable trait is the tread mark left on the bottom of the toilet bowl after you flush.* Finally, way down on the list appeared *The Horse Shit: reserved exclusively for vegans and truly the only appropriate one for fertilizer.*

For the first time in weeks, Cadence laughed out loudly. Considering how much shit had been thrown her way lately, it seemed the only thing left to do after all the crying was to laugh. Shit is, after all, life's means of allowing people to purge—emotionally, mentally, and of course, physically. It's the most basic biology. Without it, life would be one painful build-up of useless material. Cadence couldn't help but think, with grotesque fondness, of the piles Gunpowder left and of her mother's insistence on keeping them for the flowers. Thanks to her horse's contributions, the plants were always richer in color, sharper in scent, bigger in bloom than those not graced with the steed's magic. All life produces shit; death equalizes every organism in it, and the cycle begins again in bigger, better, and more beautiful blossoms. In the earth's soil, Gunpowder had returned to his origins, his massive body stripped to its skeletal core by the tiniest of powers. Once home, Cadence would plant seeds in his grave's fresh dirt, and from the wonder that was Gunpowder, the fragrance of wildflowers would drift through the pastures he once roamed—all in sweet remembrance of the incredible animal she'd never forget.

Chapter 10

Astronomy 111
Introduction to the Solar System

A black hole—at any given time, college can make students feel as if they are teetering on the edge of being whirled into shadowy oblivion, but nothing concentrates this feeling more than the stresses at a semester's end. In these days of breakdown, in this compressed space when the gravities of higher education are almost too much for any mass to hold, the universe reminds them that they are simply specks in the larger system of operation, little pieces of dark matter on the cosmic campus.

An invisible speck is exactly how Cadence felt trying to create her spring schedule. One out of five: that's how many classes Cadence got that she wanted after registration wrestling. She did not snare a coveted seat in Dr. Sessions's religion class, the one recommended by Saida and Diana, so her advisor steered her toward a communications course. The rest of her schedule was fairly unremarkable, continuations of sequences in biology and Spanish, this time with different instructors, and Intro to Theatre, which Reena suggested. Her biggest disappointment was being blocked out of Professor Mirabilis's English 102 course.

Despite the teacher's dark reputation, *CLOSED* appeared next to every one of her sections. Cadence now regretted recommending this professor to others since maybe they were the reasons why no open seats appeared. When Cadence stared at the screen's glaring rejection, panic set in. The class that she had despised the first week had become the one she really loved. Her perfect next semester was falling into imperfection, and she was powerless to fix it.

Frustrated and worried over her registration results, Cadence walked dejectedly into the coffeehouse, and Catissa, always the astute observer, asked if the loss of the girl's horse was still cause for the sad face.

"No, well, yes." She shook her head. "I'm still really sad about Gunpowder. I can't talk about him without . . ." Her voice quivered and eyes watered. As Catissa hugged her tightly, Cadence took a deep breath. "No, I'm also upset because I didn't get into the classes I really wanted for the spring."

Like an astrologer providing a horoscope, Catissa said, "You will. Don't worry."

"I don't know. They're all full. What makes you so sure?"

"It's your first semester, so you wouldn't know about the system, the system of assumptions. See Cadence, nothing is fixed; everything under the sun is dynamic—from the seasons to the seas, the heavenly bodies to our bodies, and of course, these classes. Decisions aren't final. Some students won't keep their choices. Some will fail, some won't come back. Seats will open. Which course did you want?"

"Professor Mirabilis's English class."

"Ah, my friend 'the demon.' So, you seek punishment again next semester?"

Cadence laughed. "I guess so. Her class is my hardest, but it's my favorite. I never thought I'd say I really like that the class isn't easy."

Catissa smiled at what she heard. "Well dear, if all else fails, you may ask for an override."

"What's that?"

"Professors have it in their power to provide overrides to some courses that are full. If you ask nicely and make a convincing argument of why you should be in the section, sometimes, they'll grant you a spot in the class."

"Catissa, is there anything you don't know?"

She laughed heartily. "Oh, honey. There's plenty that remains unknown to this ole gal." Catissa glanced at the clock. "Speaking of knowing, you'll have to excuse me. I'm off for some transcendental meditation lessons. Keep at it, Cadence. All will be well."

Cadence knew why the coffee matron and the instructor were friends. Leaving the shop gave Cadence the same sensation as departing English class; she felt stronger, smarter, liberated. Catissa was one of the best advisors, teachers, and counselors the school didn't employ. Days later, just as she predicted, Cadence was checking the schedule when next to one of Professor Mirabilis's sections appeared the opportunity: "1 of 20 OPEN."

While Cadence was now looking toward returning in the spring, Penny could not even see past each day; the more word got out about the rape investigation, the more of a target she became to those hell-bent on assassinating her character. Half-rubber squad members and their loyalists shamed her for being a slut and crucified her for being a whore. Their collective story became that she had been dancing seductively prior to any alleged sex—a narrative they repeated as it were absolute truth. She wanted more shots of alcohol that the players persuaded her against and willingly took on a few of them, a supposed fantasy of hers. They merely gave her the means for fulfilling that dream. Even some of the girls who had left the room turned

on her, saying they left precisely because of her lascivious behavior. Penny's closest friends knew it was all completely out
of character for someone normally quiet and shy.

Penny and Cadence met with the police officer who signed
for the rape kit when it was turned over by the hospital. He
seemed quite removed about the situation. In reading the interviews with the alleged attackers, he told Penny that the men
contended she was conscious and gave consent, even if she
couldn't remember doing so. None necessarily denied having
sex, but all rejected the notion that any assault took place. Sto-
ically, he announced that no hair or skin samples other than her
own had been recovered and that her test results were inconclusive.

Penny's head dropped and the tears followed. Putting her
arms around her friend's shoulder, Cadence asked, "How's that
possible?"

"It's possible because they may have used condoms." He
shifted slightly in his chair. "They may not have ejaculated inside her. Even if there's a DNA profile present from several of
them, it often can't be determined which specific types came
from which match, so the results are 'inconclusive.'" He looked
directly at Penny. "It may also be inconclusive because of your
mistake in taking a bath. That compromised evidence."

Penny's head lifted. "*Mistake? My mistake?*" She shot up
with such force that her chair hit the floor with a loud *clack*. "I
get the dicks of God-knows-how-many guys shoved into me
and a mop handle up my ass and I made a mistake?"

"We're going to continue investigating," he said.

"Why bother?" Penny snapped before fleeing the room.

Outside, Penny let out a scream that likely echoed into the stratosphere then went down on her knees. The spectacle attracted the attention of an Officer Seawell. With her friend in hyperventilation status, Cadence explained that Penny was upset about a private matter and that she'd be fine; they just needed to call a cab to get back to campus.

"No, you don't," he said. "I'll take you ladies wherever you want to go."

Laying his hands gently on Penny, he helped her up and into the backseat of the car. Cadence told him they were going to Albemarle, and during the drive, Penny stared at the nothingness out the window. Minutes later, they were approaching the dorm when he asked, "Would you like me to pull around the corner, so you're not seen getting out the back of a police car? I know how the rumor mills grind on a college campus."

Cadence agreed, and he turned onto a side street. When both girls got out, Officer Seawell motioned to Cadence. "I don't know what's going on with your friend, but if there's anything I can do, give me a call." He handed her his card. "You ladies take care, okay?"

When the two entered Penny's room, Carrie was talking to Saida, who held a brightly colored sheet of paper.

"What's going on now?" Penny asked, as she walked by them and fell on her bed. Reluctantly, they shared the paper with her. In big black letters appeared the message: *FIFTH BASE MEANS IT'S TIME FOR THE BENCH. GO HOME WHORE!*

"Where'd you get it?" Cadence asked.

"It was under the door when I came in," Saida said. "I wish I would have seen who put it there."

Penny, not thinking she could cry anymore, did just that. Her friends were not really sure how much more she could take, especially when Cadence relayed the investigation and rape kit results to the others. Carrie said she would try talking to some other advisors and encouraged Penny to start counseling since she hadn't done so before Thanksgiving. Their RA also suggested that Penny tell her parents since she would need their support for her recovery and in trying to get her studies back on track.

That night, Cadence lay awake thinking of the wounded girl on the other side of the wall. Penny's situation reminded Cadence of a fundraiser for child sexual abuse that she had photographed shortly before Thanksgiving. Darkness to Light's Circle of Light Gala was the grandest affair she had ever seen, and one of Charleston's best and most lavish parties. Tuxedos created a velvety backdrop against which jeweled women sashayed in sparkling dresses, their sequins throwing light like streaking comets. Champagne glasses twinkled with the finest grape juice, accentuated by manicured hands boasting gems every color of the spectrum. The women weren't the only ornamented ones, as the stout fingers of businessmen held class rings from law and military schools, gold indicators of their achievements and their brotherhoods. They strutted among the tables covered with candles and flowers, a dreamy setting, the kind that sells fantasy in magazines.

Local celebrity chefs served up splendor on gleaming plates and choreographed servers kept glasses filled and egos stoked to aid in the luxury auction. As the guests' buzzes grew bigger, so did their bidding, especially for the top item: a Labrador puppy that sold for $10,000—a sum Cadence realized would cover most of one semester's tuition. In shock, she almost forgot to take the photo of the happy couple: an exquisitely attired young woman and her much older husband, who smirked widely when the room showered wide-eyed envy on them.

Within the walls of that tent paraded concentrated success, and now Cadence wondered, how many were victims of sexual assault? Who among them had their innocence taken and how did they survive? Had any of those raped been told they made "mistakes" by their abusers? Police? Protectors? Among the starry glamour, did they carry the undeserved guilt and shame that was wrecking her friend? With the devastatingly dark power of abuse, how does someone come to the light? How does one convince a friend who's been raped that the only mistake made is the failure of some people to respect the life of another person?

The next evening, Cadence was again among the most fashionable of Charlestonians when she, Isa, Reena, and Blaze attended a Merry Sing-A-Long performed by the Charleston Symphony Orchestra. Reena had won tickets in a raffle, and it was the perfect way for them to fulfill the second of Brodsky's musical attendance demands. They were surprised this jovial occasion made it on his list of approved performances since he was the "Bah! Humbug!" type. With Schilar out of town at his own musical event, Cadence asked Isa to be her date, so the four sat high up in the music hall and watched as the festive crowd filed in, decorating the seats with their green and red attire. The holiday lights stretched like stars across the stage, their shine reflecting in smaller pinpoints from the polished instruments ready to give cheer.

When the concert began, the rudimentary knowledge of music that Reena and Cadence had managed to absorb came through, and they recognized, by name, instruments like the oboe, the timpani, the bassoon; the sections of the orchestra; and both gave themselves bonuses when they identified the ever-present arpeggios in the pronounced melodies. The revving reverberations of "Joy to the World" and "Hark the Herald Angels Sing" shook the theatre's aged ceiling even more than "Jingle Bells" and "Here Comes Santa Clause."

The entire audience stood for the encore of the never-ending and enigmatic "Twelve Days of Christmas." Reena, Cadence, and Isa joined in and sang in the exaggeratingly dramatic fashion the song requires—complete with big arms, sweeping movements, and the ridiculously long extension of the tune's best line: "Five Golden Rings . . ." While they got silly with the singing, Blaze stood with a stoic expression. After the orchestra had ensured they were imbued with the holiday spirit, Reena and Blaze left to find some mistletoe while Cadence and Isa stopped off at c.a.t.'s for gingerbread lattes before heading to bed.

It was well after midnight when Cadence was summoned from sleep by the ringing of her phone. Opening her eyes, she saw its face light up the room and answered with a sleepy, "Hello?"

"Fancy a moondance with me?"

"Schilar? What're you doing?" Cadence rubbed sleep from her eyes while trying to gauge the time.

"I'm downstairs. Come dance with me," he crooned before the line went silent.

The simple phone call threw her heart open, made her spirit rocket into the mesosphere, and prompted her feet to move as if they were walking on clouds. Cadence would meet Schilar at the end of the universe if that's what it took to enjoy even the smallest moments with him. That's how these things work, which meant his magnetic pull summoned her from bed to the lobby like gravity tugging the moon in tow with the earth. Schilar waited with a playlist, blanket, and backpack.

"Hey, sleepy head," he whispered, greeting her with a kiss. "I've wanted to do that all day. Our gig was over early, so I decided to come back here. I haven't seen a lot of you lately."

Surely, this was all a dream. It seemed like only weeks ago that she was sobbing in the park from loneliness, but now she was with this guy whose electric personality whisked her into the night to dance beneath the stars. Walking to the square, he slipped the blanket around her to guard against December's chill. Smells of fabric softener mixed with marijuana floated up from the blanket. Schilar was not one for cologne, but his scent occasionally bore the unmistakable mixture of two recreational pastimes—laundry and leaf smoking, and Cadence smiled when she recalled him confessing to writing some of his best music with the buzz in his head and the hum from spinning machines. "I get lost in the revolutions, in their cadence," he had said during one of their marathon talks. She wasn't sure how it was possible to talk about everything and nothing with someone for hours and still not get bored.

Van Morrison's voice drifted across the park as Schilar held Cadence close. They swayed warmly beneath the cold skies, illuminated by the glow of a full moon. When the singer's pitch crooned to high points in the melody, Schilar would dip his partner deeply then bring her up to meet his lips. Somehow, he knew, as if by instinct, the right amount of pressure to use that would result in the near collapse of her legs.

After a few songs, they walked over to the Christmas tree in the park's center: a towering tee-pee structure shining with thousands of lights twisted around green-tinseled strands. The best part was standing inside and looking skyward where the explosion of color created Charleston's own seasonal supernova. With Cadence's head arched back in wonder, Schilar pulled a small box from his pocket.

"Merry Christmas," he said.

She radiated at his thoughtfulness, but the glow died instantly. "Schilar, no. I, I don't have anything for you."

"Yes, you do," he replied sweetly. "Your company's all I need."

"You know what I mean."

"Go on, open it."

He had used the cover of a blue book as wrapping paper, which she gently peeled off. Inside a small box, stuffed in toilet paper, was a silver necklace and hanging from it—a small, sealed vial filled with black powder.

"It's moondust, from a lunar meteorite found in Northern Africa." He watched as she held the heavens to the light. "What d'you think?"

The glow of her expression answered him first. "It's incredible. I, I don't know what to say. Where'd you find space jewelry?"

"Where else? My astronomy professor." He hooked the gift around her neck. "He's this old guy—I mean, the man must have a cosmic lifespan. Anyway, he's collected all these moon rocks and meteorites, so he decided to make jewelry and sell it. Told us it's for his retirement, but I think he does it because the girls love it. He's pretty sweet on them, gives them discounts."

"I love it. It's beautiful and mysterious,"

"Just like you." He hugged her tightly.

"So what else did your astronomy professor teach you?"

"Come on, I'll show you."

Leading her from under the tree as far from the lights as they could get, he spread the blanket on the ground. Although the full moon made star gazing difficult, Schilar did his best in pointing out the constellations that could be seen from their sky: Orion, Gemini, and with some difficulty, the Milky Way.

In asking about the moon, Cadence was surprised to hear that it's made like lemon meringue pie. Schilar's professor explained that the moon's crustal surface rock has a low density, like meringue, but underneath, the mantle is denser than what's on top and can be warmer, so it's the lemon filling. The analogy made Cadence think of Corrine's marriage proposal, the dessert story that had left a bad taste in her mind.

"Mmmm, you've made me like lemon meringue pie again," Cadence whispered.

"What?"

"It's a long story," she said and explained it with her terrestrial tongue and celestial touches until it was nearly moonset.

Cadence was still floating from the night before, and the "Moondance" earworm—that piece of music that sticks in the mind—was firmly imbedded when she left for the last classes of the semester. The day went quickly and easily, with professors filling class time with evaluations. Mirabilis scored high marks, with Kinsdaw getting below average for stimulation. Cadence was disappointed there was no "Worst Teacher Ever" bubble to fill in for Brodsky, but she did mark *STRONGLY AGREE* next to the comment: *THE INSTRUCTOR SEEMED TO CONSIDER TEACHING A CHORE* and darkened the circle so hard she nearly broke her pencil lead. When he let the students out that afternoon, they experienced the kind of feeling perhaps Galileo would have if the Inquisition had freed him from house arrest. If it were possible to capture the sensation in a vial, like the one that hung from Cadence's neck, the harnesser would be a very wealthy person indeed.

With only exams left, she rode the high offered by Reading Day—that twenty-four hour break between the last day of classes and the first day of finals. Most students knew it should be renamed *Recovery Day* since they use the hours for rejuvenation after the succession of parties the night before. Having gone out for food and some studying, Cadence was beginning to feel better, but in opening the door of her room, she was overcome by a wave of sickness when a puddle met her feet and a collection of noxious gases that could make for another big bang affronted her nose. Rippling before her was an expanding pool of water; its undulations breaking over everything that was not saved by height. Trekking through the mess, she found the source to be the toilet, and having no idea of how to stop the water, she ran down the hall.

Luckily, Carrie was in and helped stop the rising tide that had taken over the suite and was now threatening the hall. They threw down towels, called for assistance, and soon a plumber arrived and began the grotesque task of unclogging the offending facility.

As he worked, Cadence surveyed the damage—everything at the level of a mouse was wet: rugs, books and notes she left by her bed, clothes strewn about, shoes. This could not have happened at a worse time. Blurred papers and soaked materials meant studying would be even more of a less-than-desirable activity. She was just about to chalk all of this up to bad luck when the plumber emerged from the watery hell's source.

"Uh, miss, I found what wuz causin' yer problem. Seems one a y'all been havin' lots of fun."

A scowl froze her face. "Excuse me?"

He held up a small, metal rod, at the end of which hung what looked like a shriveled balloon. "Condoms, sweetheart, condoms. Someone flushed 'em down the toilet, and well, it don't take no rocket science to know that dem things just don't go down. Air gets in 'em and will stop up a toilet quicker than a hungry beaver cloggin' a wetland. Just tell the lucky fella to find another means of throwin' away his stuff."

He belted a hearty laugh, probably at the story he had for his plumbing peers. As he began to leave, Cadence pleaded, "Sir, wait, what about all the water and the mess?"

"Sorry, darlin'. Ain't my job. You need to call dem custodials for that."

Cadence was looking up the number for custodial services when Saida passed by and doubled back to gape at the lake. "Cadence, what happened?"

"As you can see we have a little water problem. Well, you have it, too. The toilet overflowed."

"What the—! My room, too?" Rushing over to her side, she confirmed the tragedy while Cadence followed.

When they stepped in, the water had claimed another brightly colored sheet of paper undoubtedly meant for Penny: *YOU KNOW YOU WANTED MORE, SO WAY TO SCORE WHORE!!!!!*

"This deserves to be covered in shit. The person who left it sure is a piece of it." Saida picked up the wet mess and crumpled it. "I can't believe this! My fucking stuff! It's ruined!" Gathering up her leather boots, she slung water and profanity around the room.

"You can thank Corrine and her boyfriend for this."

Saida whipped around. "What?"

"It's Jed's fault. The stupid asshole flushed a bunch of condoms down the toilet. They backed it up."

"Are you fucking kidding me?" The words came out just as her roommate stepped in. Upon seeing the watery mess, Penny only added more to the puddle, as the mounting stress from all that she had been through reduced her once again. With Penny in tears and Saida beyond angry, Cadence, having wasted so much emotion on her roommate already this semester, occupied the space in between.

They did not have to wait long for Corrine—they heard her before they saw her. The phone was still attached to her ear when she stood on the edge of the watery mess. In continuing to talk to Jed and relaying the surprise of what she saw, she ignored the incendiary hints from Cadence and Saida to end the call. When Corrine didn't, Saida stomped over and snatched the phone, nearly taking off the girl's head with it.

"Hey! I was talking," Corrine said.

"That's all you know how to do! That and fucking your boyfriend." Saida turned a shade of red Cadence had never seen. "Do you see this mess? It's because of you two. Your idiot fuck flushed his condoms down the toilet and they clogged it up!"

"How do you know that?" Corrine asked.

"The goddamn plumber!"

"Just because some plumber guy says it was a condom don't mean it is. I mean, he could've planted that."

"Do you hear yourself? How stupid are you? This is exactly why you two shouldn't be having sex!"

"What's that supposed to mean?" Corrine asked.

"It means that people as stupid as you two should not even be flirting with the possibility of reproducing. If there is only a thin piece of rubber separating you and him from procreating, then God help us all! Do the world a favor and get sterilized, you inconsiderate bitch!"

Corrine looked as if Saida had just hit her with a brick. "There's not that much damage, and everything will dry."

"Is that so?" Splashing through the sewage over to Jed's shrine, Saida shot Corrine a camera-worthy look of condemnation, then ripped the heart-shaped homage to the floor. The water's liquid fingers immediately grabbed the images of Jed before seizing the teddy bear that Saida pushed off the bed into the mess. Finally, she delivered a goal-worthy kick to a nearly dry stack of wedding material, and for the final measure, she tossed Corrine's phone into the cesspool. Corrine rushed through the slop to salvage her beloved belongings.

Saida was on her way out when she sneered, "Oh, don't worry, Corrine. It'll dry."

Since the blare of wet vacuums from the cleaning crew was too much for anyone to endure, each went her separate way for the time, with Cadence taking her frustrations to the laundromat where the orbiting drums again restored some sense of relief. Afterwards, she sought the company of Schilar.

When she saw him, she practically broke down on his shoulder. He rubbed ire from her back, squeezed tension from her neck, absorbed her frustration by simply listening, and took her to c.a.t.'s. As soon as they stepped through the door, a puppy bounded over, followed by another and another. Soon, she was inhaling the uplifting scent of puppy breath and getting licked and loved as if she were the only person on the planet.

Catissa came over laughing. "I swear, I just can't keep up with these little ones."

"What's with all these puppies?" Cadence asked, as another came over to join the pack now fighting for her attention.

"Exam puppies, dear. Every semester, I bring them in from the shelter to help y'all with stress and, of course, to get them adopted. They seem to take to you, Cadence."

While Schilar stepped over to get drinks, Catissa noticed a puppy teething at Cadence's necklace. "That's a lovely piece of jewelry. Is it new?"

With a smile that could not expand any more, Cadence glanced over to Schilar. The three grabbed a table, and Cadence relayed the drama on the hall and her experiences with the roommate from hell.

"Living with someone is one of life's most difficult challenges, and it doesn't matter if that person's family, a friend, a lover, a spouse. It's even harder when it's a stranger. You're doing well, all things considered," Catissa said. "Just remember, sometimes, there is consent in silence."

In leaving the coffeehouse, Cadence felt restored and composed and was ready to face the exams and the remaining days with Corrine. As she stepped into her room, banging and screaming poured from Ruthie and Olivia's. Cadence hung back as the door in question opened and a body hit the wall with a *thud*. Olivia's hands went up in a vain effort to block Ruthie's wrath. Hair flew in handfuls, nails dug into flesh, and fists delivered the rest. Olivia screamed and Ruthie responded just as loudly with some choice words.

"You fucking bitch! I'll teach you to go through my stuff! You want something to report? Report this!" She lodged another punch to Olivia who sank to the floor where she now met kicks from her roommate.

The ruckus continued, drawing more attention, including that of Jacinda who stepped out. Ruthie was nearly out of breath from her attack on Olivia when she stopped and looked down the hall. With the speed of light, Ruthie pointed her finger at Cadence and bolted toward her.

"And you! What the fuck did you tell her?"

Ruthie's fist rose to drop down on Cadence's head, but just as it descended, a much stronger and more determined hand stopped it. Cadence had turned away to avoid the hit, and when she turned back, she saw Jacinda pinning Ruthie to the wall.

"Get your hands offa me!" Ruthie gnashed her teeth. "This is none of your fuckin' business."

"Hey!" Jacinda said, "you just need to calm your crazy self down. Hear me?"

"Fuck you, you nigger bitch! Get your goddamn hands off of me."

Jacinda's nostrils flared. "Oh no! I'm goin' to pretend you didn't just take the Lord's name in vain. You damn lucky I just got finished with Bible study. Otherwise, I'd give you an ass whoopin'."

Jacinda threw all of her weight into Ruthie, which crushed the breath out of her, and looked at Cadence with assurance just as campus police came through the doors. Once they handcuffed Ruthie, a search of her room revealed a bag of pot, bottles of pills, and a fifth of bourbon. They hauled her off to jail on simple possession and assault charges, leaving the residents in full gossip mode and Cadence completely mystified as to why Jacinda had protected her.

"I seen enough people get hurt lately," Jacinda said.

"Thanks for what you did," Cadence said softly. "And I'm sorry for what she said to you."

"Well, that comes with her dark soul. That girl, she's definitely got one," Jacinda said. "Hey, I want you to know, the photo you took of me singin' has really helped my parents. They tell me when they question where they went wrong with my brother, they look at that picture and see what they did right. Gives them a lotta pride, a lotta hope."

Cadence felt a warmth rise within. "You know I took that?"

"Well yeah, girl, just 'cause I don't call you by name don't mean I don't know who you are." She laughed. Cadence laughed too—sounds that were long overdue on their hall.

Eventually, they also heard the cause of the altercation. Olivia had been secretly rifling through Ruthie's belongings— because she was being paid to by Ruthie's mother. Seems the New Jersey girl came to college after rehab, so to make certain her daughter wasn't drawn back to the wrong crowd, Ruthie's mother deposited some nice sums for surveillance in Olivia's banking account. Now everyone knew how Olivia could afford fine luxury items on a college student's budget. When the action finally died down that night, Cadence settled in for a night of studying and she hoped, some rest, but the fear of missing Brodsky's 8 a.m. exam kept her far from deep and proper sleep.

Everyone expected the test to be positively perditious, and it was—an audibly unpleasant experience. He fulfilled their expectations by blasting the sound so loudly it was difficult to identify the composers and their scores. He also blasted their minds with ridiculously difficult multiple choice. Cadence answered C for most questions as if she were anticipating the grade she'd make. She'd be right about getting an average mark in the class. When she emerged from the darkness into the light with Reena, they hugged each other tightly. Having made it through hell together, they formed a bond melded from the fire and brimstone Brodsky spewed. Had a bottle of champagne been available, they would have cooled themselves with it.

Biology and Spanish were more of the same: multiple choice mania, with the latter also including an oral exam. Isa helped her prepare, and in the conversation, Cadence had asked about Roano and his girlfriend and what happened over Thanksgiving. Isa told Cadence that she did not see Verena over break, but for the holidays, Isa was going to Columbia to stay with Roano until he finished exams, and they were off to Mexico until January. Cadence wondered if Isa would learn the truth about her brother over break.

With three of her hardest exams down, Cadence experienced euphoria that died every time she went to sell back a textbook. Despite spending over $500 on books at the semester's beginning, the buybacks would result in only a fifth of that investment returned. Most texts were not readopted and deemed useless, unless a person desired a private library. She kept her English books, donated what she didn't need to an African literacy charity, and was thankful there wasn't a worthless text for Freshman Seminar to lose money on. For this class, Cadence spent much time on the "7 Wonders" project, especially because she simply enjoyed doing it. Most of the project's work she did in the library, but when she needed a break, she went to Schilar's dorm, where she ended up putting the finishing touches on it. It was well after midnight when she curled up next to him, and before she knew it, the alarm was blaring.

Despite being at 8 a.m., the exam for Freshman Seminar was the best because Dr. Elders brought in coffee, juice, donuts, and muffins and devoted the three-hour slot to their presentations. Some were excellently prepared, while others were hastily put together and the professor's disapproval showed. Among her favorites was an aspiring chef's "Top 7 Delightful Charleston Dishes," which included she crab soup, shrimp and grits, and oyster po' boys. It was a tasty presentation, complete with a set of recipe cards for each student.

Another interesting project was from an architectural major who guided the class through examples of fine design: The Old Exchange and Provost Dungeon; the Heyward-Washington and Joseph Manigault historic homes; the Dock Street Theatre; the Old City Jail; the Circular Congressional Church; and finally, the iron art from the incredible imagination of blacksmith Philip Simmons.

Few knew that many of the iron balconies, columns, gates, fences, and window grills they passed every day were fashioned by this skilled artisan. He learned the craft from a former slave and at the age of eighteen became a full blacksmith after a five-year apprenticeship. For some seventy-seven years, metal surrendered its rigidity and bent to the fiery commands of his hammer and anvil, resulting in creations that achieved international recognition and made him an architectural treasure in his own right.

Nervousness swept over Cadence. She was the last to go, so she popped her drive into the computer and explained that she focused on the Seven Wonders of Beauty with a focus on the letter *B*. There were so many that she couldn't narrow them down, so she grouped them into categories and hoped Professor Elders wouldn't penalize her for not following directions.

Immediately, something was wrong when the slideshow began—music issued from the speakers. When Cadence stopped the presentation, the music ceased, and she realized the sounds were tied to her photographs. She had no idea how it was there and really had no choice but to continue. When she restarted the show, the distinct sounds of blues melodies softly played, and then she knew who must have gotten up during the night and worked while she slept. Cadence led the class through the city's beauties explaining each, which she had alliteratively grouped into various "B" sections:

BRIDGES: The Ravenel, island connectors, and the one over Shem Creek.

BEACHES: The quaint feel of Sullivan's with its black and white lighthouse, the classic look of Folly's pier, surfers, bungalows; the natural sounds of Kiawah.

BOATS: The Yorktown, shrimp trawlers, the Folly bulletin board.

BUILDINGS: Rainbow Row, church steeples, the Market.

BOUNTY (from land and sea): benne wafers in a sweetgrass basket, boiled peanuts, seafood boils.

BRANCHES: of oaks, magnolias, palmettos.

BEVERAGES: a glass of iced tea, a black coffee from c.a.t.'s, a collection of Palmetto beer.

The last slide elicited applause, but Cadence wasn't certain if it was because the image of beer bottles appeared magnified or because she was the final presenter which meant they were all one step closer to break.

Cadence had moved the show forward so the beer photo wouldn't linger when another picture appeared. In black and white, Cadence sat cross-legged beneath those storied oaks on the Grand Lawn, frozen in an instance of laughter. *Simply Beautiful* was etched in the space above her. From her stunned expression, her classmates and Dr. Elders could tell the inclusion was not hers.

Moments later, their instructor thanked them for a great semester, informed them of when grades would be available, and dismissed them with well wishes for success in the semesters to come. Cadence stayed behind to shut down the slide show. In fearing that the surprise photograph would affect her grade, Cadence addressed Dr. Elders about it.

"Cadence, relax. It's okay." Her professor stopped abruptly to blow her nose. "Whoever took the photo has quite an eye for you. And I'll admit, it's nice to see such a happy face this time in the semester. You gave a fine presentation and captured the essence of Charleston with such precision. I especially appreciate the diversity of your presentation—benne wafers, sweetgrass baskets, they speak to my heritage. Did you take the pictures?"

"Yes, ma'am."

"I thought so be—" A coughing fit that lasted longer than it should have seized the teacher.

"Are you okay, professor?"

Dr. Elders took a deep breath. "Yes, yes. Just a really nasty case of bronchitis. As I was saying, I've seen your photos in *The Gator*." She barely got the words out before the coughing returned.

"I took your advice about getting involved and got a position as a staff photographer."

"Well, the quality of the photos has, has definitely improved since you have." Dr. Elders wheezed the words. "And I love the inclusion of the blues music. Really nice touch," she said, with barely audible breath.

Praise from her professor was even better than the A Cadence would get in the class. With this penultimate task down, English was the only exam left, and it occupied the very last slot during the testing period. Corrine also had one at this time and would not be leaving until after Cadence. Most people on the hall had departed: Saida was off to Miami for another pair of boots, and Reena had flown to visit her mom in D.C., but some of Cadence's friends were still on campus, including Penny who wasn't taking exams.

She had begun therapy, and her counselor had requested that her professors grant "incompletes" in all of her classes. Some were reluctant to give the extension because they were not privy to the reasons for needing one, and she certainly did not want to tell them. She was waiting to ride home with Jade, who was going to help Penny tell her parents. While everyone else was studying for and taking exams, Penny slept, watched TV, barely ate, went to some therapy, and tried to write in the leather journal Cadence and Saida had given her. Its pages remained blank.

The morning of her last day, Cadence planned to sleep in, pack, and study before her noon exam, but this was not to be. A call from TJ demanded she get up immediately. Cadence threw on some clothes and quickly covered the short distance to the Grand Lawn where the campus Christmas tree, a palm usually decorated with large, shiny orbs, stood. But on this morning, all the ornaments lay on the ground and in their places hung oversized, half-rubber balls. Stapled to the tree's trunk was a huge poster bearing the words: *All I want for Xmas? Rapists to be Punished!* Cadence began snapping immediately, anxious to show Penny, and when she shared the spectacle with her suitemate, something different, perhaps some sense of justice not present before, appeared in Penny's face. This gesture of defense had given her a feeling nothing else could.

Of course, the coaches were suddenly very interested in achieving justice for their boys. A few hours after the balls dropped from the tree, the cops questioned Penny about the vandalism. She told them she barely had energy to breathe, much less redecorate a tree on her behalf, but it was nice to see that someone was, in her words, "going to bat for me." They were not amused and assured her that the investigation regarding her rape allegations was ongoing.

For some reason, Cadence thought her English exam would be relatively easy, but she was wrong. She filled five blue books with multiple choice answers, quotation identification, short argument analysis, and two essays. In channeling the energy and adrenaline from the day's events into writing, Cadence used the entire three hours until the professor told them time was up. When she gave Professor Mirabilis her exam books, the teacher handed Cadence the graded essay on knowledge. For that moment, she felt as if it were a solar eclipse that threatened to blind her if she looked, so she waited until she had left the classroom, then peeled back the final page.

Cadence, This paper is insightful, interesting, well argued, and researched and documented precisely. A few areas still need work, but we'll address these issues in the spring. See you next year! Grade: A.

Jumping up and down, Cadence squealed in delight, a pseudo dance of sorts that Professor Mirabilis's students sometimes broke into. After grabbing one last house special and wishing Catissa well until next year, Cadence strolled the stone path on the way to her dorm, where Schilar was waiting to say goodbye. She had forgiven him with a "thank you" for the pleasant additions to her Freshman Seminar presentation. She would miss him in the weeks they would be apart. In the whirlwind of emotion that marks the virgin stages of any passion, they made promises of communication and sealed them with kisses. Cadence was waiting for Julie, the same ride home she took for fall, and as she stood outside of Albemarle, she inhaled the look of Schilar against the backdrop of the campus that had already embedded itself in her life. When Julie arrived, Cadence gave him one final kiss, and as the girls began the miles that would take them west, she turned to see her rock star, his red guitar clinging to his back, walking in and out of shadows cast from rays filtering through the oak canopies.

In peering ahead to the road that would take her home, Cadence sighed in relief. She had survived the first orbit on the long journey to graduation, the daily revolutions of the general education galaxy that tested those brave enough to explore the frontier. She had learned and laughed and cried over classes, exams, professors, friends, enemies, and strangers. The voids of loneliness and uncertainty she had felt in those first months had been filled, for now, while the ones of loss would remain swirling holes of darkness. In such brief time, she had experienced an immeasurable expansion of consciousness, an awareness of ideas, people, places, and things she had not imagined possible, but during these concentrated months, she had also known the tremendous power of condensed emotions—of anger, hate, sadness, and depression—and their devastating effects in the collisions of human natures. Indeed, it had been a short, strange, and exhilarating ride on this cosmic carousel, one she could hardly wait to begin anew in the coming year. Traveling from the city with a magnetic pull over her mind and heart, Cadence felt the mysterious tugging understood only by those who have rubbed their souls with Charleston's, and she could hardly remain looking forward without wanting to look back.

SPRING SEMESTER

Chapter 11

Theatre 101
Exploring Drama

"FREE FEELING!"

The alliterative announcement sprang across the performance hall before any of them saw its source. From the slit in the maroon curtains stepped a blond wearing a dull, brown skirt that, despite its drab appearance, seemed to dance around her Rubenesque figure.

"Sometimes in freeing your feelings, you must close your eyes to open your mind. So, please do this now," she instructed as the students sat stupefied.

"Close your eyes—*everyone*," she said sternly. This time, they obeyed. "Now, I want you to remove the clutter, all the daily concerns, conversations, conflicts. Clear your heads. Breathe deeply and s-l-o-w-ly. Find the breath. Think of nothing. Go to that place where all you hear is silence, where all you see is void. Breathe deeply and slowly. Relax." Her long exhalation sounded like wind moving through the auditorium.

She let them sit in her imposed silence until its awkwardness threatened to ruin the moment. "Now, go through your mind's encyclopedia of experiences to a time when you felt true anguish, an occasion that made you feel every fiber in your flesh, where you knew you were alive because the pain was so great." She paused, watching them flip back through their memories. "Relive those moments leading up to it—the setting. Imagine the smells, sights, sounds, tastes, and of course, the feelings to get there; go on, go there."

In sifting through her memories of torment, Cadence did not have to look back very far, only to last semester: Corrine, Gunpowder, Penny . . . the feelings were still fresh, but for some reason, her mind catapulted her back to childhood, to a Saturday afternoon, just when spring was on the cusp of giving over to summer, not too hot but just right.

Cadence had been playing outside as her parents worked in the garden. Next to it was a plot of unmown grass—wild and green, thick and fresh, the perfect place to lie down and make cloud games with the sky. The cool grass welcomed her long hair, which spread out softly around her like a pillow. Birds chirped, the breeze blew, and high above, she could see a tiny jet cutting a white streak through the aqua skyscape. She wondered how high up it was, who was on it, and where they were going. Closing her eyes, she imagined what it would be like to fly . . .

"Get to that moment when you suddenly experienced suffering beyond any you have ever felt," the teacher said.

. . . blue heavens, emerald grass, a perfect day, until Cadence felt the first sting, then another, and another to her neck, inside her ears, on her head. Sting after malicious sting spread over her scalp and onto her face . . .

"When I count to three, I want you to verbalize what you're feeling. Dig in. How does it hurt? Where does it hurt?"

. . . It hurt everywhere. Her face began swelling from the attack, tears launched and cries punctured the quiet. Her parents threw down their tools and sprinted toward her. Jumping up, she tried to shake the attackers from her, but they were everywhere. Her nails scratched through her head with such force that small cuts opened in her scalp . . . but the stinging would not stop.

"You are there. One. Two. Three!"

A single scream ricocheted across the theatre hall, but it wasn't from Cadence or Reena. It came from Reena's roommate, who did not immediately come out of her memory-induced trance.

"Excellent!" the professor exclaimed, looking at the bold responder. "What's your name?"

Miranda stared at the back of the seat until a nudge from Reena prompted the response: "Miranda."

"Ah, 'Admired Miranda, indeed the top of admiration! Worth. What's dearest to the world.'" The class looked lost. "Sorry folks, I occasionally break out into Shakespeare—comes with the job. That's from *The Tempest*, for those of you who live for the words of Dead White European Males." A few people laughed.

"Hey! When I tell a joke, it's okay to laugh and laugh out loud, even if it's not that funny. Theatre is about laughing and crying and embracing every emotion on the human spectrum. Miranda certainly got to that sense memory point, enough to aid her emotional memory, which produced the reaction. That's a part of method acting. It's one of the concepts you'll become familiar with in this course. Well done, Miranda."

It was already unusual for Reena and Cadence to be sitting in a course in which someone was receiving praise from the professor. The woman continued, "For the rest of you, we'll free those feelings over the coming months. I'm Professor Dreary. Welcome to Introduction to Drama, or what I like to call, 'The Theatre of Life.'"

After class, the trio grabbed a coffee at c.a.t.'s to do some catching up. Reena and Miranda got a table while Cadence went to find Catissa who was in the consilium. When she saw the matron standing among the ever-growing lines of writing, Cadence called to her, and as Catissa turned around, a second face greeted Cadence: that of a sleeping puppy.

"Oh Catissa," Cadence cooed, "who's this?"

"This is c.a.t.'s new co-owner," she said. "His name's Kyd. Every year, I fall in love with those darlin' babies during exams, and it was just high time I got one. But don't tell those pesky health people. He's not supposed to be here, but I can't get enough of his sweet, velvety folds."

Cadence stroked the happiness of a warm puppy. "What kind is he?"

"A white boxer," Catissa whispered. "What d'you think?"

Cadence leaned in for a whiff of his breath. "I think he may be the cutest puppy I've ever seen. And I don't think I've ever seen a white boxer."

"They're not as rare as people think. Unfortunately, breeders used to kill them. Deafness runs in the white gene, and the purebred snobs believe there's too much of the color. It violates their standards."

The bundle in Catissa's arms began to suckle the air in response to some dream running through his tiny mind. As his newly formed tongue tasted the space, Cadence thought that it must take a person of exceptional cruelty to kill a creature so sweet. As she rubbed his floppy ears, she asked, "So what are you and Kyd doing up here?"

"Just reading some of the new entries." She pointed out responses to the question: *How do you measure your life?* One read, *I measure my time here by the bug carcasses collecting in the library's lights,* and another revealed, *I measure my days and nights not by the lines I have written but by the lines I have left to write.*

"I really like that one," Catissa observed, "but these disturb me."

She drew Cadence's attention to one entry that confessed: *My life is now measured by the pain and suffering of minutes I can't remember*, and another that read, *I measure my existence by silencing the voices of those who have silenced others.* Catissa shook her head. "Pretty unsettling."

Cadence thought that Penny could have authored the first, but then again, there must be hundreds of people on campus who could have written that. After catching up, Cadence joined her friends where they had the house special waiting on her, a drink she had craved like a drug over the holidays.

It was Reena's idea to take theatre class, so she asked, "Okay, Miranda. What memory made you scream? Was it real or were you acting?"

Miranda's look indicated she had not been acting. "It was very real. I remember every detail like it happened yesterday."

On a cold winter's morning when she was in eighth grade, Miranda was riding to school with her best friend, Macala, and Macala's older sister, Shianne, who was driving. Shianne's friend Bailey was also in the car. They were just a few miles from the middle school when Shianne began to break for a stop sign but an icy patch caused the car to slide into the path of an oncoming truck. The impact crushed the driver's side, where Macala sat behind her sister, and sent the car rolling off the road into an icy pond.

"I blacked out, but when the water began filling up the car, I woke up and looked around. Macala's head was leaning toward me but at a weird angle. I reached and called for her, but she didn't wake up. I started screaming, but no one answered because they were already dead. It was so cold." Miranda pulled the warmth of her cup close to her chest. "The car was sinking. I swam out the broken window and made it to the bank. Some people were coming down to help me and Bailey. She had been thrown from the car, but she survived." Miranda bowed her head as if she were in prayer then raised it to the ceiling. "That's where I went today."

"I had no idea," Reena said gently. "Sorry to hear about your friends."

"Me, too," Cadence added. The three sat, taking it all and their coffees in.

"Cadence, what'd you go back to?"

"This time when I was little. I lay down in the grass to look up at the sky, but my head went down in a bed of fire ants."

Reena and Miranda winced.

"Yeah, it was bad. My dad snatched me up and ran to the water hose. I'm not sure what hurt worse: the ants or the jet from the water hose stinging me." Cadence's shoulders quivered at the flashback. "Reena, what's your anguish moment?"

"Um, you both know, that electroshock stuff," she replied, not needing to go into the details. "So, what do you two think of theatre?"

"It's much better than music!" Cadence laughed.

Theatre was exactly the kind of first day experience Cadence had looked forward to, but she hadn't thought drama would be the course that would give her a rush. In fact, taking it had not interested her at all, but at Reena's urging, she signed up for it. Cadence felt that she had nearly completed a degree in the subject, given all the drama of last term, especially with her roommate. It was the thought of being back in Charleston that increased her excitement—and uneasiness—with every

mile that brought her back to the city. She had missed its lei-
surely bustle and pleasurable discoveries but did not miss her
roommate. The prospect of sharing another semester with Corrine was almost enough to make her not come back, but she
knew better than to let someone like her interrupt plans. Cadence vowed to deal with it, as best she could, and even
resolved to sleep in the common room if she had to.

After bracing herself for the unwanted reunion with Corrine,
Cadence felt ready for what was sure to be a confrontation, but
she was not prepared for the stranger with fire-colored hair who
smiled at her when she opened the door. Apologizing for barg-
ing into the wrong room, Cadence checked the number on the
door only to discover that this was indeed hers.

"Hi," said the girl with a perky voice. "I'm Helena. Your
new roommate."

Cadence dropped her bag, along with her jaw. "Um, hi. I,
I'm Cadence," she said. "Sorry, I expected to see someone
else." She looked around in shock. "How, how'd this happen?"

"Well, it was all a last minute miracle, really. I'm a transfer
from Bob Jones University. My acceptance had been put on
hold, but they called right before Christmas and said I was in."

"Oh, okay," Cadence began to unpack and also started the
introductory roommate ritual all over again: "Why'd you transfer?"

"Just wanted something different. You know, a bit of excitement? BJ can be so stuffy. No watching movies on campus,
and when you do, they must be rated 'G.' No listening to jazz,
rap, rock, pop, or country. No physical contact for unmarried
people. No shopping for anything but groceries on Sunday. No
jeans or shorts worn to class." She reeled off the rules like a
fugitive who had fled a cult. "You know, sometimes a girl just

needs to put on a pair of jeans and get crazy!" She laughed and slapped the leg of her holey denims.

Cadence had heard rumors of the upstate school being intolerant of pretty much everything. A few hard-core religious people from her high school were attending, but she had not seen any of them over break. Then again, they weren't exactly the types to hang out in pastures, get drunk on homemade wine, dance in the bed of trucks, and make out.

"I went ahead and cleaned the bathroom and freshened it up for everyone, and I put some drinks and food in the fridge. Help yourself," Helena said.

A shockingly nice roommate and so far, great classes—Cadence had to pinch herself to make certain she wasn't dreaming. Not only had theatre proven to be stimulating, but Professor Mirabilis had not disappointed, either. Since fall term with the demon had prepared Cadence to expect an essay on the first day back, she was utterly surprised when her favorite teacher crossed the door's threshold, turned off the lights, and gave Cadence a second dose of Shakespeare:

The purpose of playing, whose end, both at the first and now, was and is, to hold, as 'twere the mirror up to nature, to show virtue her feature, scorn her own image, and the very age and body of the time his form and pressure.

The professor's eyes lifted from the massive book to an audience that looked as if she had spoken ancient Greek to them. "Now, who wants to explain what the Bard conveys in these lines from Hamlet?"

Cadence glanced around to see who would answer. She spotted Kirby in her section, and she also noticed that strange guy who always sat in the back of the room staring a hole into her head. A few students offered their thoughts, including a woman who seemed to be in her mid-twenties.

"Is he saying that plays just reflect the virtues and vices of people at different ages and times?"

"I don't think I could have said it better myself," the professor replied. "Thank you—?"

"Astra."

"In essence, what Astra posits is true—Shakespeare tells us that acting, and by extension, art and literature, do not invent human nature, but they work as mirrors, simply reflecting our positive and negative characteristics."

Professor Mirabilis led them through a series of pairings showing the human inspirations for some legendary characters in literature, but she held in secret those they would meet in the months to come.

After the presentation, she passed out twenty handheld mirrors and twenty markers. "Hold up the mirror, look at your reflection, and on the mirror's face, write the first word that comes to mind. When you are finished, pass the mirror two times to different people before you add another word on the mirror you receive. You should not write the same word as your last, and the word you choose must not duplicate those that already appear on the mirror's surface. Begin now, please," the teacher instructed.

"Hey, Professor Mirabilis, where'd you come up with this?" a veteran student asked.

She smiled devilishly. "Happy hour." A few laughed, but it was still difficult to imagine their teacher knocking back cocktails at a bar and coming up with assignments while doing so.

"Cool. I'm all about buzz-inspired activities," he said.

"Thanks, Dewit. Somehow, I'm sure the natures of our buzzes are probably quite different. Now, come up with some insightful words for this assignment, please."

Excited came to Cadence's mind when she gazed at her reflection, so she wrote it and swapped with Kirby who passed it to the weird guy. Cadence exchanged once more with a young lady named Aliyah who wore a perfectly color-coordinated outfit from head to toe. Her mirror had *alive* written on it.

Professor Mirabilis waited until every mirror had at least four words before continuing: "After you add the fifth to the mirror, take a piece of paper and record the words."

Cadence did as instructed, writing *fearful, shy, powerful, hungry,* and *lost* in her notebook. She wondered who felt these and why.

"From the list, you will choose one word and connect it to some pivotal event in one of the literary pieces we'll cover in the next two weeks. More details to come, but you should begin considering how the term is beneficial and detrimental to a character. For instance, if one of the words is *beauty*, how will this prove positive and negative for the character? Don't worry if you feel lost; I'll help you find direction in classes to come. Now, I'll leave you with a syllabus to read for next time. Welcome back."

Building on what she had taught them last semester, Professor Mirabilis was again exploring the dualities of words and of human nature, but not everyone was thrilled about the challenge. On the way out, Cadence heard some newbies exchange opinions about the experience.

"That was bizarre," said one.

"Uh, totally. And God, I really hate Shakespeare," said the other. "I'm going to drop. Besides, I've heard she's really hard.

I don't want to kill myself for an A." Cadence thought about how Catissa had been right—seats would open up; decisions weren't final.

"Cadence," a voice called as they shuffled down the crowded hall. "How was your break?"

"Good, Kirby. How about yours?"

"Excellent. I toured some colleges I'm thinking on transferring to," he said. "Thanks for suggesting this class. Sounds like it's going to be fun. What words did you get?"

When Cadence told him, he revealed his: *horny, stoned, pregnant, tortured,* and *fortunate.*

"*Pregnant?*" Cadence asked. "Who's pregnant in our class?"

"Not sure. Maybe the horny person had something to do with it. I didn't see anyone who looked knocked up. I guess we'll find out in time, huh?"

"Maybe. See you later. I'm off to communications class." She waved goodbye as he left for economics.

It was the course that shocked her even before she attended it. When Cadence went to buy her books, all were fairly reasonable except the text for mass communications. She checked twice to make sure she had the right price. Sure enough, the tag read $150—for one book. It was a new edition, the third one by this author who also happened to be her professor. The man teaching the class had literally written the book on the subject.

Over two hundred students filed into the lecture hall for the first class, quite unaware they had stepped into a "weed-out" course, one designed to ensure that only the most serious of those aspiring journalism, public relations, advertising, and marketing enthusiasts survived. Like an astute gardener, Dr.

Tiller would rid the field's future of slipshods who wanted only to slap together sensational feature pieces, throw promotion parties, or glam it up as ad execs. He would do so, not by delicately plucking each weed from the patch before him, but by mowing them down like a reaper wielding a scythe.

He bore a commanding presence in his custom-made navy suit and orange silk tie, courtesy of the thousands of books he had now sold thanks to multiple editions. When the TAs had finished handing out the syllabus, Dr. Tiller began.

"If you want to be a communications major, you need to learn to communicate the old-fashioned way: by listening and being attentive in the moment. In order to get a story, assess a client's needs, pitch an idea, you must be present. Not only physically, but mentally; therefore, *no cells phones* are allowed to be on in this class. You will give me your undivided attention every minute of our time together. For this reason, you may not surf the Internet for those of you with electronics," he said. "Computers are to be used only for note taking. Failure to comply will result in a zero for every day you're mentally not here."

"Excuse me," a voice whispered. "Are you saving this seat?"

"Um, no," Cadence replied, motioning for the guy to sit down.

He leaned over. "Did I miss anything?"

"Not much. He just started." She tilted her syllabus so the stranger could follow along while the professor continued with the rules.

"The seat you are in will be yours for the semester's remainder if you want to be counted as present. Yes, I take attendance; well, more accurately, my teaching assistants Winston and Julia do. They're coming around writing names in our seat chart today." Both waved their hands in acknowledgment. "It is your responsibility to read the syllabus thoroughly, but I will draw your attention to the three assignments that will constitute your final grade: two exams and quizzes. The latter will consist of assigned readings not only from the textbook but in current events. You must choose one local and one reputable national newspaper to read in addition to the campus paper and one local station to watch daily."

When the class was over, the guy next to her said, "I'm Dakota, and this class is going to kick our butts."

She laughed. "I'm Cadence, and I think you're right."

"Well, Cadence, I need to get a syllabus, so I'll see you next time since I'm permanently beside you."

It was appropriate that after the class, Cadence attended a meeting of the newspaper staff where TJ laid out the plans for stories in the spring. Because of the quality of her work, she was given the large assignment of photographing different types of dancers for April's feature on National Dance Month.

He had a few styles in mind but was open to suggestions. She would be working with Degue, who was writing the accompanying article. Cadence also needed to provide shots for Valentine's Day, the Wine + Food Festival, the Cooper River Bridge Run, and the spring training and initial games of the half-rubbers. Cadence's stomach slid into knot with the last mention.

"In speaking of the half-rubbers," TJ said, "does anyone have any leads or other information on the Christmas tree display or anything else with that situation?"

"Initial rumors were that this girl took on a number of them. Then I heard it was gang rape. Of course, the guys deny that," a reporter named Melissa said.

"Yeah, I think we have all heard that, but does anyone have any idea who was behind the tree thing?" TJ asked. "I mean, did the victim do it or what?"

No one knew, so he asked everyone to listen out and follow any leads for who was behind the stunt. Of course, Cadence knew her suitemate had nothing to do with the tree fiasco, but it was one aspect of the larger tragedy that Penny revealed to her parents over break.

When she told them, they began their own swings on the emotional pendulum. Most of all, they were distraught over her condition—the depression and dreariness that now cloaked their once happy and bright daughter. They worried about her health, all dimensions of it, and how she could recover. While at home, her mother took her to the gynecologist, who gave her another full examination, and Penny continued counseling over the phone with her psychologist. Her sisters rallied around their sibling and vowed to help her get her work done, so that when Penny returned to campus, she was mostly caught up with her assignments.

Cadence and Saida had no idea what to expect with Penny's return; both had called her several times over break, but she hadn't really wanted to talk. They were relieved to see Penny's parents make the trip back to campus. In her weariness, Penny sat through meetings with the administration, who assured them all that everything was being done to investigate this delicate matter. It was a complicated case, made even more difficult because of the alcohol. At the very least, those in charge promised they would try to bring the matter before a campus judicial panel for possible code of conduct infractions by the semester's end. Penny and her parents also met with the police and the therapist, the latter of whom suggested that Cadence, Saida, and Jade attend some sessions with Penny in order to help understand and aid in the healing process. The psychologist wanted them to be particularly cognizant of self-harm warning signs.

Penny's parents did everything they could to help their daughter recover and ensure that punishment would come upon the heads of those who did this. On several occasions, her father flirted with the idea of taking their own half-rubber sticks to the assaulters.

"Just give me ten minutes in a room with them—I'll make certain they never take advantage of another young woman again," he would say through clenched teeth to his wife. Unable to sleep, he stayed up late looking for answers in glasses of bourbon mixed with tears, which fell relentlessly when he thought of his youngest girl's pain. Sometimes, he wondered how many fathers had daughters who had been violated and how boys with mothers and sisters could cross the line of perversion in the ways they had done with his child. He entertained the macabre fantasies of revenge and wondered how many fathers had made their wishes reality. Civil sensibilities always drew him back from retribution's edge, but deep down, a part of him would always want to step off and plummet into the madness of revenge.

Before Penny returned, Saida and Cadence had a few days to hang out and talk about Saida's Miami adventures. By far, her lust life was the most exciting of any of Cadence's friends, so she was surprised when Saida reported that her break was "lackluster." Her trip ended early when it became clear that Miguel was buying boots for a number of women who continuously called and texted while Saida was with him. She departed "The Magic City" unenchanted and without any new accessories. For the break's remainder, Saida divided her time between her parents: spa days with her mother and verbal sparring with her stepmother and father, the latter produced the consolation prize of a car, which Saida drove back to campus.

When Saida asked about her suitemate's break, Cadence replied that it was uneventful, just visits with family and friends, because she really didn't want to talk about the drama of home. A few days after Christmas, Cadence made the trek to Gunpowder's grave. She took an apple, a token for the spirit she hoped still rode the farm's hills, and her journal with her. She planned to trap her lingering pain inside those lines, but pleasures with Schilar came to rest on those pages, a conscious stream of thoughts on a life already changed by her short time in college. As she wrote, she held the vial of dust around her neck and was lost in her interior monologue when a voice brought a stop to her pen. Looking up, she saw her father's most trusted farmhand, Baxley, standing beside her.

With his rugged good looks and polished manners, Baxley was the type who prided himself on his knowledge of all things manly. He lived for the dirt caked beneath his fingernails at every day's end, and he had always held a special place for Cadence, whom he had watched transform from an awkward tomboy into a beautiful, young woman. They had known each other most of their lives and had grown up exploring the barns, hay bales, fields, and folds. As children, they acted the roles of cowboys and Indians perfectly, using tobacco sticks for horses instead of riding the real steeds around them. Some of her best childhood memories were with Baxley. A few years her senior, he appointed himself her protector so that throughout school, he tried to direct her away from the hurt and pain of unworthy suitors. Recently, he sustained the part as her guardian since he was the one who searched for, found, and buried Gunpowder. He had wanted to tell Cadence in person of her horse's ill fate, wanted to hold her when she collapsed in tears, and now wanted to be there for her as she sat writing over her pet's resting place.

"Don't those professors ever give you a break?" Baxley asked as he stepped from the hollow.

Cadence gently closed her book. "Oh, this isn't homework. I was just writing some stuff."

Digging with a pen was an activity he wasn't accustomed to, so he shifted the subject to the grave in front of them. They talked about Gunpowder, of his rebirth with Cadence and his untimely death, of business on the farm and friends in town, and the changes she had missed since going away, like the end of his relationship with Shelby, a girl he had dated only a few months and one whom Cadence thought was all wrong for him. He asked about life in the city and college, and in not wanting to make her second home more important than it was here, she held back on the details and kept silent about Schilar, lest Baxley decide to tell her father of his daughter's private business. They talked on like old times, and when it was nearing dusk, Cadence said goodbye and began the walk back to the house.

She was almost out of earshot when his words, "I seen you that night," spun her around in an instant. She studied him to see if they were thinking of the same night. "One of the last rides you took on Gunpowder," he said.

It was on a night over fall break. She had gone to a party where the blanket of homecoming wrapped her warmly in nostalgia. She talked to old friends, celebrated new ones, and just enjoyed that distinct sense of being home. Baxley had been there, too, watching from the fringes with his friends—the jocks and faded football heroes from high school. He had given her a ride home since it was on his way. Not too long after, Cadence found she was the only person in the house who couldn't sleep, so she went to the barn where Gunpowder, excited that she was there, was wide awake as well. With only his reigns, she took him for a midnight ride beneath a moon so full, it shined like a flashlight in the sky.

Along the way, she thought of school and Schilar, of games and dares, and in the bizarre way that memories roll around in the mind, she recalled the first stroll around Charleston with Saida, Penny, and Corrine—the glamour and glitz of it all, especially the gleaming luxuries of the Charleston Place Hotel.

She remembered the enticing chocolate-covered strawberries and how the salesclerk had relayed the legend of Lady Godiva, the medieval woman who rode naked through the town of Coventry to relieve the townspeople of the hefty taxes her husband imposed. So intrigued was Cadence by the story that she researched the lady to discover the ride was a debatable myth but with one surviving element: a "Peeping Tom." According to the tale, the Lady requested that the residents shutter their windows and not look as she rode through, but the only person to disobey was the town's tailor, Tom, who peeped and was struck blind when he did.

The thought of the Lady's ride enticed Cadence. The night was perfect for it—she had the means, the moonlight, and the mettle enhanced by a buzz, so she dismounted Gunpowder and seconds later climbed back on in the pure power of nothing but her bare skin. Beneath the darkly lit heavens, she rode wild, free, and with complete abandon, almost like the animal she clutched between her legs. Her hair acted as a cloak, covering her when she brought Gunpowder's explosive power to a stop, and her locks flew in liberation behind her when they started again. Cadence rode him hard until they both had enough; then she circled back for her clothes, dressed in his shadow, and headed slowly home. The experience left her beaming brighter than the moon above, and she knew if the Godiva story were a myth and the ride never happened that the lady had made a mistake in not galloping nude. All that time, she thought she had been alone—just her, Gunpowder, and the night, but now she realized someone had been watching in the shadows, had seen the daringly intimate scene.

"What? You mean you followed me?"

"No, Cadence, no. When I dropped you off, I was driving home, but I needed to clear my head, so I turned off on Corkscrew Road and parked my truck in the trees. I was listening to music, drinking a beer, when I saw someone in the pasture. I walked a little closer to see who it was when I realized it was you."

Cadence crossed her arms then flung them about. "So you just stood there in the dark like some weird creep, watching me. Tell me, Baxley, did you get off seeing me that night? What, did you take pictures or some sick video?" Her mind ran through the perverted possibilities.

"I wouldn't do that to you, Cadence. I could never hurt you."

"What exactly did you see?"

His eyes never wavered from her. "The most beautiful sight I've ever seen or could ever imagine." Silence enhanced the tension between them. "What I saw that night, well, it just confirmed a lot for me, about the way I feel about you," he said.

She shut her eyes tightly and shook her head. "What're you talking about?"

"Cadence, do you know why me and Shelby split up?" Picking up a rock, he fingered its jagged edges before launching it into the hollow. "Because I can't get you out of my mind. Because I have loved you my whole life. I would give anything, I would do anything to be with you."

His words buried her in emotions she didn't want to feel. She loved him, too, but as a sister does a brother. She couldn't hear any more because she already had someone, and she wanted more with him, not with a guy she considered part of her family's fabric. "I can't deal with this, Baxley."

"Cadence," he called as she walked away. "I'm sorry!"

Later in her journal, she wrote her thoughts on Baxley's admission, and now from the safe distance of school, she recalled the scene. Initially, she was mad because she was embarrassed, but as the days wore on, the situation was sadly uncomfortable because she didn't feel the same. The journal helped to distract her from the work already piling up after the first week, especially the reading for all her classes, including biology and Spanish.

Unlike the previous term, Cadence had biology two days a week, not three, but this time with a different instructor. The sequence class was in the same room as last term, so she found it easily and settled in a few minutes before class started. Two guys sat a few rows behind her and began a commentary on the assistants preparing for the class, especially a tall, attractive one in a pencil skirt and heels.

"Hey, check out that TA," one said, motioning to the brunette down at front.

The other whistled through his teeth. "Fucking hot. I feel an
F coming on—I may need some tutoring."

"Man, I squeaked by with a D last semester, so I'll be in her
office for sure. I got lost in all that breeding shit. Gametes and
stuff? I mean hell, where I come from it's just called 'fuckin.'
Apparently, I need to know that crap if I want to be a doctor."

"Well, I wouldn't worry too much about it. Your dad can
get you into med school, right?"

"Yeah. He'll make some calls, write some checks, but he's
told me it would be helpful if I had the grades."

They both laughed. Cadence didn't find them amusing at all
and was relieved Penny wasn't in the same class to hear these
two.

Penny's start to the semester had already proved rough, especially in her biology section, since a number of half-rubbers
were in the same class. They sat like a cancer cluster at the
back, infecting the room with whispers and attention directed
toward her. It was so distressing that Penny left halfway
through the hour and immediately switched into another section, but she couldn't escape the attacks.

A steady delivery of notes under the door continued, and the
more the police investigated, the worse her situation got. She
became convinced that every person she passed on campus
knew she was the victim and that they blamed her for blaming
the athletes. She swore the dirty looks, mumblings, and pointing were part of a larger conspiracy to destroy her. Sometimes,
she was right when she'd see any loyalists or any squad members on the sidewalk, between classes, in the dining hall. It

seemed no matter where she went, the stigma of what she knew was rape and what others saw as whoredom followed her.

When the biology class began, the brunette took to the lectern and introduced herself as Dr. Mangold, and just like a cycle of life, the one about covering the syllabus began. As a continuation course, Biology 112 carried the same format as the previous term, and Cadence was disappointed when she went to the lab and found that Alex's colleague, Ms. Nina Crown, would be the TA for the section. Alex was in the midst of research and would be assisting on occasion, Ms. Crown informed the class.

Cadence had biology lab following Spanish 102, which was surprisingly more interesting than the first dose of language the previous term. All were waiting for class to begin when a man wearing a straw fedora and carrying a radio shimmied into the room. Removing his hat revealed a balding head and the hair left was slicked with shine. In his light linen pants, dark short sleeve shirt, and black loafers, he looked like he had stepped off a plane from Panama. He turned on the music and began to dance a single-man chorus line before his amused audience.

When the number was done, he bowed to the applause and announced, "That, my friends, is a Cuban dance, but you may not recognize it. You may be more familiar with conga lines and the ChaCha. I performed original Mambo. No basic steps. Instead, it's about freedom of movement. You feel the music so that the sound and the moves fuse in the body. I bet some of you are saying, is this *Español* class?"

"Well, is it a Spanish class?" someone asked.

"*Sí*! It is! You see, language is a dance." He broke into another set of moves then stopped. "Open yourself to the rhythm

and you discover amazing things about other cultures and yourself. Sometimes, it has very special steps, and sometimes, you
just go with what you feel. Learning another language increases
your freedom!" Tapping and clapping, he said, "And when you
are freer in language, you will not be trapped by your tongue."

Professor Hernandez was not too bothered with the choreographed steps of giving them a syllabus and going over the
rules. Drawing from the rudimentary vocabulary of last semester, they introduced themselves in Spanish and told of their
likes and dislikes. Since he had just stepped from a plane and
driven from the airport after a trip to Cuba, he did not have a
syllabus ready. He bid them "*hasta luego*" and exited the room
with his radio livening up the hall with Cuban music.

Students around campus were stepping into routines again,
especially with reunions, which gave them that sense of settling
into their old lives in a new year. Jacinda seemed better after
the holidays, which she told Cadence were tough without her
brother. Madison and Malinda returned with deep tans
achieved by hours on Bahamian beaches courtesy of a private
jet trip with one of their sorority sisters. They weren't interested
in anyone else's vacations but only in bragging about their own.
Olivia had no new bags to boast about, as she had been ostracized by everyone for the spying incident with Ruthie. Her new
roommate, River, had no idea of the paid informant she was
now living with, and no one wanted to tell her. Enna, Myla, and
Althea were freshly back from protests and were energized for
new strategies of changing the world, or at least for altering the
immediate one as they saw it.

Isa returned with her world completely altered. Roano had
waited until just days before the start of classes to tell his sister
he was gay. He said he wanted one last pleasant holiday before

he came out. He would tell his parents by graduation in May, and he fully expected Isa to become an only child as they would disown him for bringing shame to their family. In telling this to her friend, Isa noticed Cadence did not have the reaction she expected.

"Wait a minute. You knew my brother was gay? How did you know?"

Cadence took a deep breath. "When we were at that party after the game. A guy. That one from Argentina. You all had gone to the keg. Anyway, he said Verena was your brother's beard."

"What? My brother's what?"

"'Beard.' I didn't know what it was, either. Apparently, it's someone who covers for a homosexual person."

Isa rubbed her temples. "So you knew Verena was a fake and that he was keeping this from me, and you didn't tell me? All this time I think my brother has this nice girlfriend, and over Christmas I find out he's been lying, and now, you tell me you knew?" Isa paced.

"Isa, I'm sorry. I didn't know what to believe, and I had just met your brother."

"Yes, but you had *not* just met me! Maybe if you would've told me, I could have been better prepared. I thought you were my friend."

"I am your friend, Isa," Cadence pleaded. "I, I just didn't know if I should say anything. I didn't know how to say it. I was so confused. I thought it was just better to keep quiet."

"Maybe it's better if I keep quiet now." Isa slammed the door, leaving Cadence in a silence she didn't want to hear. The situation, along with the already rising work of the term, left her in need of a good party by the week's end; luckily, she and her suitemates would find one.

For as oppressive as the humidity and heat are in the summer, Charleston's winters can be just as cruel. The same moisture that makes the air so unbearably hot also makes it insufferably cold. The chill penetrates layers and settles deep in the bones. This was the type of weather that inspired the Bitchin' Bitter Cold Beach Party. Holding true to the tradition of every semester beginning with one party that goes down in school lore as epic, this one did not disappoint.

The party was thrown by friends of Blaze, so Reena told Cadence about it, and she brought the suite, including her new roommate. It would be the first time Penny ventured out since the incident, and Saida and Cadence hoped it would help her assume some sense of normalcy, albeit in the abnormal environment of a backyard made into a beach. It was a large lot and for months, a huge pile of sand sat in the corner, a project the owner intended to get around to. He never did, so being crafty, the guys decided on a beach bash, despite the forty degree weather.

With the sand spread, Tiki torches staked, and a roaring bonfire, the guys had converted the drab backyard into a makeshift shore. They even sprung for a used, inflatable hot tub. A kiddie pool was filled with rum punch, beach balls floated about, and leis added color to every neck. Ladies were encouraged to wear bikini tops beneath flannel shirts, and the usual fashion faux pas of flip flops with socks was permitted, but most opted to place their toes in the beige fluff of those ever-present tan suede boots. Some guys even came in wetsuits, with surfboards in tow, conveniently used as pick-up accessories.

Although Reena had invited them, she clung to Blaze most of the time, so Cadence didn't speak with her much. When the couple did make their rounds, Cadence realized just how quiet he was, but she couldn't determine if he was shy, brooding, or calculating something behind those dark eyes. She did see that in those times when Reena wasn't by his side, his eyes were always on her—gazing, wanting, needing—but something about his stare was unsettling. His look was one of mystery, of something no one else was to know.

Helena drank everything she could get her hands on, flirted shamelessly, and basically, had an all-around good time. Saida chatted with a few guys, zeroing in on one who attended The Citadel. Penny stood quietly, barely sipping the beer she clutched and looking as if she may never enjoy herself again. Cadence's thoughts were of Schilar. He hadn't returned to school because the band had not coordinated returning to class with their touring schedule, but he promised they'd arrive soon.

Around midnight, the rum pool was empty, the kegs were nearly tapped, and the party was in full crank. A conga line began that lasted for nearly an hour, with people jumping on and off in a continuous stream of drunken kicks and missteps. Helena hung on for most of the time and danced like an escaped prisoner who, upon having the first taste of freedom, swallows every ounce of living within reach. In this case, two guys were within her reach: one in front and another in back, whose gyrating cock met Helena's backside every chance he got. Penny averted her eyes while Cadence watched carefully.

And then, someone suggested the "conga strip," and articles of clothing began to drop with every pass around the premises. By the time Cadence got to her roommate, Helena was pulling at the strings of her bikini top. It didn't help that the crowd lustfully cheered her on. Parties last semester had taught the friends to recognize when it was time to go. Just as they were about to leave, the line got really crazy when some fool on the end kicked his leg so dramatically it felled a Tiki torch right into the inflatable hot tub. The side melted instantly, and the ocean that had been missing from the party all night suddenly arrived. Two hundred gallons spilled over the yard, knocking some people to the ground, sweeping towels and cups to the fence, and extinguishing the bonfire.

Even though the flames had gone out, there was still ample fire in the air, especially toward the guy who caused the disaster. Luxuries like hot tubs are hard to come by in college, even if they are inflatable, and the party throwers were not amused.

To make it worse, the drunken dancer said, "Dudes, relax! It's just a rubber tub. Hell, it's not like y'all were gonna get any pussy in that thing."

The "bash" began to take on new meaning when Mark, one of the hosts, tackled him full on in the soggy sand. It could have gotten grittier, but Blaze and a few others pulled Mark off the guy, and the party came to an official end.

Soaked feet made the walk home unbearably cold, and Helena was worse because her shirt had ended up in the fire, so she staggered in a bikini top, slurring away about how rad the party was. Cadence wondered if Helena thought it was still rad when her head was hanging over the toilet not too long after getting back to the room. In the same manner as it had been done for her what seemed like ages ago, Cadence held Helena's hair as the newcomer learned to worship, probably for the first time in her life, a very different kind of deity.

Cadence was not used to the room's morning quiet since Corrine's mouth was always an alarm. It was near noon when the roommates awoke, and since Helena remembered only snippets, Cadence filled her in on what she missed, especially her pseudo-tryout as a stripper. Helena seemed more emboldened than mortified at her near nakedness and giggled in "oh-my-God" denials.

For most of that day, Cadence occupied herself with the new onslaught of assignments. It was an earnest distraction from counting down the minutes to Schilar's arrival. When she finally saw him, she didn't want to let go when he hugged her, and in all actuality, she didn't, preferring to cling to him throughout the night. Alone in his room, with the cold blowing against the window, they shared the shelter of his single bed.

As romantic reggae crooned across the room, Schilar began to gain a rhythm with Cadence he had desired for some months. Kissing her produced the effect it always had, and he grew harder the more he touched her, until working his fingers into familiar places, he asked in that innocent way if she wanted to. Her answer was breathless, so he offered up that thin layer of protection, which gave them some illusion of safety as he rolled it on. Sliding into her created those moments of pleasurable friction when she felt the weight of all of him on top and inside of her. The experience was sweet and gentle, like the way the best love songs promised, and when it was over, she lay next to him curled in the pleasure of this milestone between them. Over the hours, he woke her several times, so they enjoyed each other until the morning when she kissed him goodbye and left for class.

The euphoria of their time together fueled her thoughts with more desire for him. For that week, she wore the unmistakable smile that marked the definitive change in their relationship. It was an emotional high that was amplified when Cadence checked her mailbox and discovered a letter from home.

Few of life's pleasures match the simple thrill of a handwritten letter, particularly when the receiver, far from home and wrapped in solitude, yearns for connection. Every sense seems magnified: from the time the envelope is viewed to the feel of pulling it out of its shadowy chamber to the smell of the paper and the ink loops lolloping on the page—the resplendent experience is often one of life's purest pleasures. Letters are mementos clasped in the hand and in the heart, but on this occasion, the missive Cadence held did not produce these euphoric effects.

Dear Cadence,

I'm not good at writing so I'll make this short. I still feel the pain of watching you walk away after what I told you. It always hurts to see you leave and deep down, I have wished so many times that you'd come home. But that's selfish of me, I know. You deserve better and I want you to have that. I just wish you could have it with me. I hope what I told you won't change things between us because I can't lose you. For what it's worth, I am here and I will wait for you. All you have to do is tell me.

Love, Baxley

Although the page remained mostly blank, he had opened his heart to her in these few words, but she had already closed her mind to a future with him. She wanted more than Baxley could provide, not in material terms, but something beyond him, even if she hadn't fully discovered what it was. But there was more. In this unfolding drama of unrequited love, she was playing the part of the unwilling villain. Giving her heart to someone else meant taking it away from a person who had always held a special place in hers. In freeing his feelings, Baxley had changed everything between them so that now Cadence felt trapped by the affection, and dread surfaced when she thought of him wrapped in his loneliness, waiting for her. He did not know how the world's stage was changing, transforming, expanding for her, so that now, she felt happiness was not to be found necessarily at home, but in the many places and players that awaited miles beyond it.

Chapter 12

Psychology 310
Perception and Behavior

Scars measure life's tragedies and triumphs. As reminders seared so solidly in the flesh, they provide instant portals to that moment of yielding. Some are visible, many fade, but the tattooed lashes of trauma are mementos of times when the body battled a foreign force and survived. Although this is true of human skin, it is not always the case with the landscape's scars. With their scraped and dented trunks, trees carry roadside crosses signifying life's departure sites and the cruelty of random selection. Even long after loved ones are laid to rest, the lines of collision remain as tangible evidence of power abruptly halted. At times, nature collides with itself, so that rocks, hills, grass, and bark bear the burned blemishes, impacts, and indelible impressions of her fierce temper. Even one of the oak trees on the Grand Lawn proudly bore the erratic groove signifying an explosive instance that left its creamy interior exposed.

Cadence had never noticed the gaping wound or the small ferns hanging like long green beards from the tree's limbs.

"We've been tryin' to save it," a raspy voice said.

"Lightning strike?" Cadence knew it was since the crevice was the unmistakable cousin of so many she had seen on the farm's trees. Standing high on the hills alone, those wooden wonders that raise their knotted fists in competition with the sky are the favorite targets for the angry heavens.

"Uh-huh. Happened right before last semester started." The woman took a long drag from the cigarette poised perfectly between her calloused fingers. "I'm Tap, the grounds supervisor. You with the paper?"

"Yes ma'am. I'm Cadence."

"I've seen you 'round taking pictures. I usually enjoy seeing your work, but this week's was rough."

"It was." Cadence bowed her head slightly. "So Tap, you know a lot about trees and plants?"

"I know my share."

"What are the green ones growing on the bark? I've never noticed them before."

Tap gazed at the specimens under her care and smiled as a mother would on her adoring children. "Those are resurrection ferns. You probably didn't notice them before 'cause when it's hot and dry, they turn gray, curl up, seem dead. But when it rains, ohhhhh, they rise from the dead and look like they do now—lush and green, even in winter." She trained in lovingly on the little wonders. "Some say they can stay dead for a hundred years and magically come back to life with a little water. They're my favorite." Glancing over to the workers who were arranging tables and chairs around the reflection pool, she asked, "You covering this thing tonight?"

"Yes ma'am." Cadence looked at the set-up on the Grand Lawn and back at the split tree. "It's all really depressing."

Tap's eyes lingered on the scar. "Yep. It sure is," she said, before returning to work.

Cadence watched Tap, whose ruggedly feminine looks contrasted her mostly male crew, moving through the lawn and checking the preparations for the event. The gathering marked the end of a hectic week that began with a ridiculously early call from TJ demanding that Cadence get over to the religious studies offices. Because he lived off campus, he would meet her there, but she needed to hurry; this was urgent.

The morning light had just begun to warm the peninsula when Cadence set out for the destination. Rounding the corner, she saw a police car and a campus security bicycle parked outside of the office building, one she knew from the steamy scene she had seen a few months back.

She didn't see much to photograph, so she nonchalantly walked by, but when she looked up, the sight of the man hanging from the third floor piazza jolted her into stillness. Instinctually, she recorded him with clicks. His face was bluish and swollen, the tongue protruded from his mouth and his eyes bulged from the pressure. He was dressed in a black suit and crimson tie, but his feet were bare and his toenails thick and overgrown. The single strap of his bag was slung diagonally across his chest, but when the body turned, Cadence stopped shooting. Attached to the strap wasn't a bag but a military-style weapon like the kind carried by soldiers. A cream-colored piece of paper with black writing was stuck to the gun. Cadence zoomed in on the note which read: *Consider Yourselves Lucky.*

"Hey! Have some respect. Put that camera away!" A voice yelled down.

Before she could respond, a police officer grabbed her elbow and escorted her away from the house. As soon as he did, the first responders showed up and quickly covered the porch's end with a sheet.

"Ca-dence!" TJ yelled between breaths as he ran to her side. "Is this, is this, what I think it is?"

Still staring at the ghostly barrier, she quietly said, "It's a suicide."

"Did, did you get some shhh—ots?" He bent over, struggling to breathe.

Without looking at him, she pulled up the shot, advancing slowly through the stills until she reached the one with the message.

"Holy shit!" His eyes shot up to the sheet.

"TJ, how'd you know about this?"

"Police scanner. Any idea who it is?"

"Not a clue."

The campus was abuzz with the news, and everywhere, speculation erupted as to the deceased's identity and to what drove him to commit suicide in such a public fashion. Most thought the victim was from the religion department, considering the location of his death, but later in the day, the lifeless form that swung from the porch was revealed to be psychology professor Jonathan Savage. No one knew why he chose the religious studies offices as the place to kill himself.

When Cadence walked into biology lab, she was surprised to see Alex directing students to the task at hand: measuring photosynthesis and cellular respiration in plant species. Dr. Mangold had already lectured on the subject, and in delivering the explanation, she did so with complete admiration for the power of spruces and spores, mosses and maples. Since all modern plants descended from algae, she spoke of it as if it were slimy, green gold, and pointed out the phenomenal resiliency of plants, especially their ability to adapt.

"They're not necessarily transient," she said. "Where they are rooted is where many must stay, so they learn to use the environment to their maximum benefit. They adapt, evolve, and change, often while remaining stationary. Perhaps they are the ultimate examples of Darwinism. But despite their tremendous abilities to adapt, plant species are disappearing, so efforts are underway to house them within the earth's frozen belly, thousands of miles from here."

Deep in the recesses of a frozen Arctic mountain on the Norwegian island of Spitsbergen lies the Svalbard Global Seed Vault also known as the Doomsday Vault. Dr. Mangold explained the maximum security, temperature-controlled facility near the North Pole is being stocked with seeds and sprouts in an effort to preserve and protect the world's plant life in the event of a world-wide catastrophe. Capable of withstanding bomb blasts and earthquakes, the vault extends 500 feet beneath the permafrost, with no one person holding all the codes for entering. Not top-secret, but certainly designed to resist forces that may try to destroy its genetic treasures.

In describing photosynthesis, the professor made it sound so exotically powerful: sunlight drops through the spheres after hurtling through space, and green leaves rise to catch it. In taking the sun's gift through their spindly stems, plants direct a phenomenal chemical transaction by using the light's energy and carbon dioxide to create molecules, sugars, and starches they need to survive. The "waste" product is oxygen, so the magic of plants allows humans and animals to breathe. She wrote the equation on the board:

$$6CO_2 + 6H_2O + Energy \rightarrow C_6H_{12}O_6 + 6O_2$$

"Try living without the waste product," she said. "And just to be clear, we all come from plants. Our cells were created from the nutrients our mothers ate—fruits, vegetables, or meats from animals that fed from grains or plants. We all go back to the soil." The simple point was one Cadence would carry with her into lab and beyond.

When she had completed her plant assignment, Cadence approached Alex who was busy preparing lab materials. "I didn't think I would see you this semester."

"I was surprised myself, Cadence. My department head gave me the labs just a few hours ago, after everything," Alex said solemnly to her student's surprised look. "The professor who committed suicide this morning," Alex glanced around, "was Nina's husband."

"No." Cadence's hand covered her mouth. "I, I didn't make the connection."

"Well, they have different last names. Anyway, she's understandably a wreck. I'm taking the lab classes for the semester's remainder."

"Does anyone know why he did it?"

Alex kept her voice low. "There are rumors about tenure. He didn't get it. That may be the reason." She shook her head. "At this point, no one knows for sure. It's just really sad."

"Has anyone said anything about the gun and the note?"

Alex's expression changed instantly. She put down the equipment. "What gun and what note?"

Cadence stood silently, as if she hadn't heard the question.

"Cadence—what gun and what note?"

After telling Alex what she saw and knew about the scene, Cadence headed to *The Gator's* office where TJ was holding an emergency meeting about the developing story. A source told him that in the professor's office authorities found a 9mm Glock, more rounds of ammunition, and his wedding ring stacked on top of his tenure materials. The note that was hanging on the body had been written on the back of the official letter denying him tenure.

"It appears this incident is being hushed. Here's what I want," TJ began. "I want colleagues, students, former students, and friends interviewed. I want to know more about the tenure process and what it does to professors—what's at stake? I want numbers on professor suicides. How often does this happen? Dr. Savage's specialty was self-harm and post-traumatic stress disorder, so why would he commit suicide?"

TJ passed a photo of the teacher taken from the faculty directory. His was a handsome face, barely resembling the one Cadence had seen on the porch only hours before. Prior to that, she did not recognize the man.

"Are the authorities sure it's suicide?" Degue asked. "This isn't some situation where it's a murder made to look like a suicide, is it?"

Melissa snickered. "Seriously? This is pretty obvious. Other than in the movies when does that *actually* happen?"

Degue ground his teeth and tightened his grip on the pen. "It happens."

"Humph!" She smirked and tossed her preened head about.

"Okay, you two. The official report has not been released. From what my source tells me, the preliminary investigation points to suicide, so there's no evidence of homicide—yet. I guess we'll see."

TJ directed assignments to different reporters before telling Cadence: "We're going to run one of the photos you took this morning. I need you to go with Degue when he interviews this professor's friends. Get shots of people remembering this guy and anything else that'll work."

Before he dismissed them with a midnight deadline, TJ insisted on another angle: "And somebody find out why he chose to hang himself at the religious studies offices rather than in his department. Was he trying to get closer to God or make some faith statement?"

Cadence was certain she knew why Professor Savage chose that building. She doubted it had anything to do with God but felt it had everything to do with what she had seen that November night in Dr. Heath's office.

With a ton of work to do, including accompanying Degue to some interviews, Cadence had to squeeze in some reading for theatre. As if the traumatic stories of the present weren't enough, those from the past were just as gruesome, especially in Shakespeare's *Titus Andronicus*.

This disturbing mirror of misery tells of Titus, a Roman general who mercilessly kills the son of his enemy, Tamora. In return for his cruelty, his precious daughter, Lavinia is raped by Tamora's two sons, who sever her hands and cut out her tongue. In a heart-wrenchingly pitiful scene, Lavinia, holding a stick in her mouth and working it between her stumps, writes the names of her attackers in the dirt. Deranged by rage, Titus murders the rapists, bakes them into a meat pie, and serves the fleshy meal to their mother. Because Lavinia is dishonored, Titus kills her, and exacts more revenge by slaying Tamora. Ultimately, the stage is a platform of absolute slaughter with Titus joining the death toll.

When she finished, Cadence put down the book and sat helplessly while her skin crawled against the cloak of carnage in which Shakespeare so effectively wraps his audiences. She pondered the mayhem of massacre as her thoughts moved to

Penny, whose tongue, while not physically removed, had certainly been silenced. Perhaps the counseling sessions would give Cadence a better idea of how to help her friend regain her voice. Although a meat pie mutilation was extreme revenge, if justice proved elusive in her friend's case, she couldn't help but think of the deviant delights Penny's avengers would get from payback of the Titus kind.

After her time in the library, Cadence met Degue outside the psychology offices. Not many of Dr. Savage's colleagues would talk to the paper, but Degue managed to find a tenured untouchable who opened up about the perils of being a professor.

Degue got straight to business. "Dr. Sedinn, why would a man dedicated to studying why people harm themselves commit the ultimate harm on himself?"

Leaning back in his chair, the professor touched the tips of his fingers together. "Many say they enter the field to help others, but a large number embark on the study in hopes of solving their own disorders. Their education becomes a means to self-diagnosis, self-medication. But sometimes, I think people expand their issues by absorbing more of the conditions they're studying. For instance, a troubled person can pile being bipolar onto ADHD and add sides of anxiety and manic to the personality issues."

"So like a psychochondria?"

"Ah, similar to hypochondria? Psychochondria? I like that. I like that very much," he said. "In terms of what has to happen for a person to go through with suicide, two factors have to align: a fearlessness of death that defeats the physical pain killing oneself entails and the perception that one's a burden, hopelessly isolated from others. If these perceptions fully develop, then the behavior that results can be highly destructive."

"Was he isolated from others?"

"It didn't seem so, but isolation doesn't have to be physical."

"Did he have marriage problems?"

"I don't know nor would I tell you if I was privy to that information."

Degue gave the professor a stony look. "Okay. Can you tell me why Dr. Savage was denied tenure?"

"I wasn't on his committee, so I cannot tell you the specifics; however, failure to publish, poor teaching evaluations, lack of community service. These are standard reasons for being denied tenure. But those are the obvious ones."

"So what are the not-so-obvious reasons?" Degue asked.

Professor Sedinn leaned over the desk. "Your colleagues simply don't like you. Or your research creates rivalry. Perhaps you outshined someone or you're reaching superstar status in your field. Maybe your politics, race, gender, religion, sexual orientation, even personal projects or your personal life clashes with theirs."

Degue and Cadence glanced at each other.

"What? Why the surprise? You two think professors are beyond this pettiness? Hardly. They perfect it. Don't think for a moment they left their cliques or cruelties behind in high school." He shook his head with a tsk-tsk-tsk. "Nooooo, in higher education, they're enhanced with bolder egos, bigger degrees, and better vocabularies."

Degue scribbled furiously. "So even if a person fulfills the standards, makes a name in a field, tenure can be denied?"

"Oh yes. Understand, you work, teach, eat, play, and sometimes sleep with these people. You share birthdays, weddings, funerals, and graduations. They will smile in your face and pat you on the back, but behind closed doors, they play like damned villains." He stood to straighten the framed degree displayed on his wall and peered over his spectacles at them.

"If someone has it out for you, that person will lobby hard to destroy any chance you have at a future. The effort may deliver the most destructive F of your academic existence. Many people will never know why they are denied. There's little transparency in the decisions, and for those who don't achieve tenure, it remains an enduring mystery. Make no mistake—within academic departments here or in any college for that matter—you're bound to find the ultimate quivers."

Degue's pen stopped dead on the paper. "Quivers?"

Professor Sedinn's eyes narrowed. "Groups of cobras—the kings of all serpents. Ultimately, you've got to be one hell of a snake charmer to get tenure. Blow on the wind instrument, move it around seductively, stroke the velvet hoods of the venomous ones in just the right ways." The way he drew out the words sounded as if he were hissing. "And if you can't make it past the snakes, you don't get to the Holy Grail of tenure."

"Can I quote you on that?"

He grinned. "I would prefer you didn't. I still have to teach in this nest, but you can quote me on the rest."

Although he could tell them no specifics about Professor Savage, Dr. Sedinn provided some very insightful perceptions on the dark side of academia. In walking back to the newspaper office, Cadence ventured upon a question that had been on her mind since the staff meeting.

"Degue, when you asked earlier about the suicide being a murder—"

"Yeah?"

She paused at his abruptness. "You said, 'it happens.' What did you mean?"

He stopped. "Look, I'm a reporter, so I'm supposed to be skeptical."

"You just seem pretty passionate about it."

Studying her in earnest, he said, "Personally, and for a lot of black people, hangings are always suspect. Let's just say it's in our history. Every now and then a case will surface of a black man, usually fairly young, who has apparently committed suicide, but if you look a bit closer, it's a lynching disguised to look like suicide." His eyes focused on the dark canopy above them. "Where you from anyway?"

"A small town upstate."

"Born and raised?"

"Yep."

"Your people ever tell you about the hangman trees there? You know, the South, especially this state, is littered with trees that bore the strange fruit of human flesh."

She shook her head. "'Strange fruit?'" She thought he sounded like a poet.

"From a song by Billie Holiday. Actually, it was a poem first then she recorded it. Anyway, I grew up in this area hearing about the trees haunted by spirits of black folks who were murdered on those limbs. You know that beloved Angel Oak out on John's Island?"

"Yeah, I was there not too long ago."

"It's said to be haunted by the souls of slaves and others who hung from its branches. The Gullah people believe the spirits are angels. That there's magic in trees because of the lives lost on them."

Cadence pictured the famous tree with its meandering branches, some the size of tree trunks themselves. For Dr. Elders's wonders project, she had included a shot of it and was struck not only by the enormity of the tree but by the eeriness of the cool, shaded grove where it lived like a creature with infinite arms. While she and Schilar were there, they learned the tree is between 500-1400 years old and provides shade that covers over 17,000 square feet. It's a historian in its own right, but nowhere on the information plaques were lynchings mentioned. Turns out, this majestic tree of life is also one of death.

"My point in questioning Professor Savage's supposed suicide is that things are often much more than we perceive them to be. I try not to believe all of what I'm told. Like, I bet there's a reason why he chose that porch. It doesn't appear random to me. He seems to have calculated everything else."

"Um, I think I may have the answer to that." She told Degue what she saw that night and the possible connections between the deceased professor, his wife, and her lover.

"Hmm, that may explain a lot. Maybe the 'yourselves' in the note refers to the wife and lover and wasn't intended for anyone else. I'll see what I can find out."

At the day's close, Cadence was utterly shattered and couldn't wait to wrap herself in Schilar's arms, which she did, and promptly fell asleep while trying to study for her communications quiz. She had read up on all the current events, even as she was in the midst of reporting on them. In her exhaustion, she set her alarm incorrectly, and so, when Schilar summoned her from sleep the next morning, the therapy session she was supposed to attend for Penny was over.

Cadence rushed to the counseling center, only to learn that she had missed them all. Later, she went to her suitemates' room and saw Saida who was getting ready for class.

"Nice *not* going this morning, Cadence."

"I'm so sorry. I had a hell of a day yesterday. I stayed at Schilar's and my alarm didn't go off."

"That's your excuse? Penny really needed you, and you slept in with your boyfriend? Whatever." Saida threw her brush on the desk and popped off the cap of her lipstick.

"I feel terrible. Can you please fill me in on what I missed?"

"No, I can't. It was a private session." She smacked her lips to even the color. "If you wanted to know, you needed to be there."

"Saida, what's your problem? I said I was sorry."

"My problem is that I sat through a therapy session where all kinds of shit gets unloaded. It's exhausting. And it's draining to see my roommate go through her own personal hell. So please, spare me the hell of your yesterday," Saida said. "Oh, and because you missed today, the psychologist says you can't attend the other sessions." She slammed the door on her way to class.

Minutes later, Cadence was settling into her seat in Dr. Tiller's class when Dakota sat next to her.

"Hey, are you paparazzi or what?"

She looked down at the camera on her desk. "Not quite," she muttered quietly, her eyes drifting over his copy of *The Gator*.

"Good morning, class," the professor began. "After your quiz, we're going to stray from our regular routine and begin with a more localized topic. But first, please answer the questions being passed to you."

Panic swept over Cadence as she didn't feel especially caught up on any other news except for the teacher's death. Like many quizzes last semester, she was prepared to fail until she saw that most of the questions were about the suicide. When students had unsuccessfully completed it, Professor Tiller said, "I want you to consider the ethical questions surrounding the front page feature story of this morning's school newspaper. That would be *The Gator* for those of you unfamiliar with the publication."

He clicked the screen at the front to life and there, magnified hundreds of times, was Cadence's photo. The hall's silence was as lifeless as Professor Savage's body with everyone absorbing the shock and the foreboding note, which had been blown up and featured as an inset in the larger picture. The photo credit listed "C. Cooper," as was the paper's style, and a multi-author article titled, "Professor's Suicide Shocks Campus: Ominous Death Note Left," accompanied the shot.

"So, what are your initial thoughts about this front page?"

An arm overloaded with silver bangles shot up immediately. Dr. Tiller couldn't help but acknowledge the jingles. "Yes, Miss—?"

"Hazard. I think it's sensationalistic and disgusting. It exploits this poor man to sell papers. Photographers and editors need more moral compasses." The squeaky voice seemed quite pleased with her answer.

"*The Gator*, Miss Hazard, is a free publication, partially paid for by your tuition." He searched for another hand. "Yes, you sir, in the back."

A guy with straggly hair and slow speech indicative of a hazed lifestyle said, "I think there are times when people taking pictures should put down their cameras and help out."

Cadence shifted in her seat while Dr. Tiller responded, "And what help could be rendered to an individual who is already dead, if indeed this is the case at the time this photo was taken?"

The future of the field contemplated his question. "If I am not mistaken, the photographer is sitting in our class. Where is Miss Cooper? Miss Cadence Cooper?"

Cadence sensed Dakota turning toward her, his brows arched in surprise. Her heart kicked at the wall of her chest, and slowly, Cadence lifted her hand as hundreds of eyes trained in on her.

"Ah, Miss Cooper, would you please tell us a little about the circumstances under which this photo was taken."

She gripped the edge of her desk top. "Um, my editor called me early and told me to go to the religious studies department. To the offices. When I showed up, I saw the professor on the porch. I snapped a few shots. The body swung around and that's when I got that photo." She briefly pointed to the screen.

Dr. Tiller glanced at the ghostly image behind him. "Okay, tell us more. Specifically, please address your colleagues' comments about the sensationalism and your apparent lack of a moral compass and compassion."

She felt as if she were suffocating. "I, I'm not sure about it being sensational. Um, I don't think I lack a moral compass." Lowering her head slightly, she continued, "I'm sorry to say the professor was already dead when I got there."

"Do you see any ethical problems with plastering a photo of a dead man across the front page?"

"Sir, I didn't choose the photo." Sweat began to slide down her back.

"That's convenient. You provided the photo, but you have no responsibility regarding its use?"

"Um, I wasn't trying to exploit anyone or be disrespectful." Her hands ached from gripping the desk. "My editor told me to get a photo. I did."

"Miss Cooper, the policy of most newspapers is not to report on suicides. Is this newsworthy or is this *The Gator's* attempt to exploit the tragic end of an educator so more of the people sitting around you will read the rag?"

Dr. Tiller was in weeding mode, and the more Cadence became visibly shaken by the confrontation, the more he swung his invisible scythe.

"Sir?" the voice beside her called out. All eyes shifted inches from Cadence. "The story is not necessarily about suicide. From the close-up of the note, this could have been a mass shooting. The note and the gun imply he was thinking of hurting more people than just himself, and for whatever reason, that didn't happen or hasn't happened. So it seems suicide may be the secondary story here."

The professor studied Dakota carefully. "Very keen observations, Mister—?"

"Shout."

"And I agree. Everyone look at the note." Professor Tiller zoomed in on the message. "It says, 'Consider yourselves lucky.' For whom is this message meant? Other professors? Students? The administration? Furthermore, were we prepared to handle the possibilities that this note suggests? Look at the gun, a semi-automatic rifle."

Some jotted down the ideas while others just gaped in blank comprehension. Dr. Tiller said, "All in all, it *is* newsworthy and brings awareness of the everyday dangers of living freely among people with mental disorders and access to weapons. I can assure you this story has sparked some discussion among faculty about safety as well as staff and student well-being." He leaned on the podium. "And frankly, while many of you were sleeping, Miss Cooper was on the scene getting news—good job. And for the record, I do not consider our student newspaper a rag. In fact, perhaps more of you should think about doing something to build your experience."

When their teacher moved on, Cadence released a faint, "Whew," and grinned at Dakota who reached over and squeezed her hand.

At the day's end, Cadence decided to close the distance with Isa. When Cadence walked into the language lab, Isa was not very happy to see her, but Cadence insisted she needed help on an assignment, so the tutor reluctantly found the two seats.

"How do you say 'I'm sorry' *en Español?*" Cadence asked.

"*Lo siento.*"

"Okay, *lo siento.*"

To Cadence's relief, Isa said, "*Lo siento tambien,*" but explained that clients were coming in for appointments. She wanted to talk, so they planned to meet for coffee at c.a.t.'s on Friday.

Later, Cadence was in the newspaper office when Melissa came stomping through gripping a stack of papers. Moving so fast she could barely maintain balance in her heels, Melissa stopped abruptly at Degue's desk.

"What the hell is this?" She rattled the offending documents in his face. "I don't need your shit."

"Shit?" He laughed. "Is that what you call news? I only provided you with some documentation refuting the fact that some murders are made to look like suicides. I thought you would appreciate being informed. Oh yeah, I forgot—you usually write about fashion. You can't be bothered with any hard headlines. Would you like to review what the dead were wearing?"

"Fuck you!" She launched the papers toward the ceiling, where they twisted about in tornadic fashion.

"I don't think so. Didn't you read those? Really wouldn't be a good idea."

"I don't need educating from you!"

"You need it from someone. You're about as blind as they come!"

"Blind to what?" Melissa asked.

"Realities. Your pie-in-the-sky, rosy-colored fantasy world is not real. Melissa, somewhere out there is a himbo looking for his missing bimbo."

"You're an asshole!"

"I guess to you I would be, but tell me something I don't know."

"All right, you two. That's enough!" TJ said, stepping between them. "We've got a lot of work to do. Melissa, why don't you take a seat in my office. Degue— "

"I'm going to get some fresh air," he said, grabbing his coat and making for the door.

When the office storm had settled, Cadence picked up the papers, which she saw were articles with the headlines: "A Suicide or Lynching—Answers Sought in Florida"; "'Not a Suicide': Black Man Lynched by Racists"; "Mississippi Hanging Investigation: Suicide or Lynching?"; "Suicide or Lynching? Death of Young Black Man Puzzles San Francisco Suburbs." There was even a copy of a book cover, *Imagery of Lynching: Black Men, White Women, and the Mob*, which featured the skeletal silhouette of a spooky tree, with shoes of all shapes and styles dangling from its deathly boughs. He had included the first chapter, too. Rather than trash the pages lost on Melissa, Cadence took them to read herself.

After returning from a late evening catch-up session in the library, Cadence fell face first on her bed. As Helena made small talk, Cadence was drifting off when Saida walked in with what had now become the most famous copy of *The Gator* ever printed. Cadence rolled on her side to make room, and Saida sat down.

"This was your day yesterday?" Saida held up the paper.

Cadence's eyes fell yet again on the lifeless image. "Mhmm."

"Your morning started with seeing this poor man? I'm sorry," Saida said to Cadence's nod. "Did you know Diana had him last semester? She said he was a great teacher, but that after fall break, he changed, started to lose it. I remember her saying something like the class thought he was walking the fine line between sanity and insanity." She looked down at the pitiful figure. "It's terrible you had to see that."

"Oh my God, Cadence, I had no idea," Helena added. "I've been so crazy with classes and stuff."

Saida looked vacantly at Helena then back to Cadence. "I'll talk to you later about what you missed this morning, and I'll keep you updated."

"I feel horrible about missing it."

"Don't worry. Get some rest. You look like shit." Saida smiled and rubbed Cadence's shoulder.

"Thanks," Cadence said, as Saida flicked off the lights on her way out.

When Dr. Tiller's assistants handed back the week's quizzes on Friday, a collective groan arose from most in the auditorium except for Cadence and Dakota, who were both up to date on current events. One guy made the mistake of verbalizing his displeasure a little too loudly, so his "This is bullshit!" was promptly addressed.

"What exactly do you find a steaming heap of bull dung, Mister—?"

"Havacheck. The name's Havacheck. This is frustrating! I mean, I'm paying good money to get Fs on these quizzes?"

Dr. Tiller stepped out from behind the podium. "Ah, I see. Your model of education is akin to the customer service one, yes?" He did not give the student time to respond. "You believe that you—or most likely, your parents—are paying for your professors to deliver a product, and you expect complete satisfaction for your purchase. Am I correct?"

"Yeah, that's how I see it."

"Allow me to realign your perception," Dr. Tiller said. "Here's how *I* see it: this class is more akin to an employer and employee analogy. I am your employer and you work for me. You show up to this job, i.e. this course, and you create products: papers, presentations, exam results, and the like that demonstrate and build your knowledge and experience. What's your paycheck? Your grades. Do poorly and I cut your pay, or you are eventually fired with—an F. Hopefully, you'll be promoted to the next class and ultimately, retire from this institution into your next life."

Some in the class smiled at the parallels, but the student whose outburst sparked the tangent did not. "I don't think I like that," he said.

"It doesn't matter if you like it or not; that's the way it is. I expect you to arrive punctually, prepared, and ready to deliver excellent work to this *job*. In the professional world, if you want to keep employment, that's what you're expected to do, but if you think you're ready for the job market, you don't need to be wasting your time with these quizzes so there's the door." Although he pointed to the steeled ones in the back, no one moved.

After she did step through those doors, Cadence dropped by the newspaper office where Degue was continuing to work on follow-up stories to the professor's death. No one else was around, so they could discuss the affair topic openly. Degue told Cadence he had not been able to confirm the adultery of Dr. Savage's wife or that it was the religious professor, Dr. Heath, who was her supposed lover. In fact, Dr. Heath had been on sabbatical last semester in Egypt, so he wasn't in the country.

"I'm not sure who you saw that night, Cadence, but it doesn't sound like it was Dr. Heath," Degue said. "I'll keep checking it out. See if we can figure out who it is."

"Okay," Cadence said. "Hey, do you want these back?" She pulled out the articles he had intended for Melissa.

"Are you mocking me?"

"Degue, no. I read them. I had no idea." She placed the stack on the corner of his desk. "I'm curious, why the animosity with Melissa?"

"I got no time for people like her—spoiled white girls who have no clue or can't see past their shopping to recognize the realities of other people's lives. It pisses me off when some privileged one like Melissa doesn't know what she's talking about and says, 'like that ever happens.'" Curling his lip, he imitated her sassy tone.

"Do you blame her for being privileged? I mean, would it have been better if she had some terrible upbringing?"

"No. I can't fault her for fortunate circumstances, but I can blame her for keeping her sheltered view because she hasn't bothered to consider that others haven't had the same."

"What do you know about her?"

"Only what I see and hear, why? Is there something I should know?"

"I don't know. Just thought I'd ask."

With the week over, Cadence met Isa at c.a.t.'s for a much needed talk. They spoke softly, easing back into their friendship. In realizing she was directing her shock and confusion onto Cadence, Isa apologized for the attack, and equally, Cadence offered her apologies for her silence. Isa and Roano had a lot to discuss. She just wished he would have been honest with her from the beginning. At times, she had thought he might be gay but dismissed her suspicions when women like Verena came along. Just as she had loved her brother all her life, she would continue to love him. Her greatest concern was that her family would not accept the truth and would disown him, choosing instead the stasis of their Catholic tradition over the dynamism of his life. As she spoke, tears slid down Isa's face into her cup. In reaching for Isa's hand, Cadence offered assurance that she'd be there in the time to come and that she was here now, sharing coffee and conversation, fears and tears.

It had truly been one of those weeks when everyone needed to get crazy just for the sake of staying sane, so when Helena held up a flier for a Psytrance Dance and asked if Cadence was in, there really was only one answer. Cadence recruited Saida and Diana as well, but Penny had no interest and made plans to see a movie with Jade.

Helena was the last to get ready, and when she walked out of the bathroom, she already looked like she had been to a rave and stolen the colors from the lights.

"Call me 'Amethyst.'" She laughed and primped her purple hair.

"I'm going to call you 'Rainbow Bright.'" Saida joked and handed her an equally colorful cocktail, which began helping them get in the raving mood.

They strutted over to a warehouse where psychedelic music and strobe lights streaked from wall to wall, floor to ceiling. DJ Head Doctor pumped sound prescriptions like he was a pharmacist. The crowd sucked in the cures from the vibes he spun and from the iridescent beams streaking across the room. On that flashing floor, they let go and danced with the type of unrestrained power that starts revolutions and fuels rebellions. Showered in their own sweat and bathed in that of others, they swapped moves and looks, jumps and smiles, and stomped their feet and raised their fists until every toxin of trauma had been expelled and they nearly collapsed from it all.

But they were not done—the chill of the early morning air smacked them like an elixir when the group shimmied through the parking lot up onto a retaining wall several feet high. No one recalls whose idea it was to imitate the synchronized high kicks of the Rockettes, but they did, and for a few seconds it was going well, until someone lost her balance and sent everyone tumbling over the wall, down an embankment covered with gravel and broken glass. Somehow, Helena and Diana were unscathed, but Saida and Cadence staggered up with ripped jeans and bleeding knees and elbows that would turn the color of Helena's hair. Their painful howls were broken with fits of laughter. Drenched in the aftermath of a purely good time, the four helped one another perform the hobble dance all the way home.

On Sunday evening, Cadence moved carefully through the candlelight glowing beneath the Grand Lawn's oak canopy. Because he had taught many introductory courses, Professor Savage's memorial service drew hundreds of students. They came because he was a good teacher, an educator who led his pupils through some of psychology's dizzying possibilities: abnormal, cognitive, forensic, physiological, behavioral. Despite being armed with the knowledge of the mind, he could not resist surrendering to an early death.

Cadence saw Nina near the front, dressed in obligatory black, her head bowed in prayer before a large portrait of her husband. A man held tightly to the widow's arm, but Cadence did not recognize him. She wondered about Nina's pain—about guilt, sorrow, fear—wondered if a bigger void existed now than the one that had prompted her to take a lover.

With each delicate step Cadence took around the gathering, her knees and elbows burned and ached from the rawness of the cuts scraping against her clothes. Her wounds would scab and scar and eventually fade, but they would always serve as reminders of a carefree night in college, one capping a week of sadness that began with a man so overcome by the emotional and mental scars no one could see that he left his own across the campus psyche. Stepping far back from the gathering into the corner, Cadence bent as far down to the earth as she could, and positioning her camera upwards, she froze the silhouettes of sadness in time's smallest fraction. As the mourners sent prayers and light heavenward by the glow of their candles, the souls of the trees stood as silent witnesses to yet another tragic occasion. In their magic, the wooded wonders captured the whisperings of pain and sorrow, just as they always have, and released the power of breath in remembrance of those no longer fortunate enough to enjoy this luxury.

Chapter 13

Dance 234
Communities in Dance

Feet together. Step back right foot. Kick back left foot. Step forward left foot to beginning stance. Kick forward right foot. Return to start. Repeat. Arms out, elbows bent, hands pointed up. Swing arms from elbows right then left. Combine feet and arm movements. Project emotion. Wide eyes. Big smile. Dance!

Fringes on their dresses flew while long strands of glistening pearls swung around the flappers dancing The Charleston. Cadence led her digital partner in a tango of timing and light, clicking away while Catissa shared one of her favorite pastimes with one of her favorite patrons. When she learned Cadence needed photographs of different dances, Catissa invited her to an exhibition. On the way to the show, she gave the brief history of the dance that originated during the early 1900s in a black community on an island near Charleston. By 1913, the dance was being staged in Harlem, and in 1923, the black comedic musical *Runnin' Wild* appeared on Broadway and featured the jazz tune "The Charleston" by James Johnson, who heard the beat from dockworkers. From there, the dance dominated the Roaring Twenties with flappers and patrons of speakeasies taking up the moves to mock those "dry" citizens who supported Prohibition.

Throughout the performance, the dancers demonstrated variations of The Charleston: contemporary, tap, solo 1920s, '20s Partner, '30s and '40s Partner. Each time, the performers moved as if they were back in the days of clandestine cocktails.

After hours of entertaining themselves and the enthusiastic crowd who praised the historical steps back, Catissa and the troupe cooled off with the pre-Prohibition favorite, the Sidecar.

"Well, young lady, did you enjoy the show and get the photos you needed? Catissa here says you've got a good eye," asked Olin, a life-long "native" in every sense.

"Oh, yes sir. The dancing was fantastic. I'll get Catissa some copies of the photos," Cadence said. Since Catissa had already given her the history lesson in dance, Cadence turned her attention to the setting. "So, this bar has a strange name. Why's it called 'The Blind Tiger'?"

The group looked to Olin who, like most original Charlestonians, learned history before knowing the basic alphabet and was ever eager to educate anyone on the subject of the city. He explained that during Prohibition when selling alcohol was illegal, establishments called *speakeasies* opened and sold booze illicitly. So named because of the hushed tones patrons would use so as not to alert police, these places were also called *blind pigs* or *blind tigers* because they'd advertise some unusual animal attraction so people would pay to see it, which of course wasn't there, but complimentary cocktails were.

"So Miss Cadence, the pub you're sitting in used to be one of the city's speakeasies," Olin said. "But I will say that even before federal Prohibition, Charlestonians frequented these parlors in defiance of the Dispensary Act. Now this law, well, it was the baby of an upstate, one-eyed teetotaler named Ben 'Pitchfork' Tillman, who unfortunately became governor of our fine state."

"And remind us, Olin, why he was one-eyed and carried a pitchfork," encouraged Sally, one of the dancers.

"'Cause one day after swimmin' in a mill pond, he contracted a bacteria. The doctors had to take his eye. The pitchfork is for his agrarian tendencies. He thought that the Holy City was a hotbed of filth and vice, so he decided to regulate alcohol. Only state-owned dispensaries could sell it. For us, it was one puritan step too close to Prohibition. That temperance mess didn't sit too well here. The night before the law went into effect, citizens hung an effigy of him right there on the corner of King and Calhoun, complete with a popped out eye and a whiskey bottle hung around his neck."

"Well, truth be told, Olin, Lady Charleston has always been a bit naughty." Catissa winked.

"Don't I know it, Cat, but cities are like the people who inhabit them—they all have dark sides." Olin grinned. "You see Cadence, for all our genteel manners and formal facades, we have a less-than-tame history. Charleston's been called 'the residence of the devil.' And indeed, she's had her fair share of demons, but as I always like to say, 'dancing with a little vice is much more fun than dancing with a lot of virtue.'" He tossed back the remainder of his drink and ordered another round.

"Oh, Olin, you would say that!"

"Well Sally, ain't it the truth!" he remarked. "Besides, some of my favorite stories of this town are about the wild and the wicked who walked these streets. Let's face it, they make for better storytelling."

"Do you have a favorite?" Cadence asked.

Leaning back, Olin thought for a moment before spinning the tale of one of the Holy City's most hellish bootleggers.

Frank "Rumpty Rattles" Hogan was deemed king of "Little Mexico," an area of blue-collar workers near the city dump where men made extra money selling moonshine to blind tigers and women turned tricks in upstairs rooms. Short-tempered and mean to the core, Rumpty ruled by his fists and the pistols he carried. He opened several blind tigers of his own: Knock Down and Drag Out, Bucket of Blood, and Robbers Inn, all names that seemed to reflect his taste for violence. He imported corn whiskey from the White brothers out of Hell Hole Swamp, but when they decided to raise the price of their $4 gallon liquor in 1927, Rumpty's former business partner Leon Dunlap and son-in-law, David Riggs, went along with the brothers to inform Rumpty of the cost increase. He was none too pleased at the news and threatened to beat the hell out of Dunlap and Riggs.

To counter the looming threat, the two took a proactive self-defense strategy. They purchased a shotgun and late one night waited behind an upstairs window on Market Street amid the revelry of flappers, sailors, prostitutes and college boys. Although Rumpty was married, he always kept a girlfriend, and on this night, he was picking up Myrtle Carter from her job as a waitress at Peking Chop Suey. It was near 1 a.m. on October 25, 1927, when Rumpty approached the restaurant's door. Shouts came down, followed by gunfire and Rumpty crumpled in the doorway.

"So, while the country was dancing to The Charleston in '26 and '27, Rumpty Rattles was swinging fists and slinging moonshine in blind tigers. Eventually, he danced with a devil named Dunlap a few nights before Halloween," Olin said. "And that jury found Rumpty's murderers 'not guilty' on Christmas Eve two months later."

"Olin, whereabouts on Market Street was this?" Catissa asked.

"You know where the Godiva Chocolate shop is? That's about where he was shot. In the 1920s, it was that Chinese restaurant, and the upstairs window across the street where the killers ambushed him is still there. God bless ole Rumpty's soul out in Magnolia," Olin said, referring to the grand cemetery built in what was Little Mexico where famous Charlestonians are laid to rest. The cheery group raised their glasses and pronounced, "Amen!"

Cadence had gotten one photo for Degue's story, so she marked that off the list, but she still needed shots of jazz, hip hop, ballet, ballroom, the shag, and belly dancing; the latter wasn't exactly a class the school offered. She thought finding a troupe of mid-drift swayers would be difficult, but a little snooping proved her wrong. The belly dancing club performed regularly, so Cadence showed up at one of the city's stately homes to see an afternoon performance.

When Cadence sat down on the floor, she recognized her Spanish teacher across the room, who nodded in her direction. She wondered about his presence until the dancer sashayed into the center of the room and Cadence saw it was a girl from her class. Beneath the gleaming chandelier and gilded moldings, the audience watched the performer spin the sensuous and suggestive dance in the peach-colored parlor.

Her bedlah, consisting of an intricately beaded bra and a sheer skirt flowing with sequins, rivaled the embellishments of the Victorian-inspired décor. Her torso-centered movement, bare feet twisting into the rug, and arms twirling in snake-like motions enchanted her admirers at whom she smiled with each pass. Cadence watched as all in the room watched the dancer whose curves responded to the Arabic pipes, drums, and cymbals beating allure into her exotic routine. Her moves also seemed to charm the snake she pulled from a basket and wrapped around her neck. As she dipped back, it moved up and over her shoulders, seemingly looking for a nook in which to curl.

After the demonstration, Cadence remained to talk to Professor Hernandez, who had trouble remembering her name. He introduced her to the performer, Camilla, who was thrilled they had come to watch and that photos had been taken. Cadence learned her Spanish professor's area of interest was dance in Latin America, and in observing the surge of belly dancing in some countries, he decided to see a local performance.

Watching so much dancing gave Cadence a longing to let loose on the floor, even with her limited rhythm, so she and Helena went to a Stone Miles show at the College Pit. It was a gig for all ages, and surprisingly, a number of high school girls frolicked in front of the stage. Cadence could not imagine her mother letting her go to a concert on a school night, let alone dressed the way some of them were—in skyscraper heels and spandex that barely covered their most intimate parts.

Many looked as if they were ready to mount stripper poles. Trying too hard, they couldn't be blamed for wanting to achieve that most coveted goal of teenage years—attention. Others fully engaged in the dance floor make out, and the groupie faction was especially fierce that evening, with a number of scantily clad women bumping and grinding in dirty dancing style.

After a night of moving to the music of her favorite musician, Cadence needed some horizontal recovery as did Helena. Cadence found it such a pleasant change to hold a conversation with a roommate before sleep, to talk about the day's events in normal fashion. This is how she had imagined dorm life would be: two friends trading thoughts in their shared space, but she did not anticipate the doubts that could be planted from Helena's observations.

"So, does Schilar's music playing bother you?" Helena asked.

"Bother me? No, why would it?"

"I mean, all those girls throwing themselves at him," Helena said. "I don't know if I could handle groupies hangin' all over my guy all the time."

"I guess I just have to trust him," Cadence said, although the threat of what Helena was saying had been hovering heavily lately.

Tonight as she stood watching him from a distance, Cadence heard one girl say, "Mmmmm, I'd like to inspire him," while her friend followed with: "His lips can sing into my microphone any day!"

At first, Cadence reveled in knowing that the guy on stage knew her in the most intimate ways possible, but as quickly as she celebrated that fact, the fear of it no longer being the case crept in. What would she do if he gave in to the temptations available every time he performed? The thought made her insides twist. It had occurred to her that other girls must be attracted to him for the same reasons she was, but their pursuits of him were realities she conveniently chose to ignore. Considering that his sex appeal had grown exponentially since last semester, it was a possibility she had a harder time trying to overlook. Keeping the madness of jealousy from transforming her into the clingy, needy, possessively suffocating type of girlfriend was becoming a challenge she had not anticipated.

Just as the roomies were about to turn off the lights, Helena's phone buzzed, and moments later, she was getting somewhat dressed and making for the door.

"Hey, who're you going to see?" Cadence asked.

"Why, Miss Nosey? Or should I call you 'mother'?"

Cadence didn't know where to walk the line between invading her roommate's privacy and being a protective friend. "Um, I don't want to pry. It's just some really bad stuff happened to a friend last semester," Cadence said. "I was asking in case someone needs to get in touch with you."

Helena dropped the defensiveness. "Oh, yeah. That really sucks about Penny."

Cadence's eyes widened. "How do you know about Penny?"

"I'm not stupid. I can put things together. I've heard some gossip, and I hear Penny crying a lot. I don't know the details, and it's really none of my business, but it's bad isn't it?"

"Yeah," she said weakly.

Helena's phone vibrated again. "Anyway, I can handle myself. Nothing's going to happen, but if you must know, here's the number where you can reach me." She wrote it on the cover of Cadence's notebook. "Don't wait up."

Cadence didn't. Although she was concerned about her roommate, there's only so much a friend can say to another who's in the throes of enjoying freedom, especially considering the prison-like existence Helena once led. Tonight, she had even said before hitting the floor: "You know, Baptists aren't supposed to dance or drink, but damn if I'm not going to. Life is for the living, so let's dance like we're running from death!" The comment was strange, but Cadence was learning that phrases like that were simply part of Helena's nuttiness.

The next morning, Cadence was getting ready for class when Helena came in with a goofy smile and a languorous stagger. Plopping down on her bed, she gazed up at the ceiling and sighed deeply. That's when Cadence saw her roommate's neck.

"What happened? Did you get in a fight with a vacuum?" Cadence pointed to the reddish-purple blemishes covering Helena's skin.

"Yep." She laughed with a girlish grin.

"I won't ask the details."

"Good. Because I don't kiss and tell, but it was fabulous!"

"Well, at least your neck matches your hair. Way to accessorize," Cadence said, referring to the dye job Helena had given herself to match the month of love. "You're quite the chameleon."

"I know. Always have been," she said, bringing the covers over her head to sleep.

It was another of those Friday mornings in which the weekend had started the day before and students in Professor Mirabilis's class were recovering. More than a few times, the teacher had allowed Schilar to attend a different section when he had a late gig the previous night, so Cadence smiled when he came in.

Sitting in a circle, the class was in the midst of reading Ntozake Shange's choreopoem, *for colored girls who have considered suicide/when the rainbow is enuf,* a work meant to be danced, when one student rose, presumably for a bathroom break.

But something wasn't right about her jagged movement, and her eyes, glazed by the alcohol still in her system, became fixed on a spot in the corner. As if weights were attached to her feet, she trudged through the circle's center, and just before stepping to its edge, brown liquid shot from her mouth, hitting the floor and bouncing onto the legs of those nearest. Horrified, a guy blocking her path slid his desk into another. The ill one reached the trashcan and vomited again. With her feet spread and hands above her head, she leaned into the wall over the can as if she were preparing to be arrested. For some reason, Professor Mirabilis tried to keep teaching, but as the retching sounds grew louder, it became impossible for anyone to focus.

"Kayla," the teacher asked. "Are you okay?"

Obviously, she was not, but Kayla answered, "Ye—p. I got this," and continued to spit and drivel into the can.

"All right, let's take a break," the professor said. "You all who may have, um, been splashed, please go get yourselves cleaned up." They could tell this scenario was a new one for Professor Mirabilis. "Um, let's see, Linda, could you walk Kayla to the restroom and would someone bring me some paper towels?"

As some students exited with the sick one, those remaining began to laugh. "Hey!" Professor Mirabilis said, "That's not funny. I don't know if any of you have been in that condition, but it's not pleasant. It especially won't be pleasant in a few hours. So please, save your jokes."

After wiping the floor, she pulled hand sanitizer from her purse and slathered it on. The memory of their professor cleaning up a student's vomit was one that would stick, but it wasn't long before they were past puke and back to poetry.

Kayla opted to return to her dorm, so her peers continued navigating the characters' vernacular, frowning at their pain, smiling at the sassy lines that cut through the men they knew weren't good enough for them. The students imagined how the poem would looked performed—with its colorful dance streaking sadness and strength, horror and happiness across a stage. The professor asked about light and dark, sickness and healing, and encouraged them to read deeply, to understand what it must mean and feel to discover god in oneself and to love her intensely. In the circle of class, they contemplated what it would take to move toward the end of their own rainbows and what they would find if they ever got there.

When they finally saw each other again that evening, Cadence asked Schilar: "So, what'd you think of class today?"

"There are some interesting people in there," he said.

"You mean the girl who threw up? Yeah, that was crazy. It was so gross *I* wanted to puke. Funny, she's always been fairly quiet. Has never really said much."

"Well, that was different, but that's not what I meant. This woman in your class. The older one. I've seen her before."

"Oh, Astra? She's really smart. Always says the most intelligent stuff. You've seen her at one of your shows?" Cadence asked.

"I've seen her at a show all right, but not one of mine," Schilar said. "She's a stripper."

"What? How d'you know?"

"Well, how d'you think I know? I saw her at a club over Christmas. The guys took me to Sapphire's for my birthday. Parker bought some time in the VIP room with her."

"You went to a strip club over break?"

"Yeah. Just innocent fun. Nothing happened."

"I'm not worried about anything happening. I was just curious as to what it was like."

He smiled. "Why? What do you want to know for?"

She had no particular reason for wanting to know, just a simple curiosity about what went on there, what the women were like, and how the men who watched them reacted. It got her thinking, so when she saw her editor on Monday, she mentioned the idea.

"TJ, what if we included stripping as part of April's dance feature?"

"No," he said abruptly. "But I like the story possibility. How about a feature on girls who strip their way through college? You know, the ones who do it to pay tuition?"

"Oh, okay. Who're you going to assign the story to?"

He looked around at the mostly empty newsroom. "I'm sure some of the guys would love the assignment, but they're all too busy. So," he said, turning to Cadence, "you."

"But TJ, I'm not a writer."

"Do you mean you can't write? If that's the case, we need to talk to your English teacher. If you mean that you haven't tried, that's not an excuse. I want an article including photos I can run—all done by you."

Cadence rubbed her forehead. "When? And how many words?"

"Um, a week and a half. A thousand words. A picture and a thousand words."

With a short deadline, she needed to approach Astra soon to get started, but Cadence wasn't sure what to say, so over the weekend, she procrastinated doing work with some erotic dancing research. She was not surprised to read that women have been removing clothes to excite men since ancient Babylonian times. It seemed obvious that men would have been itching to remove the fig leaves and frocks as soon as they became fashion trends. She was astonished to learn that the modern symbol of stripping—the pole—has an ambiguous history with the phallic symbol appearing in Maypole dances dating back to medieval days, in the male-dominated Indian sport of Mallakhamb, and as a sideshow circus attraction that utilized the tent pole as entertainment.

Another bit of symbolism, the G-string, originally referred to the loincloths worn by Native Americans. And in her life's ever-expanding vocabulary lesson, she learned of nudity's apotropaic powers, of how revealing the breasts and genitals was believed to ward off evil spirits. The great Roman statesman Pliny the Elder thought a woman could calm a storm out at sea by stripping, and in Balkan folk tales, women could frighten the gods and end rainstorms by running into the fields and exposing their breasts.

In contrast to these positives, Cadence read about how some African cultures view stripping as a curse. Removing clothes, especially when done by married or elderly women, is invoked in extreme situations as a way to shame men. Men who witness this act are considered dead and are ostracized and isolated from their communities. This metaphorical execution extends to foreign men who are rendered impotent or will experience suffering after viewing a naked mother. Nigerian women have effectively used the "curse of nakedness" to protest the unethical practices of oil companies that destroy the region's landscapes and lives.

As interesting as the history was, it didn't address the more personal questions of money, motive, and the mysterious realms protected by blackened windows and bouncers. Armed with some knowledge of the profession, Cadence approached Astra, who was sitting on a bench after class smoking a cigarette.

"Hi," Cadence said hesitantly, "mind if I sit down?"

"No, go ahead." Astra motioned to the empty space while exhaling in the opposite direction. "Some class, huh?" she said, referring to Professor Mirabilis's especially fiery teaching of poetry today.

"Uh-huh, she knows how to make you think," Cadence said. "Did you know there was such a thing as 'astraphobia' before she told you today?"

"Nope, no one's ever told me my name could mean a 'fear of thunderstorms.' That's wild."

"Did you have her last semester?"

"I didn't. My teacher talked to us like we were in first grade," she explained. "It was so far from being intellectually stimulating that my brain was numb from disuse. Then I get into this class and she rips my first paper to shreds, but I'm learning, so that's good."

"Yeah, she's definitely got a serious case of OCD—obsessive composition disorder. She's nuts when it comes to tearing up writing." Cadence was relieved that Astra laughed at the humor and made more conversation before getting to what she needed. "Um, I was wondering if I could talk to you about your job."

Astra's eyes flashed with fire. "Why? You want some tips for your bedroom?"

"What? No, no. I'm doing a story for the paper."

"Oh, great. Another exposé on the low lives of pole dancers? Save it; it's been done." Astra stomped the idea out like her cigarette butt and stormed off.

Cadence ran to catch her. "Listen, it's not like that. I'm focusing on the college aspect, you know, how you balance the job and school." Cadence struggled with her breath as Astra increased her pace. "I wanted to ask someone who could tell me the way it is. You always say the most incredible things in class. The points you make are so interesting. I was hoping that in talking to you, I could get some different ideas."

Astra stopped suddenly. "I don't want to be in your article." She was prepared to leave it at that, but something about Cadence made her change her mind. "Look, there may be some girls at the club who'll be willing to help you. I have a shift tonight, so I'll ask and let you know during the next class."

Encouraged by Astra's response, Cadence was jotting down some interview notes for the stripper story before communications class when Dakota came in.

"You're early today," Cadence said.

"Yeah well, class was CRA—ZY. This girl passed out. Totally went down. They had to call the paramedics and everything."

"Really? That's awful."

"I know. Natalie seems so nice, but I'll tell you, she has looked painfully thin lately. So skeletal in those exercise outfits. I guess not eating finally caught up with her or at least that's my guess."

Cadence thought the name sounded familiar. "Wait. Did you say her name's 'Natalie' and she's always dressed in workout clothes?"

"Uh-huh. Why? You know her?"

"If we're talking about the same person, she lives on my hall. What class was this?"

"Dance, modern techniques."

Cadence looked at him in surprise. "You're taking a dance class?"

"Yes, girl. It's to help improve my style. For my shows."

"What're you talking about?"

"Here, take a peek." Reaching into his bag, he produced a photo of a woman with vibrant make-up, donned in sequins from heel to crown, the latter topped by a fashionable feather headdress. Cadence's eyes shifted from the picture to Dakota and back again. She held it closer.

"Yes, honey. I'm a drag queen in training. What d'you think?"

"I think you're one of the most interesting people I really don't know."

"We'll have to change that." He gently took the photo and gazed at it. "This was for a show last year. Oh, girl, the dieting I did to get in that dress." He joked, but the humor hit closely to the truth of what he had just witnessed.

"Are you serious?" Cadence asked.

"Oh, yeah. There's plenty of that eating disorder mess in the LGBTQ community too," he explained. "You know, I was all worried about the freshman fifteen, but it's a myth. Apparently, we're more likely to gain weight right before graduation. My seminar teacher told us that. Crazy huh? Anyway, I hope Natalie's coming back to dance class soon."

Above all the dances found in Charleston, the Charleston Shuffle is performed hourly, but it requires no formal training, choreography, or practice. Coming at the most inopportune time, it isn't encouraged but has a long tradition extending from the cobblestones of colonial times to the brick-laid present. Cadence was on her way back to the dorm thinking of Dakota's photo and of his interesting life when she heard the familiar sounds of hooves on the pavement. *Clop, clop, clop* was the work of a stunning black carriage horse pulling his load of ogling tourists. Instantly, the sadness she had been concealing following Gunpowder's death swept in. Precisely at the moment the first tear fell, so did she, executing her most dramatic rendition of the Charleston Shuffle to date, and one so wildly done, it sent her books and papers leaping across the pathway and reopened the knee wound that had just healed.

Normally, when a person does this particular dance, spectators are known to look up into the trees or even away with straight faces—a "no big deal" form of empathy, but this time, assistance came.

"Hey, are you okay?"

With the tears of a flashback in her eyes, Cadence saw a blurry figure wrapped in camouflage flannel standing over her. "Uh, yeah, I think so."

"Damn, it looks like you've busted up your knee. Here," she said, extending her hand to pull Cadence up from the bricks.

Other passersby stopped to gather Cadence's things, and when she had slightly recovered, she got a better look at the stranger. Cadence recognized her as the person who had taken up space in the room formerly occupied by Ruthie. The girl introduced herself as "River" and said that she was adjusting nicely to life with Olivia, a pairing that was infinitely better than last semester's situation. River's first roommate turned out to be a breathing biohazard: she threw everything on the floor—crumbs, dirty underwear, drink cans, used tissues—and never cleaned or took out the trash. The worst was the great wall of Chinese food containers she would leave for weeks until the foulness could penetrate the cinderblocks. Even worse, she didn't wash her clothes, sheets, or towels, and the latter barely got use since she rarely showered. The filth was so extreme that the Palmetto bugs began to move in, too. Unable to reason with the "Diva of Disgust," River filed for a room change. As she was now a neighbor, Cadence suggested River stop by the room sometime to meet some others on the hall.

Later, Olivia was coming out of her room as Cadence was headed to check on Natalie. "Hi," Cadence said, "I met your roommate earlier."

Olivia wasn't really in the mood to talk to anyone who deserted her because of the spying incident, but she decided to speak. "Oh, yeah, she's great. Somehow, I've had the best luck of rooming with freaks both semesters."

"What do you mean?" Cadence asked.

"Well, you obviously know about Ruthie and all her crazy drug shit. Now, I get roomed with a professional knife-thrower."

"I'm sorry, what?"

"K-n-i-f-e-t-h-r-o-w-e-r," Olivia sounded out, as if the response should have been obvious. "She throws knives competitively. Total weirdo. I mean, who does that?"

"Wow. That sounds interesting."

"Oh yeah, it's fantastic. She also hunts, fishes, does archery. She's a regular Daisy Crockett."

"So, um, any word on what happened to Ruthie?"

"Rehab, but like I care. That bitch broke my nose. I was going to file assault charges, but I didn't."

"Why not?"

"Just didn't." She darted her eyes about the hall. "I gotta go."

As Cadence watched her leave, she felt for sure that Olivia wouldn't be pulling any of her spying work on River: just seemed too risky with a knife-wielding woman sleeping feet away. Intrigued by Olivia's roommate, Cadence thought

River's skill would make a good feature for *The Gator* and was beginning to understand that stories, like photos, were everywhere. Narratives just needed the right angles and light to imbue them with the power to make others pause.

When Cadence knocked on Natalie's door, it cracked a little, and a swollen-eyed Darla stood there blinking. "You okay, Darla? Can I come in?"

Darla nodded, and Cadence stepped in to see that Natalie's side was immaculate with everything tucked neatly into place. Three cases of bottled water were piled beside the small refrigerator, and atop the stack perched a basket filled with rice cakes, low-fat snacks, and flavoring powders for the water.

Darla pointed to the goods. "That's what she lives on. I should have said something. This is all my fault."

"This is *not* your fault."

Falling back on her bed, Darla clutched her head in her hands. "Cadence, I'm studying to be a nurse. I should know about these things. How am I supposed to help people if I can't even help my own roommate?"

Cadence put her arm around Darla. "Hey, hey, don't get upset. I don't know a lot about eating disorders, but if they're like any other addiction, it probably takes more than a friend saying something to make a person stop. Darla, you can't blame yourself for this."

Something broke inside and leaning into Cadence, Darla let out a series of wails that lasted for minutes until she was calm enough to breathe again.

"Hey, is something else going on? This isn't just about Natalie, is it?"

Darla wiped her tears with her sleeve. "My classes. They're so hard, and I have so much work to do." She stood up and began pacing. "I never feel like I know enough. I think I'm prepared for a test but when I take it, I don't do well. I am failing miserably."

"Have you tried getting a tutor or going to the learning labs?"

"Nothing's helped. I study so much. I don't even go out anymore. I just feel like I'm drowning," she said. "All I have ever wanted to be is a nurse, but I'm throwing money and my life away on classes I'm not going to use. I am soooo frustrated!" She dropped back on the bed.

Cadence didn't know what to say. She was also beginning to think that the elective courses required for a degree were ridiculous. Like most, she had bought into the argument that these were necessary in producing well-rounded students. Besides, she wasn't sure what she wanted to do, so the variety was a good way to get some ideas of majors; even if she hadn't been impressed with some of the choices, at least she could rule some disciplines out. But for someone like Darla, who knew exactly what she wanted to do, why should she have to do the wandering dance through a tangle of courses that had little to do with her envisioned career?

"Maybe you should talk to your advisor."

Darla took a deep breath. "Maybe. I don't know. I guess I'll figure it out."

"You will. So, um, is Natalie at the hospital?"

"Yeah. I just got back from seeing her. They've got her on fluids. Her parents are on the way here. I would have stayed, but the doctor wanted her to rest. Her dance professor is there."

"What's going to happen to her?"

"I have no idea, but I hope she rethinks dancing so much. It's sucking the life out of her."

Cadence thought that Darla's life-sucking comment may be a storyline to follow, so she added it to the list of questions she'd ask Astra's coworkers if she got the chance to interview them. Her preparation paid off because during the next class, Astra told Cadence to come to the club that night, but before hopping a cab to meet them, she went for a coffee and to review her notes.

"How's the dancing story coming?" Catissa asked.

"Oh, that's not mine; I was just getting the photos for it. But I did get assigned a different kind of dancing story."

"Really? What's it about?"

"Um, I think I'll wait until it comes out and surprise you."

"Ah, okay," Catissa said. "It wouldn't have anything to do with what's written on your hand, would it?"

Cadence had forgotten about the reminder, and Catissa, ever the one to mind the details, saw *Sapphire's* underlined in blue ink as the girl clutched her coffee cup.

Cadence laughed. "You got me. I'm doing a story on women who pay for college through stripping. I'm headed there in a few minutes."

"Interesting." Catissa looked sternly at Cadence. "And how will you get there?"

"I was going to take a cab."

"No, you won't. I'll drive you, and when you're done, I'll pick you up."

Cadence began to protest, but Catissa was having none of it. "So, if you're ready, we'll go. I have some dancing obligations myself. I'm off to shag," she said, within earshot of one of her baristas, an English-born lad complete with good looks and charming accent.

"Catissa, love, what have I told you about that? A lady of your standing should not go around bragging that you're going to 'shag.' It's truly unbecoming," Andrew teased.

"Oh, how do you say it? 'Bugger off,' Andrew!"

"What's he talking about, Catissa?"

"Something he shouldn't be. 'Shagging' is British slang for 'having sex.' Whenever I talk about dancing the shag, he always gives me grief. Imagine that: I get chided for doing the state dance." She let out a cackle and shagged toward the door with Cadence following.

Stepping outside, they were greeted by a very bouncy Kyd. He went straight for Cadence, jumping to greet her and straining to lick her fanatically. His dance of love consisted of hopping in place and wagging his nub until Cadence brought her face within reach of his anxious tongue. Kyd christened her with slobber and snorts from his mushed nose.

The sun was still cutting a warm swath across the cold sky when Catissa dropped Cadence off in the dull, gray area of industrial parks not too far from the colorfully picturesque downtown. In entering the club, Cadence was immediately blinded as her eyes struggled to adjust to the darkness. Before she could even see, a deep voice welcomed her into the den and asked if she was applying for a job or signing up for Amateur Night. The inquirer was a sinewy man in an ill-fitting gray suit, his long white hair slicked back in a ponytail. As the door closed behind her, shutting out the last bit of natural light, another voice said, "Lay off, Haywood. She's here to do a story for the paper."

"Damn! She's got that classic girl-next-door look." Haywood moved his elevator eyes over Cadence.

"Yes, she does, so let's keep it that way," Astra replied.

"Well, if you change your mind, here's my card." He pulled one from his pocket, and Cadence took it without saying anything as Astra led her to the backroom where some of the women were readying themselves with make-up, lotions, glitter, and perfumes. Astra introduced her classmate to Inanna and Hari, dancers who were also stripping to pay for their educations. Inanna was studying to be a chef at the local technical college while Hari was training to be a physical therapist at another. Because they were students at other schools, Astra agreed to be interviewed as long as her stage name, Essence, was used and her face obscured in any photos.

"That may sound like I'm embarrassed about what I do, but that's not the case," Astra explained. "There's such condemnation for strippers, especially here in the buckle of the Bible belt. It's easier for me to function outside of this place if people don't know who I am. Once you've been baptized in erotic sweat, the sin of stripping never washes away."

At a table next to the stage, Cadence listened as Astra, Inanna, and Hari described life on poles, laps, and platforms. Their jobs could earn them several hundred a night, and on especially great nights when businessmen, big golf spenders, bachelor partiers, and birthday celebrants hit the naked and naughty scene, a grand was easily made. Each year, the women brought in tens of thousands, and they knew friends of friends in larger cities who pulled six figures, but every entertainer knows that while the stage is great for being in the spotlight, the serious money comes from lap dances and VIP room time.

"Let's be clear," Astra said firmly, "this is a job. One that needs no formal training, no preparation. You can make a lot of money, get compensated for what you do, but the amount you're paid is based on performance. You have to be able to read a client. You learn what he needs in order to communicate with your body the fantasy he wants, to make it come true without fulfilling it through sex. We are, after all, in sales."

Hari added, "But to keep going in this job, you have to detach yourself. In traditional dance classes, they teach there's knowledge in the body and to be a great dancer, you have to connect the emotional part with the mind's rational part. They have to comprehend each other, but in stripping, you have to disconnect those in order to survive."

"So you're mentally not there when you're dancing?" Cadence asked.

"We're somewhat there," Hari said, "carrying on conversations and communicating nonverbally, but in our minds, we go to some other place to block out what we're doing. It's a coping technique. This business gives you a lot of those skills."

"I agree," Astra said. "Stripping teaches you how to work a room, to talk up customers, and to figure out who has the most money to spend."

"How do you know that?" Cadence asked.

"You study them. Shoes, eyeglasses, suits, wristwatches, even what their money clips or wallets are made out of says a lot. We pay extra attention to the vulnerable ones who are here to spend, to buy themselves some confidence," Inanna said.

"And there's a psychology to this," Hari said. "Men come in here for the flesh, but that's the surface. Some want what we call the 'GFE' or the girlfriend experience. Others really just want to talk. They want someone to listen to them to make them feel wanted, or stronger, or smarter. There's a lot of loneliness within these walls, and on any given night, we're therapists."

"Who are your clients, the types?" Cadence had her pen poised to record the list.

"Who's not?" Inanna said. "Single, married, divorced, widowed. Professionals, preachers, company presidents."

"College boys, doctors, judges, lawyers, professors, even the occasional gay man who's bored," Hari added.

Cadence stopped writing. "Professors?"

"Yes, and they especially like Essence," Inanna teased.

Astra leaned back in her chair, crossing her arms. "Again, lonely men. Professors have too much head on one end and not enough on the other. They're looking for something other than cerebral stimulation."

"There's this one, he comes in every Thursday. Sits in that spot over there." Inanna pointed to a small table on the stage's opposite side. "Brings his favorite red wine, and watches her for hours. He's not interested in anyone else."

"What does he teach?" Cadence asked.

"Physics," Hari answered with a giggle.

"Go on, Hari, tell Cadence your joke," Inanna said.

"Whenever he comes in, we like to tease Astra and say he's here to observe the basic laws of physics." She playfully eyed her coworker. "A body in motion continues in motion unless acted upon by a professorial force."

"Clearly, he's here to watch Essence defy the laws of gravity," Inanna said.

Cadence chuckled. "That's good."

Astra didn't seem too amused. "I doubt Newton would be impressed."

"I'm sure the 'sir' would appreciate the gravitational forces at work in here," Hari said.

"I think she gets the point," Astra said. "As you can tell, Cadence, some humor helps to survive in this business. But not all the guests are as pleasant as the professors."

While the more sophisticated clientele were always appreciated, the women also told of the other types: drunks, drug dealers, pimps, perverts, ex-cons. They, too, came looking for pleasures, and the dancers were never certain when they'd cross paths with one of these customers. Some strippers were known to carry .38 Specials, especially if a client developed a fixation. These were just some of the issues they dealt with. The three explained that the rewards were good, sometimes great—the money, meeting very influential people, the high of being the center of attention, the exercise from dancing all night, and street education, which was rarely found in a classroom or taught from a textbook.

But stripping had serious downsides: the temptations of cocaine, heroin, meth, prostitution. Eating disorders, erratic sleep cycles, aching feet, muscles, legs, and joints from the heels, back issues from the stunts, no insurance or workplace benefits, guys who don't understand "no." Each recalled times when *slut* or *whore* was hurled at them, and despite their rough-hewn armor, the names dented their confidence, diminished them. They described pimp-like managers who expected employees to put out, violence, harassment, propositioning, and of course, the perpetual scarlet letter each wore for being a stripper.

After the interviews, the women took turns on the pole, staging various positions and dance moves so Cadence could get the type of shots she needed for the paper, which meant the subjects were clothed and the photos not overly suggestive. The girls were accommodating and helpful since, after all, this was promotion for their business, and this type of exposure usually meant an upsurge in clients.

When they were finished, Astra asked, "So did you get everything you needed?"

"I think so."

"Well, you can ask me after class if you find you missed something," Astra said, but Cadence's perplexed expression indicated there was something more. "Okay, what else do you need?" Her offer was met with embarrassed silence. "Ah, I see. You need to see the show in order to write about it?"

Cadence blushed. "I think it would help. Is that too weird?"

"No, I understand. You're a visual learner like me. You must write like I draw. You have to take in the sensory experience to, um, get its essence? We'll get you a table in the corner so you can take in the whole room."

"You draw?" Cadence asked.

"Yeah, I'm a studio art major." Astra turned to go get ready for the night. "With a business minor," she said with a wink.

In the shadows of a rainbow-hued realm that smelled like wildflowers and musk, candy and the curse of nakedness, Cadence watched men take their seats in the arena of erotic experience and briefly vacate them for the intimacy of backrooms. Every few songs, the dancers would rotate from the stage, each presenting her own acrobatic feats upon the pole and across the platform and each displaying the endurance, strength, control, and poise needed to perform. In their eyes, Cadence saw the distance, windows which betrayed the escapes their minds made even as their bodies remained physically present.

Soon, the black curtain parted once more and Essence took to the pole, wielding it like a tool of art. She moved in a fury of fluidity, in a way that highlighted the powerful confidence of her female form. Her skin glistened from the tiny specks of glitter clinging to her curves, the kind master painters would desire to stroke onto their canvases. Contrary to ancient belief, Essence certainly didn't lull any storms when she removed her clothes. Instead, in this sea of men, she caused them to stir, especially the learned professor who sat in his regular spot, sipping his wine and the sight of her. He gazed at the form that resisted gravity as if she were a hierarchical problem he was working out silently. He wanted to possess the knowledge her body carried and combine it with his. During the thundering performance, when she began untying the strings of her costume, one black feather floated down onto the stage in front of him. His hand, shaky from years of clutching chalk and pens, pulled it to his nose. As he inhaled his angel's scent, he closed his eyes, escaping to some other place to contemplate the mysteries of magnetism and dark matter.

In her nakedness, Essence didn't need to curse those watching; in many ways, their loneliness already was enough to render some socially impotent. Slumped in chairs, the men within the mirror-walled space were reflections of the women dancing before them—each craving attention, companionship, and some power that was beyond what flashed in sequins and feathers, esteem and sadness. For as potent as Essence was in the spirit of her dance, in the beauty of her bare skin, and in the eyes of those admirers, Cadence realized it was a fleeting feeling—that outside the walls of this place, Astra's own walls of defense went up against those who judged her means of living, her way of surviving using what was naturally given to her.

Legs apart. Bend right leg slowly. Hold position. Bend left leg slowly. Straighten to beginning stance. Swing pelvis right side up. Slide feet to floor. Repeat. Arms up over head, grasp pole, swing legs out long and fast, wrap around steel, float down. Pull up with one arm, straddle shaft, gyrate hips, wave other arm. Switch and repeat. Conceal emotion. Separate mind. Cut eyes suggestively. Smile seductively. Dance!

Chapter 14

English 102
The Composition of Love

Certain phrases express universal truths that slide so fittingly into the soul they leave listeners speechless, burning with envy that the muse didn't inspire them to pen such memorable words. "Love is not love which alters when it alteration finds" was one of those lines that slapped the students' ears with such force that they'd remember Shakespeare's poetry for all time.

"What does 'alteration' mean in the context of 'Sonnet 116'?" Professor Mirabilis asked.

"Can it be a relationship change?" said a girl with taps of her brightly colored shoes. "Like when someone else comes into the picture?"

"Of course. Thanks, Aliyah. What else?"

"Economic?" Astra answered. "Perhaps when money comes between people?"

"Great observations. And let's not forget the fun physical changes that come with age," the teacher suggested. "But there may be something else here. Most of his 154 sonnets are written to a young man. Does this poem subvert the traditional ideal of love and marriage as defined by the church? Is it hinting at love between two men?"

"Whoa teach, that's heavy," Dewit said in his normally spacy way.

"Love's not a light matter," she said. "This poem prompts me to ask questions about this concept. Is love constant, fixed, unchanging? Or can it be inconstant, free, dynamic? Is it possible to love different people throughout one's life and still call each instance 'love'?"

"What's been possible for you?"

Professor Mirabilis focused on Kirby. "Ah, turning the mirror on me, are you?"

"Seriously, professor. What's love been like for you?"

As if searching for truth outside, she looked over to the window and smiled. "Illuminating and disillusioning; delightful and devastating; soul-crushing and soul-creating." She could make even her own experiences sound Shakespearean. "But it has changed over the years. I have loved different people at different times in different ways. I have loved intensely, but aspects changed: ambitions, beliefs, locations. According to the speaker, those times when I thought I was in so deeply must not have been love."

"What about the mind part? The poem starts with the marriage of two people with 'true minds'?" To everyone's surprise, it was the guy who never spoke up, the one always staring at Cadence. "Are you married to your true mind now?"

"Great question, Corey. I am married to my everyone. He's my completion—the halves to my soul, my mind, my heart. He completes my life."

She peered outside again, inhaling as if she were lost in a sensory moment somewhere with him. "Whew! Let's move on, but one last thing: I will say that I cannot imagine being married to the people I was in love with when I was your age. If you happen to be head over heels at the moment and it ends, your world should not end—don't allow yourself to think it has. One example of Romeo and Juliet is enough for all humankind," the teacher said. Cadence wished Reena's ears were in range to hear this advice.

A bed that goes cold qualifies as one of the most jarring temperature changes in the spectrum of human experience. Since the beginning of college, Reena had gotten used to waking up in the warmth of one that was not her own but a space she had certainly made hers through a number of sleepless nights and mornings. Ever since they met, she had spent nearly all of them with Blaze, except on those occasions when he was away on business or had gone home for the weekend, which had become more frequent as of late. She had thought everything was going well; he had always been someone of few words, but the way he looked at her spoke loudly about what he wanted and how he felt, even if he didn't admit it, so she was struck with paralysis when, lying beside her one February afternoon, he said: "I think we need to take a break."

"Mmmmm, I agree." She purred and planted one more kiss on his chest before resting her head in the groove of his shoulder. "I'm exhausted."

Just as she said it, he moved his arm, leaving her without his comfort. He stared at the dizzying loops made by the ceiling fan. "I need some time."

She sat up. "Time to do what?"

Glancing at her then back at the spinning blades, he said, "To think—about us."

"What does that mean?" Her voice began to shake.

"It means we don't need to see each other for a while."

It would have been easier telling her not to breathe, and his timing could not have been worse with Valentine's Day approaching. Considering the intensity of their relationship, his excuses were weak. Having embedded himself so deeply into her life, she felt he was nearly impossible to extract, but Reena thought about doing just that.

Only days after the breakup, she sat alone in her room, razor poised on the edge of returning to the scarring solutions of her past. Tears prepped the place on her wrist as she pressed the razor in, flirted with release and ruin, but did not pull. She had come so far and worked so hard to distance herself from destruction that she wasn't ready to open those wounds—not yet. Somehow, recovering from the temptation, she tucked the blade into her velvet-covered journal: a gift from Cadence who asked Reena to cut her pain on its pages with a pen and not into her flesh.

Jilted in the month of love, Reena took on the identity of a benevolent pseudo stalker. A burning curiosity to know what he was doing started every morning and kept her tossing through the nights. Finding excuses to walk by his place too often, she was comforted when she saw his car there, but only for a few moments until her mind began reeling out the scenarios of who could be inside and what they could be doing. Even when his car wasn't there, her reaction was the same. She thought about calling and did a few times, until he asked her not to. Complying, she showed her feelings in restraint although she would have preferred screaming them from Charleston's highest points. Blaze even made her miss his birthday; she had already bought his gift, so she mailed him the package hoping that when opened, it would fix whatever had broken between them. But there was no mending, and all she received was a message from the post office letting her know the box had been delivered.

School was the last subject on her mind as the torturous analysis of every angle of what went wrong wracked her brain to the point of insanity. She cried, got angry, cried again, threw things, but mostly, she fell into an impenetrable darkness. Like a child clinging to a security blanket, she clutched a shirt that still carried his scent; day and night, she'd bury her face in it, desperately wishing that in opening her eyes, the fresh smell of him lying next to her would be her restored reality. Cadence and Miranda grew increasingly worried about Reena who insisted she'd be fine. They wanted to believe that she would survive, but her history suggested otherwise.

Cadence learned more about Astra's history following the publication of the stripping article. It was so well done she wanted to treat Cadence to coffee, but instead of going to c.a.t.'s, they chose another place. Crowded and noisy, the shop had none of the charm or intimacy of Catissa's place, so they decided to walk and drink. The article had already begun to generate more business for the club with the dancers seeing a surge in college guys and a few more educators who came in for the anatomy. Each would be given the measured attention necessary to keep them coming back.

"I'm glad you liked the piece," Cadence said. "It was my first."

"Really?" Astra asked. "Wow, I thought you might be an old pro. Are you happy with it?"

"I am. But I still have questions."

"Like what?"

Cadence ran her finger around the cup's plastic lid. "How'd you get into exotic dancing?"

"Well, that's another story. Let's find a place to sit down." Astra pointed to the ruins in Cannon Park. "How about over there?"

They had come upon the borough of Harleston Village where four Corinthian columns stood, ghostly gray features of the Charleston Museum. On land that was once a sawmill pond, the ornamental Thomson Auditorium was built in the late 1800s for a Confederate Veterans' convention. Eventually the structure housed the museum for decades, but the building burned in 1981, and all that remains are the weathered pillars that tower over its portico.

On those concrete steps, Astra lit a cigarette and told of her past, of the man she fell in love with too early in life and with whom she had stayed far too long. At the time, she thought he had rescued her from the hell of high school by making her a teenage bride, giving her a home, providing for her. It was already too late when she discovered the real hell she had entered: one of hate, horrific abuse, and a constant fear that any breath she took could be her last. Foolishly, she thought a child would somehow make him more gentle and caring, but she found out that would never be the case when he delivered a punch that ended the life inside her. She fell into excuses for staying and listened to his lies about loving her, needing her, and not being able to live without her. He vowed and never to hurt her again, and the promise lasted until the next time she felt his fist against her face. The last beating gave her a broken jaw, nose, and arm, fractured ribs, cuts so deep they scarred, black eyes, a concussion, and a lacerated liver. Astra lay unconscious in a hospital bed while her husband reclined in a cell thinking of when they'd be together again.

When she awoke, Astra barely remembered what happened, but her friend Gina Lee was at the bedside. She had been hanging out with Astra before Mason came home and went crazy over gossip that his wife had been talking to some guy she worked with. Running Gina Lee from the house, Mason locked Astra in a bedroom and held a shotgun to her face before he beat her senseless. Gina Lee called the police, and a standoff ensued for hours, but Mason finally relented when he thought Astra was close to death.

For weeks, she struggled with accepting that the man she had given everything to had nearly taken everything from her. She knew he loved her and loved her madly and that he really didn't mean to lose his temper and take it out on her. Maybe if she went back he'd change. He promised it would be different—he had *always* promised that. In listening to her heart, she didn't want to listen to reason, to the dying voice inside her that desperately wanted to live differently. The officer assigned to her case tried to persuade her to cooperate with the investigation and the prosecution. Astra didn't want to send the man she loved to prison.

Through lips busted and dried with blood, Astra mumbled, "We'll work things out."

"You really believe that, don't you?" Officer Warring asked. "So nothing I say will convince you to help us put him away and save what little bit of life you have left?"

Exasperated again at the pattern she had seen all too often, Officer Warring slammed her black book closed, threw her contact card on the hospital table, and walked to the door. Before leaving, she turned to Astra.

"I've been doin' this a long time. It's still a mystery to me. Say something to make me understand how a beautiful, young woman like yourself carries so little value for your own life that you would let a man destroy you." She kicked at the floor with her black boot. "I just don't get it. I see so many of you. *Too many* of you." She looked through the window to a field in the distance. "The next time we have to be called because he has a gun to your head, it'll be too late. The coroner will bring you out of that house." She turned the door handle. "You don't have any children, do you?"

Astra thought of the one she could have had and shook her head.

"That's good. There won't be any little ones missing their mom when you're dead." The click of the door as it closed sounded like the cocking of a gun.

Astra stared off into a different distance now, as she sipped her coffee and blew smoke in the direction of her past. "Her words haunted me. I knew I didn't want to die; I just wasn't sure how to live. He had already killed a part of me, and it was only a matter of time before I was next. A few weeks later, I called Officer Warring and agreed to cooperate. She got me counseling and took a lot of risks for me. One day, she came over and drove me to her parents' place, several counties over. She taught me how to shoot. I bought a gun because he had been bonded. Even though there was a restraining order, Warring knew how flimsy those things are. She became my friend, my protector. I probably wouldn't be here without her."

"Do you still keep in touch with her?" Cadence asked.

"No. I broke all ties with everyone back in Mississippi. I had to. I don't want him to know where I am." Astra dragged the butt of her cigarette across the concrete. "He got ten years for what he did to me, but he'll make parole one day. I guess I'll deal with that when it happens."

"What about your family? Do they help?"

"I don't have any family." Although Cadence felt there was another story beneath the reply, she left it alone. "When I moved here, I had no job, no money, no education, a little bit of hope. I needed a way to survive, so I started dancing. I got my GED, applied to Charlestowne, and well, I'm making it," Astra said.

"Why Charleston?"

"I knew I wanted to be near the water. When I left, I got in the car, and drove until it felt right to stop. This feels like home." Astra looked up at the columns. "I think I'm going to draw these. They seem like they've withstood their share of trouble."

A theme of surviving life's troubles permeated the campus for Darwin Week, and Professor Mangold reminded everyone to celebrate the important contributions of the father of natural selection and evolutionary thought. Panel discussions featured academic, religious and social leaders verbally sparring over who had the fittest argument. Promotional posters with a large photo of a peacock littered the campus. With his Argus-like train fully spread, the bird appeared above Darwin's words: *The sight of a feather in a peacock's tail, whenever I gaze at it, makes me sick!*

Why the male birds had developed such elaborate tails, especially when they seemed to be a hindrance to their existence, perplexed the naturalist. He wrote it up to sexual selection—feathered boys with the brightest colors compete and get the most girls. The theory's been debunked, so the cocks with the flashiest colors don't necessarily get to have the most hens or fun in the farmyard.

In the case of flashy cocks, Ren and his half-rubber cronies were being promoted as a Christian-values, feel-good group, which made daily functioning for Penny even more difficult.

She thought her case had been all but forgotten; the investigation had devolved into circular discussion with the accused continuing to steal chances to trash her reputation, and nothing had come of the interviews except "they said, she said." Surviving every day was a struggle despite the support of her close friends, and when the half-rubber season got into full swing, seeing the team in their glory made Penny sick. Apparently, it made someone else nauseous, too.

Cadence was beginning to think she should buy a tent and just sleep on the Grand Lawn since it seemed she was getting called there far too often. In the middle of Darwin Week appeared the most scathing indictment yet of the half-rubbers. Hanging from the flagpole was an enormous penis that had been fashioned from stuffing one leg of a pair of pantyhose. The inflatable half-balls from the Christmas tree made a return and were being used for the testicles. Plastered on the building below this spectacle was a gigantic banner: *Celebrate Darwin Week: Help Women's Survival—Castrate Rapists!*

Cadence took a picture of the explicit scene but knew TJ couldn't run it, so she also got ones of the sign and just the balls. Whoever had it out for the team was showing no love by creating a public relations nightmare for the school, so the administration launched an all-out hunt to find those responsible for sullying the players' reputations.

With Valentine's Day approaching, local businesses were in seductive sales mode, and Professor Dreary was selling something too—tickets for the opportunity to hear vaginas sing, scream, laugh, curse, and cry. She encouraged all her students to see the production of Eve Ensler's *The Vagina Monologues*, and she called special attention to Miranda's role as one of the vaginas, although she wouldn't reveal which one.

"Remember folks, attendance to this counts as one of your theatre requirements, and proceeds go to the V-Day Movement, an initiative to end violence against women. So see me after class if you want to get some vagina action on Cupid's holiday."

"Dr. Dreary, why aren't there penis monologues?" one guy asked.

Professor Dreary laughed. "Dear heart, we've been hearing those since the beginning of time. Let the vaginas have their turn, okay? Don't be stingy with the stage of human experience."

The guy sat up straighter in his seat. "I think that's sexist."

She glowered. "Let me make this easy for you. Name a famous female playwright other than the one I just mentioned or the woman who wrote *A Raisin in the Sun*."

His face went vacant, to which she replied, "Exactly."

"Uh, who did write *Raisin*?"

"Lorraine Hansberry."

After theatre, Cadence found time to hang out with Schilar. Although mid-terms were on the horizon, they distracted themselves with each other. Out of nowhere, Cadence asked, "I want to know what turns you on."

"You."

"Seriously, Schilar. Tell me."

"I am telling you. *You* turn me on." Brushing her hair out of his way, he nibbled her neck. His lips forced her eyes shut, but in opening them again, she persisted.

"Okay, if you must know." He grinned. "Yoga pants turn me on. They're just fucking hot."

"I don't own any yoga pants," she said, poking out her bottom lip.

"That's because you don't need any." He focused on her neck again.

"So is there something about me that really turns you on?"

"What is it about you that *doesn't* turn me on?" He stroked her face. "Your beauty, passion, your mind. The way you bite your lip, like you're doing now. So freakin' sexy. Makes me crazy!" Turning on top of her, he whispered, "The real question is—what turns you on?"

She laughed. "I'm not telling you."

"Hey, that's not fair." He rolled away for the moment. "I'll get you to tell me." His fingers began a frenzied search for a weak spot.

She crossed her arms. "Won't work. I'm not ticklish."

"Damn! But seriously, tell me." This time his approach was much more persuasive. His tongue found places he had come to know by heart and his hands returned to the areas he had memorized on the map of her body. He enjoyed the journey and with each new location stopped to ask, "Does this turn you on?"

With each pause, she responded, "Mmmmm." When his fingers reached the button of her jeans, she whispered, "Trains."

He stopped. "What?"

"Trains. Trains turn me on. Trains and Shakespeare."

"I like the trains answer better."

"So you don't want to hear about Shakespeare?"

"No." He reached for the button, and at the sound of it popping free, Steve and Nikki came in.

"Hey you two, get a room," Steve said.

"This is a room." Schilar flopped on his back to stare at the ceiling. "What're you up to?"

The two had been walking around town, checking out the red, white and pink window displays on King Street. Mannequins in scantily clad lingerie threw fantasy into the imaginations of passersby. Steve and Nikki inquired at a few places for dinner reservations, but most were booked for the early and late seatings, tables that would turn and burn on the day of required dining for couples.

"It looks like cupid shit everywhere downtown," Steve said.

"So what *are* we doing for Valentine's?" Nikki pressed.

"Are we *supposed* to do something?"

She kicked at him. "We better."

"What if we don't?"

"Then I may have to find another honey."

"Good luck with that," he said. "You know what the girl-guy ratio is in this city."

It was true. The area lacked a plentiful supply of available males. Although the largest concentration of them resided at The Citadel, these men in uniform were bound by rules and available only at certain times. Dating choices on the peninsula were so dismally pathetic it was a wonder more women didn't consider temporary lesbianism during their college years.

A quick knock preceded the entrance of the suitemates, Parker and Dale, and the latter's girlfriend, Darcie, whom he had been dating since just before Christmas.

"What's happenin'?" Parker said as he plopped down at Schilar's desk and began rummaging through the drawers.

"Nothin' much now," Schilar flinched at the jab from Cadence's elbow. "Just shootin' the shit about all the V-day craziness. Hey man, do you mind?" Schilar said.

"What?" Parker asked. "Oh, sorry, man." He shut the drawers but continued snooping over the things on the desk. "Yeah, great occasion. You get to spend an assload of money to take some girl to an expensive dinner, buy some chocolates, roses, and hope you get some pussy. Fuckin' fantastic night," Parker said, "but without the fucking."

"I think guys should treat their ladies like every day is Valentine's." Dale delivered several pinches to Darcie's side, making her squirm and giggle in a manner most sickening.

"Oh whatever! Guys are such liars," Nikki said. "You'll tell us all that romantic stuff but you don't mean it! You just want to get in our pants."

"Yoga pants," Schilar whispered to Cadence.

"Are you kidding? We're liars? Y'all say all kinds of crap in your padded, push-up bras and thongs. Make us think your tits are three times their actual size and that you're walking around commando. Puh-leeze!" Parker said.

"Hey now, don't be knockin' the ladies' underwear choices," Dale said. "The truth is we all know they look better on the floor." The guys high-fived while the girls' eyes rolled collectively.

Dale soon found out just how unsightly his girlfriend's underwear looked lying on the floor. He didn't come to college with a lot of money; in fact, what he had to survive on was pretty paltry compared to his roommate's lined pockets. Parker would often pay their way to a buzz. Before the holidays and short on cash, Dale discovered that donating sperm proved a good way to finance the luxuries of his life, including presents for Darcie. Whipped as he was, he donated often in condoms and at the clinic. Having just purchased some hot little selections, which were wrapped in a very distinguishable pale and hot pink striped bag, Dale worked extra hard to keep Darcie decked in lace that he very much liked removing.

When his Monday class was canceled, Dale returned to the dorm to hear his roommate getting it on in the bathroom. Their pleasurable sounds turned him on, so he called Darcie for a morning romp of his own. With the first ring, he could have sworn he heard her phone. The second and third were quite distinct, and the fourth confirmed that the sound was coming from the bathroom. Busting through the door, he found some of the lingerie he bought in a crumpled heap on the floor while the rest was hanging loosely from his girlfriend as she straddled Parker atop the toilet.

Dale lunged at Parker, and Darcie, wrapped in what was left of her gifts, screamed at both of them, but her pleas fell on ears deafened by blood and brawn. The commotion moved into the hall where neighbors finally got the two separated, a division that would last forever since Parker moved back with his parents while Dale licked his wounds alone in a room filled with memories of lost love and friendship. In the end, Dale had been shot twice by Cupid: once by the golden arrow of love and once by the leaded arrow of hate.

In keeping with February's theme, love and lust were the topics of discussion in English, with Professor Mirabilis trying to bridge the similarities between the expression of feelings in Shakespeare's time and now. She embarked on this effort in response to a complaint.

"Man, teach, how much longer do we have to read this stuff?" Dewit said. "I can't take much more. It doesn't make any sense. Can't we read something we can relate to?"

"It's not a matter of relating. Shakespeare should not have to conform to your experience, but you should extend yours to meet his. It's a matter of identifying, and what connections can't be made to a protagonist who has mommy issues, hates his stepfather, and is on the rocks with his girlfriend? Granted, it's a little more complicated with the murder, mayhem, and madness, ghosts and graveyards, and souls hanging on the verge of hell, but all in all, I don't see what's not to identify with in some capacity. Unless, of course, you're not human."

"See, when you talk about it, it makes sense, but when I read it, I don't have a clue what they're saying," Dewit admitted, to which the majority nodded in agreement.

"Perhaps I should decode a few lines, just to show you how interesting and naughty Shakespeare can be," she said. "Let's start with Act Three, Scene One when Hamlet commands Ophelia: 'Get thee to a nunnery.' What do you think he means?"

"That she should go to a place where she can protect her innocence," Kirby responded. "Because nuns aren't supposed to possess carnal knowledge."

The professor nodded. "Okay, good. That's the traditional way of reading it, but here's another. Some scholars suggest that in Shakespeare's day, 'nunnery' also meant 'brothel,' so is he really telling her: 'Get thee to a whorehouse?' After all, by this point, he's feigning madness, and well, he's not exactly happy with any women in his life. That's one dual meaning to think about."

They lent her their ears as she relayed the denotations of words many of their high school teachers didn't dare discuss. When Hamlet later asks Ophelia, "Do you think I meant country matters?" they were surprised to learn he means physical lovemaking, and to unlock the pun, she asked them to consider the first syllable of "country." They grinned. In the same scene, Hamlet continues his bawdy suggestions by answering "nothing," as the "fair thought to lie between maids' legs." Eyes widened when she told them that "nothing" usually means something, especially in the case of the "no thing" that distinguishes female genitalia from that of males.

"'Nothing' is often used as slang for 'vagina,'" she explained. "Gives a new reading to the play titled *Much Ado about Nothing*, yes?"

"Now this is the kind of education I'm talkin' about," Dewit said.

"I'll take that as a compliment. This is an apt tie-in for those of you going to see *The Monologues* tonight. I'll close our vocabulary lesson by telling you that the *Oxford English Dictionary* lists one definition of 'to die' as 'to experience sexual orgasm,' so sometimes, when the Bard's characters talk about dying for each other, well, they don't exactly mean leaving this life for the grave. On the contrary, it's much more about achieving life's pleasures."

Professor Mirabilis's students filed out of the room with an appreciation for Shakespeare and a new language of lust and love to use in impressing their friends.

Within the wide realm of pleasures, there are few as innocently pure as the love given by a puppy, and Cadence looked forward to this every time she went into c.a.t.'s. Kyd was getting bigger every day in that crazy way that time quickly ages all lives, but especially those of dogs.

Cadence had a way with animals, and when she came in for her caffeine fix, she ducked in the office to get her doggie one, too. Sometimes, she'd walk him when the shop was busy, but the baristas often fought over this duty, especially the guys, who took him on extra-long outings because Kyd was the optimum tool for attracting women. The pup's panting tongue simply reflected the internal expressions of those who held his leash. When the guys returned from walks with him, their faces held grins bigger than the boxer's and, on occasions, the phone numbers of would-be dates. On Valentine's Day, Cadence bought a heart-shaped toy for Kyd and was meeting Schilar for coffee before she was going to see Miranda in her vaginal debut.

Although she intended to get the day's special, Love Lattes, Cadence was undecided at the coffee board and contemplating the irresistible choices when a voice broke her trance.

"Been in any dark closets with strangers lately?"

She turned to see Walker smiling at her. "Hi," she said softly, her eyes darting about the room.

Reading her worry, he asked, "You looking for someone? My crazy girlfriend, perhaps? She's not here. In fact, we're not together anymore."

The news set Cadence at ease. "Oh, I'm really sorry to hear that."

"No you're not. I heard what she did to you. I'm the one who's sorry," he said. "So, you didn't answer my question."

"Hmm? Oh, no. No dark closets, no strangers."

"Well, you have been in some other dark places." To her confused expression, he held up the copy of *The Gator* that contained her stripper story. "Intriguing, Cadence Cooper. Very intriguing. Did you have fun writing that?"

She blushed. "It was interesting."

It was as if they were back in the quiet of the closet with only the sounds of their voices in the space. Walker relayed how he had stopped in to see Professor Mirabilis who admitted she was having a lot of fun with Cadence's class. All in all, the term was going well.

"Hey, I think you're up." He pointed to the barista waiting to take her order. "Always nice to see you, Cadence."

Cadence got the drinks and settled into the seat next to Schilar. "Who's the dude?"

"Just a guy I met in the library last semester. He lives with Reena's boyfriend. Well, her ex-boyfriend since they broke up. Anyway, he had Mirabilis, too, when he was a freshman."

"Tell me, do you study him as much as he likes studying you?"

Cadence almost spit out her drink. "What? What *are* you talking about?"

"The way he looks at you. Can't say I blame him. It's a lot like the way I look at you." Wrapping his arm around Cadence, he pulled her to him for a passionate kiss in plain, public view.

"Schilar!" She playfully resisted.

"What? Just staking my claim."

"I bet whatever look he gave me doesn't even compare with the looks those groupies give you."

"What groupies?"

"The ones that flock in front of your stage. You can't tell me you don't notice them."

"I see them, but I'm not interested in them," he said, shifting the subject. "So, I got you a Valentine's Day gift." He pulled a CD from his backpack. It had a specially designed label with the title: "Ten Songs that Remind Me of You."

Cadence read the list, smiling at each selection. "Hey, there's only nine songs on here."

He took the disc. "Oh, damn. I guess I miscounted. Good thing I'm not a math major. You still like it, right?"

She leaned over and kissed his cheek. "I got you something, too," she whispered.

He waited for her to present it, but nothing appeared. "Well, where is it?"

"Look around."

Schilar's eyes moved about the shop and back to Cadence, who urged him to look slowly throughout the space, to take it all in. He had never really paid attention to the paintings and photographs by the student artists whom Catissa so faithfully supported. As he scanned the framed works, his eyes were drawn to one in particular. It was a photo of a guitar that looked all too familiar. His chair slid across the hardwood, and Cadence watched him walk over to it.

She had captured the polished instrument leaning against a tree on the Grand Lawn. The smooth, red and vanilla body provided a striking contrast against the aged oak's rough, gray exterior. Positioned so that it threw the afternoon light behind it, the guitar reflected pieces of the park from all angles. In the background appeared another tree, its sprawling arms lit by a ghostly glow that seemed to add some magical aura to the photo, a sensation similar to the one the guitar emitted when Schilar strummed it.

Cadence came up behind him. "Do you like it?"

He kissed her on the forehead. "It's incredible. But how'd you get it?"

"With a little help from your roommate."

"Cadence," he said, wrapping his arm around her shoulders, "I've been wanting to ask you something. I've been thinking about it for a while. Would you mind if I named my guitar after your horse?"

She pursed her lips to stem the tide rising in her eyes and nodded her head into his shoulder. "I didn't mean to upset you," he said. "I've just thought about how you described him being full of fire and life with a little bit of the devil inside. That's powerful. It's exactly how I feel when I hold that instrument. It is Gunpowder."

Wiping her eyes, she whispered, "The name's all yours."

"You know," Catissa said, stepping over to them, "I've come to like this photograph very much, Schilar. I don't think I'm going to let you take it down."

"That would be trouble, Catissa. It's the coolest gift I've ever gotten."

"It *is* incredibly cool. So, what do you two lovebirds have planned for the night?"

"I'm going to see my friend in *The Vagina Monologues,* and he's playing at a little Italian restaurant."

"Oh, sounds good for both of you, except for the not being together part. Cadence, that's such a fabulous production. You'll love it. And Schilar, I must get you in here one night to play for us," Catissa said. "Now, you two sit back down and admire that photo over a piece of my ridiculously romantic red velvet cake."

The flavor was indeed ridiculous; it was the kind of treat that creates addiction on the first bite. But Catissa, knowing that too much of good cake makes it less tasty, offered it only one week a year so that lovers would wait in longing. In some ways, the annual performance of the monologues created a similar anticipation.

A rainbow of identities filled the auditorium that night, and Cadence was surprised to see that nearly half of those in attendance were guys. Of course, this should not have been too shocking since males find women who are in touch with themselves a fascinating attraction. The monologues portrayed just how funny, frustrating, erotic, exciting, controversial and comforting the relationship between a woman and her supposed "nothingness" can be.

Of all the monologues, Miranda's one of the lesbian vagina was delivered with such dramatic sensuality it left many wondering if she didn't have first-hand knowledge of the material. Cadence marveled at her friend's performance and could see that Miranda had found a place under the theatre's spotlight, in the loving company of her fellow players.

By the night's end, the monologists had made much to do out of nothing. They projected the smells, sounds, tastes, looks, and feelings of a woman's essence. They inspired vaginas to wake up, get dressed, go out and talk to the world. They reclaimed *cunt*, repurposed *pussy*, renamed *down there*, and reimagined the sadly sterilized way of viewing vaginas. They made the mirror a happy and beautiful one to hold when gazing at the red, velvety folds of a woman's flower, and left the audience energized by the endlessly empowering ways of the vaginas.

Having missed Miranda's acting debut, Reena was curled in the fetal position of heartache, wrapped in her former lover's tear-stained T-shirt. It was after midnight when her phone began to dance across her desk; she knew it was probably her roommate urging her to join the theatre afterparty, but when she saw the number, the phone's vibrations jolted through her arm straight into her heart. She answered immediately but with a delayed "Hello." Seconds of silence maintained their separation until two simple words connected them again: "Come over." It was all she needed to hear. She didn't bother with clothes or shoes—just a black coat.

In the pouring rain, she slipped over puddles and blocks later climbed the stairs to him. Blaze was waiting in the hammock when Reena's silhouette crossed the porch's threshold. She was cold, shaking, wet. Leading her inside the dark house, he warmed her with touches so deep they cured her chill instantly, and his tongue worked as an elixir bringing her back from the edge of death. Throughout the night, he said nothing and she said nothing, but the poetry between their bodies created its own memorable language, maddening lines of longing that would draw her to him again and again and again.

Chapter 15

Urban Studies 200
Designing Dreamscapes

Gold glinting on Charleston's streets is not a common occurrence, but in a mystical place where pirates pillaged their ways to fame and misfortune, anything is possible. On this day, a trail of glitter emanated from the most unlikely of sources: a guy with a cache of formal dresses slung over his shoulder. Following this prince and his treasures, Cadence stepped into the vestibule of a church not far from campus where once upon a year, fairy tale dreams are made for Cinderellas in the area.

"Are you here to volunteer?" a young woman immediately asked when she saw a visitor standing in the doorway.

"Um, I'm not sure." Cadence glanced around. "What is this?"

"This is the Cinderella Project. I'm Alise, the director." Like a showroom model, she swept her hand across the space and extended it to her guest. "We're going to make some girls very happy tomorrow."

As godmother of the Cinderella Project, Alise was a tenacious professional who practiced law when she wasn't weaving dreams and giving old dresses new owners. She explained that in the morning, the hall would be filled with girls lacking the means to afford prom's luxuries. Thanks to donations, they would find their dresses, shoes and accessories. With her hours free, Cadence stayed and let the feel of sequins and sateen transport her back to the first time she discovered the magic in a magnificent dress.

Anything but jeans had always been foreign fashion to Cadence. She wanted nothing to do with flowery, frilly, lacy or feminine clothing. As a tomboy to the core, Cadence preferred dungarees and boots, which were also the uniform of work on the farm. Some would say she was fashion challenged, but keeping up with trends was never a concern for her until it came to the coveted event of prom, an occasion so important it rivaled graduation night in high school.

The hype over the essentials—dress, hair, nails, make-up, shoes, and jewelry—was not too dissimilar from the stress brides-to-be exhibit before their special days. Indeed, teenagers prepared for prom as if it were a wedding night, and as a consummation of sorts, it proves for some to be the "Night of Virgin Sacrifice." The routine was simple: spend the day getting primped; take obligatory photographs; ride in a fancy car to a nice restaurant; eat a gourmet meal; do a little dancing at the prom; hit all the after-parties in the post-prom outfit; make out with date and go home, or spend the night with the date and go home. Because she had a strict curfew of midnight that was guaranteed by means of a shotgun, Cadence was forced into the former option.

When prom time rolled around, Cadence was still largely wounded from Damien's desertion. She didn't have a boyfriend and was not interested in one, but as couples paired off, she feared the regret of not going and secretly wanted to attend. Prospects were dismal until Tony, a senior and distant friend, asked her.

At her mom's urging, they made an outing to Atlanta to shop for a dress. It was the first time Cadence entered a concrete jungle of this size. Being accustomed to the openness of the country, her senses were accosted by the constant noise, the exhaust-laden air, and the shadowy palette of glassy towers. Despite these displeasures, something about the constant hum, the vibrations of lives thriving in a concentrated space appealed to her, but not enough to make her want to go to college in a metropolis. Something on a smaller scale would be an ideal fit for her, a school that wasn't too flashy or modern, too tight or loose—a college that fit like the perfect dress.

Exasperated with Cadence's resistance to anything she suggested, her mother was ready to glue sequins on a bedsheet for the dress. They were circling the last store on that exhausting day of searching when a row of color flashed from a rack.

Ankle-length, strapless, black taffeta, with a spectrum of sequins vertically circling the bodice to the waist: it was a fantasy dress. She wanted it but had her doubts about how it would look until she tried it on. The euphoria was immediate, and she finally understood the fascination.

A dress is a deflated wasteland of wrinkles and folds waiting to be filled and fulfilled, and when the right figure raises the rag to life, it catapults the wearer into a defining moment. Few experiences match the thrill of slipping into fabric that becomes second skin, infusing a person with an all-conquering attitude, with superpowers that temporarily destroy opinions about the evils of materialism. The evanescent moment usually lasts until midnight or a short time thereafter, but the memory becomes its own sanctuary, a place to return when esteem bottoms out and the aesthetic identity needs lifting.

And that's exactly what happened when Cadence put on this dress—in that store, at home, and of course, on prom night. For weeks, it waited in clear plastic on the back of her door for its debut. Seemingly, it wanted to be worn as much as she wanted to wear it, and when she did, she joined her classmates, the other queens at court. The prom's theme was Bright Lights, Big City, an apt contrast for a rural high school, but thousands of bulbs strung in the rafters and the silhouette of skyscrapers helped transform the drab and smelly gym into an ethereal escape from the confines of the country. Despite the excitement of a different kind of night, Cadence's heart was elsewhere. Tony got plastered, so Baxley made sure she got home safely, and except for the incredible aura of that dress, it was a night that she'd remember to forget.

"That's an especially nice one." Alise's voice brought Cadence out of her daydream.

"Yeah, it is. There's a tag on it." A quick glance at the flimsy paper made her eyes widen. "Wow, this dress is $500! And it was donated?"

"Uh-huh." Alise beamed with pride. "Charleston is an incredible community of giving. A lot of the boutique owners send new dresses, some have gone out of season. Our girls get to choose from some of the best. Leave those tags on. They provide a little something extra."

Cadence continued sorting until a flood of other volunteers filled the room, and she decided to move on. She was on her way out when Alise stopped her.

"So you walked in on the hard part, but if you're free tomorrow, you're welcome to come back and be a part of the fun." Alise pointed to Cadence's camera. "You always carry that around?"

"Most of the time. I'm a photographer for *The Gator*, the newspaper at Charlestowne?"

"Yes, I know it well. I'm an alum," she said. "If you want more volunteer hours, you could always come take some pictures. It may be a good feature for the paper, and to be honest, it'd be great to have some mementoes, if you'd be willing to share your talents with us." Alise had superior persuasion skills because Cadence agreed to photograph the project. To remember her commitment, she wrote *Cinderella* on her hand. As she left, she wove her way through the army of volunteers scurrying about like mice to create the fashion wonderland.

Volunteering a few hours made that Friday even more perfect than it already was. It had been that kind of day when the sun sits just right in the sky—not too close, not too far away, when a cooling breeze brushes the skin lightly, when early spring begins peeking from behind winter's coat. It was a day that makes a person breathe in the pure pleasure of being alive and breathe out silent thanks for the opportunity.

For the rest of the afternoon, Cadence wandered the streets, taking advantage of the time since TJ had asked her to photograph the Wine + Food Festival. The assignment was infringing on her spring break, so he scraped some money from his budget to pay her for staying. Midterms had gone well, or so she thought; everyone except Professor Mirabilis had given them, but the English teacher preferred to keep them engaged over their hiatus with an essay due when they returned. Cadence expected her peers' papers would bear the marks of suntan oil and other liquid indulgences of their fun-filled destinations. But for her, it was back to the farm where she hoped to avoid Baxley, enjoy time with her parents, and work on her assignment. For now, her project was simply taking in the city.

Strolling down King Street can instill a sense of royalty, a feeling that echoes the aristocratic roots of King Charles II, for whom the street and city were named. Known as "The Merry Monarch," Charles's court perfected the *carpe diem* philosophy of "seize the day," by taking every available opportunity to eat, drink, and be merry. He did so with numerous lovers; within his court, he fathered twelve bastard children with seven women, and outside of his royal circle, many more illegitimate offspring resulted from his trysts. The shophouses of lingerie, shoe, and jewelry stores with apartments above would have indulged Charles's senses, and his well-heeled feet would have stumbled into more than a few of the bars.

At the corner of King and Market, Cadence looked toward the Godiva shop and up to the window out of which came the bullets that ended the life of Rumpty Rattles. Knowing some history of the pathways she now walked intensified her journey. With every step, it was as if the city whispered its secrets only to Cadence, and she felt an ethereal excitement in imaging life a century ago. Olin's stories of Prohibition were apt since she couldn't indulge in alcohol legally but still found clandestine ways to enjoy the forbidden. The Market area was still a hangout for drunken college boys and girls who loved to dance, and although not overtly seen, Cadence suspected sex-selling women visited some hotel rooms. All in all, it didn't seem as if much had changed—except everything.

Strolling past Market, she came upon King's avenue of antiques, a gilded section featuring everyday artifacts of times past. China, mirrors, silver, and chandeliers gleamed with aged brilliance; the displays appropriately led to the threshold of Broad Street, a divider marking a crossing over into a very different economic zip code. Harboring the oldest and most expensive homes on the peninsula, the South of Broad borough is the touchstone Charlestonians use to define true affluence.

Before she crossed over Broad Street, the opulence radiating from an awning-topped window held her. The fashion marquee perched on the corner announced Berlin's distinguished role in clothing the city's men and women since 1883. The majestic dresses behind this glass project a fantasy so overpowering that browsers may be suddenly seized by a desire to slip into the advertised life of luxury and elegantly glide into some fine party that is the toast of the township. In observing the exquisite finery for Charleston's society ladies, Cadence thought of how at the other end of King, Alise and her mice were working to ensure less privileged girls received the same revered reception when they made their grand entrances into prom.

Steps later, Cadence reached the oasis at the city's tip and took in the treasures of White Point Garden, a park flanked on the south and east sides by Low and High Battery. Originally called "Oyster Point" by early settlers because of the sun-bleached shells that once covered it, the green area has been the grisly scene of executions, site of a bathhouse featuring a cake and ice cream parlor on top, and a popular music venue with concerts performed in the bandstand. Meandering beneath the oaks toward the seawall of Low Battery, she came upon the bronze statue of a little dancing girl, a Willard Hirsch sculpture gifted to the city by Sally Carrington in 1962. A surprising find for the ongoing dancing story, Cadence caught the small symbol of joy in mid-step, her delicate toes forever dangling just above a trickling fountain made for children.

A walk through Charleston is tiringly energizing with every turn bringing into view a photo-worthy scene. Cadence sat on the steps that divide the promenade of Low Battery from High. In the midst of jotting down photo ideas in her notebook, she heard clops that jolted her heart. This time she fought the tears, steeling herself with the assurance that a little bit of Gunpowder echoed in the hooves of all horses. It made the sound easier to bear; she hadn't intended to look, but she couldn't help it when the massive animal stopped right in front of her.

The carriage driver, a bearded man with a white sun hat, smiled down at her. "Studying? I thought college students were supposed to be on spring break."

Cadence's eyes rolled lovingly over the horse and up to the man. "Yeah, we are. I'm not studying. Just resting. I've been walking for a while."

"Well, you couldn't have picked a better day for it." Tilting his head back, he took in the aqua sky. "Headed anywhere in particular?"

She stood, brushing grit from the seat of her jeans. "Back to campus, I guess."

"You've got some ground to make. Want me and Elvis to take you halfway?" He motioned to the white horse, a Percheron draft, whose skin twitched with shine while the breeze lifted his black mane.

"Sir, I don't have money for a carriage ride. Thanks anyway."

He chuckled. "I'm headed back to the barn, and my coach is empty. This one's on me. Hop in."

Having never been in a horse-drawn carriage, she could hardly contain her enthusiasm. She thanked the driver, who introduced himself as Garrison, a ten-year veteran of the carriage company and an architectural encyclopedia.

A slight tap of the reins propelled Elvis forward. "So, what can you tell me about the city?" Cadence asked.

"That's pretty broad. What d'you want to know?"

"Anything." Since they were passing the postcard homes of East Battery, she pointed to a pastel mansion. "Tell me about that one."

"Ah, Five East Battery," he said fondly, "that's the John Ravenel House. Built from 1847 to '49. Ten bedrooms, nine and a half baths, black marble fireplaces, two secret passages." He gently stopped the carriage. "But those have been filled in. It's in the Italianate style, and there's still a Union cannonball stuck in a wall on the second floor."

While they sat in front of the peach-colored palace, Garrison told her that Ravenel, of French Huguenot descent, was an aristocratic planter at first then a merchant and shipper. He was also the president of the South Carolina Rail Road. Cadence thought of her affinity for trains and smiled. Here she was in front of the house of a man who was largely responsible for the tracks in her home state.

Garrison also pointed out that the piazzas of the peninsula's houses were built facing south and west to catch the prevailing winds during the brutal summers, and he motioned to the house next door, a Greek Revival built in 1838 by William Roper, a wealthy cotton planter who wanted his home to be the first visitors saw when approaching from the sea.

"Now Cadence, those gargantuan two-story Ionic columns can certainly be seen from boats, and if you look real close around some of the doors, like the one on the Roper house there, you'll see a rope symbol. And yes, he may have intended the pun." Garrison grinned. "That's a Chinese symbol of wealth and prosperity. Now, just having come from White Point, well, there's an interesting history regarding rope use there. Did you know that's where they hung the pirates?"

Somehow, she had missed that historical marker, but the human one accompanying her told the story. In her early days, Charles Towne welcomed pirates like Edward "Blackbeard" Teach and Stede Bonnet the "Gentleman Pirate." The swashbucklers and their crews spent gold looted from Spanish galleons in the taverns and shops, but when the thieves began attacking British ships bound for the city, they weren't as well received. Famed for his powdered wig and fine clothes, Bonnet was the antithesis of the hardened buccaneer, but when he teamed with Blackbeard to blockade the city in 1718, pillaging, ransacking, and taking hostages, the governor had them hunted down. Bonnet was captured, returned to Charles Towne, tried, and hanged along with his crew. His body dangled for days until it was buried in the marsh below the low water mark.

"Speaking of ropes, Cadence, ever heard of keelhauling?" Garrison asked, to which she shook her head.

"It's been rumored that Bonnet liked this method for his victims when their ransoms weren't paid. They'd run a rope under the ship then tie a person to one end and drag them under the boat," Garrison explained. "With the boat's bottom covered in barnacles, if the person didn't drown, the poor soul was cut to shreds, sometimes decapitated." He turned to see if she had a reaction.

Her face scrunched in disgust. "I think I like the rope over the door better. By the way, how do you know all this?"

"Well, it's my job. The city requires all tour guides to be certified. But it's more than that for me. I want to learn as much as possible about the place I live. Knowing connects me to details I'd otherwise pass by and never think about."

"Okay, like what?"

"Good timing on the question, Cadence." He stopped the horse in front of a pink house, one decorated with ornamental wrought iron. "Okay, see that rectangular stone sitting on the sidewalk? What do you think it is?"

She peered at the unsightly block that seemed like a wart on the otherwise tidy streetscape. "Um, a cheap version of a bench? I have no idea."

He laughed. "Those, my dear, are upping stones. They're relics of a time when carriages and horses were the main modes of getting around. That one is made of limestone, but others in town are carved from brownstone, granite, marble, or concrete. Stonecutters shaped them into rectangles, half-circles, circles, and some even have dual steps."

"So that's what people used to get in and out of carriages?"

"Yep. Or to mount a horse. But they're also symbols of social status. That's why this South of Broad area has the most upping stones. As you've seen, lots of wealth was displayed here." He looked up and down the street. "And of course, still is."

Cadence snapped away before Elvis resumed his march toward the Market, and Garrison shared more, which Cadence attentively absorbed. They passed the pastel pleasure of Rainbow Row, houses that reminded Cadence of cotton candy, as did so many of the city's other colorful abodes. Garrison thought that observation fitting since many of the houses were built from "cotton" money of a different kind.

He told her that Rainbow Row wasn't always painted like that. In the early 1900s, Dorothy Porcher Legge revitalized this section, which had become a slum following the Civil War or as Southerners often call it: "The War of Northern Aggression."

Legge renovated the buildings and chose these bright hues perhaps because she liked the Caribbean color scheme or maybe the lighter shades helped keep the buildings cooler. Other homeowners followed suit, and the pretty paints continue to blossom all over the city.

Sitting high in the carriage as it trundled over the storied streets, Cadence felt a little like a princess. Her coachman informed her of the colony's condition and of her cultural inheritance, one that began when King Charles granted Eight Lords Proprietors a slice of land running between the latitudes of 36 and 31 degrees, extending from the Atlantic to the Pacific. Plans for the city's checkerboard layout called "The Grand Modell" were sent from England. At this time, creeks cut deep into today's nicely rounded peninsula, so most of the land was filled in. The street that Cadence traveled over now, East Bay, was once named Front Street because it was on the water and eventually fell within the city walls. Charles Towne became the first English walled city, protected by bastions and surrounded by a moat to guard against attacks from the Spanish, French, Native Americans, and of course, from pirates.

"And I've already told you about those brigands," Garrison said as the ride rolled to a stop in front of the stables.

Climbing out of the carriage, Cadence extended her hand. "Thanks for the lessons and the ride, Professor Garrison." She went to pull her hand away from their shake, but he held it firmly.

"Cinderella?" he asked, reading the black writing.

She had forgotten it was there. "Oh, it's a reminder to shoot photos for the Cinderella Project tomorrow. It gives girls who can't afford dresses what they need for prom."

"Ah," he said, rubbing his peppered beard. "My friend works for another carriage company and mentioned taking the princess coach down there in the morning. It's shaped like a pumpkin and loaded with lights. It's pretty cool at night, and little girls love it. So you're a photographer?"

"I take pictures," she said. "That's what I was doing today before you came along."

When Garrison asked if he could see her work, Cadence shared the shots. Many caught the sunlight scattered about the shadowy passages of homes guarded by intricate iron gates.

"I love how the light falls in the city and creates these patterns in the shade," Cadence said.

"That's called *chiaroscuro*. It's Italian for bold contrasts of light and dark. See that play of shadows? It's in nearly all of your photos. You use it well."

Before departing, Cadence took a photo of Garrison beside Elvis then stepped to the side of the horse's face. Softly, she raised her hand to his nostrils moved her fingers from the bridge of his nose over the bony tenderness of his muzzle. When she breathed in deeply, he lowered his head, splaying his ears to their sides. "Thanks," she whispered and stepped away. From a distance, she heard Elvis sigh, his deep exhalation fluttered with relaxation, a sound she had heard so many times before and was finally glad to hear once more.

Darkness had almost descended when she neared her dorm. With most of the campus cafeterias closed, she stopped for takeout at a Chinese dive famed for its savory noodles. Next to the door sat a man with a small shopping cart filled with everything he owned.

"Excuse me, miss. Could you spare a few dollars?" he asked, with lips parting into a toothless grin.

She started to walk on by, to conveniently ignore his plea. After all, she had always been told that talking to strangers was dangerous, especially destitute ones.

"Sir, I don't have any cash on me." The photos of tasty plates plastered to the window made her anxious to settle her hunger. "But if you want something to eat, I could buy you some dinner."

"That, that would be mighty nice of you," he said.

"What would you like?"

"Anything, ma'am. I ain't fussy."

Cadence bought enough food for a few meals—egg rolls, fried rice, sweet and sour chicken, lo mein—and asked for extra fortune cookies. When she handed the man the bag, his eyes widened with surprise.

"Oh, miss, this here's a lot. I'm right thankful fo' it. God bless you."

"Enjoy your dinner." She could hardly wait to eat. To lessen her hunger pains, she had dessert first. Cracking open the fortune cookie, she ate half of its crunchy sweetness and pulled out the slip tucked inside. *Doors will be opening for you in many areas of your life*, she read as she passed through the entrance of her dorm.

An early string of rings from her phone began the day: calls from her parents and family, followed by messages from friends wishing her a happy birthday. She was disappointed that she had yet to hear from Schilar when she left for the project. Turning the corner to the church's auditorium, Cadence saw chattering girls and their mothers lined up around the block. As Garrison predicted, the pumpkin coach was parked on the street; a shimmering pink dress dangled from its open door.

Girls flooded into the boutique in waves as volunteers shuffled to and fro directing the would-be Cinderellas to the fulfilling of dreams. The sparkle and glow of excited girls outshined the dresses. Cadence floated through the aisles capturing the celebration of youth, and it wasn't long before she saw the moment when one teen found the cloth that would be the cocoon of her metamorphosis. When the girl twirled in front of the mirror, a woman whose entrenched wrinkles told of hard times brought her trembling hand to her mouth. Her tired eyes found energy in this vision of her daughter, and fortunately, the moment was repeated throughout the day and would be again on that special night.

Just before she was ready to leave for her next assignment, Cadence showed a very pleased Alise the photos. "So what are your plans for the rest of the day?" she asked, her eyes still monitoring every aspect of the room.

"Oh, I have to shoot a food festival event," Cadence said. "After that, I'm not sure. It's my birthday, so I may treat myself to something. I just don't know what."

Alise raised her brows. "Your birthday, huh? Well then, allow me to treat you. The shopping rush is over, and most of these dresses will go into storage." She pointed to the unclaimed beauties. "Go pick one."

"No, no, I couldn't."

"I insist. You can always give it back next year. Now go on, pick yourself out a birthday present." Alise nudged Cadence toward the racks. Overwhelmed by the choices, she didn't know where to begin, so she migrated toward the essential color of black, and when she saw it that once-upon-a-time feeling returned.

"Ah, a great choice. Every woman should have a little black dress. I love the sexy slit it has." Alise stood back and studied Cadence's find. "Hmmm . . . but I think it may need something more. Come with me."

Over at the accessory table, Alise held a dangling pair of ruby earrings beside Cadence's face. "These will really make it shine—not that your smile isn't enough. Yes, perfect. Now, where's your prince?"

Cadence laughed. "Out of town."

"Then he'll have to take you out when he gets back."

After thanking Alise for the gifts, Cadence moved toward the door, but before she could get out, the director was on a chair holding a cupcake with a glowing candle and announcing to everyone that it was a volunteer's birthday. She led the room in the song and brought the treat over to Cadence who made her wish.

Returning to her dorm, she hung the dress carefully, admiring its simplicity but wondering when she was ever going to have an occasion to wear it. She took a few minutes to check for messages from Schilar but there were none. She didn't remain long in the room before venturing to a local cooking studio that was sponsoring the College Series Cook-Off, one of many events created in connection with the multi-day gustatory celebration. TJ wanted Cadence to photograph the Rockin' Ramen Rumble where contestants use the famed noodles to create delectable dishes. All the participants were students, the judges were local chefs, and the audience was anyone willing to watch the boiling, sautéing, and serving up of the sodium-saturated college staple.

Steam rose from the pots as the noodles rolled in liquid and sweat formed on the brows of the aspiring chefs. Cadence moved unobtrusively around the scene, snapping the action. She had stepped to the side aisle when someone loudly whispered, "Hey, paparazzi, do you ever give it a rest?"

"Very funny."

"So you're a foodie, too?" Dakota asked.

"No, just covering this event. What're you doing here?" She crouched next to his end-row seat.

"See that good looking man up there with the noodles?"

"Dakota, they all have noodles."

"Don't I know it, but the *good* looking one? That's my friend, Stefan." Cadence shot him an expression of knowing better. "No, he really *is* just a friend. I'm here for support."

They watched for the judges' expressions indicating the results as they tasted the creations. Cadence sensed Dakota's nervousness when the countdown to first place began. Third and second places went to a Ramen pizza and Ramen spaghetti with veggie meatballs, but the dish that got the culinary crown was Stefan's Hoppin' John Ramen, a delectable mixture of rice, field peas, and pulled pork inspired by the Southern dish famed for bringing luck and money to those who begin the New Year with it. In swapping the rice for the noodles, Stefan put a very different spin on the tradition and topped the creation with a scoop of collards that would have made his granny very proud. Cadence hung around to get all the necessary information for the feature and chatted with her classmate while Stefan enjoyed congratulations.

After a while, Cadence turned to go when Dakota asked, "So, what are your plans tonight?"

"Um, I don't have any. Everyone's gone." Her voice broke a little from the sadness and self-pity that had begun to surface.

"Honey, what is it?"

Cadence bit her lip. "Just feelin' a little sorry for myself, missing my family." She wiped her misty eyes. "Truthfully, it's my birthday. I guess I didn't think I'd be spending my first one in college alone. I should've been home by now, but this thing came up, so I don't leave until tomorrow."

Dakota cupped his hands on her shoulders. "Well, you're not going to spend your birthday alone, okay? Let's go out tonight. Hit this town, really get dolled up." His expression was suddenly serious. "Do you have a good dress?"

Cadence managed a half-smile. "I think so."

Snapping his fingers three times in that trademark Z formation, he said, "Well throw that shit on grrl! 'Cause we're going to prance all over this pretty peninsula."

With his instructions to "go get ready," Cadence returned to the dorm to change. She was in the shower when she missed a call from Schilar. The message was brief but sweet. She had tried to get him to stay through the weekend, but the pull of the road proved too much. Over the next week, he would call when he could, which was not often. Her attempts to reach him were answered with voice mail, so a frustrating game of phone tag ensued. Cadence longed for him, wanted more pleasant memories, but the ones she recalled were sometimes disrupted by imagining the hordes of groupies surrounding him. But tonight, on her birthday, she vowed not to let these insecurities ruin the occasion.

As if she were the male counterpart to the date, Cadence arrived on time to his apartment and rang the bell. Dakota welcomed her with air kisses to both cheeks before sweeping his arms dramatically toward the living room. His apartment looked as if it had been decorated by a professional. On the table was a bottle of Prosecco chilling in a bucket, the cheap

Italian bubbly that's pure, plain fun. Next to it was the monarch of college staples—a pizza, but in his sophistication, Dakota opted for a classic Margherita, with olive oil, basil, tomatoes and mozzarella. It paired especially well with the drink, and they toasted her birthday, Stefan's win, spring break, the class that brought them together, and college life.

When they finished dinner, Dakota said, "Now, stand over there and let me get a good look at you."

Following the steps of those she had seen that morning, Cadence twirled like a flirty model as Dakota gazed approvingly on her mane and the flashes of red emanating from her earlobes. His "Mhmms" responded to the way the dress hugged her and the sexy slit up the thigh, but when he got to her feet, horror contorted his face.

"Cadence, what are those drill sergeant things on your feet?" He pointed to the flat, black, scuffed monstrosities. The twirling ceased and Cadence looked down in humiliation.

"They're all I have."

"I'm not letting you ruin a fabulous dress with those. Come with me."

Leading her to his closet, he opened the door to a fabulous fashion collection. Of course there was guy wear: buttoned shirts, ties, pants, and jeans, and organized according to color and ironed to perfection with razor-like creases. But there was another side—one filled with dresses, skirts, and shoes that could wake the sleeping beauty in any woman or in any cross-fashioned man. Browsing his clothing buffet, Dakota pulled a black box from it.

When Cadence opened it, her eyes widened in wonder at shoes that could have transported her to Oz with the proverbial click of red glittered heels. Cadence held one up to the light as if it were glass and she was looking into a shimmering future.

Dakota watched her. "I know, they're pretty aren't they? Lucky for you, I have small feet. Here, allow me." Taking the shoe, he bent down and slipped it on her foot. At first, it resisted the feel of something other than sneakers but eventually surrendered to the indulgence. The other foot followed the right's example. Teetering inches above her normal height made Cadence nervous, but there was also an inexplicable power in the feel of the heels, one that would carry her confidently through the night in these magical slippers, even though she was shaky in every step.

"Now that we've got you primed for the ball, princess, I need to get ready. He tapped his finger to his lips and selected gray suit pants, matching vest, and a black shirt. As Cadence sat on the bed with her grape juice, admiring her feet and Dakota, he looked her over from crown to toe again, and without removing his eyes, reached in with a grin and grabbed a deep red tie from the rack.

She laughed. "Oh, we're going to match?"

"But, of course. Why not? We make a spectacular couple. Well, except for the sex thing. That's okay, though. It's not everything, right?" He waited for a response, which was given in uncontrollable giggles.

Cadence had never watched a guy take such care in getting ready. He took his time in making sure every strand of hair was in place, but when done, it was tidily tousled. Spreading cologne in all the vital places, Dakota moved the scent over his body just as a woman would her perfume. She liked the way he raised his brows and threw puckered expressions into the mirror just as a model would.

"Hey Dakota, I think every woman needs a gay man for a friend."

"Don't I know it, honey. If only to tell them they're beautiful. You know?" He turned his attention again to his reflection. "Is there anyone in the universe who doesn't want to be told they're beautiful? Inside or out, natural or made-up? It doesn't matter—people need to hear that." He skillfully finished the knot on his tie and revisited his hair.

"Dakota," she said, "you're beautiful." He froze in a vogue-like pose, and Cadence thought she saw his eyes glass over. "So where *are* we going?"

"Somewhere fashionably fun."

Strutting down the catwalk of King, Cadence looped her arm through Dakota's to steady her steps in borrowed heels. Strolling in a friendship that felt old, they had just passed a window when Cadence stopped suddenly. Like most on this street, the glass framed a dreamy setting: sweet everythings whispered over exquisite dishes lit by candlelight, a piano sounding intoxicating melodies of love. Cadence didn't want to believe what she saw.

"See that guy, the one with that woman, in the corner?" Cadence pointed discreetly to the subjects in question. "That's my friend's boyfriend. She's gone for spring break, but she mentioned he was staying here and that his cousin would be in town."

Cadence and Dakota watched Blaze pour more wine for the woman and reach for her hand. They were sitting close, very close, and although the way his eyes fell on his dinner companion was different than the way he looked at Reena, this date didn't seem like family.

"You say that's supposed to be his cousin?" Dakota squinted at the couple. "Grrl, if that's his cousin then I'm all about snatch. That guy is clearly shakin' two trees." Dakota took a disappointed Cadence by the hand. "Come on, let's go."

The temple he took her to wouldn't be considered holy by most standards, but it was certainly a place where anyone could parade like a Greek god. As a haven for gays, lesbians, bisexuals, and trans members, Club Pantheon was putting on a show in advance of Fashion Week, and Dakota scored front row seats to the event.

Cadence felt like a VIP as she watched men sporting dresses and women in suits sashay down the runway, stop, pose, pivot in stilettos, and prance off behind the curtain. It was an interesting reversal of roles to see that each time the men turned, their sequins spun sparkles across the audience like strobe lights at a disco. Sassy, sexy, elegant and enchanting—they were exactly what many women donning heels and flashy attire desired to be. As the models strutted, Dakota and Cadence responded with "oohs and aahs" when inspired and scrunched faces at particularly hideous ensembles. Being a stage-side fashion critic was new to her, but with Dakota as her seasoned guide, it was an experience she hoped to have again.

After the show, he introduced her to some of his friends. One of them, Amani, seemed especially enamored with Dakota. This queen stood close so that even the slightest movement caused friction in the fabric between them. Dakota didn't seem too interested, which caused Amani to compensate the inattention with even more exaggerated expressions and overly dramatic arm talking. Before they said goodbye, Amani plucked a red carnation from her bustier and placed it in Dakota's lapel. They said goodbye with air kisses, but Cadence got the feeling Amani wanted something more solid in their parting.

It was late when they stepped out of the club, but Dakota clutched an unopened bottle of bubbly in hand. "Is that for tomorrow?" she asked.

He held it up. "It is tomorrow and darlin', we haven't had cake yet!"

Since it was after midnight, it technically wasn't her birthday anymore, but she wasn't going to argue. They stepped into a restaurant where Dakota asked her to wait while he spoke with the bartender. A few minutes later, he had secured a dessert to-go and plasticware, and they walked over to a parking garage. As they passed the exit booth, a young woman, her brown face dismal with boredom and entrapment, glanced up from a book laying open before her. The pseudo-couple took the elevator to the deserted top deck and settled in a corner that gave them an inspiring view of the harbor.

Another cork pop began the night's end, as Dakota sang "Happy Birthday." They shared peach and ginger cheesecake against the backdrop of the bridge, its double diamonds glowed like jewels on the skyline. In between the decadent bites, they talked about dreams they never wanted to forget. Dakota aspired to own an events company, to become the guru of designing, entertaining, and hospitality. He was a communications major and a business minor, so he'd be prepared to promote and run his own firm. After that, he wanted to meet a prince charming, settle down, maybe have kids, travel, retire, die comfortably happy. His dream sounded like that of so many others.

"Dakota, can I ask you a personal question?"

"Shoot, birthday girl."

"How long have you known, you know, that you were gay?"

Turning his face to the celestial ceiling, he breathed in deeply and exhaled his truth. "Ever since I was born. I've always known I wasn't interested in girls, just like you've always known you're attracted to boys." He turned to her. "You know, Cadence, people say asinine things like it's a choice. It's demeaning when others think you choose your sexuality like you choose a pair of shoes or what you're going to eat. Yeah, I choose to be gay just like other people choose to be heterosexual. How we all feel is instinctual, a natural inclination."

"Do your parents know?"

"Oh, yeah. I had to tell them my junior year of high school when they caught me with a guy. They didn't take it well. Both think that if they pray enough, I'll get cured. You know, come around to the right choice?"

Dakota told her about faking it for nearly all his life by conforming to the religious pressures of a small town; about hating himself for not being able to be himself; about letting the mentalities of hypocrites imprisoned by the tunnel vision of a cross dominate him. In hiding his emotional truth, he lived a sensual lie when he pretended to like girls, even going to prom with a friend who suspected he was gay but kept his secret. On what was supposed to be an unforgettable night, he didn't want any memories of it since he longed to be with someone else.

When Dakota and his clandestine lover waited for the moment they thought was right, in walked his parents. They also kept his secret, so as not to be condemned by the community, but they made it a point to use words like *sinner, damned, disgrace*, and *abomination* in his presence. In coming to college, he was able to live freely, to shed the skin of enforced expectations, and to enjoy life—one defined on his terms and not those of traditions that rendered him less than human in others' eyes. As he told his personal turmoil, Cadence thought of Isa and how Dakota could help her understand Roano's struggles.

"So enough about me, Cadence. Let's get back to dreams. You never told me yours."

"I'm not sure. I don't know what I want to do. Really. I guess my dreams come one day at a time." She tilted her glass back. "I guess my dream is to be happy. Just like yours."

He wrapped his arm around her. "You will be. I just know it."

"How do you know?"

Dakota looked down at her shoes. "The same way I know those red heels look fantastic on you! Damn it, Dorothy, you're keeping those. Happy birthday, baby!" He hugged her deeply before a dulled clunk of their plastic cups sealed the final toast to parking garage dreams.

When they descended, the woman was still imprisoned in her lighted booth, still staring wearily at the pages. As they approached, Dakota and Cadence could see she was reading a large textbook that resembled the heavy ones they lugged around campus. Hunched over the words, her body sagged like a heavy load, and she looked as if her brain might explode. Her pursuit of a dream was deferred in the lackluster metal box where she labored. Dakota plucked the flower from his lapel and slid it through the cash drawer. The woman's face suddenly eclipsed the fluorescent lights surrounding her. In that soundless exchange, Cadence saw the natural beauty in this man blossoming under the artificial lights of urban life.

After hours of walking in new shoes, Cadence's feet cried out for relief. Dakota must have heard them because he hailed a rickshaw. They took in the city's dying night scene slowly, thanks to the exhausted human horse pulling their tiny cart. Along the path, women with blackened feet carried heels in their hands, while men in loosened ties and untucked shirts swayed down blocks. Shouts and yells pierced the air, drunks fell into taxis, and bouncers ushered those wanting more toward the staggering parties moving outside. The rickshaw driver navigated it all with precision, his calf muscles tightening to deliver speed when needed and relaxing at times as he coasted them home.

When they arrived at Albemarle, Dakota crawled out of the cab. Taking Cadence's hand, he planted a kiss on it and helped her out of the carriage. Another hug and he shooed her away with instructions to get some beauty sleep. He gave careful watch over her as she went to the door, and in reaching it, she turned and blew him a kiss.

Catching the affection, he slapped it on his cheek and threw one back. After she had passed safely through the door, his driver set the cab in motion again. When they were out of view, she stepped back outside, standing in the shadows to watch Dakota's chariot disappear and reappear beneath the lamp lights. On the pavement around her, she noticed traces of ruby glitter, shimmering gifts from a true treasure of a person who said the right words at precise times, even if the same hadn't been done to him. She marveled at the man who knew the magic of sincere gestures—of silent deeds that deliver love's transformative power—and admired how he embraced change and shared it with others who came within his spell. Turning her face to the twinkling stars, Cadence wished upon one, but it wasn't for her. She hoped that the story of this extraordinary Cinderfella would end happily, that he'd find a prince who'd deliver the same enchanting bliss he had given to her on this unforgettable day.

Chapter 16

Geology 296
Intermediate Petrology

Every graveyard is a library and each tombstone an abbreviated book tasking the imagination to fill in the lines of life, to conjure details of persons passed. In the shadows of the Holy City's churches lay these precious volumes of history. The headstones appear stained with melancholy, some broken but still standing in spite of the hurricanes, earthquakes, sun, and relentless moisture that do their best to ravage every face. Like their owners, the stones are as diverse as the places from whence they came, imports from upstate, the North, Europe— brought here to build a city, to provide a foundation, to make and commemorate life. Few people or places exhibit the lessons of life's importance more poignantly than a study of rocks marking the birth, work, marriage, and death milestones of life.

To make this point tangible, Professor Mirabilis sent her students into the churchyards to answer questions and compose reflections about Charleston's former residents. Inspired by their upcoming study of death-themed poetry, the assignment fell precisely as spring had usurped winter's power.

Cadence was deep into her meditation on death, listening to the bells of a church tower toll the hour when a whisper floated down to her.

"Hey, aren't you in my English class?"

A pair of bright yellow shoes cut a colorful contrast in spring's emerging green grass. Cadence squinted toward the sky. "Hi, yeah, I am. Aliyah?"

"Yes, that's right. Cadence?" Aliyah clutched her notebook tightly to her chest. "Do you mind if I sit near you? This assignment really freaks me out."

"No, go ahead. I'm almost done, but I'll wait for you."

While her classmate wrote thoughts about biographies of the departed, Cadence moved among the stones in the yard of St. Patrick's. She zoomed in on dates from the 1700s and recorded the influx of Irish immigrants in the 1800s, citizens who ultimately joined their Italian, English, and American neighbors now resting eternally. The number of buried children saddened her as did the way stories were being slowly erased by time's cruel hand. Cadence read as best she could, filling in the blanks of words stolen by weather, of life's lines ending before they had begun. Even more disheartening were mothers buried within days of their infants—evidence of birth's dangerous transaction. Yellow fever, malaria, accidents, old age, and drownings claimed them. Several victims were around her age, a mirror to the reality that young people do die, that precious breath can be suffocated at any moment.

In the back corner, three enormous stones lay separated from all others by a concrete border fighting for space against the overgrowing grass. A small engraving with the name *DELLA TORRE* announced the distinguished family resting in this plot.

Born in August of 1780, in Como, Italy, Antonio Della Torre arrived in Charlestowne in 1809, and for more than 50 years, he flourished as a respected citizen along with his wife Margaret. Son of an Italian vintner, Della Torre was a devoted Catholic who lived 77 years and 11 months—far longer than the sadly brief stories of his children.

Buried next to the parents were four of six sons aged 4, 7, 16, and 28, the last being Lieutenant Antonio Thomas Della Torre. According to this rock record, he possessed *a large and comprehensive intellect*; the chiseled narrative describing his years was a piece of poetry in itself:

> *His maturer life would have amply fulfilled the abundant*
> *promise of his Spring and his old age have been as*
> *reverent as his Youth was blameless*
> *But it is ordained otherwise; and he died young in years*
> *but ripe in Virtue, too early in deed for the hopes*
> *of his friends, but not too early for himself and Heaven*

The homage to him was long, but Cadence continued reading about a short life well spent, about duties performed, faith kept, good fights fought, and the *tranquil pious end* Antonio met.

When she had finished spending time with the Della Torres, Cadence turned to see Aliyah sitting among the stones, silently engaged in thoughts of death while the city swirled with life around her. Not too long after Cadence released the shutter on this subject, Aliyah gathered her things and thanked her classmate for waiting.

Pointing to the camera, Aliyah asked, "So is that a hobby or something?"

"Kinda. I shoot for fun, but I'm also a photographer for the paper."

"Hey, did you take the picture of that professor? The one who killed himself?"

"I did," Cadence said reluctantly of the photo that was increasingly becoming the one defining her amateur career.

"That was so sad. I wonder why he did it. I can't imagine going through all that school, getting all those degrees, then ending it. He must have had some really bad problems. Poor guy."

Just as they were nearing the entrance to the Grand Lawn, a squirrel happily hopped along in front of them; his jagged, stop-and-go movements made Cadence smile. Without warning, he darted into the street as a car sped by. They heard the *thump* then saw him twitching on the pavement. Aliyah let out a cry while Cadence stonily faced the mangled little body. He was not dead, but his injuries were grave. It would be only a matter of time. Cadence glanced around for what she needed. Pulling a loose brick from the sidewalk's edge, she went over to the wounded animal and crouched above him. She didn't have to raise the stone high but used both hands to increase the force as she brought it down on the small skull. It took only one smash. Picking up the poor creature by its tail, she took him into the Grand Lawn. Beneath an azalea bush, she dug a shallow grave with the brick and placed the small body inside. After returning the stone to its place, she rejoined Aliyah.

"I can't believe what you just did. That was crazy," Aliyah said.

Cadence rubbed her hands together, sending the dirt falling back to earth. "I don't like to see anything suffer."

As much as Cadence admitted that she didn't like to see suffering, she was still witnessing it in Penny, whose moods would swing from pseudo-normalcy to depression to anger to indifference. There didn't seem to be any particular triggers to her reactions, and since the case had essentially died and the perpetrators remained unscathed, Penny was suspended in a perpetual state of purgatory, although someone out there continued to acknowledge her agony.

When the newspaper staff returned from break, TJ called them into a meeting about the year's final stories, including the damning messages half-rubber players, coaches, supporters, and certain influential alumni had received. The emailed communications promised to expose the rapists in the case if they did not leave the squad. Moreover, the messages threatened to unleash a smear campaign to ensure that every player would be stained with the stigma of rape if the guilty ones weren't removed. And the character killings would not stop there. The senders who called themselves *The Harpies* would reveal the school's most well-guarded secrets if action was not taken.

"The harpies? What's that mean?" Jill asked.

"They're mythological creatures with the faces of old women and the bodies of birds," TJ said. "I had to look it up. Apparently, they're agents of punishment or divine justice."

"So the police haven't been able to catch these crazy people?" another staffer named Todd asked.

"No. They're quite tech-savvy but pretty simplistic, too. The higher-ups thought they had the culprit when one of the messages was sent from an identifiable account. They tracked this kid down for interrogation, only to find out he hadn't logged out of the library's computer. Whoever sent the message just used his email."

"What about the library's security cameras?" Degue asked.

"Nothing, and even if they had something, the footage is so grainy no one could make it out," TJ said. "So, let's see if we can find out the identity of these so-called 'harpies.' And Cadence, I need you to get over to the practice fields and get some shots of the half-rubbers training."

Cadence didn't want to go. She wanted to explain the conflict but doing so would betray Penny's identity as the victim. Her suitemate had already had enough harassment, especially since a lot of people were convinced she was involved in the players' character assassinations. Cadence decided just to do the job she was assigned without letting anyone know how very close she was to the story.

The next day, she caught a shuttle to the team's practice area in Hampton Park. Since she had never ridden the bus, she had no idea about how it worked, but luckily, a gregarious driver named Jerome helped her get to the destination. Cadence sat near the front, and as they moved toward the fields, she watched the road slide by in the reflection of his eyeglasses. He was an avid fisherman, a lover of the outdoors, and a man with a gilded smile thanks to sweetly placed gold teeth. Best of all was his voice, deep and seductive like a classic radio announcer. When the shuttle pulled up to the fields, Jerome reminded her of the bus times and told her to "take care."

Some players were already on the field, throwing, catching, swinging; others were in the cages, so Cadence went to work, not bothering to announce herself. For the most part, she remained unseen until the pitcher noticed her and motioned to one of the coaches who came stomping over.

He pointed his finger threateningly at Cadence. "Hey! Who the hell are you?"

"I, I'm with *The Gator*," she said. "We're covering your spring training."

A glop of brown juice hit the ground. "You sure this has nothin' to do with that *other* story? You know, that psycho tryin' to destroy my boys' futures?"

Images of Penny crying in a tub, shaking on an examination table, screaming in the police parking lot flashed through Cadence's mind. Her eyes narrowed in anger. "If you don't want any positive press, I'll go."

She was heading for the bus when he stopped her. "Miss, you can stay, if this is about featurin' our trainin'. Things have been a little tense 'round here as I'm sure you can understand." He surveyed his boys. "Come on, you can get your pictures. Be sure to get some of Ren; he's our star player."

Guilt and disgust surged inside her. She knew the coach had no understanding of the tension Penny felt when his boys pulled a train and a bat on her and the lingering stress that would affect her future. To him, Penny was just some whore trying to ruin his good ole boys' potential. Cadence despised everything about their leader. The brown juice dribbling down his chin seemed to reflect the stains of his character, a moral putridity he carried from protecting his horde of rapists like a bishop guarding molesters in his church.

When Cadence looked at Ren, she saw just a smaller version of the coach. The player strutted about and struck poses as if he were modeling for a sculptor. As is custom, he incessantly grabbed his crotch every few minutes, perhaps ensuring himself it was still there considering the Grand Lawn's castration scene only weeks ago. Since he knew he was being photographed, he flexed his muscles more in his throws, held positions longer and harder, and oozed bravado.

Not wanting to feed the beast, she snapped a few shots and moved around to shoot the others, making her last stop the cages where a lone player repeated his swing to a machine hurling the swerving and dipping half balls at him. Cadence positioned herself around the enclosure, focusing through the net at him. She was leaving when he spoke.

"Are you a reporter?"

She turned to him, her posture stiff and rigid like the small bat he held. "Not really. Just shooting for a newspaper feature on spring training. I'm not writing an article, if that's what you're asking."

He knocked the reddish dirt from his shoes. "Oh, I thought you might be here about the situation."

Cadence began to turn the color of the dirt. "And if I was? Let me guess, you'd say that girl deserved what she got? That she asked for it? She was dressed for it? Save it—that's what all you guys say." Cadence slung her camera over her shoulder and walked away.

"Actually, if it's true, I think what they did was beyond criminal. They shouldn't be allowed on this team or at this school or any school for that matter." He swung so hard it looked as if his arm would come out of socket. "But I can't say that, and I'm not the only guy who feels this way. We've been told if we want to play that we'd better keep our mouths shut. Appear united." He looked past her to the coach steaming toward them. "Just thought you should know."

"Reed! You 'bout finished talkin'? We don't have much time to chat, and I doubt she's helpin' you with your technique."

"Yes, sir!" Reed's bat thumped another hit.

"Young lady, you get what you need?"

Cadence looked over at the hitter. "I did."

When she returned to the bus stop, a smiling Jerome welcomed her on board again and dropped her back to campus where she gave the photos to TJ who began reviewing them immediately.

"Cadence, what happened to these half-rubber shots?" He tapped his pen rapidly on the desk.

"What d'you mean?"

TJ pointed to the photos. "The ones of the pitcher, they're all blurry. I can't use these."

She leaned over for a closer look. "Oh, damn. I guess I didn't have the camera on action setting. Sorry. I didn't realize, but there are others you can use. The ones of the batter, Reed, are pretty good. Besides, the pitcher always gets too much attention."

"I'm not really a fan of those. I guess next time I need sports features I'll send someone else."

"That'd be okay with me." Cadence turned to go.

"Oh, before I forget," TJ said, "this girl called while you were out. Something about needing a photographer for her wedding. They'll probably be standing still at the ceremony, so you won't have to worry about taking any action shots." He dangled the piece of paper in front of her.

On her way to the dorm, she called the number and someone named Ellie answered. A sophomore, she was marrying her fiancé, Earnest, in a few days, and they were looking to get hitched on the cheap. She wondered if Cadence would photograph their wedding. They couldn't offer her much, but Cadence agreed to give them her time and talents on the afternoon following St. Patrick's Day.

The next morning, English class seemed chattier than usual, perhaps because they were anxious to share discoveries of the city's most sacred land plots, and Dewit, who was always willing to talk, began the conversation.

"So Professor Mirabilis, check this out: I went out to that Magnolia Cemetery. I was totally into the meditation thing when suddenly this dude in a full Confederate uniform, sword and everything, was standing right in front of me."

She and his classmates sat in disbelief with one finally saying, "Are you serious?"

"Graveyard dead serious! I hollered and he said, 'what's wrong?' and I said, 'you talk too? Oh my God, I'm havin' a Hamlet moment, I've done gone and disturbed the dead with this crazy ass English assignment!'" Dewit clutched his chest. "The man said, 'relax, son. I ain't no ghost. I'm not here to hurt ya. Just visitin' some of my compatriots. I thought I'd ask why you writin' in a cemetery.' So I told him about the assignment, and he thought it was mighty decent of you to have us do this. Says it was good for us to get back to our roots."

"Next time you see your Confederate ghost, do tell him I 'preciate the kind words," Professor Mirabilis said in her finest Southern drawl.

"So why was he dressed like a Confederate soldier?" Kirby asked.

"Oh, yeah, some sort of Confederate reenactment or something," Dewit said. "But I'll tell ya' I damn near became a resident of that graveyard! I nearly shit myself!" The class's laughter could have awakened the dead.

When Professor Mirabilis regained her composure, she educated them on Magnolia Cemetery, the largest on the peninsula and the final resting place of more than 1,700 soldiers who fought in the Civil War. Joining them are members from some of the city's most prominent families. With over 30,000 burials, Magnolia is a city in itself, a treasure overlooking the marshes of the Cooper River since 1849, and a sanctified place where Spanish moss floats above tombs like ghosts in the wind.

Their teacher told them of the grave that intrigued her most, a story passed on by Ted Phillips, Jr., an accomplished attorney who admitted his obsession with the grounds ever since his job as an assistant gravedigger in the '70s. He devoted the latter years of his life to researching and writing the stories of those interred and even paid for one very special headstone.

While immersing himself in the cemetery's ledgers, Phillips discovered an entry that briefly noted the burial in 1883 of a child, one year of age, who was born in the Dakotas. At the site of an Indian camp on Ashley Street, he died of "cerebro spinal meningitis" according to Dr. E. E. Jenkins, the attending physician. Buried on December 17, 1883, at a cost of $7.50, the child is listed as "King of the Clouds." And that is all that is known of the mysterious boy with the majestic name. Phillips and his friend Josephine Humphreys, a literary treasure in her own right, surmised that the child may have made it to the coast from the Dakotas via the Wild West shows that sometimes traveled through Charleston. Something about this little soul touched them deeply, perhaps a feeling that every person deserves a stone, a marker to the miles traveled in life, however long or, in the case of this King, short they may be, so they had a gravestone made for him.

"I make it a point to pay my respects to him whenever I go to Magnolia," Professor Mirabilis said. "Now that I've shared one of my graveyard stories, let me hear more from someone."

"You have more than one?" Kirby asked.

"Many. But we'll leave those for another time," she said. "Now, which ones do you have to tell us?"

Astra raised her hand. "I got followed around by a black cat while I was there, but when I went through the gate to leave, he stopped at it, and just watched me walk away."

"Hmmm, Astra. How fitting. In Egyptian mythology, cats are the guardians of the underworld," the professor said.

"Anyone else have an unusual or memorable experience?"

"Yeah, I got a date," one guy said.

"With someone living, right?" Dewit asked.

The guy replied with a peculiar smile, leaving the class to wonder what macabre meeting that must have been.

Cadence was uncertain how to tell Reena about seeing Blaze and the mystery woman over break, but in considering how Isa reacted to withheld information, she decided to broach the subject. Surprisingly, Reena was calm, explaining to Cadence that the woman was Blaze's cousin and she had been in town for a few days. When Cadence hinted at the intimacy, at a connection that seemed more than familial, Reena insisted her friend had misinterpreted the scene, that Blaze and his cousin were very close but hadn't seen each other in a long time. Reena's mind was set, so Cadence left the subject alone.

As the spring semester moved at warp speed toward sophomore year, Cadence began feeling the pressure to declare a major, especially since she would have to sign up for fall classes soon. Like most students, she just didn't know what she wanted to do after graduation. It was hard enough seeing past freshman year, never mind into the throes of a mid-life job. Whenever she thought of it, panic arose and she felt stuck in the mire of being undecided. Writing had become an interest, and she was fairly good at it, or so said the hardest English teacher she ever had, so Cadence went to discuss what an indecisive student should do with the rest of her life.

Professor Mirabilis listened to Cadence's thoughts of majoring in English, of maybe one day teaching, perhaps being a photojournalist. Cadence expected her professor to be thrilled at the prospect of her student leaning toward a path similar to the one she had taken, so Cadence was surprised at the advice.

"I would not major in English, Cadence. Or at least I would not major solely in it," she said with a stern expression. "From my experience, many English departments are not in the habit of teaching you how to make your degree marketable. Sometimes, there is a profound disconnect between the academic and professional worlds. How will you make a living from it when you graduate? As romantic the notion, you're not here simply for the love of knowledge, are you?"

Cadence wanted to admit that she was, but that was naïve. She hadn't seriously considered what kind of job she would get after graduation, so she shook her head at the question.

"I didn't think so. Sometimes, it may be hard to connect the English courses you take into potential jobs. Yes, you'll have a solid foundation in writing and keen analytical skills, but prospective employers may see a transcript filled with classes in novel reading, poetry spouting, and research paper production."

She advised Cadence to think about a practical, applicable use for the degree since the professor had known too many English diploma holders in limbo after graduation simply because they weren't sure what they could do with the major despite brochures that promised endless career trajectories. Breaking into careers outside of teaching was a matter of happenstance since the degree wasn't exactly the requirement screaming at the top of most job descriptions—even though the skill of writing was the most coveted by employers.

"Now, if you know you want to be a teacher or go on to graduate or law school, then perhaps a bachelor's in the field will sustain you, but honestly, I'd choose a double major. Pair English with communications or business. At the very least, get a strong minor in one of the more marketable disciplines like computer science or hospitality."

"What about majoring in education? I could teach high school or middle school."

Professor Mirabilis ran her tongue across her teeth. "I cannot in good conscience recommend that major for you, especially if you want to teach English or actually, any specialized discipline for that matter."

"Really? Why?"

"Let's just say I have run into too many education majors who knew too much about teaching theories, classroom management, and bulletin board decorating and not enough about their subjects other than what they gathered from *Cliffs Notes* or the guides to their textbooks."

She advised Cadence that to be a true professional and be taken seriously in any job—especially one that requires a person to stand in front of a classroom—then at the very least, a teacher must know the subject and know it well. The professor told her to think about the differences between a transcript filled with courses ranging from Old English to Modern British, American, African American and world literature as compared to the limited courses of education majors.

"Believe me Cadence, if you're going to be a teacher of middle or upper grades, you're best served by in-depth knowledge about your discipline. Not only will it benefit you, but it will be of vital importance in connecting with your students, who will shut themselves off to learning if they suspect you don't know your subject. Some education programs have very limited coursework in core fields like English. That's not to say that you can't minor in education to get your certifications."

"Were you a double major, Professor Mirabilis?"

She sighed. "No. Only a single major."

"Do you regret your choice?"

"I wish someone would've told me what I'm telling you. I wish I would have had the prescience to learn more about what I could do with my degree rather than simply declaring. I believe I would have made different choices."

Although Cadence knew her teacher's advice would probably prove useful, it did nothing to assuage the stress of deciding a major. Instead, it seemed to have increased it since she had not even thought about a minor, much less a double major or a combination. Her head began to hurt when she contemplated the possibilities, so she was relieved when Schilar called wanting to make up for time they missed over spring break.

When she met him in front of her dorm, he was standing beside a black truck borrowed from his roommate. He wouldn't tell her where they were going, only that it was somewhere special. The ride toward the setting sun was enhanced by a copy of the compilation disc he had given her for Valentine's. She had memorized the songs and sang with a spirited surety that made it clear to him how much the gift meant.

After a seven-song journey, Schilar turned off the main highway onto a secondary road then to a long, dirt one that bore a tunnel through the mass of draping oaks. Just when it seemed it would go on forever, it opened into a small field overlooking

the marsh. Schilar cut the engine and reached through the sliding rear window to the cooler in the bed. He slipped a cold beer
into her hand and leaned over.

"Cheers, beautiful."

She clinked the head of her bottle into his. "Why're we
here?"

"Follow me, and I'll show you."

A short path that climbed a small embankment came into
view a few yards from the truck. When they got to the top, Cadence heard the grind of rocks, felt their distinct friction the
moment she stepped onto the granite-lined sides of a railroad
track. The lines of parallel steel ran eastward across wetlands,
and midway over the water, a shadowy trestle was set aglow by
the sun's dying light.

"How'd you know about this place?" she asked.

"My bandmate's in geology. He told me about it. Apparently, some woman died and left the land to the school. The
students come out here for field work."

"So, what d'you think?"

"It's great," Cadence said. "But why'd you bring me here?"

"Oh, I think you know." His lips, chilled from the beer,
warmed as they touched hers. "I thought you'd like it. Come
on."

They were careful to skip the gaps as they ventured out over
the water. The tide was coming in, so they watched the creek
slowly cover the pluff mud. Crabs scuttled in and out of their
holey homes; a crane stood frozen in the reeds, perched for a
catch. Schilar smiled at her smiling and the way the breeze
made her hair dance. Every so often, Cadence would glance
behind her to the dark bend where the tracks disappeared. It
was thrillingly fearful that at any moment, a train could come

barreling from the treeline forcing her and Schilar into the muddy water or to hang for life from the trestle's edges.

"You know what I like about this place?" she asked. "I can hear myself. It's quiet, so quiet. Not like in the city where there's a constant hum. Even in the middle of the night I hear it. Although the smell's different and the land, the silence reminds me of home."

"Not me. Being from a city, that hum's my norm. When I don't hear it, I think I'm in the wrong place. But Charleston doesn't really hum, or if it does, it's nowhere near as loud as the one I grew up with."

When they reached the point where the river flowed beneath them and the danger of the train seemed imminent, they turned back. As their feet touched the soil, Cadence picked up one of the millions of stones that filled and flanked the tracks.

She did not know what she held was called *ballast*, that many engineering mistakes were made before granite and quartzite proved the best stabilizing bed beneath a thundering locomotive. She would have found it funny that workers who once laid, cared for, and cleaned the tracks were called *gandy dancers* and would have marveled that the amount of ballast covering a rail line had to be precise based on soil and traffic. Jagged edges were preferred to round ones to ensure the rocks interlocked, like puzzle pieces snapping into place to secure a picture. The salt and pepper stone shimmered in her hand, an impermeable reminder of quality time with her rock star.

As the last light of day faded, they returned to the truck. Another beer provided cool reprieve against the heat in the cab from clothes shed and windows fogged. Lost in one another, they almost didn't hear the horn blast but certainly felt the rumble of the approaching train. Reaching behind her, Cadence

silenced Schilar's voice crooning through the speakers. He
smiled as she increased the friction between them. Closing her
eyes, she let her body take its lead from the machine now roaring past. The squeak of steel on steel hurtling energy through
the countryside's calm was absorbed by Cadence, who converted the power into grinds of pleasure. Much in the same
manner that she watched him on stage, he watched her now circling above him.

With the thunder of the last car resounding past, Schilar
tightened his hold on Cadence. A pleasurable moan brought
him to stillness, and he released his grip. She remained on him,
his face pressed against the softness of her breasts, inches away
from her thumping heart. Her lips lowered to his ear and after
a tender exhalation, she whispered, "I love you."

The words surprised even her—she hadn't meant to say
them. His hands had been laying loosely around her hips, but
now his fingers pressed tension into her flesh. She waited for
the response to match, but just as he seemed on the verge of
speaking, blinding lights flooded the space. Schilar pushed Cadence to the seat beside him and grabbed his shirt while she
fumbled for hers.

A massive truck with an antenna swaying as tall as the trees
blocked the road out. A portly man sporting a dirty hat with the
head of a buck on it and muddy boots that matched the inches-
thick smear of the truck's rim emerged from the cab. The sleek
barrel of his shotgun gleamed from the spotlight he trained on
them.

"Stay in the truck," Schilar said. Cadence quickly dressed
and cracked the window so she could hear.

"What're you kids doin' out here?"

"Nothin'," Schilar said dismissively.

The man launched a mouthful of brown spit to the ground and looked over into the smaller truck's bed. "Uh-huh. What you got in that cooler there, son?"

"Nothin'," he repeated.

"Well, you just full of 'nothin' tonight ain't you? Don't lie to me."

"A few beers," Schilar said.

"You old enough to drink?"

"No."

"No, sir," the man corrected while Schilar stared coldly at him. "But you sure as hell is old enough to trespass, ain't you?"

"Trespassing? This isn't private land."

He took a step forward. "The hell it ain't. This here's my goddamn land, and you may want to think twice before getting smart with me, boy. I've had about enough of your kind comin' down here and thinkin' they own the place."

"Hey, I didn't mean any disrespect."

"Don't 'hey' me. Learn some goddamn manners or go back where you came from."

Cadence stepped beside Schilar. "Sir. We're sorry. We didn't know we were trespassing. We're students and were told that we could come out here."

He hiked up his pants as far as the substantial gut overhanging his belt would allow. "Little lady, sumbody told you wrong."

"We were just looking for some rock samples before the sun went down. It's such a pretty place, we stayed for a while."

He met her innocent expression with the not-born-yesterday variety and pointed across the tracks with the barrel. "Over yonder."

Schilar and Cadence glanced in the direction. "Sir?" she asked.

"The land that dem students use is on the other side of the tracks. Not this here side. There's a rock depository over there. Damn young folks always gettin' the directions wrong. I been meanin' to put up a gate. Just hadn't gotten 'round to it."

"Sir, I apologize. We didn't mean to trespass on your property," Cadence said.

"Well, don't let me see you out here again. Now, I want you to get yourselves in that truck and get off this land before I call the law on you. And tell your friends to get their directions right 'cause next time I catch 'em out here, I'm libel to shoot 'em graveyard dead."

"Yes sir," she said and began to walk away.

"And one more thing, missy: you need to get rid of this here Northern boy and get you one who'll show you a bit more respect. As I see it, he's needin' some manners. I doubt your people'd be impressed with him."

Cadence could feel the heat rising from Schilar, so she grabbed his arm and pulled him toward the truck. Once inside, they had to wait for the man to unblock the road. He stayed behind them, monitoring their slow journey from the marsh to the highway.

When they were safely out of the man's shooting distance, Schilar let go. "What a fucking asshole!"

"He was angry. I mean, we were trespassing on his land. And you weren't exactly polite."

"How? By not bowing to his every whim with 'yes, sir,' 'no, sir,' 'sorry, sir?' That's ridiculous."

"No, it's respectful."

"Oh, and I guess he was showing us respect. And you lying to him was also respectful."

"What was I supposed to say? I told him that to save your ass."

"My ass didn't need saving. And fine job you did when he told you to get rid of me. You didn't even stand up to him."

"Because that's not what you do down here."

"That's fucked up and stupid."

"So I'm stupid now?"

"That's not what I said."

Cadence wasn't quite sure what was being said or how this rockiness between them had begun. All she did know was that she wanted to get out of the truck, to end what had begun as a good night. On the drive back to campus, Schilar changed the music to metal, turned it up to tune out the tension, and drove the whole way leaning on the door. They didn't look at each other, and when he dropped her off at the dorm, he muttered a good night. Slamming the door, she immediately regretted the sound, but it was too late. There she was standing alone and the guy she just told she loved was gone.

Before she knew it, the weekend had arrived as well as that celebrated time of the year when beer turns the unusual color of green or black, beads and shamrocks become necessary accessories against ass pinching, and suddenly, people begin speaking in strange accents and boasting lineage to an emerald island most of them couldn't locate on a map.

The tension from her fight with Schilar hadn't really subsided, but he had asked her to come see the band play at a St. Patrick's Day celebration. She wanted the chance to make up, but getting there required a car, so she asked Saida to come along, who recruited Diana and a newcomer, Sierra, a hallmate of Diana's.

As they approached the party, Cadence realized she had put on her one pair of jeans that had no pockets, but they hugged her figure better than any and would definitely turn Schilar's head. She handed her phone to Saida, who dropped the device in her purse. Sierra had scored a fake ID over spring break and used it to buy beer, which they all took turns chugging behind buildings and cars. Green shots followed every hour, but Diana finally declined, deciding it was best someone sobered up to drive, so she took Saida's keys while the others played.

They meandered through the crowd, gazing and being gazed at, collecting strands of green beads as tokens of their flirtations. Stone Miles was onstage, so the friends danced beneath the sun, twisting and turning as if they were engaged in some Celtic ritual. Occasionally, they'd disappear to down a beer or two before appearing again. With acts along the street, Saida and the crew decided to check out the other bands while Cadence remained to watch Schilar finish the set. She had every intention of making up and told them she'd catch a ride with him.

When the band finished, they hung around a table selling CDs and talking to fans. Schilar gave Cadence the look she had hoped for, but just as she began talking to him, a group of girls came over, tossing their locks and laughing like hyenas at anything the guys said. Cadence soon found herself pushed out of the way by their leader, a bubbly blond, who insisted on numerous photos with Schilar. A wily grin appeared when he slipped his arm around her shoulders, his hand dangling loosely over her sizeable chest as if it were reaching into a candy jar. Several photos later, Schilar still hadn't called the bitch in heat off, nor had he bothered acknowledging Cadence. Turning the appropriate shade of green for the day, but for all the wrong reasons, Cadence snatched the drink beside him and huffed off into the crowd.

She couldn't find her girlfriends but needed to find a bathroom. The lines for the Porta Potties stretched so long that she couldn't see their ends. The alcohol increased her impatience, and she wasn't about to wait for her turn at the toilet, so she set off in search of a bush.

A block from the scene, she set her beer atop a car and took cover behind some azaleas. She was in mid-pee when she suddenly lost her balance and toppled over in the grass. Scrambling up, she peeked around to see that no one was near and resumed relieving herself. Emerging from her cover with a goofy grin, she was still zipping and adjusting her jeans when she reached for the drink.

"Young lady, may I have a word with you?"

Cadence caught the glint of gold hanging from the man's shirt, but unfortunately, he wasn't dressed as a leprechaun.

"Sure, officer," she said with contrived coolness.

"Where's your wristband for what's in that cup?" He pointed to the clear container filled with liquid the color of sunshine.

"Oh, um, it must have fallen off." Cadence glanced around for the paper bracelet that was never there.

"Sure it did. Because they come off so easily. Let me see your ID."

She patted the jeans without pockets. "I don't have any ID on me."

"Then how did you purchase that alcohol?"

"My friend bought it."

"Is your friend twenty-one?"

"Yes sir."

"Then I need to talk to this person."

Her heart jolted. "Um, why?"

"Because your friend's going to jail for contributing to the delinquency of a minor."

Her buzz immediately gave way to the fear of betraying Sierra and her fake ID and by extension, Diana and Saida. "She's um, she's already gone."

"That's convenient. And she left you here? Nice friend. Since you can't take me to the person who supplied you the alcohol, and you have no ID, I suspect because you aren't of age, you're going to have to come with me." He reached for his handcuffs. "Now, put the cup on the car and place both hands on the hood."

"Can I at least tell my friends I'm being arrested?"

"I thought you said they were gone?"

"I mean my boyfriend. He's here. Can I tell him?"

The officer was in no mood for shenanigans. "No, you can call them from jail. Now, hands on the car."

Cadence did as she was told to the click of the cuffs. He led her to his car, which was parked next to an army of other black and whites. Since his shift was ending, he drove her to the county jail personally, along with a shaggy-haired drunk who, in addition to public intoxication, was also being arrested on marijuana possession. With his head back on the seat and mouth wide open, the inebriated guy was snoring away without a care in the world.

As they were about to pull away from the party, Cadence said, "Officer, please, please don't take me to jail. I'm sorry." Her voice began to tremble and tears streaked down her cheeks.

"You should have thought about that before you wouldn't cooperate. Tears don't work on me; save them for your boyfriend." In the rearview mirror, she saw the face of stony, seasoned public servant. "I will give you an option, though. What would you like me to book you for? Minor in possession of alcohol or indecent exposure?"

She looked away from him to see the scenery passing in a blur. "I don't know."

"Okay. I'll give you some advice, other than answering truthfully next time someone asks you a question. If I were you, I'd take minor in possession. Just know that technically, I could charge you with a registerable sex offense since urinating in public falls under 'sexual activity' in our codes. Then again, I probably wouldn't have arrested you if you would have taken me to your alcohol supplier."

Cadence was in no position to argue, and as they rode, she thought of how ridiculous it was that she was in the back of a police car partly for peeing, a function that had nothing to do with sex as far as she defined it. Growing up in the country, she didn't even think about when and where nature called. The only toilet was in the house, and no one walked back there to use it. Besides, her mother wasn't going to let anyone covered in dirt and hay dust inside without first washing up outside. Every truck and tractor on the farm held a roll or two of paper for natural needs. But she was a far from home and could not discount the obvious facts that holding a beer and covering for Sierra were also reasons why she was being chauffeured to the lock up.

When they pulled into the jail's parking lot, the drunk guy woke up. "Are we home?"

The cop smirked. "Yeah, you could say that. At least it's your home until you bond out tomorrow or Monday."

Cadence felt the floodgates building deep down, but she vowed not to cry, so she took the booking without breaking. With her information, fingerprints and mugshots taken, she was given her inmate number and her phone call, but the surge almost let loose again. It occurred to her that other than her parents' numbers, she had no others memorized. They were all in her phone which was at the bottom of Saida's purse. Panic started to set in because if she called the school, they'd probably call her parents, and she couldn't let that happen. She asked the attendant for a phonebook.

The barista, Andrew, answered in his charming British accent and informed Cadence that Catissa was in Savannah for the night but would be back tomorrow. Without revealing her whereabouts, Cadence gave him the number, asked to have Catissa call her as soon as she could, and stressed that it was important. When Cadence hung up, she took a deep breath and tried to absorb the reality that her life at Charlestowne College was over.

Just as she had done these semesters, Cadence thought she'd enter a small space to sleep next to someone she didn't know, but she was ushered into a large room, one set up like a military barrack, and faced hundreds of strangers clustered in groups. The second she entered, she knew she'd get no sleep.

"Mmmmm . . . look at that fresh meat," a husky voice called to her, punctuating the point with a whistle. "Nice jeans, honey. Before the night's over, I'm gonna peel you outta those." The woman ran her tongue sloppily around her lips as Cadence pretended not to hear. She had not anticipated this type of head turning when she got dressed that morning.

"Leave her alone," commanded a woman with wiry brown hair sitting in the corner with two other women.

"Or what?" the throaty one said.

"Or they'll be peeling what's left of yo' ass offa this floor." Her eyes moved menacingly over the target. Motioning to Cadence, the woman patted the spot beside her. "Chile, come over here."

Cadence moved toward those who invited her into what seemed like a safe zone and sat with her back to the wall.

"That's right. Set there, honey. That lesbo bitch won't be havin' any of you tonight. I'm Vianna, but everybody calls me 'Vi.' This is Flora and Ruella." She motioned to the others in her circle. They all wore the standard orange uniform which indicated they wouldn't be released for some time. "What you in fo'?"

"Um, alcohol possession," Cadence said in a low tone.

They laughed. "Cops got nothing better to do than bust babies drinkin'," Flora said.

"He was going to arrest me for indecent exposure, too."

"Uh-oh, do tell. You flash some St. Paddy's crowd with those perky breasts of yours?" Ruella asked.

"Not quite," Cadence said. "I was peeing behind some bushes and fell over."

They cackled like three weird sisters around a cauldron, and Cadence joined them as a fourth, trading stories and passing time in the joint. With sleeping nearly impossible, the four embarked on an all-nighter sans books, but the knowledge of lives hard lived would stay with the college girl for years, especially the story of Vi who was a habitual reoffender in again for selling rock.

"Crack?" Cadence asked.

She laughed. "Oh no, girl, you kinda behind the times on your drug vocab. 'Rock' is crystal meth now." Vi grinned and it looked as if hell had taken up house in her mouth. Many of her teeth were missing; the ones remaining were black and brown and clung to her gums like dead leaves waiting to fall from a skeletal limb. Even the skin around her lips was poisoned, but she spoke with a sweetness that eased Cadence's fears.

"You know, I had big dreams when I was your age, even before. I wanted to be a doctor," Vi said.

"Yeah, you a doctor all right, but the shit you cook and push ain't good for no healin'," Ruella said.

"What happened?" Cadence asked.

"Wrong people in my life all the time. I let one convince me I wasn't college material. But my problems started way back, honey." Vi slid her knees up to her chest, hugging them tightly. "My stepfather molested me; my momma didn't believe me. She kicked me out, so I dropped out of high school and moved from one man to the next. Thought I had finally gotten settled with the one who'd take care of me. But he got me into red rock first. That's heroine. Then into meth. And well, here I am."

The lives of Flora and Ruella revealed similar fates: minimal educations, abusive home lives, alcohol, drugs. Flora was in for larceny and fraud while Ruella was a repeat offender for prostitution and drug possession. This cozy corner of the jail was a second home to these women who were reunited too often here. They held the commonality of age: all were in their early thirties, with records, kids, and little means of ascending from the personal pits into which they had plummeted. Unsure of how to shake the sediment of self-destruction that buried them, they could only take each hour as it slowly came, hoping opportunities would appear to dig them from the rocky records of their mistakes.

"The sad thing is I knew I could be somebody. That I could get through school if I put my mind to it, but it's always easier to listen to the voices that say you can't. And then, I played with that pipe of dark magic. The first time it ever hit my lips it was over. I can't explain what it's like to inhale what you think feels like life only to realize you've sucked in death." Vi tilted her head back to the wall and closed her eyes to stop the tears. "I gotta beat this, ladies. For my kids. I sold my soul to meth 'cause I convinced myself I was caring for them. I'd do anything to buy it back."

"Where are your children?" Cadence asked.

"I got three young'uns. Two are in foster care; the youngest is with family. Not a night goes by I don't worry about 'em."

On Vi's drug-marked skin, Cadence sensed gaping wounds of regret for what she had and had not done to her children. Her eyes betrayed the futile desire to turn back time, to use the knowledge of present to change the past.

"But enough about us. Tell us about you," Vi said. "You gotta boyfriend?"

Cadence hesitated. "Well, sort of. We're having problems at the moment. You know, I'm not sure what we're doing." She could feel herself shaking. "Last time I saw him, a bunch of girls were hanging all over him. He's a rock star of sorts."

"Whooooaaaaaa . . ." They all threw up their hands, sounding in unison.

"Girl, you know what you sayin'?" Ruella asked. "A 'rock star' trades sex for crack."

Cadence covered her mouth and giggled. "Oops. No, no, not that type of rock star. My guy's a musician."

"Whew. For a minute there, I thought we was gonna have to put you on the straight path. You don't need no people messin' up your life. You get you your education then you can worry about gettin' a man," Flora said. "Tell us about school."

Cadence obliged and described life in college: her courses and professors, the ones she got out of bed for and others who made her want to crawl back into it. She talked about her position at the newspaper and what she had seen on her shoots, especially the dazzling details she had learned of the city. She shared reflections on what she and her friends had experienced and of the decisions on classes and roommates she would soon make for next year.

"We'll be your roommates. Count us in," Vi said with her mostly toothless grin. "My, my. All that sounds exciting." She glanced up at the clock, which was well past the witching hour. "Here, chile, lay down and try to get some sleep. We'll watch over you. You need some rest 'cause I know you got lot of studyin' to do when you get out. Ruella, thow me that blanket. You can do without it for one night." The woman tossed Vi the cover, which she draped gently over their guest.

Cadence decided to take the women up on their offer of protection. She closed her eyes and was surprised when she felt Vi gently shake her hours later. The ladies had made the time fly for Cadence so that she awoke to the reality of her release after breakfast. When she stood up to go, she thanked them for their company and wished them well. She was moving toward the door when Vi called to her.

"And Cadence, honey, one more thing. Don't let any of us catch you back in this place. Us three come and go, but you better go and not come back. You hear?"

Cadence answered with a nod and a smile. She appeared before the magistrate who set her court date and released her on a personal recognizance bond, and when she walked through the jail's locked door, Catissa was waiting.

"Oh, Cadence, I'm so sorry you had to spend the night in there. Are you okay?" Catissa's hug nearly squeezed the breath from Cadence.

"Yeah, I'm fine. Tired, but fine."

"I brought you some coffee and a sandwich. Come on, let's get you home."

The ride to campus was short, so Cadence quickly relayed the day's and night's events. Catissa said she'd ask some of her law enforcement regulars for advice regarding the upcoming court date. With it being over a month away, they had some time to figure out what would be best in putting the infraction behind Cadence.

When Cadence got to her room, Helena rolled over. "Well, well, did someone have a good time? I haven't seen you since yesterday."

"That's because I was in jail."

Helena sat up. "What? What happened? Are you okay?"

Cadence had her hand on the door on her way to the other suite. "Yeah, I got busted for drinking. I didn't have my phone and didn't know anyone's numbers, so I couldn't call. I'll tell you in a minute; let me go get it."

Saida and Penny were still sleeping when Cadence slipped into their room. The purse was on the floor, so Cadence fished her phone from it. Some missed calls from Schilar appeared, and it was strange that the device was somehow on silent.

Helena was full of questions, so Cadence conveyed the story again then said she needed sleep because of the wedding she was photographing that afternoon. Helena turned off the light so they could both rest. As her lids closed, Cadence breathed in the dank smell of jail and of Vi, whose scent and shattered self finally made it to the comforts of a college dorm, only without her.

"Psst, Cadence. Hey." Helena was bent over her roommate, delicately shaking the blanket. "Um, I didn't want to wake you, but what time's that wedding?"

Cadence rubbed her eyes. "Um, 4:00. Oh shit, what time is it?" She flipped over to see that it was 3:00. "Damn! I've got to shower." She was already stripping off her clothes as she stumbled into the bathroom. "Do me a favor; see if Saida's in and ask her if she can give me a ride to the Battery."

Fifteen minutes later, Cadence was recounting the events to Saida, who had thought all along that her friend was with Schilar. Saida forgot the phone was in her purse, especially since its charge had died by nightfall.

Cadence arrived at White Point Garden in plenty of time to snap shots of the twenty or so guests who showed up to watch the couple get married in the bandstand. It wasn't long before a white horse pulling a carriage appeared. A slight wind blew in from the harbor, flirting with the hem of the bride's short white dress, tickling the petals of her daisy bouquet, and shaking the oaks' arms so they seemed to wave upon the happy occasion. Ellie and Earnest were young but seemed so in love, firmly entrenched in those all-consuming feelings that seize days, nights, and every second in between. For this couple, there was no imagining love tomorrow without declaring it today. Cadence wondered about the fine lines separating this couple's happy moment from the unfortunate ones of the women languishing in jail, about fate's delicate demarcations that determine joy for some and misery for others.

The wedding witnesses listened to vows and waited through those moments made for objections. Apparently, no one knew of any impediments barring the two from togetherness. No dissensions were voiced, but even if they were, it was doubtful destinies would be altered or mistakes made in love's tarnished name would be undone. Finally, the justice of the peace reached that defining sentence, the one line echoed in ceremonies over the centuries and etched by date on the gravestones of lovers before them: *till death do you part?* If they stayed together, the soil would welcome them at their lives' ends where they would unite side by side in hallowed ground, embraced by mysteries beyond tombs recording their births, deaths, and undying love. But if they divorced, loving promises would turn to ashes, a future together to dust—a divide leaving them with a different set of stones, markers chiseled with stories greatly altered from the one told on this day.

Chapter 17

Biology 112
The Cycles of Life

Beneath its delicately hard exterior floats a globe of yellow so brilliant that few colors rival it. Suspended in the clear fluid of life, it awaits the opportunity to become something more, to break from its incubating chamber according to nature's clock. As a tiny testament to the power of life, it assumes many uses: breakfast staple, baking essential, holiday decoration, vandals' weapon, ancient fertility symbol, and in labs across the world, it's a favored choice to study life's progression after fertilization.

It takes roughly twenty-one days for a chicken egg to hatch, and although the lab students were supposed to keep detailed track of the different stages, they found it difficult to concentrate each time they broke open another specimen. Up until day thirteen, they observed the yolk's vibrancy and the blood vessels snaking through the mass like streaks of crimson lightning. Beyond this day, the tiny misshapen thing assumed form with a beak, feathers, scales, and feet, but with every shell's crack, they watched the veins pump frantically then taper into stillness. They measured the weight, the time it took to expire, and coldly recorded the nascent traits. Fascinatingly morbid, the experiment was enough to make most of them ward off eating eggs in the near future, but others would swear off the perfect food permanently.

After the trauma of lab, Cadence hung around to talk to Alex, who was reviewing reports. Some students had been wondering about Nina and if she'd be back before the semester's end, so Cadence asked.

"Nina's not working at this school anymore," Alex said. "I saw her over break when she came to clean out her desk."

"How's she doing?"

"She seemed okay. Said she was moving because she needed a change of place. Too many memories here." Alex scanned the room. "She wanted to be closer to her family, so she'd have help when the baby comes."

Cadence's mouth fell open. "She's pregnant?"

"Yeah. She wasn't hiding it when I saw her." Alex put down the pages and studied Cadence like she would a specimen beneath a microscope. "Cadence, what's going on? I've seen that look on your face before, when you knew something more to a story."

Degue was the only person Cadence had told about that November night and now her expression hinted there was more to Nina's situation. Cadence told Alex about the scene through the window.

"Wow," Alex said. "That explains a lot. Come to think of it, she was working on a project for Darwin Week with this visiting professor in the religion department. I forgot his name, but they were spending a lot of time together. I really didn't think much of it."

After they discussed Nina's perplexing situation, Cadence asked about classes for next year. Alex recommended a course in young adult literature that her boyfriend still talked about from his undergraduate years as well as any religion class with Dr. Sessions. Cadence had heard he was phenomenal, especially from her suitemate who had mentioned his hotness factor more than a few times.

In browsing the offerings, Cadence found the suggestions, and with her advisor's approval, signed up for them. Another course with Professor Mirabilis seemed in order, but she did not see the teacher's name on the schedule. Ultimately, she looked forward to a schedule of history, religion, English, logic, and another communications class.

In addition to academic decisions, the ones regarding living arrangements needed to be made. Cadence and Saida had talked about rooming together, but the issue of excluding Penny might be more than she could handle, so they decided to be suitemates again and Penny was relieved they didn't abandon her. Since Helena decided to pair with a friend, Cadence needed to find a new person to live with. She filed through the possibilities: Isa, but she was moving in with the international students; Enna and her crew were going off campus; Miranda and some actress friend were coupling; Diana and Sierra were together. There was Reena, who Cadence thought would move in with Blaze considering how much time she spent with him, so she was surprised when Reena agreed to be her roommate. Relief set in as the future fell into place, and Cadence felt good about August's prospects.

She wasn't feeling so positive about her strained relationship with Schilar and still wasn't sure what was going on. When he learned of her arrest, he apologized for not being there, for not knowing she had been hauled off in a cop car. As they talked over drinks at c.a.t.'s, Cadence asked about his classes for next semester.

Looking around, Schilar rubbed his hands on his jeans. "I haven't signed up for any yet."

"You better hurry. The ones you need will be full."

"I'll get to it."

His vagueness prompted her to reach for his hand, which he briefly surrendered. "What's going on, Schilar?"

"Not much. I just don't know if my parents are gonna pay for my ride next year. Out-of-state tuition is killin' them." He pulled his hand away.

"Is there something I can do?"

"Nope, not unless you win the lottery and wanna be my sugar momma."

"What about your gigs? Don't you have money from those?"

"I have some, but it gets split between all of us and we've got to pay for gas, food, promotions, stuff like that. In the end, it's not much."

"What're you gonna do?" She bit her lip to stop its trembling.

"I'm not sure. But when I am, you'll be the first to know."

The feeling of her heart falling out of her chest stayed with her so that even lighter moments of laughter quickly sank. Every time she thought about starting next year without Schilar, she felt sick and tears flooded her face, a condition she hadn't dealt with much since first semester, which seemed a lifetime ago. The possibility drained her at a time when she needed all the energy she could muster considering what remained in the weeks before exams. She had projects and papers galore and a stack of photo assignments, including instructions on shooting one of the oldest and largest events in Charleston.

She wasn't certain what 40,000 people moving through downtown's streets would look like. The number only accounted for those participating in the Cooper River Bridge Run and did not factor in the cheering legions lining the race route. Even the day before the race, it seemed the entire world had descended upon the city, a population upsurge so dramatic it felt as if the peninsula would snap from the mainland and float out into the Atlantic.

Cadence didn't even know how far a 10K was until Isa told her as the two went to pick up the race packet.

"It's 6.2 miles. That's not too bad, distance wise, but the incline is tough. That's why the slogans say 'Get Over It.'"

"How do you feel about it?"

"I'm excited. It's my first race of this size and distance. I can't wait to cross the line."

"Have you run the bridge before?"

"Just in training on the pedestrian walkway. You know, before that new bridge was built there was apparently nowhere to run to prepare."

"I remember the old bridges from when I was a kid," Cadence said. "There were two. One was old and rickety. Really creepy, just two narrow lanes into Charleston. The other was bigger, but it could still put a pit in your stomach if you looked down when you were going over it."

"Hopefully, I won't have time to look down."

"Well, I'll be looking out for you," Cadence said.

"I'll be the one with the race number on." She laughed. "Look for me behind the Kenyans."

At the time, Cadence did not realize how much truth there was in Isa's humor, but in positioning herself at the corner of King and Calhoun early the next morning, Cadence stood in front of a doctor and his friend who talked about injuries that sidelined them as they enjoyed steaming cups from one of Catissa's competitors.

Their conversation topic shifted after a spectator remarked, "Here come the winners." He rose up on his toes for a better view. "Yep, it's the Africans. They always win." His voice betrayed a tone of disgusted admiration.

Cadence looked up to see muscles accentuated by the tension of motion. Grouped tightly together, the runners bounced like a flock of birds over the road. Seemingly weightless, their sinewy legs, shaped by the long miles they covered across continents, enabled them to fly from view as soon as they came into it.

"God that guy sounds racist," the doctor's friend said.

"He may sound racist, but there's truth to what he says. They've won most of the major distance races for a few decades now. It just may be in their genes."

"You still studying that stuff?" The man's eyes followed the second group racing by—a mixed-race cluster of impressive evolution.

"Somewhat. I've got a colleague who's into the research, tries to prove biological predisposition."

"Hmm. What's the finding?"

"Apparently, fast and slow twitch muscle fibers," the doctor answered. "See, long distance runners from Africa have slow twitch fibers, which means they're more aerobic. Their bodies have an oxidative capacity that's higher than that of whites. It helps with fatigue resistance."

"Hey, translation please? It's kinda early for a lecture."

The doctor rolled his eyes. "The bodies of these runners use oxygen more efficiently because of these muscle fibers."

"Humph. I've always heard African runners are faster because they run long distances to school barefoot."

"Myths mostly created by whites," the doctor replied. "Africans' athletic superiority comes down to a lot of hard training and determination, but body morphology thanks to genetic drift also gives them an advantage."

"Genetic drift?"

"I'll explain later." The doctor pointed to the running field. "There she is. She's looking good. On pace."

Cadence spotted the woman he was watching, who appeared to be struggling to keep up with the group of black women surging ahead. Cadence was not certain if Isa had been serious about being behind the Kenyans, so she watched in earnest for her, but as the race clock sprinted forward, the field thickened so that now the runners appeared like cells moving in, out, and around each another through the city's arteries.

Some were fast, others slow; struggle showed in some faces, effortlessness in others, but an emerging sense of triumph surrounded each. They would funnel into Marion Square where stacks of bottled water, bananas, oranges, muffins, and beer waited to revive them. But most of all, each would ride the runner's high of accomplishment and spin stories of pace and pains, the weather and the weird wonders with their mile-marking colleagues.

"Come on, let's go find her," the doctor said to his friend, but no sooner had he gotten the words out when a collective gasp arose from the crowd. The two moved like sprinters toward a man lying motionless on the pavement. When they rolled him over, blood trickled from a gash in his head. The physician ripped his own shirt, handing it to his friend who held it over the wound. Clasping his hands on the runner's chest, the doctor began the rhythmic pounding against death even as runners pounded past. He worked with precision and determination, eventually beating breath back into the man's body. When the first responders arrived, the doctor remained with his patient, and the hands that only minutes ago held a steaming cup of coffee now clutched the cool rubber of an oxygen mask. The clear plastic provided the focal point of Cadence's photo that would make the paper's next printing.

On Monday morning, the students knew something was wrong. Professor Mirabilis was late—she was never late. They discussed how long they could wait for a teacher before leaving and launched into debate over the existence of any rules. Some said ten minutes was the limit while others cited fifteen and a few pushed it to twenty. They settled on ten but were silenced when she entered nine minutes past the hour.

Lacking the usual ebullience that accompanied her teaching of literature, she announced in shaken words that one among them was gone. Their classmate, Aliyah —the one with the bright shoes which were only outmatched by her beaming smile—had been killed in a car accident. Their teacher seemed uncertain about the course they should take for class, but she simply followed the syllabus, a crystal ball now foretelling that on this day, the class would need the solace of poetry. Aside from the obvious void in the room, even their schedule was an eerie reminder of life's ephemeral nature.

In forming a circle, they left one desk empty, a void also symbolizing the one in their hearts. When their professor's eyes were not fixed upon that blank space, they lay hidden behind her lids as she soaked up the verse issuing from the mouths of her babes. They read for her, for their colleague, for the ones who had gone before, and for themselves. At first, images of scythes and hooded figures, long nights and longer sleeps rose from the pages like ghosts stalking them, but more melancholy selections lulled them into contemplations of the mortal coils encasing every soul.

Professor Mirabilis ended class with John Donne's "Meditation XVII." Kirby's deep voice boomed the words softly about like the sermon's church bells, and in those lines echoed the timeless struggle to understand the end of existence and the possibility of beginning:

No man is an island, entire of itself; every man is a piece of the continent, a part of the main. If a clod be washed away by the sea, Europe is the less, as well as if a promontory were, as well as if a manor of thy friend's or of thine own were: any man's death diminishes me, because I am involved in mankind, and therefore never send to know for whom the bell tolls; it tolls for thee.

It was one of the toughest classes, and it had nothing to do with a test, exam, or presentation. Life and death were proving the most difficult and mysterious of matters to master. Their inexplicability brought questions for which even scholars and the most erudite of teachers could give no definitive answers. Why Aliyah? Why now? Why wasn't she allowed to finish the project of college she had begun? Unwillingly, they peered into the mirror of mortality death holds up for all, and they didn't exactly like their powerlessness in the reflection. Their teacher ended class with a moment of silence and told them she'd inform them of funeral arrangements.

In the hall, Cadence, Kirby, and Astra were discussing attending the service when a voice interrupted.

"If y'all decide to go, can I catch a ride with you?"

They turned to see who wanted to join, but instead of their eyes meeting her face, they were drawn to the protruding belly hidden beneath her oversized sweater. Kirby thought of the first day of class, of *pregnant* written on the paper, and now felt he knew the author.

"Um, sure," Astra said, since she would be driving. "What's your name?"

"Haven," the girl replied. "I'll pitch in for gas."

"Don't worry about it," Astra said. "We'll let you know our plans when the professor tells us."

Later that day, Cadence stopped by Professor Mirabilis's office. The door was slightly ajar, and through the crack, Cadence could see her teacher reading from an old, tattered book in the barely lit room. Cadence knocked lightly.

"Come in." The woman dabbed at her eyes with a tissue and motioned for her visitor to take the seat. "So Cadence, what brings you by? Do we need to talk about the final paper?"

"No, I just wanted to stop by and see if you're okay."

The teacher smiled sadly. "That's very sweet of you, Cadence. I appreciate your concern. Losing students is the hardest." She sighed deeply. "Just last week, Aliyah was sitting in the very spot where you are with paperwork for me to sign. She was declaring a major in English. She wanted to be a teacher."

Cadence felt goosebumps rise when the professor's voice began to crack. Like her classmates, Cadence perceived Professor Mirabilis as one incapable of crying, as if tear ducts had been purposefully left out of her steely anatomy.

"She told me she wanted to become a teacher because I inspired her." The trail of tears indicated not only the loss of a student but of a future colleague. "She would've made a wonderful educator."

For half an hour, the two talked about the incident and strange timing of the poems about death and dying. Before she left, Cadence pulled out a card she had struggled to pen some hours before. Just as her professor had written sympathetic words upon Gunpowder's loss, Cadence made a similar attempt with something more.

Professor Mirabilis's breath escaped her when she saw the graveyard picture of Aliyah lost in the meditation of the English assignment. It was eerily beautiful and sadly foretelling of the type of place the young woman would permanently visit only a few weeks after Cadence captured the image.

"All photos are *memento mori*," the professor whispered.

The funeral was set for a Saturday afternoon, so Astra picked up Kirby, Haven, and Cadence in front of c.a.t.'s in plenty of time for the drive to the tiny country church. It took them over an hour to arrive at the antique structure of peeling paint at the end of a winding dirt road. The sanctuary was packed, and as they settled on a well-worn pew that creaked with every movement. Professor Mirabilis nodded in recognition to them; she sat a few rows from the front where a closed white casket lay beneath a spray of brightly colored flowers that reminded everyone of the shoes Aliyah was so famous for wearing.

It wasn't long before the young minister instructed them all that Aliyah had been "called home," and while her death did leave a void, faith in God and constancy to His plan assured them she was ready to begin a different type of schooling.

"Yessss, I'm tellin' ya. Gawd has called Miss Aliyah to a much higher education." Wrapping every word with fire to sear his message into their hearts, he raised a finger to the ceiling. "This young sista is now enrolled in courses of love, charity, and goodness. She faithfully arrives to those great halls of everlastin' knowledge on time, ready, and willin' to learn. Yes! Miss Aliyah is now a spiritual scholar!"

"Amen," a voice called from the back and another responded, "Praise Jesus!"

"Everlastin' learnin', my bruthas and sistas—that's what I'm talkin' 'bout. That's what the good book, the *only* textbook you'll ever need in this life, tells us. Yes, I tell ya, sista Aliyah knows that book now. She studied it well here, among us, yes, she sure did, but she knows it by heart now that *the word* has been *truly* fulfilled for her. Who knows the word?"

He looked to them for an answer, but none gave it up.

"Salvation!" His voice bellowed the promise as his arm shot high to heaven.

Aliyah's classmates sat in astonished attention. Throughout the sermon, Cadence noticed Astra's eyes drift down to Haven's belly more than a few times. Haven must have felt the gaze because she seemed to shift in response each time the stare fell upon her.

"Yes! Praise the Lawd!" called a woman wearing a velvety purple hat while echoes of "Amen" and "Thank you, Jesus," rang around the room.

"And sista Aliyah is well on her way to a degree in glory, one that the rest of us up in here can only hope to achieve. She's listenin' to the lectures of saints, and studyin' in the presence of angels, and the king of all teachers, our great professorial power, well, he's in charge of that classroom—of all classrooms! He only wants the best students. Those who make the grade."

He pointed his finger menacingly out over them. "And I ask you folks here—how's your transcript to heaven lookin'? Let's just say that in this life here, you want to make the almighty A's and avoid the Fs like an Old Testament plague. In admissions to the pearly gates, A is for ascendancy and F, well that's for FIRE!—the kinda home you don't want fo' all of eternity! Now, who's gonna follow Miss Aliyah's fine lead as the model student into the Promised Land?"

Bodies rose and hands shot up, with every church member shouting, "I am!" before breaking into song. A revelry of joyful noise erupted with clapping and swaying and praising, the decibels of which would surely make heaven's gates come unhinged. None of the classmates had ever been to a black church, but they walked out in wonder at how a ceremony marking death was transformed into a celebration that felt like a birth.

The service lasted for nearly three hours, yet despite this seeming marathon of emotional release, the congregation had much more in reserves, which they took out to the small graveyard behind the church. Prayer and words of promise rang out as Aliyah's casket disappeared into the earth.

On the drive home, the group was not as quiet as they were on the way to the funeral. The classmates traded opinions of the service until the subject turned to Haven's situation when Astra asked when she was due.

"In three months," she said. "That's good because I won't be in school, so I can deal with letting her go."

"What do you mean?" Kirby asked.

"I'm giving her up for adoption."

Through the rearview mirror, Astra fixed hard on Haven. "Do you think that's the right decision?"

"I think it's what I need to do at this time."

"What about the father?" Kirby asked.

"What about him?" Haven shifted in her seat. "He doesn't want it. Wanted me to get an abortion. He's just a sperm donor. Nothin' more."

"And what are you, an incubator?" Astra snapped.

The comment slammed the conversation to a halt and left everyone looking awkwardly at the passing scenery except for Astra, whose eyes remained fixed on the highway all the way to campus.

Haven got out of the car without saying a word while Kirby muttered thanks. When they were out of sight, Cadence remained in the passenger seat with her hand resting on the door handle. Astra fumbled through her purse for a cigarette.

"Astra," she began with hesitation, "I hope you don't take this the wrong way, but that was really cruel. Downright brutal."

The lighter's flame briefly illuminated Astra's face. She leaned her head back on the seat, took a long drag, and closed her eyes as she blew out the burning inside of her. "I know."

"It just doesn't seem you'd judge her like that."

"You couldn't know what's going on with me. What day this is. I didn't remember until I was in the church."

"What're you talking about?"

"Ten years ago today, I miscarried." Astra inhaled deeply as if she were drawing in the memory then let it go. "I guess I can't imagine being pregnant and not wanting to keep it. I say this because I'm not even certain I can have children."

Cadence touched Astra's shoulder and felt the overwhelming weight of the day's sadness. The sorrow followed Cadence back to her room where she thought of Schilar, of him leaving, of the uncertainty that was their relationship, and she felt guilty. She had just been to a funeral, seen her classmate's casket buried in a churchyard, learned of her friend's painful anniversary, yet she was wallowing in self-pity because she was losing a college boyfriend. As Cadence walked in, Helena emerged from the bathroom, not looking like herself. Perhaps it was her hair's freshly dyed shade of raven that made her skin look more pale than usual. Cadence wasn't sure, but whatever it was, her roommate did not appear well. Helena thought she was coming down with a bug or maybe it was bad Chinese food she had eaten the night before. Whatever it was caused her to crawl from the day's light into bed.

During the week, Helena's mood aligned more with her hair color, and as she retreated into the darkness beneath her covers, Charleston blossomed into spring. With temperatures rising quickly and the big ball of golden in the sky preparing for its full-time summer appearance, women embarked on pilgrimages in search of the perfect beach attire.

With her morning class canceled, Saida set off to shop for a swimsuit, and although she liked having the convenience of a car, she hated the competition for parking, a gross oversight for which schools never seemed to legislate enough space. She complained about circling the streets like a vulture waiting to swoop down into a spot but resigned herself to parking at a lot over a mile away. On this day, her mood turned especially nasty when she got to her car and discovered a flat tire. Luckily, a city maintenance worker happened by to help and recommended a garage that could patch it for her. So instead of heading to the mall, she drove to a cinder block building to purchase some rubber work.

Saida's bejeweled flip flops had barely slapped the parking lot when her serviceman, Warren, introduced himself. She told him what she needed, and he directed her to the patio waiting area where she watched him work from behind her overly large sunglasses. His uniform's short sleeves revealed tanned triceps smeared with grease and expertly shaped from wielding impact drills, turning wrenches, and wheeling tires around asphalt that, at times, was hotter than the South's sun on a tin roof. Warren and his coworkers made the work seem as if it weren't a job, as if they were boys on a playground of man-tools just having fun.

Once he patched her tire and mounted it, he spun the lug nuts until the drill popped against their resistance. With the air pressure checked and set to the perfect PSI, he said two of the language's sweetest words: "No charge."

Saida couldn't resist leaving an impression. "So what do you use to get the grease off at the end of the day?" It wasn't her best line, but perhaps the toxic perfume of oil and rubber had temporarily rendered her senseless.

"Just soap and water, ma'am."

"And what do you look like when you've cleaned up?"

"Oh, 'bout the same," he replied, opening her door.

Getting nowhere and in need of air conditioning, Saida abruptly got behind the wheel. As she reached to close the door, he leaned over.

"But if you'd like to find out, I get off at six. On Wednesdays, my buddies and I usually have a few beers at The Scene; it's a bar not far from here. Would you like to join us?"

Her face maintained a blank expression, but if he could have seen her eyes, he'd have known the answer.

"So, will I see you? Miss—?"

"Maybe." She quickly pulled the door closed.

Twenty minutes after six, the blackened glass of The Scene's front door swung open. Warren was sitting so that he faced it and watched as the light from outside accentuated every curve of her silhouette. Her entrance was enhanced by the rush of air that swirled her hair about. His coworkers had been watching, too. They each handed a five to Warren—a bet he had won when she strolled over to their table.

"Well hello, Miss Maybe." He winked at her and raised his bottle in toast to his customer.

She cut an annoyed smile and exchanged names and greetings. Taking the seat across from him, Saida listened as the guys talked shop, racing, hunting, and other topics she found no interest in. There was only one subject that held her attention, and she studied him at length, noting the day's greasy traces: black nails, dingy skin, and the unmistakable smell of sweat, all tangible proof of manual labor. When happy hour ended and drink discounts were no more, the coworkers began leaving.

"So, do you have plans for tonight?" Warren asked.

"Maybe some studying later," she replied.

"I figured you were a college woman. Studyin' anything interesting?"

"Not really, but when I am, I'll let you know."

He laughed. "Miss Maybe, you seem like a hard one to handle. If your studying can wait, I don't live too far from here. Want to come back to my place and hang out while I get cleaned up? Maybe we can go get something to eat?"

Saida answered by sauntering toward the door, to which he moved after throwing some cash down for the beer. Meeting at her car for the second time in a few hours, he asked her to wait while he got his ride. Soon he reappeared, his hands tightly gripping the handle bars of a tangerine-colored speed machine. He motioned for her to follow, and they arrived at a garage apartment tucked behind a business.

Sparsely furnished, the place was neat and save for the books about cars, trucks, and motorcycles, and countless stacks of supply catalogs, it seemed as if no one lived there.

Saida picked up one of the books. "Is this what *you* study?"

"Pretty much. It beats all that biology and stuff you have to take."

"Chemistry," she corrected. "I take chemistry."

"Oh, okay." He handed her a beer. "I'm going to take a shower. Make yourself comfortable."

"Fine. I'll just amuse myself with . . ." She randomly flipped to a page and squinted at the words. "Vulcanization."

"One of my favorites." He laughed. "Tell you about it later. Hey, why don't you put on some music?" He passed her the control to a stereo tucked in the corner.

Seconds later, the sound of running water rushed to her ears. Saida gripped the device tightly. She had been thinking about him all day and now he was warm, wet, and naked in the next room. The thought of joining him crossed her mind a few times, and just as she was about to move on her urge, the water stopped.

"Warren? Could you come help me with this thing?"

He stuck his head around the door. "What was that?"

"I can't figure out what buttons turn this thing on." She held out the control helplessly.

When he emerged in a crisp, white towel, his physique was just as she suspected—lean, well defined, and with a form that rivaled Michelangelo's greatest sculptures. After a string of boyish bodies and the beer guts of college beaus, she pursed her lips in anticipation. Gently taking the remote, he attempted to show her, but Saida wasn't interested in his instruction. She fixed her eyes on what she wanted and waited for him to acknowledge her.

Finally, he did. "So, I get the feeling there are other buttons you'd like to push?"

Her tongue was on him faster than the legendary service at his garage. She pulled him to her and soon felt what waited beneath. Moving her mouth down his chiseled chest, she paid ample attention to the lines that defined each muscle. She smiled when she heard him inhale deeply, but when she reached for the tucked corner of the towel, he pulled her back to his mouth.

"What's the rush, beautiful? We have all night." Turning the music on, he placed the control in her hand and disappeared again.

She plopped on the couch, exhaling loudly. Even though she didn't smoke, she wished she had a cigarette or something to quell her excitement. Between sips of her beer, she sulked.

Warren emerged in faded jeans, the classic kind worn threadbare in all the right places, and a button down shirt. The way he dressed only increased the heat coursing through her. "It's pretty hot in here. How about a ride?" he asked, sliding on his mirrored sunglasses.

"Fine." With feigned nonchalance, she swept past him and out the door he held open.

Being turned on by the sight of him nearly naked was bad enough, but straddling him from behind on the motorcycle only made it worse. Safely beneath his helmet and wrapped in a spare jacket he had given her, Saida quickly discovered that the orange machine humming between her legs was like jet fuel to her tension. Her knees tightened against the bike with the force of a metal compactor, and her nails dug deeper into his side with every swerve between cars.

His traffic maneuvering eventually led them to a tiny island where a decades-old seafood dive overlooked the marsh and served up some of the region's best bivalves. Over a steaming pile of them, Warren told her he was from Texas and that he came to the coast with dreams of starting his own business. When that didn't work out, he took a job as a mechanic and had been figuring things out ever since. He thought about college but couldn't bear the thought of being in a classroom for hours a day, so he vowed to scratch out a living by some other means that revolved around anything with wheels.

"So that's the reason for all those books and catalogs?"

"Yep. It's knowing my trade."

"Okay, so what's vulcanization?"

A fiery grin cracked across his smooth face. "It's when rubber's heated under pressure to make it more resilient and stronger."

Saida didn't remove her eyes from him as she traced the letters of graffiti carved into their table. "Sounds molten."

He leaned forward, mimicking her gesture. "Want to know more?"

She lied and said she did, but she couldn't have cared less about the language of rubber. She did think, however, that it would make for fun bed puns—when she got him there, so she filed away *wet traction, vertical bouncing, tramping, corner force,* and *eccentric mounting* for future use. In a few hours, she'd twist these terms into a lusty jargon, so when they arrived back at his place, she began climbing the stairs to do just that.

"Hey," he called from below. "Where're you going?"

"Isn't it obvious?"

Warren positioned his right foot on the first step and leaned on the rail. "I don't think that's a good idea." He extended his hand. "Please come down."

Saida turned. "What's your problem?"

When she stomped down to him, he hoisted himself up to meet her and cupped his hand under her chin. "I want to date you," he whispered.

In the ears of most women, his words would have been enough to make knees melt like candle wax, but in Saida's case, it was against her anatomy to flinch at these sentiments. For the moment, his uttering extinguished the flames between her thighs, but she'd play the waiting game, at least for a while.

"Now, go home and rest. You'll need it for another time." Walking her over to her car, he checked his handiwork on her mended tire and kissed her sweetly. "If you stayed here, you wouldn't get any." He gently closed her door, which made her only more determined to open him to her possibilities.

In the weeks to come, Saida, occasionally forthcoming with the juicy details of her escapades, would reply only, "We're just havin' fun," when any of her friends asked about Warren or her "tangerine play machine," as she took to calling him. They knew she especially liked the motorcycle and began to wonder whether it was the man or the machine that was working her into a fever.

The looming semester's end was throwing everyone into a frenzy, especially Helena, whose usual jovial demeanor grew alarmingly darker. Pacing, hand wringing, and bouts of crying became daily activities. Any time Cadence asked her what was wrong, she'd brush off the question or make an excuse to leave, but one Sunday afternoon, she finally broke.

Cadence had returned to the dorm to find her roommate huddled on the floor in a fitful state while a friend Cadence had never seen was holding Helena.

"Helena, enough of this," Cadence heard the girl say. "You're worrying yourself to the point where you can barely function. Just find out."

Cadence looked at the two and introduced herself to the stranger.

"I'm Chance."

Cadence darted her eyes from one to the other, unsure of whom to direct her question. "So what's wrong?"

Helena buried her face in her knees, letting out staggered sobs. "I'm going to tell her," Chance whispered. "Helena thinks she's pregnant."

The sobs grew louder. "No, no, I, I'll give it just a few more days." She lifted her head. "It'll come, I just know it."

"Enough of this. I'm making an executive decision. We're going to buy you a pregnancy test and you're taking it tonight. Got me? I'm tired of seeing you like this."

Pulled into the situation by default, Cadence agreed to go with Chance to get the test. The odds of running into someone they knew at the closest pharmacy were too high, so they walked to an out-of-the-way grocery store over a mile from campus.

"I don't mean to pry, but can you tell me a little more about the guy and the situation?" Cadence asked.

Chance paused to press the crosswalk button at the intersection. "She'd been hooking up with some guy she met at a party when she first came here."

"I wonder if that was one of the guys from that beach party we took her to."

"I think she mentioned that's how she met him. Anyway, a little over a month ago, after they had done it, he had this weird look on his face, saying he had put a condom on but then he couldn't find it. They looked all over the bed and in the sheets for it. Nothing." Chance screwed up her face. "She pulled it out of herself a few hours later."

"Ugh, that's terrible."

"The gunk was still inside it, but she wasn't sure if some had come out. She's tried to put it out of her mind. She hasn't had her period since way before that, but she's convinced stress is the reason."

"Could it be?" Cadence asked.

"I guess. But I'm worried about her. She's been really nauseous this last week or so."

"Has she told the guy?"

"They're not hooking up anymore, and he was bangin' some other chick, too."

"Poor Helena," Cadence said. "This does explains why she hasn't been herself lately."

Once inside the store, they walked nonchalantly about, picking up a few extra items—cheese doodles, a box of cereal, bottles of soda, quality toilet paper, and the Easter special of bright yellow Peeps—to camouflage the main purchase. They studied the signs, searching for clues that would lead them to the right aisle. *Feminine products* held promise, so they scanned the shelves, but amid the douches, pads, and tampons, Cadence and Chance could not find the test that would deliver the truth about what was happening inside Helena's body.

"Shit, they're not here," Chance said. "What kind of grocery store doesn't carry pregnancy crap?"

They looked at each other in beleaguered confusion and back at the goods before the answer popped into their heads.

"Pharmacy!" they said in unison and scampered toward the front.

"Wait!" Cadence turned back. "I need some of these." She grabbed a blue box of crotch corks before searching for the drug area.

The choices were too confusing: digital or standard stick tests; one step or two; three or five minutes wait time. All promised fast, accurate results, an ensured detection of hCG, a pregnant woman's hormonal calling card. The sticks would communicate in lines and signs cheerfully colored in dark and faint hues of blues and pinks. Cadence and Helena read quickly, compared prices, and finally decided on the stick version.

With the test tucked loosely among the goods, they went to the checkout, but just as they were feet from an open lane, Cadence heard her name. She wheeled around, only to hear the slap of something hitting the floor. Chance's hands were full, too, so neither could pick up the strayed good.

"Here, I'll get that for you."

"Walker," Cadence said with a tight-lipped smile. "Hi. I, I didn't know you worked here."

"It pays the bills." He fingered the box with interest. "I'm applying for an internship at a law firm, so I might be able to give up this glamorous attire." He stroked his apron and turned his attention to the package in his hand. "Peeps, huh? Personally, I like the hot pink bunnies or the purple ones, but the yellow chicks will do." He reached to tuck it among the items in Cadence's arms.

Chance stepped toward him. "Here. I'll take those."

"Oh, okay." He placed the candy atop her goods. His attention returned to Cadence who in shifting to hide the test had made it only more visible.

"Walker, this is my roommate's friend."

"I'm Chance. I'd shake your hand, but . . ."

"Yeah, between the two of you, you don't have one to spare. Want me to get you a cart?"

"No, no thanks," Cadence said. "We were just going to check out."

"Okay, then. I won't keep you. Nice to meet you, Chance, and Cadence," his voice trailed off. "I hope you're doing well."

Walking away, she felt certain his eyes held pity for her, that he had seen the test tucked among its strange companions of doodles and tampons. She shuddered at what he might be thinking, but when she peeked over her shoulder, he was gone.

Back in the room, Chance and Cadence hastily read the instructions, told Helena to go pee on the end of the stick for five seconds and bring it to them. She did as she was told, placed the oracle of her future on the desk and assumed her customary pacing but with much more speed than usual. Cadence and Chance hovered over the little chemistry set, waiting for it to deliver the lab results. At any other time, the clock would have raced forward, but at this moment, it crawled from second to second. It was one of the most pressing tests Cadence had never taken; her nerves were wracked, but not to the degree of Helena, whose life was about to be defined by thin blue lines forming in a small plastic window—two for a positive result, one for negative.

Turning from the door to complete another lap, Helena looked up to see Cadence cover her mouth and Chance drop her head.

"Nooooo!" The floor seemed to disappear beneath Helena and she went facedown to the rug.

"I'm sorry," Cadence said, but her words were drowned by the sobbing.

"Shhh, we'll figure something out." Chance knelt beside Helena.

Cadence cast her eyes from her wailing roommate to her desk where the package of yellow chicks peeped out of their neat package. Beneath the shiny cellophane, they sat in perfect rows, all ten with their fat sides squeezing into one another, their beady eyes vying for a view of the drama. She looked from them to the test, which lay a few inches away. The two blue lines that had sent Helena to the floor had faded, leaving a single mark. Cadence snatched the stick and blinked incessantly against the trick her vision was playing. She scrambled to find the directions and this time, she read them slowly—*Wait three full minutes before reading the results.* Cadence looked at the test again: one thin, blue line. Just one. Negative.

"He, Helena! We, we were wrong. We didn't wait long enough!"

Helena sat up, trying to catch her breath. "What? What are you saying?"

"You're not pregnant! The test is negative—not positive. We were supposed to wait three minutes, but we must have looked too early. See?" Cadence rushed the stick over.

Chance grabbed it and peered into the window. "She's right! One blue line! You're not pregnant!"

Following a joyous outbreak of dancing and a group hug, the three camped on the floor, devouring cheese doodles and washing them down with soda like schoolgirls at a sleepover.

Pulling three of the chicks from the safety of their package, Cadence gave one to Helena and another to Chance. They squeezed and stretched the little yellow birds into misshapen mallow while retelling the mishaps of failing to follow directions on one of the most important and easiest tests of a woman's life. Perhaps someday, one of them would relish a positive result, make plans for a new life, embrace the duties of motherhood, but for now, they all celebrated the negative, the joy of a single line representing nothing and everything. As they bit into the sugary fluff, the treats brought such gritty sweetness to this infertile occasion—a time they celebrated with great relief precisely because life would go on without life.

Chapter 18

Communications 184
Perspectives on Mass Communications

Eyes are everywhere: observing, ogling, occupying inconspicuous spaces above and below, from angles all around. With electric eyes that magically open doors to the flashing red irises beneath dark bubbles protruding from ceilings—the Orwellian vision of optical oppression is too much with the world.

Professor Tiller's students had no realization of this truth until it was too late for the majority of them. Like a reaper moving through a field, he effectively severed their existence in his class, not by a swing they saw coming but by means hidden behind them since the beginning.

In the semester's first days, he made the presence of his teaching assistants Winston and Julia obvious; the two always sat up front taking attendance and passing out papers when needed, but the students were unaware of another: the individual sitting in the back posing as one of them. He looked like a conscientious note taker, but secretly, he was taking account of each time a laptop screen wandered from the topic. Unbeknownst to those off in cyberspace or otherwise not absorbing Dr. Tiller's knowledge, they were being kept track of by O'Brien—the third teaching assistant, the one they never knew about.

By April, O'Brien's reports had successfully cut the communications class to less than half of its original count as most students were forced to drop when they learned that for every day their attention strayed, a zero had been recorded. Rather than languish with a grade in the teens, most unwillingly dropped the required course and did so railing against Tiller's secret tyranny. The octopus-eyed professor took no heed; although he had announced his policies loudly and clearly, most chose to ignore the warnings.

"In your reading for today," Dr. Tiller said to those who survived the slashing, "who has an assessment of the Kew Gardens community as reported by Martin Gansberg in '37 Who Saw Murder Didn't Call Police'?"

Hands shot up and Dr. Tiller acknowledged one. "I think it's horrible that all those people watched that woman get stabbed and no one called the police," Miss Hazard, the jingle-braceleted one responded. The noise maker, unfortunately, had not been eliminated.

"One person did call," a classmate countered.

"Yeah, but a lot of good it did. She was already dead," she snapped back.

"You both make valid points, based on the fact that you simply read the article but did not pay attention to it," the professor said. "The headline reveals that 37 people saw this woman being murdered. The lead tells us that for more than half an hour, these 'respectable, law-abiding citizens' watched the killer 'stalk and stab' the victim. Is this what happened at 3:20 a.m. on March 13, 1964, in Queens, New York?"

"It was printed in the *New York Times*," one student said. "They have lots of editors and fact checkers, so I think it's safe to assume it's true."

"Mr. Havacheck, you should never assume that what you read is true—no matter the publication," Dr. Tiller chided. "Here's why . . ."

The professor led them through the account of twenty-eight-year-old Catherine "Kitty" Genovese returning home following her shift as a bar manager. Shortly after three in the morning, she parked her car in a lot next to a railroad station and made her way toward the entrance to her apartment, which was at the rear of a row of shophouses. As she walked, she noticed a man following her; apparently, she headed for the call box or the bar at the block's end, but he stabbed her before she got there. Her scream caused a window to open, and a neighbor yelled down for her to be left alone. The stalker left; she got to her feet and struggled toward the door in the building's rear. She made it into a hallway before he caught up with her again and delivered the fatal stab wound. Days later, Winston Moseley was arrested for the murder.

"Tell me: Why were 37 people awake and peering out their windows in the middle of the night?" Dr. Tiller posed.

"That does seem weird," someone responded. "But if a few people were up and they didn't help her, that's really callous."

Dakota raised his hand. "Someone did come to her aid. The man who called down. He verbally intervened, and Moseley left. Maybe that neighbor didn't know she had been stabbed, especially if she had gotten to her feet."

"Excellent point, Mr. Shout."

"And wouldn't it have taken time for most people to wake up after they heard her scream, if they even heard her at all?"

"I would think so. Anything else?"

"Yes. If the entrance to her apartment was around the back, she would have been out of most people's sights for the other attacks. How were they to help if they couldn't see?"

"Exactly," the professor said. "And by the way, there were only two attacks, not three as reported. Yet sloppy reporting would have us believe that no one came to her aid. This is simply not true, as Mr. Shout has highlighted."

Their teacher explained how the reporter didn't get it right. And because he didn't, a neighborhood was held up as an example of urban decay, crucified in newspapers across America, and taunted by a killer who claimed, in a 1977 opinion editorial, that his crime had served society. By murdering Kitty, Moseley bragged that he had exposed human indifference and showed how people must come to the aid of others."

Dr. Tiller slammed his fist on the podium. "When you're a journalist, when you have the power to destroy reputations and lives, you have a responsibility to get the story right. You must deliver the truth because millions of eyes will read what you have written and take untruth for truth—to the devastation of others."

A photo of Kitty Genovese, standing demurely in a white dress, her hair perfectly coiffed, flashed up on the screen. Seconds later, a mugshot of Winston Moseley settled next to the picture of his prey. The apathy in his expression supposedly reflecting the indifference that defined a community, a group of people who also became victims. Two lives, one night, zero eyewitnesses who saw *everything.*

"I'll leave you with this to ponder," Dr. Tiller said. "Because we so easily believe what we read in print, students and educators alike, we still have psychology professors teaching this case as a classic example of the bystander effect, that social phenomenon that hinders an individual from rendering aid to a victim because of the presence of other bystanders. How many of you have been taught this in a psych class?"

A few hands rose, with one student adding, "I was taught it's called 'diffusion of responsibility.'"

"It is, but it's also famously known as 'the Genovese Syndrome' made popular by social psychologists Latané and

Darley following this case. Clearly, now you all know that the story of Kitty Genovese is not an example of the bystander effect." Leaning toward them, he narrowed his eyes. "It should make you wonder what else you're being taught that's not the truth." He let the silence settle over them before his designer shoes tapped across the stage and to the exit.

Dakota turned to Cadence. "That was heavy, huh?"

"Yep," she said, glancing down at the visage of a man tucked inside her classmate's book. Cadence reached for the flier. The figure on the paper was Dr. Foster, a visiting scholar, who was giving a lecture titled: "'It's a Jungle Out There': The Ethological Evolution of Truth, Lies, and Survival in the Animal World."

"Cadence, you okay? You look like you've seen a ghost."

She didn't answer him, but stared at the face she recognized from that night when she was stuck outside Dr. Heath's office.

"Cadence?"

"What?" She looked up. "Oh, sorry. Where did you get this?"

"My philosophy professor gave them out. It's for a lecture we have to attend. Why? Are you okay?"

She handed the paper back to him. "Yeah, I'm fine."

"You want to come to the professor's talk?"

"No, it's not something I'm interested in."

"Speaking of interesting, anything going on with you?"

Cadence averted telling Dakota what she had just realized and said there was nothing to report about her life, which was especially true in the romance department. Her relationship had gone devastatingly lukewarm with Schilar, but she tried not to wallow in pity and remained hopeful it could be rekindled. He still wasn't sure if he would return to school in the fall, and she hadn't seen much of him since he'd been busy recording songs for the band's first big release. One of his friends from home was visiting to help with the music, and they were throwing a party on the weekend to celebrate the project's completion. Other than the upcoming get-together, nothing interesting was going on. As she thought about it, the only friend with anything exciting happening was Saida, but she wasn't saying much about her motorcycle guy.

Saida had been working for weeks to ensure that the white towel her tangerine machine donned every day after work eventually hit the floor, just as she had wanted it to on that first night. Warren was turning out to be a tease with his insistence on dating. He wanted her almost as much as she wanted him, but he just didn't want to admit it. He needed their time together to be slow, not rushed, not frenzied.

On an afternoon of final project work when Saida had grown tired of studying figures and formulas for her business course and needed more invigorating material, she headed over to Warren's apartment—intent on learning all she could about him. He had just gotten off work when she arrived, so he popped the tops on two bottles of beer, handed her one and the music remote before heading for the shower. Saida waited until the water was sufficiently flowing before entering his room. The steam swirling from behind the curtain only added to the allure, but she sat on the edge of the bed, out of view from the small space he occupied and waited.

It wasn't long before he appeared in that terry cloth—wet, warm, and for the taking. He was surprised to see her on his bed.

"What're you doing?" He titled his head to shake the water from his ear.

"Right now?" Saida looked from side to side. "Nothing. What're you doing?"

"Getting dried off so I can get dressed and take you out."

"I'd prefer you didn't."

"Didn't what?"

"Get dressed." Saida stood up. "Come here."

He obeyed and steps later, her tongue was studying the map of his muscles. She retraced it down his chest, savoring the lines fashioned from lifting, pushing, pulling, pounding. His was the most exquisite six pack she had ever tasted. While she worked, he laid his hands softly on her head, not directing her, as he knew exactly where she was going, but just running his fingers through her long, silky hair. Moving down, she came to the towel line, where she could feel him hardening beneath it. This time, when her fingers reached to untuck the covering, he did not stop her. She smiled when it fell to the floor and was delighted at her discovery. He was impressive. At first, she carefully worked her tongue around the edge of him—her way of promising what was to come.

When she had gotten him to a state of wet traction sufficient enough for vertical bouncing, she directed his hands to her clothes, which soon made acquaintances with the towel. Pushing him onto the bed, Saida positioned herself above and reached over to the nightstand where her purse sat. Pulling a condom from the side pocket, she opened it with her teeth and expertly rolled it on him.

She eccentrically mounted him as she did the tangerine machine parked in the garage beneath them. When he opened his eyes, he could hardly believe the vision: moving to the music pounding from the next room, the dark-haired beauty writhed in and out of the day's last sunlight, which cut the blinds' shadows in stripes across her breasts. He shut his eyes and tried to concentrate on her moaning, but her sounds of pleasure were soon silenced.

Her motion stopped. "Wha, what's wrong?"

"I, I don't know." He reached for the limpness between her legs.

"What do you mean? What's going on?"

"Maybe we're going too fast. I'm not sure." He moved his hand to her thigh and squeezed.

Slightly sliding back, she raised her fists, slamming them to the sheets as her forehead smacked his chest. "I don't think we're going fast enough!" she yelled into the wall of muscle.

Her ride was over before it began—he was deflated just like a punctured tire. They tried again and again and again, but no amount of vulcanization was bringing him back to life that night. Exhausted from frustration, she left for the dorm. On the drive back, she thought about the disaster. She was communicating her every feminine wile to a body that wasn't responding. It was a damn shame that nature would get the equipment so right in form and so wrong in function.

It was early morning when she stepped onto the exceptionally quiet floor of their hall. Gently shutting the door so as not to awaken Penny, Saida was slipping into bed when she heard a noise outside. Just as she turned toward it, a piece of paper shot beneath the door.

Like a cheetah, she sprung into the empty hall then into the stairwell where she stopped. Breathing ever-so-slightly in hopes of detecting the tormentor, she crept toward the rails and peered down. Nothing. But in looking up, she saw a shadow on the wall above her. She bolted up the stairs, taking them by twos and leaving the figure with no chance of fleeing in time. Before the prey knew it, her face was crushed into the concrete with hellish fury on her back. Saida rolled the offender over and was stunned.

Jerking Malinda off the floor by the hair, Saida marched her down the stairs to their hall where Penny stood in the doorway holding the paper.

"What does it say?"

With a forlorn look, Penny held it up. In the same black lettering as the others appeared: *Our Half-Rubber Squad is Worth MORE than your HOLE Lies.*

Spinning Malinda into the wall, Saida snatched the note, shoving it so violently under Malinda's nose that the paper left a torturous cut on her delicate skin.

"It, it wasn't my idea. It was Madison's. She's behind this," Malinda cried.

"Is that so? Where is she?"

"In our room, I guess." Malinda wiped the small smear of blood beneath her nose.

"Let's go see." Saida pushed the messenger from the wall and sent her down the hall with a slap to the back.

"Saida, wait," Penny said, but her roommate continued marching the captive to their destination. When they got there, Malinda hesitated going in but caved under Saida's demands. The door swung open to reveal Madison sitting on the bed, her face brightly lit from her computer's glare. She peered over the screen at the intruder. "What're you doing here?"

"Cut the shit! You and your little crony know why I'm here." Crumpling the paper, Saida threw it at Madison's head.

Madison caught it just like a player and unfolded it. "I don't know what this is. Get out of my room or I'm calling the police." Madison reached for her phone.

"You fucking liar! Malinda already fessed up." Saida eyed the phone with a smirk. "And call them. I'm sure they'd be interested in all the letters you've been slipping under our door for months."

Madison's eyes narrowed on Malinda as if she were trying to vaporize her roommate. Saida watched the silent exchange.

"Just own what you did, bitch!" Saida shouted.

Madison jumped to her feet. "So what? I sent some messages because your roommate's the one who won't *own* what happened."

"What're you saying?"

"Those guys on that squad are my friends, and I know they wouldn't do something like that. That slut from up North is just comin' down here stirrin' up trouble. How're they supposed to live with their reputations ruined?"

"*Their* reputations? A bunch of rapists? You don't know what you're fucking talking about." Saida's voice shook almost as much as her body. "Were you in that room?"

"Well, no." Madison brought her hand to her hip. "Were you?"

For a moment, everyone seemed struck by the obvious truth that no one, save Penny and the players, had been present. Despite the fact that Penny's anguish told the truth of what happened, the incident had become a matter of perception— loyalty forced sides to be taken.

"No, but I was there with her in the hospital while she was in pieces after being raped. That's proof enough for me."

"Did it occur to you that she may have wanted to take on more than one guy? Some girls like that you know—'specially y'all Northern hos."

Saida balled her fist to strike, and just as she did, the RA cut through the crowd that had gathered at the door. "All right, that's enough," Carrie held out her arms between the two. "Everybody needs to cool off. Someone want to tell me what's going on?"

"Yeah, I'm getting ready to slap the Southern accent outta this bitch." Saida grabbed the paper from Madison's bed and handed it to Carrie. "She's been tormenting Penny with these for months."

"No, I haven't." She pointed to Malinda. "She's been delivering them."

Malinda's mouth dropped. "But you're the one who's been writing them."

Madison huffed. "That's my freedom of speech."

Carrie grimaced at the paper. "Anonymous notes of harassment are not protected by freedom of speech."

"That's freedom of perverted speech, you stupid bitch." Saida moved for Madison but Carrie's arm blocked her path.

"Saida, please! We'll deal with this in the morning. It's the middle of the night and most of the hall's awake. I want everybody to calm down and go back to bed. We'll sort this out tomorrow."

Saida backed away, but as she turned to go, she stopped in front of Malinda. "You're a pathetic excuse of a person. If she tells you to wipe her ass, do you?" Saida's stare dug into the girl. "If so, I hope the shit under your manicure stains forever."

Carrie forcefully guided Saida to the door where Penny stood surrounded by most of the hall. Saida put her arm around her roommate, who shunned the embrace inside but fell within it nonetheless. As they stepped over the threshold, Saida whipped around. "Hey Madison! Next time you're going to exercise your freedom of speech, you should at least get the spelling right. It's W-H-O-L-E with a W. You dumb cunt—and that's with a C!"

Madison smirked. "Bitch, you think you're so smart? It's a pun."

When Saida and Penny disappeared from the corridor, the witnesses were left exchanging awkward glances. The confrontation had revealed a secret harbored on the hall for months—their neighbor was at the center of the half-rubber rape rumors. From what the hallmates had seen tonight and heard from behind Penny's door on many others—muffled cries so painful they sounded like those of a wounded animal—most felt they knew the harsh truth even if those beyond the hall denied it.

The end of their first year and the cruelty that accompanied it couldn't come fast enough. As the days marched to the term's close, parties blossomed like spring buds bringing energy and colorful fun to the tiring and unpleasant ways of late.

Schilar and the band held the party at a friend's house on the edge of the city, a small bash within reason since fewer people usually meant longer party times. The bigger the crowd, the more likely it was to get busted sooner by the cops. Cadence invited everyone in her suite to come along, but Penny had plans with Jade, and Helena was going to a bash with Chance. Saida recruited Diana, and as they were leaving, River emerged from her room looking like she could use a night out. Olivia had given her the silent treatment all semester, and River wasn't sure why. So on the walk to the party, Saida and Cadence filled

River in on the Olivia-spying-on-Ruthie debacle of fall semester and the fight that ended it all. The story explained a lot for River since her roommate always seemed wrapped in suspicious silence.

The party was humming when they arrived. Cadence looked around for her rock star, but he wasn't there. A bandmate mentioned something about Schilar being on a beer run, which was strange since the keg was fully tapped. With their signature red cups in hand, the ladies huddled in a group waiting for the guys to take interest. From across the room, Cadence spotted Schilar's roommate Steve and his girlfriend Nikki. Next to them, Kirby was standing alone, so Cadence went over since they hadn't had a chance to talk since that awkward car ride following Aliyah's funeral.

"Yeah, that was a low blow from Astra," Kirby said. "I don't know her, but I get the feeling there's a lot behind that comment." He looked to Cadence for hints, but she averted answering by sipping her beer. "Anyway, I talked to Haven after class a few days ago. Astra apologized."

"That's good." Cadence was relieved at the news but changed the subject. "Do you think Mirabilis's exam is going to be hard?"

"I don't think it's going to be easy, but it won't be the worst."

"What's that going to be for you?"

"Calculus. Total brutality. Yours?"

"I think my communications exam is going to kill me. My professor wrote the book on the subject." Cadence replied to Kirby's skeptical expression. "No, he really did. I think he's a bit of a legend actually."

"Speaking of legend, how about that poem today?"

"You mean the one about the mariner?"

Quicker than the crossbow that flew into the albatross, Kirby transformed into a professor of Coleridge's work:

> *Water, water every where*
> *And all the boards did shrink;*
> *Water, water, every where,*
> *Nor any drop to drink.*

"Maybe you should replace that with 'beer.'" She laughed at her classmate reciting poetry at a keg party.

"Well, there's plenty of that here, right?" He laughed, too, and tipped his cup into hers.

She decided to play along:

> *Alone, alone, all, all alone*
> *Alone on a wide wide sea!*
> *And never a saint took pity on*
> *My soul in agony.*

Cadence swept her hair off one shoulder, having remembered the lines from her high school studies.

"Impressive." Kirby's eyes remained fixed on his classmate. "How about this?"

> *One after one, by the star-dogged Moon,*
> *Too quick for groan or sigh,*
> *Each turned his face with a ghastly pang,*
> *And cursed me with his eye.*

"You're really into this stuff!" Cadence said. "You really are quite the poetry pro."

"I like words. Words matter. I want to make sure mine always do."

COMM 184 · 489

"Hey, hey, what's all this?" Schilar slid around the corner and landed a kiss on Cadence's neck.

Kirby forced a smile as Cadence's face turned a shade of her cup. "I'm Kirby," he said, extending his hand.

Schilar met Kirby's grip. "You two have English together?"

"Yeah. We were just talking about class," Cadence said.

"The craziest shit happened in ours today," Schilar said. "So, Professor Mirabilis gives back our papers. It's quiet. Everyone's reading the comments, and all of a sudden, this chair goes flyin' across the room and hits the front board next to her. And this guy just loses it. He goes off. Calls her 'a fuckin' bitch.' Tells her she doesn't know what she's talking about—that she's trying to ruin him."

"You are joking." Cadence's eyes widened at the story.

"I kid you not. Anyway, he grabs her, so a couple of us pull him off and wrestle him to the floor."

"Oh my God," she said. "Is she okay?"

"I think so. She was pretty shaken up."

"What happened to the lunatic?" Kirby asked.

"Arrested. But check this out. When the police searched his bookbag, he had a knife in there. Not a pocket one, either. A big fuckin' blade. Needless to say, I don't think that asshole's gonna pass."

Kirby tossed back the last of his beer. "Whew, I need another after that story. Can I get you two a refill?"

"No, I'm good," Schilar said. "Just goin' to spend some time with my lady here."

"All right. See you two later."

With Kirby gone, Cadence stepped away from Schilar.

"Your 'lady'?" Cadence asked.

"Well, yeah. You sound surprised."

She kicked at a piece of trash on the floor. "It's just that I haven't felt much like your girlfriend lately."

"I'm sorry. I've been busy with this new record, and I want you to meet my closest friend from home. He's been managing that. Got a lot of great ideas for the band. He's around here somewhere."

Schilar briefly brought his lips to hers and smiled at the gift dangling from her neck—a memento she had worn every day since the night he had given it to her. He stroked it lightly. "Nice necklace." As he threw back his beer, his friend appeared seemingly out of nowhere. "Jacan! My man. I was just talkin' about you!" Schilar wiped the liquid dripping down his chin.

"Didn't I teach you not to waste good beer?" Jacan sounded like a father dismissing his son.

Schilar laughed. "I'm sure you did. Jacan, this is Cadence." Schilar hugged her closely to him.

"So this is the one I've heard so much about?" Jacan offered his hand to Cadence. "Pleasure."

His touch was cold and slimy from the cup and luckily, didn't stay wrapped around her skin for very long. As the three began to chat, Cadence soon found herself on the fringes of a conversation about music, so she excused herself to go find her friends.

Although Saida hadn't entirely given up on Warren, she was on the lookout for a new subject but found the choices limited. Baggy pants and the musty scents of patchouli and cigarettes did not attract her or Diana who shared the same taste in guys but who was less successful in her conquests. River wasn't interested in their hunts, so in wandering around, she met Kirby, and the two were conversing about the finer points of her knife-throwing skills. Even though it was her boyfriend's party, Cadence felt like a stranger, so over the night's course, she took much comfort in the keg.

Eventually, she found a comfy spot on the couch and was taking in the party when Jacan slid in the space beside her and began watching the crowd, too. They laughed at the antics of some drunks, the slurred pick-up lines they heard, and how a number of guys approached Saida only to be rebuffed with a single look. Schilar drifted through the room, moving among circles. He was like a magnet to Cadence's eyes, and every so often, he'd return her gaze with a smile and a wink—gestures that did not go unnoticed by Jacan.

"I see you're the muse of the moment," he said after observing one of these silent exchanges.

"I'm what?"

"His muse." Jacan titled back his cup of dark brown liquid. "Damn, that's good." He seemed to ignore her question.

"What did you say?"

His gaze swept from her feet to her face. "His muse. He needs it. Always has ever since I've known him." He cocked one leg up on the table in front of them and settled back into the couch. "He always finds a beautiful girl to be with. Charms her with his words and usually some trinket. Has some great times, waits for the bad ones—it's all for the lyrics, for the music."

In reaching for her neck, Cadence found the metal to be warmer than usual.

"He gave you that, didn't he?" His laugh sounded like a cackle. "He never changes. Same routine, different place."

The chain suddenly felt as if it were choking her. "I, I need another beer." Before she could pull herself from the couch's suffocating clutches, Jacan's hand gripped her knee.

"Hey, before you leave, I'd like to know something." His tongue flicked like a snake's. "What would it take to make you my muse?"

She jumped up, but before she crossed the threshold into the next room, she glanced back. His eyes remained fixed as his body shook from a silent laughter only the two of them could hear.

Cadence kept close to her friends and to Schilar when he wasn't absorbed in talking up the record. She thought it best not to mention the incident with Jacan, as she didn't want to ruin her rock star's night. Near midnight, the band made the living room a stage. Lights went low for the melodic highs, and the musicians began to rock the old, wooden house.

An hour later, drunkenness snuck up like a thief and stole Cadence's sensibilities. Her world began to spin, so she sought the instant remedy of fresh air, but her feet felt like they were stone blocks as she trudged through the kitchen to the porch. Stepping out, she saw Kirby and River cozy in a corner still talking away. A scattering of people were around the fire pit, but even with the orange glow, she couldn't tell who they were. The smoke shifted her way, surging her dizziness, so she slipped around the side of the house and steadied herself against it. She shut her eyes and focused on breathing.

She thought she had conquered the spins, but when she opened her eyes, they intensified precisely because Jacan was standing inches from her. His hand brushed by her ear, coming to rest on the same board as her head. He smelled of smoke and sweat and whiskey and trouble.

"Cadence, baby, you okay?"

"Yep, yep. I'm ffffine. Wait—" She gulped for air then covered her mouth. "Waitin' for Schilar."

"Hmm . . . have you thought anymore about what I said?"

"No, no. I havennn't. Not goin' to." She raised herself on her toes and tried to look over his shoulders but swayed back into the wall. "Ple, please go. Just leave me alone."

Jacan grinned into her closed eyes. "You know, Schilar's still playin'. He will be for a while. He's up there in a room full of girls, singin' to them. There's plenty of time for us to do a little playin' of our own. Come on, just a kiss or two, that's all I want."

Hot breath turned her neck moist, and Cadence pushed at him, but her aim was off, and her hands slid past his sides so that she fell into him—the semblance of a passionate embrace she never intended. His scraggly goatee scratched her face like sandpaper as his tongue churned in her mouth. Somehow, the cold metal of her necklace melted away under the heat of his touch.

She got her hands to his chest and started to push; her own strength amazed her when she heard him hit the dirt. Somehow, her mind paused the spinning long enough for her to see Schilar looming over Jacan, who was crawling away like an insect. She breathed relief and called her rescuer's name.

"Shut up." His icy response was accompanied by a more chilling stare. "Don't say a word to me."

"Sch, Schilar, you, you don't understand."

"You're right. I don't understand how my girlfriend's out here makin' out with my best friend."

Cadence stumbled toward him, but he stepped back and pointed to the street. "Get your friends and go home!"

"Wait. I, I need to explain." Just as the tears began to roll down Cadence's face, Saida pulled her away for their walk home. The group contemplated a cab but decided the cool night air would help Cadence's condition. The trek was long, staggered, and punctuated by pauses to puke. Holding her hair, her hand, and what was left of her heart, they watched a sobering sadness settle in their friend.

April was turning out to be a very cruel month indeed. Far from measuring her life in the joy of Prufrock's coffee spoons as promised on the wall in c.a.t.'s, Cadence was measuring it with heaping helpings of misery, proof of which she was shedding on the couch in the sanitarium late one evening. Communication with Schilar was nonexistent, and because of the void, her eyes looked like a wasteland of woe from unrelenting tears.

Her face was buried in a pillow when a warm tongue found its way into her ear, and soon she was trapped beneath four paws and a black mask of slobbering concern. Cadence laughed, and the more she did, the more the boxer's tongue worked its magic on transforming her mood.

"Kyd! Kyd! Are you up here?" Catissa called. Rounding the corner, she saw the puppy on the couch over Cadence looking as if he had just been caught stealing treats from the jar. His nub fluttered furiously as he laid down on his victim. "I should have known it was you up here, Cadence. I swear this dog goes crazy when you're around. Now Kyd, get down."

Cadence put her arms around the dog. "It's okay, Catissa. I love this guy."

"But I don't love him on my furniture. Now Kyd, get down." Catissa ushered him to the floor where he stretched out below

Cadence. "So, a little late night studying?" Catissa sensed that books were not the reason the girl was alone in the room. "Want to talk about what's troubling you?"

Glassiness appeared in Cadence's eyes. "Guy problems." Cadence hugged the pillow to her chest and Kyd, sensing the distress, sat up and nudged her with his smushed nose.

Catissa rose. "I'll be back in a moment. Kyd, you stay."

Cadence remained seated, stroking Kyd's sleek white hair and admiring the jewelry jingling on this collar. She grabbed the black tag shaped like a bone that read *K-Y-D*. It was the first time she had ever seen his name written out.

"What's up with the spelling of your name, boy?" she asked, but he must not have wanted to answer because he ran off at the question.

The only other presence left was Shakespeare, his visage peering down in empathic delight at her melancholy. She wondered what he really knew of love and heartache and the pain of silence, but the sound of Kyd's nails moving toward her broke the contemplation. An oversized, red marker hung from his mouth, which he dropped next to her leg.

Cadence picked up the slimy instrument. "You're a silly boy, Kyd, and a smart one, too. I should write about it, huh?" She laughed and shook her head at Shakespeare who seemed to approve of Kyd's suggestion.

"Okay, dear, here you go." Catissa handed her guest a steaming cup of tea perched on a delicate saucer. "Now, let me take the chill off," she said. With the turn of a key and strike of a long wooden match, the fireplace's logs exploded to life. Catissa glanced up to the portrait. "Ah, good evening, Bill. Eavesdropping as usual I see." Kyd left Cadence's side to curl up in front of the warmth.

Catissa pulled a chair next to the hearth and sank into it. Cradling her cup, she said, "That's Maggie's Elysium Elixir, a recipe sure to send you into Elysium."

"Elysium?"

"In Greek mythology, it's the underworld where the souls of the heroic and virtuous rest." She brought the cup to her nose and inhaled. "Mmm. Maggie is a very dear friend who gave me this recipe during a very difficult time when I couldn't sleep." She turned to the flickering glow and Cadence saw a mirror of her own distress.

"Catissa, what's wrong?"

Pulling a tissue from her pocket, Catissa dabbed the tears. "So sorry, dear. Anniversaries are always hard." She blew ripples across the tea's surface. "Ah, essence of lavender. Maggie smuggled the seeds out of France many, many years ago. We studied together in Paris and used to stroll along the Champs-Élysées dreaming as girls do of our futures—careers, husbands, children." In an instant, her voice shifted from soothing to serious. "Cadence, fifteen years ago today, my husband disappeared."

Only the sound of Kyd snoring could be heard. "Disappeared? Catissa, I don't want to pry if you don't want to talk about it."

"I don't mind sharing the story. It's good to talk about these things, but let me take you somewhere more appropriate for the telling." Catissa stood up, but before she moved toward the hall, she grabbed the hook-shaped poker from a stand next to the fire. Although set out for decoration, the steel rod was really a key of sorts.

Cadence followed Catissa into the hall with Kyd at their heels. Just before the door to the piazza, Catissa set her cup on a small table and raised the rod to a loop sticking out from the ceiling. With a slight pull, the door creaked open. Catissa pulled down the ladder and began the climb, but stopped to look back at Kyd. "Be a good boy and stay. Cadence, this way, dear."

Cadence placed her cup next to Catissa's and patted Kyd as he assumed his guard position. She ascended until she reached the floor where Catissa had lit a candle. Its light bounced off the window panes in the house's cupola, and beyond the glass, the wonderland of the port city stretched out around them.

"Now you know where the best room is." Catissa took a seat on the window bench that connected all sides of the quaint space. "Welcome to my widow's peak. The irony is too much, don't you think?"

"I guess so. That's a morbid name for such a beautiful look-out. Is it yours?"

"No, no. Back in the old days, lookouts similar to this one were given the name. Wives would watch for the return of their husbands who had gone out to sea. But as I know, the ocean makes wives into widows all too often." Her words seemed to drift out towards the Atlantic as if to remind it of the treasure it withheld.

"So what happened to him?"

"I don't know." The sadness of earlier returned as Catissa began her story of loss.

His name was Halsey, and it was his fortieth birthday. Although his wife wanted to throw him a big party to celebrate "midlife," he wanted a quiet day on the water and dinner with a few friends. Catissa got up and cooked him an early breakfast, made him a thermos of coffee and a bag lunch, and kissed him goodbye. At the marina, the dockhand wished him a good day of fishing and listened to the motor's humming fade as it moved toward the horizon.

Catissa spent the day preparing her garden and getting ready for the dinner. By late afternoon, Halsey had not returned. His absence wasn't of concern since he sometimes stayed around the docks until dark, puttering about and talking to boaters who'd arrived in port, but when guests began arriving for dinner, Catissa called the marina. In checking Halsey's boat slip, the dockhands found it empty, so the Coast Guard was called, and the search began immediately. The friends who came for dinner drove Catissa to the marina, but the vacant space where her husband's boat should have been safely tied was an emptiness she could not bear. She asked them to take her to the lighthouse on Sullivan's Island, a place where she thought she'd be closest to him.

"I just knew if he could see the lighthouse he'd feel me looking for him, and he'd find his way home. For hours, I stood on the chilling sand and stared at that black water. The way those waves beat the shore sounded so angry. I remember telling them: 'just bring him to me; lay him up here on this beach. Let me have him.' They never did." Catissa turned toward the wide expanse of water in the distance.

"Was anything ever found?"

"A few days later, pieces of his boat washed up on Kiawah, but that was all that I ever got. He's been lost ever since."

"What do you think happened?"

"I wish I knew. You know, the mystery is the worse part. Disappearance may be worse than death. An imagination can be a cruel gift. It will fill in the possibilities of what happened, and the habit kills you. For a long time, I would ponder all the ways he could have died—slipping beneath the surface after treading water for hours, a rogue wave, heart failure, a shark attack. Perhaps if we could have found his body, I would know. I am most certain he's dead, but I would have definitiveness of his end."

"You'd have some closure." Cadence nodded slightly.

Catissa turned to her. "No, no, I don't believe in closure. It's a woefully inadequate word for dealing with an incident that becomes a defining moment in life. 'Closure' makes me think that someone can shut the door on tragedy, walk away from it, when really, the disaster lingers every day. Some remnant of it shapes you, transforms your mind, informs your decisions— reminds you of life's fickleness. It changes your identity, even when you don't want it to. I am a widow, but Halsey's disappearance would be no more closed for me than if I had shut the lid on his coffin."

Catissa stood, stretching her arms out toward the city as if hugging in all of it. "Enough of resurrecting the pains of the past. I have something I want to share with you, but it's downstairs."

Cadence began the descent while Catissa cast one last look toward the ocean that refused to surrender the man she still loved. She blew the flame out in its direction and peered down to see Kyd anxiously waiting for her.

Stepping from the ladder, she motioned Cadence toward the consilium. Once inside, Catissa said, "You know I like to come in here from time to time and see the conversations. Well, the other night, I noticed a musing that might be of interest to you." She pointed to the question: *How do you measure your life?* and placed her finger on a winding, dark red line coming off one of its letters.

"Come here and follow it," Catissa urged.

Cadence touched her finger to the line and traced the path as it looped and dropped, swerved and curved across three walls until it reached the French doors. Resting at chest level next to the window, appeared: *In the glimpses I see of Cadence.*

She gaped at the writing on the wall. "Me?"

Catissa chuckled. "I've been on this campus for quite a while. You're the first Cadence I've ever met, so I figure it must be you. Think your guy wrote it?"

Cadence studied the script closely. "It's not his handwriting. Besides, we're having problems at the moment." Considering the tale of lost love Catissa had just revealed, Cadence tempered her sadness but couldn't help feeling a little elation at the message.

"I'm sorry to hear that. I hope it works out the way you want." Catissa nodded toward the message. "But if it doesn't, there's possibility out there. You seem to be having a tough time, so I thought it would brighten your evening."

"Catissa, you always know what people need, even when they don't."

After gathering her things, Cadence said good night, positioned her pepper spray in hand, and headed the short distance home. Catissa remained in the sanatorium putting away markers Kyd now retrieved as toys and occasionally stopping to review more of the year's chronicles. She smiled at the lines pulsing with energy around her. Heading downstairs, she grabbed the cups from the hall table, but when she stacked Cadence's on hers, Catissa nearly dropped the china. Formed from the loose leaves of fortune in the cup's bottom was the image of a bird—a raven—an ominous omen in the ancient practice of tasseomancy.

For a long time after her husband's disappearance, Catissa explored ways to communicate with him. In her search, she met psychics, clairvoyants, and mediums, all of whom claimed connections with the spiritual world. Nothing came of their attempts, but her experience with psychic divination created a keen interest in the future. She studied the Tarot and palmistry, and reading tea leaves became a hobby. Although she tried not to place too much faith in the happenstance tellings of leftover leaf fragments, she recalled the times her predictions had been right. She peered again at the black figure perched in the cup that seemed ready to fly after Cadence. Catissa hoped she was mistaken, that the shape could resist definitive form like an ink-blot's options under the scrutiny of different eyes.

Alone on the brick path to her dorm, Cadence was intrigued by the notion that somewhere, someone was thinking of her—someone other than her rock star, whose distance from her seemed about as far away as those orbs in the night sky. The moon was absent and those familiar dots Schilar had helped her name months ago did not shine as brightly as they once had, their light dwindling at the end of the long-years' journey to earth. But one star fought its way past the others, and when it reached her, Cadence basked in its dreamy promise. As she did, she did not see the piercing eyes lurking in the darkness—spheres of emptiness anxiously watching as she disappeared through the doors to the safety inside.

Chapter 19

Spanish 102
Intermediate Translation

The curvy script resisted identification, holding tightly to secrets it refused to reveal on a document created in 1539. Browned with age, the paper locked its mysteries in criss-crossed red lines and jagged yellow borders. Nothing was clear except that it was a map boasting *TIERA DE AYLLON*. Translating the phrase into *Land of Ayllón* was easy for Professor Hernandez's students but deciphering why they needed to and what relevance it held to them was proving more difficult.

The group struggled with the task of reading the work of cartographer Diego Ribero. Some words were clear: *aquí, poblar, barco, frío, trabajo,* as were their English equivalents: *here, populate, vessel, cold, work.* Putting them together to make sense of a message without their professor's advanced knowledge was like trying to read ancient Egyptian hieroglyphs without the Rosetta Stone. For however murky the story of this paper was, the language learners were certain of one aspect—the expedition did not go well. *Murió*, Spanish for *died*, ominously revealed the fates of those who followed dreams into Ayllón land.

In hearing their disgruntled mumblings about bothering with an old drawing and hating the requirement for straying from their native tongue, the professor called for their attention.

"I sense that some of you think this work is *estúpido*." He glared at the ones who held the opinion. "I will explain to you this story in English so you comprehend how *muy importante* this translation is. Does anyone know precisely what this map details?"

"It looks like a coastline," someone replied. "*Playa* means 'beach' and it's written a few times."

"*Muy bien*. What more?"

"It's a coastline, definitely, but which one?" another student added.

Their teacher grinned like the Sphinx. "The document you are examining charts the land you're sitting upon. More precisely, it includes an area about sixty miles north of here that may be the most significant site in the history of early America."

"Wait, do you mean Georgetown?" a guy named Sandy asked.

"Ah, Señor Beckham, you know of it?" Dr. Hernandez asked.

"That's where I'm from, and it's already historic. Third oldest town in the state."

"Is that the extent of your knowledge?"

He scowled. "Well, what else is there to know?"

"Allow me to tell you . . ."

In relaying the life of Spanish explorer Lucas Vázquez de Ayllón, Professor Hernandez sounded more like a tour guide than a language teacher and held his audience entranced by the eerie tale of men and women sailing into the mystery of a new world. In August of 1526, Ayllón steered six ships carrying 600 men and women and nearly 100 horses and livestock into an area believed to be Winyah Bay. Records indicate the initial landing was 10 miles north of the "River Jordan," a waterway likely to be the Santee River. Perhaps the bay's dangerous shoals or sandy fingers reaching up from its depths dragged down the fleet's flagship The *Chorruca.* It foundered, but the passengers survived to build a replacement. Eventually, Ayllón moved his party south toward Georgia where on September 29, they established the first colony in America—San Miguel de Gualdape—a settlement that did not last and for which no archaeological evidence has been discovered.

"Or so that is what was believed," Professor Hernandez said.

"What do you mean?" Sandy asked.

"Well, the location of the colony has always baffled historians. Some thought it was near Cape Fear, others claim Savannah. But we have new translations of a work called the *Chaves Rutter*, which suggests Ayllón's settlement may have been on the shores of Winyah Bay in a place called Hobcaw Barony." He paused to see if they were putting the clues together. "Can anyone explain why this is important?"

"Hold on, if nothing survived then how can they prove it?" someone asked.

"We don't know the evidence hasn't survived—it just hasn't been found. Our earth is quite exceptional at concealing her secrets. Archeological expeditions have been searching for the wreckage of the Spanish galleon."

"And if they find it?"

"Then Georgetown gets another entry in maritime history," Sandy said.

"Yes! But much more than that. Why?"

A hand went up. "Would it mean there were settlements before the ones we know of now? Like, what's the name of the one in Virginia?"

Professor Hernandez grinned. "Jamestown? Bravo! Ayllón's colony would predate Jamestown by eighty-one years and

St. Augustine by thirty nine. Even more—his would be the first Catholic mission in North America, and the Carolinas would become part of the Spanish Empire's history before those lands were English." He tapped a dance across the room, which made the class laugh.

"Hey professor, wouldn't some history books have to be rewritten?" Sandy asked.

Their teacher froze mid-step. "I think they all would have to be," he said, tapping up to the board. "Now, continue translating the passage. Then I want each of you to describe what you really see on this paper. Go beyond the obvious and give me a creative response in Spanish. Work until the period's end and turn it in for next class."

Cadence hardly knew how to express what she saw in another language, but she knew what she wanted to say in her own tongue:

Courage deeper than the depths of the sounds upon which they sail fuel these men and women. Riding the waves on wooden ships, these explorers feel the fullness of life even though fear courses through their veins as much as adventure. In arriving to lonely realms, these pioneers don't know how the sometimes hostile eyes of natives stalk them from the forest. Within the swampy abyss, reptilian monsters lay in ambush: poisonous snakes and ravenous alligators, but perhaps most deadly of all—mosquitoes carrying their lethal loads of malaria and fevers seek their own fleshy landscapes. Once these vampires strike, parasites of death course through the body and the quest ends.

When Cadence thought about the subject, she found it invigoratingly depressing; perhaps it was a subconscious reflection of her own emotional state. She considered how she would make the account more uplifting until she looked at the map again. *Murió* struck her eyes as much as it did her ears as if some ancient, aged traveler were calling to her from an unmarked place in Ayllón's land.

Cadence's mind was still clinging to the images conjured by the Spanish lesson, so she didn't see Schilar waiting for her after class until she passed by him and he called her name. He needed to talk, so they walked to the park and found a place in the sun.

"I've wanted to call you for days, but I didn't know what to say."

"Schilar, I—"

"I know." He squeezed her hand. "I know it was Jacan and not you."

"How do you know?"

Tilting his head back, he took a deep breath. "Because he's done it before. With a girl I was dating in high school. I blamed her when he told me she came onto him. I was convinced he had done me a favor by exposing who she really was."

"That's terrible."

"Yeah, it is. I almost let him do it again with you." He dug deeply into his pocket. "Hold out your hand."

She did and he dropped her necklace into the sunlight on her palm. The chain was broken, dirty, and tiny scratches appeared on the vial, but the moondust was still inside, although it seemed blacker than before.

"I found it beside the house the next day. When I saw it, I knew what had happened." His voice seemed on the verge of breaking. "Cadence, I'm sorry."

She leaned over, kissed his forehead and put her arms around him. "It's okay," she whispered. He rocked her back and forth in an embrace before pulling her to the ground with him. For a while, they gazed at the azure above and enjoyed the warmth of spring, but the moment turned cool when she brought up the future.

Schilar sat up. "I gotta have a talk with the band about what they want to do. It's me or Jacan. Technically, he's now our manager. He put money into this project."

"So you're stuck with him?"

He plucked a blade of grass and began tearing it into pieces. "For now. We'll have to buy out his share. But I can't go on the road with him, and I don't want him in my business anymore."

"What do you want?"

Schilar tossed the green pieces about. "You always ask that, Cadence. I don't know. I'm at this frustrating place between school and my music and . . ." As he stared into the distance, the people in the park filled the lenses of his sunglasses. "Everything."

She put her hand on his back. "I didn't mean to make you mad."

"I'm not mad. Just confused. I want to stay here and go. I want both. Honestly, my grades suck. I've been working so much on this new record I've let things fall apart. And I don't want to leave you. I guess I want it all."

"But you can't have that."

He tapped the ground with his fist. "And unfortunately, it's not all my decision."

"Whose is it?"

"I just told you. I have to talk to the band." He leaned to glimpse the clock face on the church spire of St. Matthew's. "In fact, I need to go." He stood up. "Want to walk back with me or hang out here?"

"I've got biology, so I'll go with you."

They didn't say much on the return to campus, and their parting was strained. He squeezed her hand and mumbled a goodbye. As the physical distance between them increased, so did the emotional one, a disconnect that was strangely appropriate since Dr. Mangold focused on the social behavior and communication of animals. She lectured on courtship, mating, caring for the young, and ended by illustrating how animals establish their rank in social hierarchies through sound and body language.

The lab following biology was the last of the semester and the one that would remain embedded in the memory of their nostrils for all time thanks to the formaldehyde that encased the fetal pig they dissected. Not many people in Cadence's group wanted to put the blade to the corpse. An exercise in ethical grotesqueness, the assignment was too much for some to take, but the threat of failure forced them to participate, so the conscientious objectors stood by fixated on their notebooks and looking on only when it was absolutely necessary.

Life on the farm prepared Cadence for the work; she and a partner named Carl cut and carved, extracted and explored. Focused like surgeons, they led their team through the fascinatingly foul innards of a pig whose life on a farm was stolen for death in a lab. During the process, Carl affectionately called the specimen "Wilbur" in homage to that famous spider and pig story he remembered from childhood. Carl was convinced the swine liked the name since the piggy sustained a blissful grin throughout the procedure. The more sensitive partners were not amused and fled the lab when the corpse desecration was complete.

As had been her routine for some months following lab, Cadence hung around to talk to Alex, who was headed to Atlanta over the summer for a graduate internship with the Centers for Disease Control.

"What're you going to do there?"

"Hopefully, I'll get to work with viruses." Alex began wrapping each pig carcass for disposal. "HIV, yellow and dengue fevers, smallpox. But I hope to get close with the real nasties— Ebola, Marburg, bird flu."

"Wait, bird flu's one of the nastiest?"

"Oh yeah." Alex's voice took on a tone of professorial wonder. "In nature, the avian virus can jump from birds to people, but it doesn't pass easily from person to person—at least not yet."

"So it's expected to happen?"

"If history is our marker, then the answer's yes. But there has to be sustainable spreading between humans for a pandemic." Alex grabbed another pig. "Cadence, in 1918, the Spanish flu infected 500 million people and killed 50-100 million of them. We'll never know the exact number, but the strain that caused that outbreak arose from an avian strain." She pointed to the specimen before her. "Although it's also been linked to a swine strain and that passes easily from one human to another."

"Okay, help me, Alex. I think that formaldehyde got a few of my brain cells." Cadence glanced down at the pitiful piglet. "Where's this going?"

"Toward another biological holocaust, maybe. If the avian and swine strains combine and mutate, they may become one of the most lethal forces ever known."

"And you wanna get all cozy with these killers?" Cadence shook her head. "You're fearless, Alex."

She laughed. "Not quite. These organisms scare the hell out of me, but that's one of the reasons I'm so interested in them. It's all about conquering fear."

"So what do you want to do in the field?"

"I'm leaning toward becoming a virologist and working in bioterrorism. You know, stopping the loonies who want to destroy the world with tiny powers that refuse to be controlled?"

"That sounds like a cool job."

"How about you? What do you want to do? You ask a lot of questions. Thought about being a journalist?"

"I have no idea. All I want to do right now is get through the end of this semester." Cadence grabbed her things. "Speaking of which, any advice for Dr. Mangold's exam?"

Alex picked up another pig and grinned. "Yeah—study."

"Thanks for the tip. Have fun with your viruses this summer." Cadence slung her bookbag over her shoulder. "Hey Alex, just curious. Why was it called the 'Spanish flu'?"

Alex's gloves froze above the animal. "That's a good question. I don't know. Sounds like something you should look up."

When Cadence left the lab it was almost dusk, so she grabbed some dinner and dropped by the newspaper to check for assignments. All the major projects had been taken care of, but a few end-of-the-term features were left to shoot. She was just about to leave when Degue flew through the office. Cadence watched as he frantically rummaged through his desk drawers.

"Hey, what're you looking for?"

"My recorder."

"Can't you use your phone?"

"No, not enough memory or charge. I don't know how long this is going to take." He slammed the metal drawer. "Damn! I just had it the other day."

"How long what's going to take?"

He shot her an annoyed look. "An interview. Cadence, I don't have time to chat. I have to find this thing." He picked up stacks of paper and tossed them down.

"Uh, Degue?" Cadence pointed to the filing cabinet next to him. "Is that silver box in the basket there your recorder?"

"Yes! I knew it was here somewhere." Grabbing the device and his notebook, he sped past her then whirled around. "Hey, do you have your camera with you?"

"Of course."

"Come with me. I'll explain on the way."

As they rushed to the basement of a classroom building, he showed her the note left on his desk earlier that day: *If you want to know of the madness behind the harpies' method, meet us tonight.* It gave the details of time and place, and when Degue had filled Cadence in on what he knew, they were descending the stairs to room 100. The window was blocked with a piece of cardboard but the door was unlocked. Before going in, he told Cadence to wait in the hall. She could hear muffled voices, and after a few minutes, Degue stuck his head out and motioned for her to come in.

"Lock the door behind you," a voice called down.

Cadence clicked the silver knob to secure the door and followed Degue to one of two chairs on the stage. The spotlights blinded them from seeing the lecture hall, but when they were settled, the front lights dimmed and others higher up brightened slightly to show the profiles of three figures in the last row of seats.

Following ancient tradition, the individuals wore masks of old women's faces atop black feather shrugs. Each held a rigid posture and seemed perched in her position as if ready to swoop down in an instant. They spoke in low, almost manly tones and explained that their purpose in sabotaging the half-rubbers' reputations was to avenge the victim and draw attention to a hushed problem—but one not necessarily particular to this campus.

"So is that all you wanted me to know? Your reasons for the spectacles?" Degue was unimpressed. "How do you think setting up displays and attacking these guys is going to get change?"

"It gets attention," the harpy on the right answered. "And that's just the beginning."

"This is where you come in," the one to the left said.

The harpy in the middle rose and pointed a black object at them. "There's always a story behind the story."

Degue and Cadence heard the grind of a motor as the projector screen behind them rolled up. Beneath it, a green chalk board appeared covered in names:

PENNY, IRIS, CARLEE, KELLEY, EVIE, DELIA,
FAITH, OCTAVIA, REBECCA,
FELICIA, IMANI, CATHY, TANYA, ILLANA, OSCAR, NOEL

Cadence's eyes almost refused to move beyond the first word, but she and Degue read the list while the harpies observed.

Degue turned to the women. "This list, it's of sexual assault victims?"

"Yes," they called down in unison.

"But we believe there's more," the middle harpy said. "Dig and you just might find the story of your college career."

Degue studied the board again. "Is this all I have to go on?"

The harpies whispered to one another before the middle one said, "No. Follow the moonshine!"

The room went black and a streak of light appeared as the harpies made their exit. He jumped up in pursuit but got no farther than the aisle's second step before he tripped. Cadence found the light switch and began snapping photos of the board. After she was finished, Degue erased the names, and the two discussed what they had seen as he walked Cadence home.

"You know," Degue said, "it's really hard to know whether or not the names are true or even if those people are rape victims. Those harpy things could be lying."

"Why would you think someone would lie about a rape?"

"Because it happened—to my cousin. In high school, he had sex with this girl. It was consensual. But afterwards, she lied and cried 'rape.' He was charged, convicted, and sent to prison." Degue's pace quickened.

"How do you know she lied?"

"Because after he was in the joint for a while, she admitted she lied because he didn't want to date her after they had sex. A life ruined all because that bitch wanted to get even."

"Where's your cousin now?"

"Trying to put his life back together—what's left of it. He's out and working to get his record cleared. So forgive me if I'm not fully trusting when it comes to rape cases."

Cadence stopped as he continued along the path. "Degue, I know one of those victims on that board."

He turned to her. "You recognize one of the names?"

She nodded. "I've seen what she's gone through. She can't remember the details, but she's positive several guys had sex with her. They did some pretty horrendous things, which they bragged about then denied."

"Wait a minute, are you talking about the half-rubber case?" He saw the affirmative answer in her face. "So you've known about this and haven't said anything? Why exactly are you working for the paper?"

"I'm a photographer, Degue. And this situation's really personal. It's not my story to tell."

"It *is* when you work for the media. It becomes yours when you know the details. And now this incident is really political." Degue stood inches from her, a towering interrogator in the dark. "Damn, Cadence. How are you at the heart of these cases? Same thing happened when Professor Savage died. You knew about his wife and the affair."

"You make it sound like I want to be in the middle. It's not a place I asked to be."

"What else do you know?"

She crossed her arms. "I don't feel right telling you about the assault. I can tell you she's been harassed since it happened." Cadence paused as a couple passed by and resumed when they were out of ear range. "That day I took pictures of the team's practice, one of the players said they were told to keep their mouths shut, to put on a united front."

Degue looked up into the trees. "That doesn't seem out of the ordinary. Groups close ranks to protect each other. But there does seem to be more here. I wonder what moonshine means?"

"I'm not sure, but I think that's what my friend said she drank with those guys."

"Then that's where I need to start. Cadence, did you notice anything else about the names on the board?"

"No, why?"

"There was at least one guy's name, maybe more."

"What are you getting at?"

"Don't know. But I do know it won't be easy finding out. It's all a matter of digging. I guess I need to sharpen my shovel. I think you should, too. You're already a part of this story, whether or not you wanted to be."

Back in her room, Cadence's mind spun the possibilities of what Degue would uncover. Ready to tackle her remaining work, she pulled out the Ayllón map and thought of her conversation with Alex. The curiosity over why the flu was named the Spanish one lingered, so Cadence set out to settle it.

Through her research, she learned that although the geographic origins remain unknown, some historians claim the contagion began in China and spread through Canada by way of migrant workers. These itinerants may have worked as contractors at the army base of Camp Funston in Fort Riley, Kansas. In March of 1918, one cook complaining of a bad cold was followed by over a hundred similar cases the same day. Soldiers bound for fighting in Germany, France, and England carried the virus, where it exploded in the perfect storm of poor conditions brought on by the war: crowded camps and trenches, stress, cold weather, humidity, fear, close contact with animals, even chemical weapons aided the virus. The mystery of the pandemic's genesis continues. It certainly did not begin in Spain, nor did it end there, but that's not what the world believed at the time.

La Grippe, Spanish Lady, La Pesadilla—the Spanish flu had a number of names, but most were synonymous with death.

Spain was the first Western European country in which the disease affected a significant number of the general population. Because of its neutrality during the war, Spain was not subject to wartime censorship, so the press reported freely about the disease, especially the coverage of its most famous sufferer, King Alfonso XIII. While other countries stifled information about the epidemic to protect war morale, Spain became a reliable source for news about the disease, so the illness was dubbed *Spanish flu*.

The virus proved particularly unforgiving to the young and healthy who succumbed to a cytokine storm. Within the victim, the body waged its own war on the invader and on itself. Being healthy became a liability for many when their immune systems overreacted and destroyed the lungs to kill the virus. The sick spewed pink froth as they fought to breathe, skin turned blue from oxygen deprivation, and ultimately, they drowned in their own bodily fluids.

After hours of reading article after article on nature's smallest assassins and their time travels across continents, Cadence had answered her question, but others came in its place. Studying the map of Ayllón, she wondered how many of those first explorers died of similar infections. What were the origins of their black plagues and fevers? Did they know, like those WWI soldiers, that the lethalities within them crossed oceans to new lands? Did they care when they brought a new language of suffering—the Old World contagions of smallpox, measles, typhus, and cholera—to the natives in paradise and brought back the horrors of syphilis to their homelands? For Cadence, it was a night of searching for answers where an inquiry resulted in a journey through history, one reflecting the centuries' old struggle to survive nature's reverently ruthless selections.

Ruthlessness shamelessly stalked the stage before Miranda, Reena, and Cadence when they attended a production of the revenge play *The Spanish Tragedy*. It was the second of their two required drama attendances for theater class, and Miranda was especially keen on critiquing the performance of a certain actor, named Pierre, whose acquaintance she had made recently and who was playing the protagonist, Hieronimo.

While the friends waited for the curtain to open, Cadence read the program and smiled when she connected the playwright's name with one of her favorite dramatic characters as of late. Thomas Kyd was a contemporary of Shakespeare, and Catissa must have named the playful boxer after the dramatist. The biography mentioned that Kyd may have written a precursor to *Hamlet*, which the Bard borrowed from and morphed to ink his masterpiece.

The convoluted plot of love, lust, madness, mutilation, and murder was all directed by the chorus of a Spanish courtier's ghost and the character of Revenge. Dr. Dreary required her students to write a memorable line on their programs, so Cadence scribbled:

> *The heavens are just; murder cannot be hid.*
> *Time is the author both of truth and right,*
> *And time will bring this treachery to light.*

The treachery Hieronimo brings to light is the murder of his son, the suicide of his wife, and the diabolical dealings of the Spanish duke's son and the Portuguese viceroy's son. Driven to near madness over his losses, the protagonist concocts a plan to use a play of "sundry languages" to enact his revenge. He assigns his enemies varied roles in Latin, Greek, Italian, and

French, and their babblings bring about their supposedly feigned deaths.

As the performance neared its climax, Miranda and the others watched in disgust as Hieronimo, standing among the corpses, reveals how he has truly slain the foes around him. He runs to hang himself, but when the King of Spain realizes his nephew is among the dead, attendants stop Hieronimo from suicide. In a ghastly move, Hieronimo bites out his tongue rather than speak the names of those who aided in his revenge.

The spectators recoiled in horror when a rubber tongue bounced on the stage from Pierre's mouth. Blood gushed down his shirt, but the mutilation wasn't complete until they witnessed Hieronimo get a knife and stab the duke of Castile and himself.

Absolute carnage covered the stage while the entire audience applauded it. After the show, Miranda dragged Cadence and Reena backstage to meet Pierre.

"Mmmiranda." He rolled her name off his lips. "So good of you to come see the performance. And you brought friends? How very supportive. So, what's your review?" He directed the question to Miranda as if she were the only critic in the realm.

"Bloody," she said, "but brilliant. I see you got your tongue back."

He wiggled it at her in confirmation. "Indeed. I need it for other pursuits."

She giggled while Reena and Cadence watched another drama unfolding—maiden Miranda coming under the spell of the actor with smoky eyes, a dreamy voice, and a sex appeal that straddled the lines of preference. He appeared to be a character much more than the ones he played, with an artistic earnestness that could be detected a stage length away.

Although they were on the outskirts of the conversation, Reena and Cadence took the hint when he hid his lips and whispered to their friend: "Listen, I'm going to change for the after party. Want to come? I'd love to invite your friends, but you know how these gatherings are—really for our group." Turning back to the others, he said, "Ladies, thank you for coming," before sauntering away.

"Miranda, Cadence and I are leaving, but why don't you stay and hang out with him."

She looked over at Pierre who was the center of an admiring circle. "No, I should go with you all."

"But you don't want to. Just stay and have a good time. There aren't many days left in the semester to do so."

"Are you sure?"

"As sure as if I had just seen a tongue fall out of a guy's mouth."

Reena was certainly right about not many days being left for fun in the semester, so Cadence was pleasantly surprised when her friend announced that Blaze and his roommates were throwing a *Cinco de Mayo* party—one of the final bashes of the year. Cadence was getting ready when there was a knock at the door. On the other side, Isa looked as if she were on the edge of breaking, and the second her eyes met Cadence's, she did.

Isa was a quiet crier, her tears pacing slowly down her face as if they were in for a long run. "I need to talk to someone. I didn't know who else to come to." Isa glimpsed the make-up on her friend's face. "But this looks like a bad time. You are going out?"

"I am. But that can wait. Here, sit down."

"It's my brother."

"Is he okay?"

She shook her head. "No. My parents know."

"How? What happened?" Cadence handed Isa a tissue.

"These men from our town. They went to Columbia on business and were out at dinner. Roano was at the same restaurant." She stopped to blow her nose. "My brother and his partner were having a celebration dinner. They were very close. And these people started talking and they went home and told people Roano's secret. My parents found out. They called him and he finally admitted it."

"Isa, that's terrible. He had to tell them over the phone?"

She nodded. "The worst part is that my father said to him: '*Ya no eres mas nuestro hijo.*'"

Cadence tried to translate. "Isa, *no comprendo.* Something about 'son'?"

"He told Roano—you are no longer our son." She broke again, and Cadence reached over to hold her together.

"Isa, I, I don't really know what to say."

"There are no words, Cadence. My parents are not coming to his graduation. I am the only family he has right now. It's so awful. This should be a happy time for him, but it's the worst."

Cadence listened as Isa laid out the difficult road ahead for her brother. He'd traverse new territory as an outed gay man. Isa wasn't sure if he'd ever return to their hometown. He'd celebrate commencement with only her and she'd return to Mexico alone. Her parents had made it clear that he was not welcome at home. Cadence offered as much comfort as she could, but nothing would adequately quell her friend's pain.

Isa took a deep breath. "I've kept you long enough. I will go."

"You're not going anywhere unless it's out with me."

"No, I really don't feel like it."

"I insist. Listen, you'll sit in your room and obsess over this. Come on, blow off some of this stress. Besides, aren't you required to celebrate *Cinco de Mayo?*

"But *Cinco de Mayo's* not for a few days. And you know what's funny? Americans go *loco* over the holiday, but it's not very important to most Mexicans."

"Isn't it your Independence Day?"

"No, that's on September 16."

"So what's *Cinco de Mayo?*"

"It's about a battle in a place called 'Puebla.' Some Mexicans defeated the French. That's about all I know, but I've heard the holiday's called the 'Mexican St. Patrick's Day.'"

Cadence laughed but the reference was painful since her court date for her Irish partying was coming up. "I guess we Americans will take any reason for a party. So go get your *olé* on, *señorita*. I'll wait for you because we're going to a *fiesta!*"

It was one of those gatherings where the universe came together—one where friends of friends of friends realized their degrees of separation and connected under the common cause of making merriment. The party was well jumping when Cadence and Isa stepped up to the house, and in weaving through the crowd, Cadence was surprised at whom she saw.

"Dakota! I can't believe you're here." Cadence threw her arms around him.

"Paparazzi!" He kissed her on the cheek. "You look naturally gorgeous, as usual." Dakota eyed Isa. "And who is this lovely Latina?" He offered his hand. "Hi."

"I'm Isa." Her face brightened for the first time in days as Dakota helped them get drinks along with Stefan, who was still enjoying his crown as the Ramen noodle king. It wasn't long before Dakota and Isa were chatting away, so Cadence went to look for Reena but was stopped not too far into her search.

"So I hear there's a mean game of Truth or Dare later. You in?"

"I think I'll pass. That game gets me in trouble."

"Then we'll have to find another game for you to play." Walker glanced around. "Speaking of games, where's your boyfriend?"

"Playing a show out of town." Cadence tilted her head. "How did you know I had a boyfriend?"

"Reena mentioned it."

"Speaking of, have you seen her?"

"Hanging on Blaze, as usual. They're around here somewhere."

Cadence laughed. "They are pretty inseparable." She sipped her drink. "Hey, did you get that internship you were telling me about?"

"As a matter of record, I did. I have to practice up on my legal jargon, you know?"

"So are you going to law school?"

"That's the plan. I've been studying for the LSAT, getting my financial aid together."

"Well, congratulations." She held up her cup which he met with his.

Without moving his eyes from her, he took a long chug of his drink. "Hey, there's someone I want you to meet." He motioned for her to follow. "Come on, this way."

"Where're we going?"

"Up to my room."

She stood still. "Walker, I'm not falling for that. I'm not going to your room."

Genuine hurt appeared in his eyes. "Cadence, that's not what I meant. Tell you what, stay here. I'll be right back."

She waited in the hall as he ran upstairs. It wasn't long before she was meeting the acquaintance of a large black lab. Walker smiled down at the two as Cadence dropped to her knees for kisses and the lab's tail beat the wall wildly.

"When did you get a dog?" Cadence asked.

"Oh, back in high school. This is Lady, my love. I've had her since I was a freshman, but she lives with my parents. They're away for a few weeks, so she's staying with me."

"And how do you like college living, Lady?" Cadence dropped to her knees in a playful exchange of affection with the dog.

"Well, she seems to like curling up to me every night. I've heard no complaints yet."

"I'm sure she's a lucky dog, Walker." Cadence stood up. "Thanks for letting me meet her." She peered down into her empty cup. "I'm going to get a refill and find Reena. See you later."

As she moved away through the crowd, the dog began to whine. Walker reached for Lady's ears and in stroking them lightly, whispered, "I hear you girl. I don't like to see her leave either."

Once Cadence had replenished her cup, she searched for Reena, whom she found outside with Blaze and his friends. Reena's exaggerated greeting exceeded the bounds of happiness—she was on top of the world and feeling beyond fine. She and Cadence toasted the near end of another semester and recalled how far they'd come since the torment of Brodsky's class. They had traded the hell of music for the heaven of theatre, although the characters in most of what they read and watched seemed bound for damnation. In their buzzed states, the girls declared their undying love for one another—a temporarily permanent devotion that would last longer than the alcohol in their blood.

Reena wandered back over to Blaze just as Dakota came out of the house and over to Cadence. "Can I just say that I love your friend Isa. She's so fab."

"I'm glad you two met. I think you'll be good for her."

"Me, too, and I already think she feels a little better about her brother, you know?"

Cadence looked surprised. "She already told you?"

"She did. Look, people need to talk about what's troubling them. I happened to ask the right questions and she opened up."

"That's great. I think she can really connect with you."

"I know she can. We already have a coffee date next week."

"Where is she?" Cadence glanced over to the people hanging on the porch.

"Oh, she and Stefan are inside chatting with some mutual people they know. Weird, huh?"

"Yeah, you never know who you're going to meet at a party in Charleston."

Dakota and Cadence remained outside, observing the parade of partiers. The two were perfectly positioned for the piñata entertainment around a tree. Blaze tied a blindfold on Reena, positioned a long stick in her hands, and turned her around three times as the tradition goes. She managed to hit the motley-colored donkey once, but she wandered far off course, leaving the paper animal swinging with glee at being spared. Another volunteer stepped forward and managed to smack the figure a few times, sending its smirk into a tornadic spin. The third hitter was a guy whose brawn sent him to the dirt when he applied too much of it. Cadence and Dakota laughed so hard they nearly fell on the ground with him. When the next whacker stepped up for a try, Dakota nearly dropped his drink.

"Oh snap, Cadence! Haven't we seen that woman before?"

"The piñata player?"

"No, the one over there." Dakota pointed to a woman moving toward Blaze. "Remember, his cousin?"

Cadence saw the figure swerving through the crowd then watched as she went up to him, placed her arms around his neck, and laid a kiss on him that had nothing to do with family. Blaze turned paler than the white car he was leaning against. Reena was standing a few feet away with her back to him, so she did not see the initial greeting, but when she turned around, her face lost all direction at the sight of someone else's arms wrapped around her lover's neck. Feet away, a loud crack sounded across the yard and the donkey's contents—condoms, lubricants, and Blow pops—spilled onto the ground.

Reena huffed. "Excuse me, but who do you think you are?"

The woman's hands slid down Blaze's chest and to her sides. "I'm Blaze's girlfriend. Who're you?"

Reena thought she had heard wrong. "I'm sorry, what did you say?" Her vision volleyed from the woman to Blaze and back again.

"I'm Jane, his girlfriend." She shot her left hand toward Reena and a stunning ruby ring flashed like a demon's eye.

"What is that?"

"*That* is a promise ring. He's promised that we'll be together forever."

Reena's knees were barely holding her up. "Since when?"

"Since about middle school, off and on. We have a lot of history, and we're back together now." Jane shook her finger at

Reena. "Wait. He's mentioned you. You're the one who won't leave him alone. Look, don't be desperate. Take the hint. He's taken."

Reena searched Blaze's face for the truth, but the only truth forthcoming was the lie that stood between them. "Is this true?" she asked.

Lowering his head slightly, Blaze touched Jane's side, and Reena went numb. He was barely looking at her when he muttered, "Yes, we got back together. I was going to tell you."

She did not hear his words as if they were in the language she had spoken all her life but as if they were in a tongue she would never understand. The message was clearly conveyed in the jewel that hung on the finger of the woman she wanted to be and in the way Blaze laid his hand on the promise he had made. Instantly, the night sky collapsed on Reena, plunging her into shadowy confusion and stirring a sickness deep inside. She suddenly felt like a foreigner in a land she had known since those first days of exploring college. Rather than fight for the territory she desired, she fled into the blackness and away from the calls for her to stop, the pleas for her to come back. Reena ran without direction since the map of her emotions was suddenly, once again, without a compass. She didn't care about her final destination as long as she could outpace the ghosts chasing her when she blazed a trail of tears that would never be forgotten.

Chapter 20

Criminal Justice 319
Deviance and Social Control

The glowing cross cut a hallowed reminder in the night, one among many that crown the spires reaching for the celestial ceiling above Charleston. These holy antennae transmit messages of love and loss, wealth and woe, appreciation and angst into heaven's sometimes deaf ears. When the sun slips behind the earth's curve, spotlights illuminate these everlasting symbols of power, promise, and punishment. For as the story goes, a man was brought to justice on gallows of timber, sentenced to death for the religious and political crimes of blasphemy and insulting a head of state. Humiliation, scourging, suffocation— one person paid in pounds of flesh for multitudes to receive spiritual passage into paradise.

From the comfort of her bed, she never saw the echoes of death emanating from the rood but chose only to bask in its radiating positives. It was the first vision she awoke to, the last she spied every evening, and her habit was to whisper prayers up to it ever since the beginning of her senior year when she rented the carriage house. She had always felt the cross watched over her, protecting her from evil like an amulet she wore in her heart and not around her neck.

But tonight was different. More than ever, she needed it, called to it for release from the hell above her. Although she threw silent prayers of desperation up to it, the stoic metal did not respond to her plea to stop the stranger who held the chilling blade to her skin while violently heaving himself into her. A mask hid his face and gloves made no fingerprints, but he did leave clues to his identity—in the foreign fluids that now invaded her body.

His grunting and thrusting etched his presence into her memory. To her prolonged horror, he lasted longer than most men she'd been with, and this slow, torturous eternity would take up infinity in her mind. When he was finished, he told her not to call the police until he had vanished. She waited as commanded then wailed hysterically into the emergency dispatcher's ear. Officers arrived, and the gossip began with each onlooker who stumbled on the scene.

In the days following, news of the crime came in fragments, as breaking stories always do. First, rumors spread that the victim had been assaulted while walking home alone from the library. Details then morphed into the version of her having too much to drink and venturing home alone, only to be snatched from behind and dragged into bushes near the library. By midday, people were shaking their heads at the scantily clad girl who passed out on the library's lawn, leaving herself easy prey for the predator and for criticizers quick to throw the stones of reproach.

The ugliness of those who judged this victim was outdone only by the horror of the facts. After celebrating a birthday at a local restaurant, the victim and her friends made their ways home. She made it safely inside, crawled into bed for a champagne-induced slumber but was not aware of the intruder lurking in her closet until the weight of his body and the weapon on her throat startled her from sweet dreams into the rancorous nightmare. For now, she would remain unnamed unless she chose to reveal her story as a survivor, perhaps if the villain was brought to justice. She had enjoyed the freedom of living alone, but this terror altered that independence as it does for anyone whose sanctuary is stolen by those who force their wills upon others.

When Cadence cut through the Grand Lawn a few mornings later, the incident was not on her mind. Skipping class was not a common occurrence, but since it was her judgment day, she didn't have much choice. She was on her way to court by means of the bus when she spotted Tap and her crew standing over a foamy mass covering the reflection pool.

The last time Cadence had seen the grounds supervisor, the area was being prepared for the sad occasion of Professor Savage's memorial, but now this space was being transformed for the celebration of graduation. Every year over the reflecting pool, Tap's crew built a bridge for the commencement ritual of graduates walking over the water, a symbolic passing into their new identities as degree holders, job seekers, career professionals, adults. Upon crossing the stage, each student dropped a coin into the pool—for wishes, thanks, good luck, but mostly for tradition. The money funded scholarships to ensure future scholars continue the passage over, but this year, the bridge was blocked with a banner reading: *CLEAN UP THIS CAMPUS— WASH AWAY RAPISTS!* The soap that had been poured into the water created a frothy mess, making the sign appear as if it were floating on a cloud.

"Hi, Tap."

The woman turned and pulled the cigarette from her mouth. "Mornin' Cadence." She blew the smoke skyward. "You here to get a photo of this?"

"I didn't know anything about it, but since I'm here . . ." She took out her camera and snapped a few pictures. "Do you think this has anything to do with that rape the other night?"

"I don't know much about that, but I doubt it. I think those damn harpy things have struck again." The cigarette hissed when Tap snuffed it out in the foam. "Every time they do something, they make more work for my crew. As if we don't have enough to do. We're going to have to drain this thing, clean it, and refill it before graduation. It's a damn shame, wasting all that water and work time." She looked at Cadence. "How long before you get to walk that bridge?"

Cadence smiled. "Three years. I can hardly believe my first is almost over."

"Believe it, honey. Time—it never slows down, never stops. It's the most precious thing we all don't have." Tap glanced at her watch. "Speaking of which, I gotta get my guys in gear for this job. Another on the list I didn't intend for. See you, Cadence."

She said goodbye to Tap and headed to the bus stop where to her surprise, Jerome, the driver who had taken her to the half-rubber practice, was behind the wheel.

"Hello, Cadence." The shine of his gold teeth greeted her as she paid her fare.

"I can't believe you remembered my name."

"I do. Knowing my passengers' names is important to me. So are you going to photograph more sports this morning?"

"Not exactly." She lowered her voice. "I have a court date."

"Uh-oh. Nothing too serious, I hope." He could tell she didn't want to talk about it, so he asked her about school and her photographs, which lightened her nervousness by the time he pulled to the stop near the courthouse.

"Cadence, good luck in there. Everything'll be okay." Jerome smiled. "I'll pick you up soon."

He was true to his word. In a few hours, Jerome welcomed her again when she climbed back on board, happy to report that everything was, as he predicted, okay. In fact, she was surprised at how well it went.

William Whetstone was the presiding judge, and Cadence sensed a book of some sort would come flying her way. Her arresting officer was present and fully prepared to ratchet up his quota, and with every defendant called forward, the lawman noted whether the accused had been respectfully cooperative or a loathsome leprechaun who made his job more difficult. The bench was full of minors busted for imbibing forbidden liquids—even if it was an Irish requirement on the day they were all arrested. Cadence waited hours until her name was called. She was guilty and pleaded so, answering all the judge's questions with every bit of reverence her Southern upbringing could supply.

Before announcing her punishment, Judge Whetstone grabbed a piece of paper from the stack on his bench and passed his glasses over it. "Ah, Miss Cooper," he said, moving his eyes from the document to her. "I understand that you have quite a talent in photography. Is this correct?"

Her eyebrows arched at the question. "Um, I guess. I mean, yes, sir."

"I want to offer you a punishment that would make use of your skills and benefit this community's charities. The court requests you choose one you want to work with, provide them with 100 hours of service, and we'll consider this matter closed. Do you have any questions?"

Cadence wrung her hands. "Sir, the semester's over, and I'm going home for the summer. I won't be back until August."

"The court recognizes your dilemma and will defer your service until you return. Your hours must be completed by the first of December. Will this work for you? If this does not, I hope you have some money ready today."

"No, sir. I mean, yes, sir. That works for me. Thank you, judge."

"And Miss Cooper, I remind you that according to the laws of this state, you are not permitted to drink alcohol legally until you are twenty-one years of age. Please refrain from doing so until you meet the law's condition for legal consumption."

"Yes, sir. Thank you again."

As Cadence replayed the scene on the bus ride back to campus, she knew she had someone to thank for the judge knowing about her photography. The punishment would keep her record from being tarnished by youthful indiscretions and save her bank account from being wiped out by a several-hundred-dollars course in alcohol education.

Cadence heeded the judge's advice for a few hours, but it was the last day of school, and with Reading Day tomorrow, stress relief was as much of a requirement as taking exams. Although she wanted a night out, Cadence was hesitant because exams were looming, and she could use the study time. Saida needed a night out, especially since she had grown frustrated with her roommate's refusal to report Madison and Malinda's harassment. Penny was going to let the two get away without paying for their nastiness, and Saida, who appreciated eye-for-an-eye justice on occasion, could not understand why. What she did understand was the necessity for some fun, so she convinced Cadence that a final blow out at the College Pit was in order. They were joined by Helena, Chance, Kirby and River— the latter two becoming somewhat of a couple in the last week.

Sierra popped in for the occasion with some bottles of J. Rogét, the bubbly brut guaranteed to make celebrants as silly and giggly and fizzy as what was in their plastic cups.

When the crew arrived, the groupies were already swooning in front of the stage. On it, Schilar played to them in a mode so electric he was like an adhesive to the eyes. Cadence preferred to remain in the shadows and swayed in the back along with Saida who wasn't in the mood for hunting—particularly in a room largely composed of beer guts and juvenile physiques. She and Sierra remained by Cadence's side while Kirby and River danced and Helena and Chance played the floor for what Saida didn't want.

As the night moved toward morning and cups were sucked dry of their courage, flesh flashed more deliberately, and those closest to the stage began reaching up to claw at the calves of these local celebrities. Cadence couldn't blame them; after all, Schilar was moving with more vitality than ever, and the sight of him made her wish she wasn't there. She held back her heart from the edge of breaking, and feeling as if it were too much for her to take, she told Saida she wanted to leave and, in fact, insisted on it. Saida made excuses for staying but finally agreed to walk home with Cadence. They waited for a break in the music, and when it came, they made for the door through applause and cheers. Schilar waved his hands up and down to hush the house.

"Thank you, thanks very much." He grasped the mic stand tightly, as if he needed its support. "Um, with this next song, I'd like to give my own thanks to someone very special." He shaded his eyes from the spotlights. "Cadence? Are you out there tonight? I think you're here. I hope you are."

Dragging Cadence immediately in his direction, Saida yelled, "She's here!" and pushed their way to Schilar who asked the crowd to part for them.

When he could finally see Cadence fully, his grin took up the whole stage. Looking down at her, he announced, "You inspired this one. It's called 'Strummin.'"

And then he played and sang as she'd never heard him do before. Every note, key, and chord was perfect, and of all the people packed in that room, Cadence felt that only she, Schilar, and Gunpowder occupied it.

In my darkness, trying to write a song,
Words somehow fail me, it all goes wrong.
Oh I suffer for my passion, it's true I need the muse,
I hope that she'll come back soon,
But it's just no use.

At the moment, I wanna give up
And quit this dream,
But then I pick up my guitar
And then my heart comes clean—
In memories of you, I strike the right key—
For a moment in sound I want you to see.

When the world's too much
And I just can't pull through,
I get by, just strummin'
To the rhythm of the thoughts of you.

I try but I cannot explain it,
No, the mystery is strong,

And I cannot be without you, oh for very long.

When the world's too much
And I just can't pull through
I get by, just strummin'
To the rhythm of the thoughts of you.

Our friction gives life to my lines;
They flow best in our trying times.
If the miles keep us apart, the pain's too much—
Let your soul feel my touch.

When the world's too much,
and you think we're through,
Just know I'm always
Strummin' to the rhythm of the thoughts of you.

The last note shook the room but not as much as it did her heart, and the feeling intensified when Schilar jumped down to her. Pulling his muse as close as that fiery instrument between them would allow, he kissed her with the potency of an artist fully inspired. The crowd was so loud she couldn't hear, but when his mouth left hers, she opened her eyes and read the words leaving his lips: "I love you, Cadence."

She had waited so long to hear him say the words, but now she almost wished he hadn't because they marked a new beginning in a relationship Cadence felt was coming to an end. The moment was a confounding blend of elation and emptiness— the happy but hollow result of an intoxicating romance that could shatter in a future of separation. In the back of her mind, this sobering reality lurked, but in front of her was her rock star performing a closing song to a rowdy throng celebrating confessions of his heart.

Lights eventually blinded the partiers, and the bouncers bid them all a "Good morning." Cadence, knowing the band would be a long time in packing up, decided to go back to campus. She needed to since a mountain of study awaited. Considering exams began in one day and all she had read was bathroom graffiti and a champagne bottle's label, she knew crashing in her own bed seemed best.

As Cadence went to tell him good night, Schilar said, "Don't leave. Come with me. I've already made the arrangements for this stuff, so we can leave now. All I need is you."

"Where're we going?"

"You'll have to come with me to find out."

Cadence looked to her friends and back at him. "How can I say 'no' to you, especially after that song?"

"I would hope you couldn't. Now you have the tenth song—the one I left off on your compilation."

She smiled. "I guess my collection is complete. Let me tell them I'm going with you."

Within the hour, they were pulling his roommate's truck next to the dunes on the very secluded north end of Folly Beach. Not only had Schilar made arrangements to leave right after the show, but he had packed a cooler and a sleeping bag. They sat on the tailgate tasting stale sandwiches against the scents of salt and sand. Strolling on the beach afterwards, they listened to the soundtrack of the wind's song and the waves beating their own rhythm into the shore. Enjoying the beach life, they were not to know the sandy grains between their toes held the ghosts of a place once called *Coffin Land*. Before entering the harbor, ships bound for Charleston's port would leave plague and cholera victims on the island. Those who survived were picked up on the return, and those who didn't were buried.

In the distance, the two could see the shadowy outline of a lighthouse, the one struggling to survive the ocean's relentless appetite for its destruction. Although they saw only water now, three islands once covered the four miles between Folly Beach and Sullivan's. But time's cruel hand played too harshly with the delicate sand, leaving the Morris Island beacon treading on human efforts to keep it above water. Its stony resilience remained a testament of deviance—even now lightless as it was and replaced by its black and white neighbor to the north, the lighthouse refused to surrender its red and white stripes to the depths.

Returning to the truck, they took up space between the warmth of blankets. In those quiet hours beneath the witness of celestial eyes only, they created a perfect night of remembrances—touches and whisperings of such potency they vivified a realm that once belonged exclusively to the dead and barely living. Tonight, though, it belonged to Cadence, her rock star, and no one else.

In the morning for breakfast, they devoured the bowl of fruitful hues offered by sky. Cadence could not recall ever watching the sun rise over the water, but the shades of tangerine, strawberry, and peach were seared in her memory as much as the exhilaration that came from sharing this happiness with him. Although she didn't really want to face days and nights of cramming for exams, the time with Schilar helped prepare her to do just that.

During Reading Day, Cadence stopped into *The Gator's* offices one last time. As she made her rounds bidding the few left in the newsroom goodbye, she saw upon a huge vase of flowers on Degue's desk.

"Those aren't from Melissa, are they?" Cadence joked as he shot her a deadpan expression. "Okay, is someone else sweet on you, Degue?"

He looked up from his writing. "No, they're not for me."

"Hmmm, a new lady in your life?"

Tossing his pen on his desk, he tucked a card in an envelope and licked its seal. "They're for a friend who's ill. My professor from last year, Dr. Elders."

"Dr. Elders?" Cadence repeated with surprise. "She was my Freshman Seminar teacher. What's wrong with her?"

Degue stood up. "She's had a rough semester. Been in and out of the hospital, but this time looks bad." He began gathering his things.

"Wait, can you tell me what's going on?"

Glancing around, he said in a low voice: "She's having HIV complications."

He grabbed the vase, and when he walked by Cadence, she reached for his arm. "Degue, please tell her I'm thinking about her and that I hope she gets better. Students really need her."

His eyes fell on the hand touching him and he nodded. "We sure do."

The news of Dr. Elders's hospitalization stayed on Cadence's mind for the day's remainder. By the evening, it lingered even as she met Diana, Jade, and Darla in the library for a reunion session to study more about the subject of life. For biology, they focused and plowed through endless notes and diagrams on the phylas of the animal kingdom: invertebrates and vertebrates; fish and amphibians and reptiles; birds, mammals, and of course, primates. The scope of material was so intimidating it left each one feeling as spineless as a sponge.

"Isn't that in the Porifera phylum?" Cadence asked.

"I don't care anymore. My brain feels like a jellyfish." Diana sunk her head into her hands. "What's that one?"

"Um, it's . . . Cnidarian," Darla answered. "Someone please tell me again why I need to know this?"

"'Cause you might be on a game show someday and you'll sweep the category." Jade grinned.

Darla threw her pen at Jade. "That's not going to happen. I just need to be done with this class and this place, and in a few days I will be!"

"What d'you mean?" Jade asked.

"I'm not coming back next year."

"What're you going to do?" Jade tossed Darla's pen back at her.

"Nursing school. I'm going to a community college. I hope to be working in two years. This four year thing isn't for me. I just want a frickin' job!"

"Sounds like a good plan," Cadence said. "By the way, is your roommate Natalie coming back in the fall?"

"Where've you been, Cadence? Natalie never came back after spring break. Took time off. Last time I talked to her it didn't sound like she had any plans to return."

"Oh, wow. I had no idea." Cadence tried to recall when she last saw her hallmate but couldn't think of it. The ghost of the gaunt figure must have fooled Cadence into thinking Natalie was still on campus.

"What happened to her?" Diana asked.

"She's bulimic and a total workout addict. When she collapsed in class, her parents thought it would be best if she went home for a while."

"One of my suitemates has anorexia. Or had it. She's better now but still obsesses about what she eats." Jade shook her head. "Not me, my butt has packed on some pounds this semester. Too much stress, you know?" She glanced at Cadence who understood Jade's worry stemmed from Penny's situation.

"Ugh, I want to be done! In fact, I am!" Darla slammed her book closed. "Who's with me?"

Everyone was except for Diana who needed to start on a paper for religion.

"Wait, wait, one more before you all go." While the others were packing, Diana flipped through her notes and spotted a blank. "Okay, what's an ungulate?"

"I got this one," Cadence said. "Ungulates are hooved mammals. They eat plants and have toes that are called . . . um, phalanges! Those are covered by a hard casing." Kissing her fingers, she raised them to the ceiling. "Miss you, Gunpowder."

They smiled and bid Diana good luck and good night. Before beginning the trek home, they warned her not to walk alone, and for good measure, Cadence loaned Diana the can of pepper spray.

Diana's paper took longer than expected; it was close to three in the morning, and her lids were heavy from the constant zigzagging between books and her computer screen, but at least she was still upright. Glancing around, she noticed bodies everywhere—on desks, under them, slumped in chairs and over them. Those who remained awake had peaked complexions like zombies. Some even let out the occasional moan at work that resisted devouring. Finally, Diana decided it was time to leave the wasteland of cramming.

She stepped on the pathway home, assuring herself that the walk was short and people were bound to be out. Because she was so utterly drained, any thoughts of threats were as distant as her bed, which she wanted more than anything on the planet to be in. A few paces into the shadowy gauntlet, she stopped to dig in her purse for the spray. As she did, a voice came out of the blackness.

"You really shouldn't be walking alone, miss."

"Oh God!" Diana's hand held what was left of her heart. "Officer, you almost scared the life out of me."

His bike rolled up next to her. "I'm not going to apologize for that. Maybe fear will cause you to be more careful."

"So you want me to be scared?"

"Cautious," he replied, "I want you to be cautious."

Diana pulled the spray from her bag and held it up.

"That's good but is probably not enough."

She frowned. "Then what would you suggest?" She leaned slightly to read the name pinned to his chest. "Officer F. Harden?"

"An escort. Where're you headed?" As he asked, the dispatcher called for a check-in. "Forty six," he answered.

"Is that your age?" Diana asked.

"Not quite." Dismounting the bike with a smile, he began walking the blocks with her.

Despite her exhaustion from hours of studying, Diana was surprisingly awake. With every step, she became keenly aware of muscles refined by activities that kept him outdoors when he wasn't tending to drunken college kids, arresting the unruly, unlocking buildings, and rescuing the stranded. His dark gray and red uniform was still spotless in these wee hours. Metals of all brilliances flashed whenever he passed beneath a street lamp: the bronze of his badge, the silver of his handcuffs, and the gold on his left hand that told of another set of laws he was bound to obey. A ring of steel keys jingled with his every step, while a flashlight, baton, and the instrument that got between him and lethal problems—a Glock—clung tightly to his sides. As the distance to their destination decreased, Officer Harden asked about her studies, her plans, her interests. He gave her the kind of genuine attention women find overwhelmingly addictive.

So until she departed for summer, Diana studied late in the library then requested the services of Officer F. Harden to ensure she arrived safely to her bed. She knew he'd be giving escorts as he had mentioned he was stuck with the graveyard shift throughout exams.

In the early morning hours as they retraced the brick path to her dorm, she learned more about him. Born and raised in the state's second oldest port of Beaufort, he grew up in a family that had run shrimp boats for generations. Since that way of life was under constant threat from tasteless foreign imports, his father encouraged him to break tradition and go to college. He did, married a girl he met there, and they returned to his hometown for a while. Eventually, they moved to Charleston for jobs and had been living their dreams ever since. By her last chaperoned stroll, Diana even knew that the initial in "F. Harden" stood for *Felix*.

He was an alluring presence Diana could not get out of her mind, a distraction she mentioned to Saida as they prepared for Dr. Sexy's religion exam.

"Mmmmm, a man in uniform with a gun, a pair of hand-cuffs, and lots of keys. Impressive."

"I get why the gun and handcuffs impress you but keys?"

"The more keys on the ring, the harder they are to score. It's simple. More keys equals more responsibility, more risk. That's a lot of doors to unlock. It's just a guy theory of mine."

"How many theories do you have?"

"I'm still working on some but probably enough to fill a good-sized read. About like this." Saida held up a chunk of pages in her textbook. "Anyway, sacking a cop is a major coup."

"Sacking? I don't want to get him fired."

"I meant getting him in the sack, dumbass." Saida let go of the pages, and they flopped back into place. "Then again, sleep with him and he's bound to get fired. They have rules against that, and I doubt you're up to breaking them."

Diana crossed her arms. "Are you daring me?"

"Not necessarily. I'm just saying that's a, a high-profile se-duction. Not your average bedding. Is he married?"

"Yes."

"Then he has a separate key ring—even more responsibility. The stakes are much, much higher. I'd leave him alone."

"No you wouldn't—not if you wanted him." Diana leaned forward. "I know you, Saida. The space between your legs burns hotter than hell sometimes. By the way, how's it going with Warren?"

"Pretty cool, actually. So much so that I've put the brakes on it—every pun intended."

"Uh-huh, I see." Diana cut her eyes. "Anyway, you seem to think you're the only one who can get a guy like the one I'm talking about."

Saida cracked a smug smile. "I'm not the only one who can. I'm just the best at it."

"Are you saying I can't?"

"No, you're the one saying that." She relished stoking the rivalry in Diana. "But if you want a challenge, I'll bet you can't seduce your handcuff hunk by . . ." Saida tapped her lips with her pen. "Let's see, you'll have to take up this project next semester, so I'll give you until Halloween to snag this treat."

"I accept. And what do I get if I win?"

"Hopefully, multiple orgasms and handcuff burns." Saida laughed. "What do you want?"

Diana's eyes drifted around the room and came to rest on a box of items Saida had packed. "Shoes. My choice."

"Hang on, you need to cap that request. That could be really expensive."

"So could this affair."

Saida leaned back. "So it could be. Okay. Shoes of your choice. But I'm not going over a grand. If you lose, you buy me something of equal value. Deal?"

"Deal." Diana reached over the desk covered with books on religion and met Saida's grip. They sealed their bet with a vigorous handshake not too unlike the testosterone holds that men close their gambles over sports, cars, and women with. The winner of this wager wouldn't be rewarded for some time, and until then, Saida and Diana taunted each other over the unfolding drama of what they had already dubbed *The Great Handcuff Heist*.

Drama was the first exam Cadence faced, and what turned out to be easy for her and Miranda was nearly impossible for Reena. Sleeplessness, anxiety, and the pain of disloyalty caused her to twist answers into indecision on questions of acting methods, stage terms, and play identifications. The only thing she could focus on was coloring the rectangles on her answer sheet as black as her being. She was, after all, only following the directions clearly stated on the form: *MAKE DARK MARKS*. Sadly, they had already been made within her thanks to Blaze.

As the hours crept on, Reena stared at the blank boxes, wavering between answering *A* for *asshole, anger, agony*; *B* for *Blaze, bastard, betrayal*; *C* for *crushed, confused, chaos*; *D* for *deviance, despair, death*; or *E* for *end, empty, embarrassed*. Fragmented language was just the way her brain functioned, and no matter how much she needed to concentrate on the test in front of her, she couldn't, so she marked every blank with a *C*.

Before turning in her answers, Reena took one last look at the slender sheet of failure. In the box labeled *IMPORTANT*, she noticed another set of directions—*ERASE COMPLETELY TO CHANGE*. She laughed out loudly. If only she could erase him completely from her life, she thought change would come.

"Something funny, Miss Mayrant?" Dr. Dreary asked.

"Just my life, Professor Dreary. Just my life." Reena flung the paper and its advice into the drama box.

Having finished far before Reena, Cadence and Miranda waited outside the classroom for her. When Reena emerged, she looked as if her soul had been stomped into the pluff mud. Knowing she needed them, the friends took her to the Grand Lawn for some rejuvenation via means of fresh air, c.a.t.'s coffee, and a glimpse into the future. Cadence and Miranda called Reena's attention to the bridge over the pool that awaited her crossing in a few years. They promised to walk the passage together, to help each other through the difficulties to come and the ones they faced—whether they be trials of the heart, body, or most commonly at this time of year, those of the mind.

One word described the exams for biology and communications: *grueling*. They took the full three hours to complete. Multiple choice, fill in the blanks, and short answers made up both tests, but Dr. Tiller tacked on three essays, the latter of which would be placed under the scrutiny of the TAs. The professor wouldn't waste his vision on them unless there was an issue Julia, Winston, and O'Brien could not resolve themselves.

Dakota and Cadence finished their exams at the same time, both using every second to turn thoughts into tangibility. Outside, they hugged one another goodbye, a sending-off ritual that both would repeat innumerable times in the days ahead. He was heading to New York for the summer, a last-minute internship he managed to snag with an events company. Cadence looked forward to hearing of his big city adventures next semester, and she would since they were taking another class together.

"I hope the Big Apple's ready to be bitten!" Dakota nibbled at the air.

"Be careful, it might bite back."

"I'm countin' on it, sweetie. See you next year. And good luck with your next final. I'm going to take a hot bath and pamper myself."

Her Spanish exam had two parts: a written one, which she stumbled through, and an oral portion. Cadence's appointment for the verbal trial was near the end of finals—the penultimate test of her freshman experience. The conversation seemed to be going well with Dr. Hernandez exchanging pleasantries about food and beverage preferences, travel interests, and school studies. He sat facing her, arms relaxed on his chair. Cadence answered him in a staggered style until one question gave her pause. He read her perplexed expression and repeated the sentence.

"*¿Tú quieres que yo sea tú novio?*"

Flipping through her mental dictionary, she struggled to determine if she had heard him correctly.

"Do you understand what I asked you?" he said.

"I, I think so." In her mind, she went over the translation again. "Um, you asked if I want you to be my boyfriend?"

His eyes pressed her for the answer before his tongue did. "*Sí. ¿Cuál es tu respuesta?*"

Cadence straightened her posture and strung the answer together as best her shaky tongue would allow: "*Yo no quiero tú.*"

Instantly, he swung his chair away and faced his desk. Scribbling furiously on a yellow pad, he said nothing, but she listened to the angry sound of his pen and to the voice whispering in her head—*you just told your Spanish professor that you didn't want him.*

Briefly, Professor Hernandez announced the exam was over. "I will post your grade in a week or so. *Adiós.*"

His dismissal left her feeling slighted and disappointed. She didn't understand how a professor whom she genuinely liked could destroy her perception of him with one question. She couldn't help but think he crossed some line in conversation, but with one exam to go, she didn't bother asking anyone's opinion—she just wanted to be done.

Before her final exam, Cadence dropped into the coffeehouse with a gift for Catissa and a bag of treats for Kyd. He was in the office and bounced like a kangaroo when she opened the door. Cadence grabbed his jowls as she would a child's chubby cheeks and kissed his cold, wet nose. His nub went wild, and his front paws found her shoulders. Soon they were hugging like old friends when Cadence heard a laugh from behind.

"I thought I heard someone in here." Catissa wiped her floury hands on her apron. She had been in the kitchen making cheese wafers and sautéed pecans for the onslaught of graduation visitors. "Kyd, I swear, you get more love than a harlot on the night before Lent." The boxer just continued licking Cadence. "What brings you by, dear, other than puppy love? A shot of energy for your exam?"

"Yes, I'll need that, too, but I have something for you." Cadence retrieved a package wrapped in brown paper from around the corner.

"For me?" Catissa looked genuinely surprised. "Goodness, what for?"

"It's just a little thank you—for all you've done for me, especially in talking to the judge."

Catissa grinned. "It wasn't me." Unwrapping the gift one piece of tape at a time, she answered Cadence's surprised expression. "My dance partner Odin made that call. When I mentioned your case, he insisted on helping. Seems he was quite taken with you and your article. Even has a copy of it hanging in his office. Personally, I think he likes the photo of the belly dancers that's beside the one of us. Makes him feel half his age."

Catissa's hand covered her mouth then slipped to her heart when she saw what was inside the paper. Holding the frame away, she got a better glimpse of the coffeehouse captured in black and white. Sunlight filtered through the oaks, casting the signature shadows that permeate the city's paths. The photograph was evidence of c.a.t.'s pull on Cadence's heart, a locale she'd remember for always, especially when the miles divided her from Charleston.

"Cadence, I love it. Thank you dear, thank you. Come here." Catissa wrapped her arms around Cadence. "Oh, I can't believe your first year is over. Where, oh where, does the time go?"

Cadence remained in the kitchen with Catissa chatting about summer plans until the exam hour drew near. Before leaving, Cadence was stocked with homemade goodies, a house special, well wishes, and a promise to visit immediately upon her return next year. After one last embrace, Cadence was off to the final for the class that began her college experience.

Fittingly, Professor Mirabilis's exam was the last that stood between Cadence and summer, and it challenged her not in the manner of regurgitation, but in a complete test of the knowledge she had gained from great works of literature, love, and life. Just as on their first day, the teacher repeated the request to *SKIP LINES*, so Cadence duly wrote the command on her hand.

After testing their argumentative and analytical abilities, Professor Mirabilis threw in a personal reflection request—*Examine your evolution from the year's genesis to this moment.* Unlike the first day of class in which she had no time to think, Cadence sat back in contemplation and glanced around. She could see the pens of Kirby, Haven, Dewit, and a few others scribbling furiously. Corey, the guy in the very back whose stare seemed permanently fixed on Cadence since those first days, was following tradition. She looked the other way toward the empty desk where Aliyah once sat. An aura of sadness had filled the space ever since her death. Cadence also noticed a vacancy where Astra should have been and wondered what could have kept her friend from taking the final. As time was ticking away, Cadence set out to describe her transformation. She wasn't even certain if words existed to convey the experience, but she wrote with all the craft and passion she could supply and told her audience how she was inspired to read and write and learn as much as she could for as long as she could.

Putting the period on the final sentence was like crossing the finish line after an arduous race, even if she didn't know personally what that felt like. Just as she was about to pack her things to leave, Cadence realized she had not said all she needed to. Her pen touched the paper once more and she scribed—*P.S. I'll always remember you as the teacher who helped start my evolution.*

Now she was done. Walking past a few classmates who were still unloading, Cadence handed in the exam. Professor Mirabilis flashed Cadence a look of approval. "Have a good summer."

"Thanks, Professor Mirabilis."

To her surprise, the teacher quietly returned, "No, Cadence, thank you. You have enriched my work in ways you may never know. I'm very fortunate you've been part of my teaching experience." The appreciation struck Cadence as unusual, but she brushed it off as her teacher's sentimental way of sending her pupils on their next journeys. *She probably says that to most of her students*, Cadence thought.

The sound of the door's heavy metal handle giving way was like a cannon firing independence. Despite her exhaustion, she burst into the May afternoon, feeling more alive than ever. She was savoring the moment when Astra came rushing toward her accompanied by a police escort. The usual calm that was Astra had given way to a storm of anxiety.

"I'm so glad to see you." Astra held Cadence so tightly she felt as if her friend would never let go. She smelled of smoke and fear, sweat and danger.

Cadence watched the officer scanning the area. "Astra, what's going on? Why did you miss the exam?"

"It's a long story. I didn't miss the exam. I have it here." She held up a stack of blue books. "I had to take it in a secure location. Mason, my ex-husband, he's out of prison. No one knows where he's at."

"What? How?"

"Some kind of early release. If he's knows where I am, he may be headed here. Officer Narona's providing protection while I take exams."

"But what about when you're not on campus?"

"Well, you know what kind of protection I carry. I'm moving to an apartment with security in a few days." Astra glanced at the guard who signaled it was time to go. "I have to go give this to Professor Mirabilis, but I'll talk to you soon, okay?" Astra moved toward the door being held open by her temporary guard.

"Astra," Cadence called to her friend who stopped at the entrance. "How long did he serve? You know, prison time?"

"Two years of ten." Astra stepped past the officer.

Cadence returned to her dorm to perform the final walk-through before shutting the door on the first room of her college career. Its walls were now bare, but it was full of memories—some of Corrine and Jed she'd like to wash away as she did on that October day when Reena called down from a porch and lifted Cadence's spirits. She was unsure what would happen since the relationship with Blaze had been extinguished. She wasn't even sure about her own with Schilar, but in time, she'd find out if he'd make Charleston his home again in the fall. In addition to Reena and Schilar, the fates of Astra, Isa, and Penny worried her. The latter had just received notice that a campus judicial hearing regarding her assault case had been scheduled over the summer, so perhaps justice would prevail. Cadence could only hope for the best in all the difficulties.

In her usual clumsy fashion, she was busy twisting her room key off of her chain and did not see Enna stepping into the hall. They collided, sending the papers and books in Enna's arms tumbling in all directions.

"Enna, oh no! I'm so sorry." Cadence bent down to gather the scattered materials.

"Don't worry about it," Enna said. "I thought everyone was gone. I didn't know you were still on the hall."

"Besides you, I think I'm the only one. Was lucky enough to have an exam in the last slot. My mom's downstairs waiting."

"Go on then. Really, Cadence, I've got this. Just go."

Not heeding her friend's command, Cadence continued picking up the pile. She was not paying attention to the pages until she grabbed one featuring an ancient etching of a wooded scene and something unusual stuck to it. Carefully, she pulled a black feather from its face and held it up in front of her own.

Enna, who was busy collecting the items closest to her, stopped suddenly when she saw her friend stand up. She rose, too, and looked past the feather deep into Cadence's eyes. Gently, she plucked the evidence from her friend's fingers, picked up the papers, and slipped silently into the stairwell.

With her things packed, Cadence and her mother circled through campus on their way out of town. Their car stopped at a light next to the Grand Lawn where Cadence could see the reflecting pool cleaned of soap and on its way to being refilled. In three years, her journey would end across that water alongside her friends—individuals who began as strangers only months ago but who now defined the most remarkable experience of her life. She had quite a distance to travel before she would complete the pursuit, but she knew how far she'd already come.

As they drove west, Cadence breathed in the marsh air, absorbed the sun's soaring rays, and recorded the wheels' echoing grind across the drawbridge's grate—imagery she sealed into the yearbook of her memory. Propping her bare feet in front of the side mirror, Cadence recalled the words she had written only minutes ago and what she had really learned since that first day back in August. She looked down at the message on her hand then licked her finger and began erasing the reminder—*SKIP LINES*—from her skin. As she did, she thought of all the lines she'd studied, written, and spoken, but most of all, she thought of the ones she'd heard and seen—those with the power to jar her mind, shift her soul, and shake her heart in ways that would forever reshape the self she once knew.

Smiling at what she now possessed, she inhaled accomplishment and exhaled relief at having passed the multitudinous milestones that marked her freshman year. The contemplations gave way to a sad awareness that months stood between her and the return to the Holy City that had become a second home within her. With eyes closed in absolute satiation at what waited ahead, Cadence could not see the loosing of a blood-dimmed tide rising behind her that threatened to drown the spires in darkness.

DEAN'S LIST

A Novel Begins with the Hands—it's an idea that explains the genesis of this project, and while the narrative's creation certainly began with my own, it could not have been completed without the hands of others. I am indebted to many who have given me critical advice, encouragement, support, and most importantly, their time.

Matt: As is my pattern to make stories circular, you're on the "Dedication" page and at the top of the "Dean's List." I cannot explain all the ways you complete my life. My experience with you has been truly *extradictionary*—I want more memories with you for which there will never be words.

My parents, Thurston and Wanda: Without the education you provided both at home and in sending me to USC, this book and the ones to follow would not be possible. Thank you for the sacrifices you made in giving me knowledge and the privilege of being a college graduate.

Maggie and John: I never imagined that in marrying Matt I would be gaining a second set of parents who have loved, supported, and guided me in so many endeavors. I appreciate the time you spent reading my unpolished words and all the suggestions you gave to improve them.

Granny Lee, Nanee Cooper, Aunt Donna, and Aunt Margaret: My "rocks" of feminine strength, love, and unwavering support. I am a better woman because of the examples you provide.

Angie Howard—reader extraordinaire. I appreciate your interest, tips, and encouragement. Our family is beyond fortunate to have you as part of it.

Fran Butler: We've reached quite a number of educational milestones together as graduate students and English instructors. You believed in me and this project and offered invaluable comments to make it better. I owe you, so anytime you want to take a "History of the English Language" course, grab the *OED* and meet me at the bar.

Lissa Block, Judi McCabe, and Kimberly Tall—my earliest readers who encouraged this endeavor and were always willing to tell me what worked and what didn't. I am grateful for all you have brought to my life and lines.

Mike Tall, Darragh Doran, and Scott Walls: Thanks for always being available for a pint and providing me with enough guy material to write a thousand books.

John "Rock Star #1" Shields, James "Rock Star #2" McNally, James "Keon" Masters (also a Rock Star), Jaclyn Niller, Erica Peterson, Hannah Ashe, Rachel Feinberg, and Lucy Remitz—the "8 Wonders." Each of you is a testament to why I value the profession of teaching and treasure my time in classrooms. Thank you for being with me during the last English 101 and 102 classes I ever taught and for the friendships we share. And a special thanks to Rachel and Lucy for your readings and suggestions; to Keon for a tune fit for a book's opening; and to John—for making an earworm I never want to get out of my head.

Elise Darrow, Alissa Collins Lietzow, Kornelia Kostka, Asia Spellman, and Marla Cochran Robertson—all former students and now among the most intelligent, perceptive, professional, and savvy women I am fortunate to have in my life. In many ways, I am your student because you have certainly proven to be my teachers.

Angela Doyle, Natasha Liggons, Margaret Lacey, and Elise Lasko—I thank each of you for your interest in my work and for taking the time to read that first chapter and offer your thoughts. You are among the finest I have ever had the pleasure of instructing.

Maggie Nolan: Thank you for lending me your hand—literally—for the opening photo and for your copious edits and enthusiasm for this project.

Eliza Jones and Lucas Judson: Your comments and notes have been invaluable, and I am thrilled to have you both and Maggie join the Boxer Publishing team on this momentous venture. I look forward to our long friendships.

To my former students who have kept the lines of communication open long after our semesters have come to a close—thank you for continuing to be a part of my life and for your support in telling this story.

Dr. Trish Ward, Dr. Bonnie Devet, and Dr. Dianne Johnson: I had the privilege of sitting in your classrooms and because I did, I am enriched for it. Thank you for sharing your knowledge and passion with me and for encouraging this novel.

Professor Gary McCombs: I met you through casual conversations about teaching, politics, religion, and just life in general. Collectively, I think we've solved the world's problems through words. I value my friendship with you and relish the stimulating topics we wander into whenever grading papers can wait.

"Bubba" Gillard: many thanks for being the "law enforcement" encyclopedia, and to Tristan Hill: *Gracias por comprobar mi Español y por ser un excelente profesor usted.*

My family and friends (especially Niles, Jackie and Brian, Paul and Michele, Pat and Richard, Jodi and Neil) who inquired, "How's the novel coming?" I can finally answer: "It's done." This reply would not be possible without your interest—Thank You!

Lee "Schuyler" Collins: Although you're gone and have been for years, the letters, drawings, and photos you shared with me remain. Wherever you are, I hope the words I've written in memory of you echo into peaceful spheres. You asked that I never forget you—I assure you I never have.

Huxley, Lyra, and Isis (and the long-departed Anfield)—my writing buddies for countless hours. Thank you, pups, for making me take breaks from work to go outside and play, for always being at my feet when I'm at the keyboard, and for reminding me about what's important in life: slobber, sleep, belly rubs, bike rides, treats, and most vitally—love, loyalty, and happiness.

You—the reader—who took a chance on the words of an unknown author: thank you for sharing your intimate, space, precious time, and perhaps, your connections with me. I appreciate what you bring to this work and hope we can start a conversation about your experiences. Let's talk at www.thecollegechronicles.com or visit me and my team on Facebook, follow us on Twitter, or pen an old-school letter and send it to: Boxer Publishing, 3642 Savannah Hwy, Suite 116 #319, Charleston, SC 29455.

2 ½ degrees and 20 years—that's how long Kelly Owen has been in higher education: as a student and an instructor of English composition and literature. With two degrees in English, she was studying for a third when something happened on the road to getting a doctorate—a novel idea, literally, that changed the course of her quest and resulted in *The College Chronicles: Freshman Milestones*, the first book in a series of four. Informed by her studies at the University of South Carolina, the novels fictionally reflect some of her experiences as a student and educator. For nearly two decades, she has shared her knowledge of literature and passion for writing with thousands of students at Georgetown High School, James Island High School, Trident Technical College, City Colleges of Chicago, The Citadel, Columbia College of Missouri, and College of Charleston. Kelly enjoys reading, writing, running, cooking, and gardening. She resides in the Holy City with her husband Matt, who hails from Birkenhead, England, and their two devilishly angelic white boxers, Huxley and Lyra.

80 Courses,
4 Years,
1 Series . . .

The journey at Charlestowne College has just begun. As sophomores, Cadence Cooper and her friends return to a city seized by terror and a school on the brink of ruin. With the help of the Harpies, Cadence investigates the biggest scandal in the school's history while dealing with a troubled roommate, feuding friends, and her own relationship turmoil. Demanding professors, dangerous discoveries, and extraordinary education await in the second book of the series: *The College Chronicles: Sophomore Keystones.*

Watch for these future titles from Boxer Publishing:

THE COLLEGE CHRONICLES
Sophomore Keystones

THE COLLEGE CHRONICLES
Junior Touchstones

THE COLLEGE CHRONICLES
Senior Capstones

THE COLLEGE CHRONICLES
Resources

Want to See "Cadence's" Photographs?
Hear Schilar's Song?
Interested in Teaching Materials?
Need Book Club Discussion Ideas?
Want to Know the Story Behind *SKIP LINES*?
Looking for Tips on Writing and Self-Publishing?
Desire more Details about Charleston?

Visit: www.thecollegechronicles.com
Like us on Facebook
Follow Us on Twitter:
@collegechron   #whatsyourcourse

THE COLLEGE CHRONICLES
Evaluations

In the publishing world, these are known as "Reviews."
Please take time to visit Amazon, Barnes and Noble,
Goodreads, or your favorite review site and post your opinion.
Recommendations are always appreciated.

CPSIA information can be obtained at www.ICGtesting.com
Printed in the USA
LVOW07s0345150814

399257LV00002B/2/P

9 780996 061711